# BLOODTRAIL

# BLOODTRAIL

David Lewis

Leonard Press

Leonard Press
Bolivar, MO 65613-0752


For other titles, prices, and order information:
www.leonardpress.com




ISBN 0-9769114-3-4
Library of Congress Control Number: 2005927971

Cover Art: Kristina Cox

Unload'er Udell.
Today we race.

# PROLOGUE

SHE WAS WELL INTO MISSOURI, the Jeep's oversized tires singing on the cement, when hunger became a factor. At a rest stop on I-44, she grabbed a Snickers and took a couple of hits of speed, then ran her fingers through her short hair and put the top down to better enjoy the afternoon. Early September surrounded her as she pulled back onto the interstate, heading southwest.

Gunnar and Felene had wanted her to stay a while longer, but people were waiting for her at home. She'd loved prowling Lake Shore Drive, enjoying the cliff dwellers on one side and Lake Michigan on the other. Something was going on nearly twenty-four hours a day. She'd walked for miles, day and night, prowling the drive, the side streets, the alleys. Time had flown by. She had arrived in May and, almost in a blink, she was in the first week of September. Time to go home.

She'd left Chicago shortly after dawn, Felene and Gunnar walking her out to the street from their digs deep in the second sub-basement of the Field Museum. They'd found the Jeep and kissed her good-bye, Gunnar adolescently patting her butt and growling in her ear, Felene licking her on the upper lip and nipping her with lovely little teeth, both of them promising to return the visit. Sorrow surrounded her—recollections of another era—as she left the city. Once upon a time, when they'd still been together, she and her father had lived in Chicago, but she hadn't seen her dad in years. The memory hadn't faded. Her memories never did.

When she reached Rolla, she turned south on 63, not really caring about making time, just driving in the general direction of home. Small towns slid by, and Licking came up after a while. She smiled at the name, remembering Felene's tactile enthusiasm. Houston was next, then Cabool and a low gas gauge. She filled up at a 7-11, ate another Snickers, and crunched a little more speed, but she knew it wouldn't be enough. Soon she would need to stop and eat.

She took 181 out of Cabool, smoked half a chubby reefer, and was snaking through one of the Mark Twain National Forests as dusk fell. With tourist season over, traffic on the narrow Ozark two-lane was sparse. Only the occasional passenger car, rusty pick-up, or the odd logging truck doing the red oak rumble at half the speed limit joined the Jeep on the asphalt. Finding a Forest Service lane disappearing off into the undergrowth, she pulled the Jeep back into the weeds out of sight and stopped. Opening her suitcase, she stripped off her chinos and long sleeved shirt and wiggled into a pair of jean shorts cut off at the crotch and a white tank top. Barefoot in the dim light, the need dripping from her sinuses down the back of her throat, she returned to the road, squatted in the ditch, took three or four hits off a roach, and waited.

A minivan full of Baptists and brats rolled by, followed five minutes later by a tall pick-up with two motorcycles in the bed and three rednecks in the cab. She peed in the grass and killed another ten minutes, her appetite gnawing with anticipation, before she saw the old red Chevy. Weaving slightly, with only one person on board, the raggedy mini-pickup groaned and rattled around a curve. She stepped out beside the road and stuck out her thumb. The dumbass behind the wheel almost locked up the brakes trying to stop in time. Smiling, she licked her lips wet and walked to the driver's window, shoulders back, hands in the rear pockets of the shorts.

"Hi."

"Evenin', Ma'am," he grinned, beer on his breath, a flabby tattooed arm resting on the window frame. "Whatchoo doin' out here all by yer lonesome this time a night, little lady?"

"My boyfriend dumped me 'cause I wouldn't put … 'cause I pissed him off," she said, leaning forward a bit and crossing her arms, pushing her breasts together with her biceps.

"Hell, you doan look old enough to know what ta do with no boyfriend."

"Old enough to wear that pissant out if I wanted to," she snorted. "Fuck him."

The good ol' boy leaned away from the steering wheel, belched, pushed his ball cap back on his head and let his eyes roam over her.

"Ain't yew awful young ta be out all by yourself? Little bitty girl like you could git took advantage of."

She laughed and swished her butt. "Well, yeah, Dummy! That's why I need a ride. Walking around out here in the dark, almost anything could happen. You sober enough to rescue me, or what?"

Fantasies of butterscotch hair, pebbled nipples, and pink tongues rippled behind his moist eyes.

"Wanna beer?" he asked, stifling a belch.

"Sure, if it comes with a ride."

He leered, licked his lower lip and took a chance.

"What if it comes with more'n a ride?"

She grinned, cocked her head to one side, and ran her tongue along her upper lip. "Then I might need more than one beer."

She could smell his sweating accelerate, alcohol misting his breath. Too dumb and too drunk to realize this was too good to be true.

"I got half a case a Bud Lite in a cooler in the bed," he said around the growing lump his throat.

"Got someplace we can drink it? I ain't ridin' around with no drunk at the wheel."

"Whatcher name?"

"Cat," she said, rocking back and forth on slim muscular legs.

"Cat? That short for something?"

"I ain't short on nothin', Hero. You got eyes."

In the near blackness of the cab, she could see his hand drop to his lap.

"Yer kindly short on pants," he said, trembling a little as he fondled himself.

"You gonna stare at my crotch all night, or we gonna drink some beer?"

"Damn!" he said, tearing his eyes away. "Ain't you something!"

"More than you know," she said, trailing a hand lightly across her breasts.

He gave a strangled snort and she caught the sour scent of his seminal fluid. "Well, git the fuck in, Cat. I'm Leon. Let's go drink some beer, or somethin'."

Cat grinned. "Or somethin'," she purred and walked around the truck.

Leon watched her ass pass the headlights. Shit! Earlene with them saggy tits and them three kids, only one of 'em his, waitin' back at the trailer house, bitchin' all the time about ever damn thing they was to bitch about. Fuck her. He was tired of her flabby ass. This little piece didn't look like she was mor'n thirteen years old, but damn, she was some hot shit. Once he got her off the road and a beer or two down her neck, this was gonna be like nothin' else in his whole life!

Cat sat on her side of the seat, amused as she watched him struggle not to paw her and strain to see her legs in the pale green of the dash lights. She swiveled to lean back against the door and parted her knees, her left hand slowly stroking the inside of her thigh. He dropped the right front tire onto the shoulder and wrenched the truck back on the roadway.

"Damn!"

"Whatzamatter, Hero? Havin' trouble concentrating?"

"How fuckin' old are you, Girl?"

"Older than you think. Just keep your eyes on the road. You wreck this piece of shit, and you're gonna fuck up my plans. How much farther we got to go? I'm thirsty."

"'Bout this fuckin' far," he said, slowing the Chevy and easing up a narrow, rock-studded lane.

The logging road widened after only a short way, and he turned the truck around, facing it back down the shallow slope. He shut off the ignition and peered at her silhouette against the open window.

"C'mere," he said.

It was pitch dark, but Cat saw him clearly. Dirt in the creases of his crow's feet, lower lip wet with spittle, patchy beard stubble, pot belly sagging over a cheap plastic belt, greasy blue jeans, soiled t-shirt, worn cowboy boots, filthy fingernails, massaging his fly, sure that the dark gave him privacy.

"What about the beer?" she asked, keeping her distance.

"Beer can wait. C'mere, Little Girl."

She smiled. "My name's Cat, you know, like pussy?"

"Goddamn!" he grunted.

She could smell fresh discharge and hear his heart-rate climb. "I ain't never come across nobody like you before!"

"You got that right," she said. "I guarantee it."

"Well, slide your tight little ass on over here, Pussycat!"

Cat laughed. "I don't think so, Hero," she said, opening her door. The dome light didn't work. "You promised me beer."

She scooted out the door and walked to the bed of the truck, reaching for the cooler that had slid up against the tailgate. Leon weaved his way next to her, breathing heavily through his nose. Cat drew a longneck Bud from the water and ice as he pressed his bulk against her and put an arm around her waist.

"Slow down, Hotshot," she said, slipping away from his grasp and body odor. "Let me tell you the way it is. It's gonna take one beer before you lean on me, two beers before you put an arm around me, three before you grab me, and at least four before you get next to this sweet little pussycat. The way you're pantin', you'll probably come all over yourself in a minute anyway, you dumb fuck." She unscrewed the top and took a deep slow hit of the Bud, enjoying the amount of verbal abuse he was prepared to absorb as long as he thought it might be part of foreplay. "While I'm still sober, you don't stand much of a chance. So just slow down and let me get ready."

Leon looked at her in the moonlight; his vision blurred by booze and need.

"What?"

"You got anything to eat, Hero?" she asked, tossing the suddenly empty bottle into the undergrowth. "I'm hungry. I haven't had a good meal in days."

"Have another beer," he said, plucking one from the cooler and twisting off the cap. She drained it in four long swallows.

"Damn, Girl! Can you fuckin' drink, or what?"

Cat shouldered him aside and grabbed another bottle. In five seconds it was empty.

"Jesus," Leon said, trying to see her ass in the dappled moonlight.

"Just keepin' my word, Hero," she said, stepping in front of him and leaning against his belly. The top of her head was three inches below his chin. "I said that after three beers you could grab me," she said, dropping her hand to his fly. He sucked in a sharp breath as she stroked him. "Wanna grab me, Hero? Do ya?"

She thrust her other hand deeply between his legs and pressed upward, feeling his sphincter tighten and the rhythmic pulsing begin behind his scrotum.

"Fuck!" His hands flew to her backside, each grasping a cheek, and pulled her roughly against him. She turned her face up.

"Gonna come, Hero?" she growled, her eyes shining with amusement. "Gonna come for me? C'mon, Hero, shoot your hillbilly wad. Come, Baby!" she squealed, rubbing against him in feigned urgency. "Come!"

"Jesus!" Leon roared, and she felt the spasms beneath her hands.

He pushed his face against hers, his tongue probing her lips. On tiptoe, she opened her mouth for him and sucked his tongue in between her teeth. Leon snorted. Leon wheezed. Leon bucked. Leon shivered. And, as Leon came, Cat struck.

So far gone in the most thunderous orgasm of his adult life, Leon didn't immediately realize what had transpired. He felt the crunch of Cat's teeth as they entered his tongue, but his pleasure at that moment was so intense, so rock-hard, sperm-spurting, prostate-pulsing, gut-wrenching good, for a second his reptile brain overrode pain, and the terrible trauma of the event did not register. A second was all Cat needed. In the first half of that second she released her hold on his crotch, grasped each of his wrists, and removed his hands from her backside. During the last half of that second she extended her arms out from her sides to keep Leon from scratching or tearing at her, bit completely through his tongue, grasped the stump between her teeth, and began to suck.

Leon's orgasm was shattered by what felt like fire in his mouth. He wrenched backward to escape it, but it came with him, searing pain and scalding agony that clung to him, tore at him with flames shredding through his face. He attempted to claw at it, but couldn't move his hands to his head, only dimly aware of the bones in his wrists splintering as they broke under amazing pressure. He lurched and fought to no avail—his screeching blew snot from his nose and ruptured an eardrum as he whirled like a pathetic dervish attempting to fling a bloodlust banshee from his face—finally crashing to his back on earth he could not feel, staring at the stars with eyes that could not see.

For a while during their dance, Cat was suspended from Leon only by the strength of his tongue, her one hundred two pounds swinging freely in front of him. As he spun and struggled, she broke both of his wrists and dislocated his right shoulder. After he collapsed she spat out the meat that was once part of his tongue, wiped him off her eyelids and face, and—using her knee to pump his dead heart—drank from his hollow mouth as if it were a blood-spring filling a sacred vessel. When she had her fill, she thrust herself off of him and stood upright, life coursing through her veins, the darkness as light as day. From the sheer joy of it, she threw back her head and howled, giggling as coyotes answered from the distance, hugging herself with ecstasy, fulfilled, happy, supercharged with life, rich from the kill, radiant with the purest of nourishment. Then she came, the orgasm clawing its way through her with ivory talons, ripping her apart with its intensity, fusing her back together with its power. She lay on her side in the grass and shook, laughing with glee at the battle, the kill, the meal.

After a few moments she urinated the excess moisture from her system and sipped briefly from Leon's mouth for a final taste. She grasped the body by the pants and the cheap plastic belt and, one-handed, tossed the two hundred thirty pound corpse casually into the rear of the truck. Finding the keys in the ignition, she drove back to the Jeep and parked.

Cat stripped off her bloody shorts and top, washed with the ice water remaining in the cooler, and dressed in her chinos and shirt. She carefully slipped the bloody clothing into a plastic bag along with a sizeable rock and put it on the passenger-side floorboard of her Jeep, awaiting a lake or river. Checking Leon's wallet, she found nearly ninety dollars which she slipped in her purse. She left the body in the truck, started the Jeep, and pulled back out onto 181, heading for Arkansas. The cool night air warmed her as she chased her headlights through the hills. Looking at her watch, she noticed it was barely ten o'clock. She lit the last half of her last doobie and wished she'd brought the rest of Leon's beer.

# ONE

Doc

"SOMEBODY HERE to see ya, Doc."

Joseph Casey opened his eyes and looked toward the voice from his position on the bottom bunk. Through the bars Butler appeared upside down.

"What?"

"You got a visitor."

"Butler, I don't have visitors."

"First time for everything," Butler said. "C'mon, get up."

Casey lurched to a sitting position, remembering to keep his head low to avoid the steel frame of the upper bunk.

"It's too late for visiting hours."

"Special deal, Doc. The assistant warden set it up. Some gal with juice wants to see you."

"A woman?"

"Yeah. You remember them, doncha?"

"Not very clearly," Casey said, rubbing his face with his palms.

"This one'll sure as hell refresh your memory."

"Butler, how long we known each other?"

"I dunno. Ten or twelve years, I guess."

"Have I ever had a visitor that you recall?"

"Nope."

"Piece of mail from anybody but a lawyer?"

"Nope."

"Phone call?"

"Nope."

"Gotta be a mistake."

"Mistake or not, I'm not the one who's gonna make it. I'm supposed to take you over to the administration building. Get your shit together."

Casey sighed and slipped into his shoes. A visitor? He didn't want a visitor. He didn't want his life messed with at all. He'd carved himself a nice little insulated niche that he was going to outgrow soon enough. An intrusion from the outside could only make things more difficult. He preferred his memories, as bad as some of them were, over any contemplation of the future. Rising to his feet and wondering what the hell was going on, he grabbed a blue cotton shirt with his number sten-

12

ciled over the single pocket and put it on, buttoning it to the neck. He finger-combed his hair straight back and turned to the guard.

"How do I look?" he said.

"Like a convict."

"Just the effect I was going for. She'll be impressed."

Butler chuckled. "Let's go, Doc."

Casey stepped through the open cubicle door and out onto the second floor catwalk, tucking in his shirt. A woman. What the hell would a woman want with him? He hadn't been near a woman since before he'd dried out. He hadn't had a normal relationship with a woman since his wife died, and that was too painful to dwell on even after all these years.

Located in central Indiana not far from Indianapolis, Macon Detention Facility was constructed in 1995. One of several project prisons, Macon was privately owned and administrated. Built with a faux pink marble exterior and green tile roofing, it was supposed to resemble an industrial park or large condominium complex. Guard towers were cleverly concealed in rooftop cupolas, wide expanses of lawn were graced by ponds and flowerbeds. Exercise yards were hidden from view by hedges reinforced with razor wire. The double row of sixteen-foot chain-link fencing and concertina wire surrounding the entire two hundred acre complex did little to sustain the ruse. The illusion failed.

The positive side was that local, state, and federal governments had nothing to do with the day-to-day management of the place. Because Macon prison was privately run and competing with other facilities of its type, it was considerably more progressive than conventional prisons. The food was better, the staff more efficiently maintained and trained, the bunks softer, and visitation more liberal. From time to time inmates even filled out comment cards. Cells became "cubicles," guards, "administrative assistants," and prisoners, "contained population." The prison's goal was "to reinstate disenfranchised individuals back into the general population as contributive members to the societal norm." Despite the classroom, educational, medical, and sports facilities, despite the color coordinated detention areas, despite the larger cubicles, and despite the un-military uniforms of the administrative assistants, it was a prison: a place where society assigns those of whom it is afraid, of whom it is ashamed, and of whom it wants to rid itself.

The population consisted of eight to nine hundred detainees at any given time, kept in four maximum-security buildings and in one total lock-down, mega-security building. Joseph Casey had resided in maximum security for almost eleven years. He was a model prisoner, admired by inmates and guards alike.

Joseph was one of the few in his building who was not under lockdown unless working or in an exercise period. No matter how crowded the facility became, Casey never had a cellmate, but he was permitted to live privately. He alone was allowed to leave his cubicle after nightly lockdown should the occasion call for it. He never asked for any privileges but received them anyway. Why? The same reason he was called Doc. Casey was a healer.

He worked in the prison hospital six days a week. So did other inmates, but they did not receive the same considerations he did. They did not work with terminal

AIDS patients. Casey moved among the dying without hesitation or fear. He brought them comfort; he eased their pain and their minds. He touched them and they felt better. He sat with them and they relaxed. He cared and they responded. A few that were hyper-religious considered him second only to Christ. Some that would have gleefully spit in God's eye, smiled when they saw him coming.

Recuperating from a shank wound to the kidney, Theotus Lark—at six-seven and three-thirty-five, the baddest HIV positive sumbitch in the valley—got to know Casey. "That Doc," he said, "is one natural-born muthafuckah. Anybody fuck wit his ass, dey fuckin' wit me. They doan want ta be fuckin' wit me."

Nobody fucked with Doc anyway. When he first arrived at Macon, several tried, but without success. In his early forties, at about five-ten and one-sixty, Casey was not an intimidating physical specimen. He belonged to no group and had no protectors. Soft spoken and usually polite, he was not social, kept his own council, and stayed out of the way. In spite of that, he caught Theotus Lark's attention in the yard one afternoon as he walked past him and his group.

"Hey, Whitemeat!" yelled Theotus. The surrounding yard grew quiet. "C'mere, Boy. Step on over here an' let me get a look at yo' ass."

Casey stopped, looked at the immense black man, and grinned. "It's a damn sight prettier than anything you've ever seen in a mirror, Shithead," he said. "Close your fuckin' mouth. Your breath stinks." He continued his walk.

Two days later, Theotus caught Doc alone in the shower. When it was over, Casey had a small scratch on his cheek that healed in moments. Theotus had four broken ribs and a dislocated hip. Both participants in the fight were punished. Theotus spent five days in the hospital and two weeks in solitary. Doc was fined twenty-five dollars and found a carton of Camels on his bunk when he returned to his cell. Accounts were square.

The administration building sat across a grassy lawn about seventy-five yards from the chain-link fence that surrounded the maximum-security containment area. Butler got them buzzed through the main door, and then he led Casey up to the second floor and down the hall to a reception room. "Right in there, Doc," he said. "I'll wait here in the hall until you're done. Just knock and go in."

Casey smelled the lie, but he knocked and went in anyway.

The windowless room was about twenty feet square with mauve walls and a light gray ceiling. Indirect lighting gave it a quiet glow. Two long tables and several desk chairs on casters sat near the center of the room. A large mirror was set into one wall. On one of the tables were several cans of soft drinks in ice and a coffeemaker with foam cups. Behind the other stood a woman. Casey looked at her.

Not tall, not short, not thin, not fat, not young, not old. Thick, auburn hair to the shoulders with a natural wave; pale, almost translucent skin; not enough makeup to cover the freckles across her nose; eyes the color of limes. A silk and wool pantsuit two shades lighter than her hair, with a cotton blouse two shades darker than her eyes. She'd bathed with Dove soap and used Oil of Olay to moisturize. Short and natural nails. He couldn't place the scent of her shampoo. She'd just finished an Altoid. She smoked. She shook him to the bone.

"Joseph Casey?" Her voice had gravel in it. A silky contralto with character.

14

Casey willed himself not to tremble. "That's correct," he said.

"I'm Moira Flynn." She extended her hand across the table.

He took it. Dry, firm, pulse over ninety. Nervous meeting a real convict one-on-one.

"Thank you for consenting to talk with me," she said.

Casey smiled at her and did his best to collect himself. "I didn't consent to anything, Miss Flynn. I was told to come here and escorted to make sure I'd comply. It is, however, nice to be in your company. You are a welcome addition to my regular fare. Why am I here?"

"I need your help."

"Got a flat tire?"

She snorted and sank into a chair. "Look, Mr. Casey …"

"Call me Joseph." He popped the top on a Coke and walked slowly around the room to keep moving and to put some distance between them. She smelled so good.

"Mr. Casey, I am not here to engage in a verbal battle with you. I am here to attempt to persuade you to be honest with me. There are some questions I'd like you to answer. I can assure you our conversation will be held in the strictest confidence. Of course, there is no way I can compel you to be candid with me. I can offer you no threat or promise of reward. The best I can hope for is to present you with the opportunity to possibly contribute to a higher good by appealing to your better nature."

"Better nature?" Her choice of words made him smile. If she only knew.

"Yes."

He looked past her. "Do you know why I'm in here?"

"I fail to see why that should influence …"

"I'm in here because I killed four people while attempting to locate my daughter. What makes you think I have a better nature or care about a higher good?"

"That seems to be the consensus of opinion here at the detention facility."

Avoiding her eyes, Casey went on the offensive. "You always talk like you got a textbook shoved up your butt?"

"I beg your pardon?"

"Chamomile, right?"

"Chamomile?"

"Your shampoo."

"Mr. Casey," she said with exaggerated patience, "if we might return to the subject at hand."

Her scent ricocheted through his nostrils. "And mint, and macadamia, and wild cherry, and, ah, dandelion?"

"Mr. Casey."

He looked at the mirror and saw dimly into the small room behind it. "You said our conversation would be in the strictest confidence?"

"Yes, of course."

"Then how would you explain the fact that there are four people watching us and listening to our conversation from the other side of this wall," Casey said, pointing at the mirror.

"What?"

"Count on it," he said, allowing himself to become irritated for focus. "One of them is a guard named Butler. Nice guy but a pathological liar."

She rose to her feet. "Mr. Casey, I can assure you, I had no idea our meeting was being monitored!"

"Relax. I know you're telling the truth." He heard a door close nearby. She didn't notice.

"Allow me to apologize," she said. "It was never my intention to mislead you, or to allow myself to be misled by people I was told I could trust."

"Go away," Casey said, not wanting her to. "Raise hell, get us a privacy guarantee, and come back tomorrow. It's Sunday. I usually only work a couple of hours on Sunday. You can tell me then what this is all about and maybe we'll talk."

"Really?"

"They were spying on you, too, Miss Flynn."

"I suppose they were."

"That makes us almost co-conspirators," Casey said, looking directly into her eyes for the first time. "I haven't conspired with a woman in years. Wanna conspire with me, Moira?" He could feel her pulse accelerate a bit as she flushed and fought a smile.

"Thank you, Mr. Casey. I'll return tomorrow, and we will have no more privacy issues."

"Good, but I make you no promises, Miss Flynn," he said, opening the door.

"None expected," she said. "I would just like a chance to explain."

Moira Flynn was a little shaken as she drove back to her motel. She hadn't wanted to do Casey's interview in the first place, but she thought a male prisoner might be more open with a woman, and secrecy demanded that she involve as few other Proteus Trust staff members as possible. She had thought of sending Melvin Foltz, her head researcher, but Melvin was not well suited to fieldwork. Although he was loyal and discrete, he was a lab man. In the real world Melvin couldn't find his way out of a crowd of three.

Finding out the staff at the penitentiary had lied to her, made her angry. Casey made her curious. More than curious. She found him attractive although not in any conventional way. He was fairly average in appearance, but his eyes were compelling. Something flickered there, something that could easily become a flame, like being watched by a big cat in the zoo.

You could look at a cougar for an hour, pacing back and forth, lying around and yawning, and then, for an instant, actually feel the gaze of the cat. In that moment, in that second, the predator arrived. The power, the assurance, the essence of that creature, smoldering out from beneath half-close lids, could stop breath.

Casey didn't frighten her exactly—Moira was not a woman easily frightened—but his eyes did chill. He was obviously intelligent and self-confident. He even teased her. And somehow he knew there were people behind the mirror. Educated guess, perhaps. She'd call the senior administrator's office first thing in the morning and get everything straightened out. Proteus owned a significant amount of stock in the company that controlled the prison. She had leverage, and she wasn't afraid to use it. The good ol' boy network had never stopped her before. They damn sure weren't going to start now.

Arriving at the motel, she slugged to her room with her briefcase and recorder, and immediately stripped and showered. Being in the prison had left her feeling soiled. Out of the shower and into lightweight sweats, she bought some Bugles from the machine in the hall and sat cross-legged on the bed, trying to read a little of the work she'd brought with her, but she couldn't keep her thoughts away from Casey. Something kept niggling at the back of her mind. Finally, she got up, went into the bathroom, and looked at the label on her bottle of shampoo: chamomile, mint, macadamia, wild cherry, and dandelion.

Damn.

Butler was waiting in the hall when Casey walked out of the interview room. "Shit, Doc," he said. "Sorry. I was under orders."

Casey grinned at him. "Finally there's truth between us. Our relationship will never work if it's based on lies, darling. You may walk me home."

"Eat shit," Butler said.

"You're just jealous because I have a heavy date tomorrow."

Sleep wasn't much of a factor for Casey. In the more recent years of his life, he'd found that a couple of hours of deep sleep was all he needed. He spent most of the night thinking about Moira Flynn and examining his reaction to being in the company of a woman. Between thirty-five and forty, she was obviously well educated and used to having a certain amount of power, but only a certain amount. Casey had noticed a bureaucratic feel about her, as if she were someone in the chain. Near the top but not at the top. She didn't feel like an executroid drone—she was used to making decisions and giving orders—but being in the unfamiliar world of a prison put her off a bit. She was uncertain as to her place and didn't like it. After the privacy debacle he was reasonably sure she would chew heavily on somebody. Casey smiled. Never piss off a woman with red hair.

What did she want with him? Since his first day in Macon Prison, Casey had concealed the vast majority of his abilities, giving just enough away to make himself valuable to both the guards and the inmates. Prison was a closed and cloistered society. He could afford to let a little of his power out. No one asked questions. What went on inside, stayed inside. Nobody looked his gift horse in the mouth. He had no fear of the population—he was beyond their abilities—his only fear was of discovery, so he held back his abilities to a large extent.

Over the years, he had developed the desired reputation working in the Macon Prison hospital, and he garnered a certain amount of respect as someone who helped when help was needed. He moved across racial and social lines, something very difficult to do in prison. Macon, even with its cosmetics, was a violent place. The blacks hated the whites, the whites hated the blacks, everybody hated the Latinos, and the Latinos hated everybody right back. Racial tension constantly bubbled just beneath the surface. Within each racial group were social groups that bickered among themselves, flying different colors, professing different codes, exercising their own version of the territorial imperative. It was stupid. It was sad. It was necessary. Oddly enough, the split-second potential for violence was what tended to keep the peace.

Through the maelstrom, "Doc" Casey moved on his own course. Gangs made no difference to him, race made no difference to him, position or power made no difference to him. In an environment where friends and rank meant almost everything, he didn't seem to care. In a society where violence, or the threat of it, was one of the prime motivators, nobody messed with Doc. On the few occasions when someone had, things had ended quickly and badly for the aggressor.

Theotus Lark was a case in point. Less than six months after Theotus had attacked Casey in the shower, several members of Los Lobos had surrounded Theotus in the yard, and Jesus Martinez had stabbed him in the kidney with a shank made from a soupspoon. For the next week, Casey had tended to Theotus in the hospital, changing his dressings, cleaning the wound, giving a damn about whether Theotus lived or died. Every time Casey touched the huge man, Theotus felt better. The thorn had been pulled from the lion's paw, and the lion knew it.

A couple of weeks after Theotus went back into the general population, he approached Casey in the yard. "Doan hurt me, Doc," he rumbled, a grin spreading across his ebony face.

Casey returned the grin. "Fuck you want, convict?"

"Ah'd a keel you in a minute, an' you know it, but ah come up in dat hospital an' you hep me. Doan axe nuthin', doan wan' nuthin'. How come?"

"Beats me, Theotus," Casey replied. "You're too fucking ugly to live. I must have lost my mind."

Theotus chuckled. "You alright, Doc."

Casey smiled up at the huge man. "Thanks, Theotus."

"S'okay, Doc. Wanted you ta know."

"This doesn't mean we're gonna be taking any long showers together, does it?"

Laughing, Theotus slapped Casey on the shoulder. "Ah ain' never gittin' in no shower wif yo' ass agin'!"

After breakfast, Casey was jumpy. When he realized that he was nervous about the possibility of Moira Flynn's return for another chat, he clipped on his building pass and headed over to the hospital wing in the custodial services building to stay busy. It was Sunday and he had the day off, but on Sundays he almost always stopped by for a while. On the way he passed through three checkpoints, undergoing a cursory body search at the first two. He knew the guards; they knew him. Their greetings resembled pleasantries between co-workers. Not so at the third checkpoint. Tuesday through Sunday, it was manned by Evans.

Evans was a guard because he liked the power and didn't have enough ambition to do anything else. Manning the booth outside the custodial services building, Evans surveyed his own little kingdom through stereotypical, mirrored sunglasses. He chomped five or six sticks of gum at a time because chewing tobacco made him sick to his stomach, he twisted his straw hat in a western roll because it was cool, he puffed himself up and wore two-inch lifts in his boots because he wasn't a tall man, and he spoke with a slow drawl even though he was originally from New Jersey.

"Well, lookie here," he said, leering as Casey approached the booth. "If it ain't ol' Doc. Where ya goin', Doc? Up ta take care of yer faggot friends?"

"On the way to the hospital, Evans."

"Up there to that AIDS ward to check out all them buttfuckers you love so much?"

Casey unclipped his building pass and handed it over so Evans could run it through the reader.

"You a fudgepacker, Doc?" Evans asked. "You like wiggling yer bean up some nigger's poop chute?"

Casey looked at him, watching the throb of his carotid artery and easily smelling two-day-old sweat through Evans' Old Spice deodorant. "Get on with it, Evans. You make me itch."

The guard reddened. "Hands on the wall, feet back and spread 'em wide, convict!" he spat and shook Casey down, being excessively aggressive around the upper thighs and crotch. Casey endured in silence. When it was over, Evans handed the pass back. "Go ahead on, Doc. Go see all them queers you got dyin' up there."

Casey smiled and let a little of what he kept behind his eyes show. "Everybody dies, Evans," he said. "Even you."

The smile hit Evans like ice water. The guard shivered and goose bumps rose on his arms as he watched Casey walk toward the building.

"Motherfuckin' faggot," Evans muttered, his left hand groping deep in the pocket of his pants.

Casey did a rapid walk-through of the wards, killing time, putting in an appearance, saying hello, letting his charges know he was around, then stopped by the office to catch up on the medication charts. Doctor Lamb, the weekend resident, greeted him casually and went on about his business.

It was well after noon before Casey put the paperwork away, made his daily visit to the blood cooler, and left the building, walking slowly back toward Evans' checkpoint.

"Hey, Doc!"

The shout came from behind him, and he turned to see Butler striding his way, carrying an M-16. He stopped and waited. "Musta just missed ya in the ward," Butler said. "Your visitor is back."

"No shit?" Casey asked, feeling his heartbeat increase.

"No shit."

"What's with the rifle?"

"Aw, that lady kicked some major ass. I'm your official guard. You an' her are gonna meet out by the south pond at them benches where you can have some privacy. I'm supposed to lay back a hundred yards or so an' shoot ya if ya get fresh and pat her knee or somethin'."

Casey laughed. "I'll try to resist."

"Thanks," Butler said. "I can't hit shit with one of these things."

# TWO

THE SOUTH POND WAS A MAN-MADE DEPRESSION of about a half-acre in size near the edge of a large, manicured lawn. Outside the fenced compound sections, but inside the chain-link and concertina-surrounded complex next to the visitor's parking lot, it had been dozed from the earth and filled with well water as a concession to the softening of the prison's image. A twisting gravel path meandered around its perimeter, flowerbeds lined its shores, cement and redwood benches graced its banks, and, in August, mosquitoes rose in angry gray clouds and made anyone in the visitor's parking area fair game. Intended to be a lovely, uplifting sight, it was about as appealing as the backside of a billboard. It was there that Casey met Moira Flynn the second time.

Wearing a white, cotton, man-tailored shirt, a light beige silk and wool blend skirt, hose, and bone two-inch pumps, she was sitting on a bench holding a clipboard. Beside her was a large briefcase. On the gravel behind the bench sat a portable stereo. She watched Casey approach—occasionally shifting her gaze to Butler and his M-16 in the distance—and extended her hand.

"Mr. Casey," she said. "Good of you to come."

The sudden warmth of her touch made Casey glad he hadn't tucked in his shirt-tail. "Pretty day," he said. "Nice to be outside."

"Again, I would like to apologize for my naiveté relative to the insured privacy of our last meeting. I assure you, it was not my intention to mislead or deceive."

"Be at ease," Casey said. "It was intuitively obvious to the most casual of observers that you were not party to the ruse. I maintain complete confidence that you have exercised influence to ameliorate the circumstance relative to our current encounter. That is to say, I believe you have chewed some ass."

She blinked at him, and a grin chased the puzzlement from her face. "I'm sorry. You've made your point. The past few years, I've worked in an environment where speech and communication are not necessarily the same thing. I'm afraid I have succumbed."

"No shit?" Casey said.

They smiled at each other until Moira nervously pulled back from the intimacy. "Well," she said, "to put your mind at ease, I have swept our immediate area with a device I am assured would find any hidden microphones or recording machines. Have a seat."

Casey leaned back at the far end of the six-foot bench. "And the boom box?"

"Insurance against any parabolic devices directed at us from the prison." She flipped a switch and classical music filled the air. "Plus, I am not recording our conversation."

"I believe you."

"So easily?"

"You have an honest face. Who are you, Miss Flynn, and what do you want from me?"

Her demeanor shifted a bit and she squared her shoulders. "I," she said, "am an investigator and analyst for an organization called the Proteus Trust. My function is the tracking of the AIDS virus and the interpretation of that data."

"AIDS? I thought it was backburner stuff these days. Treat 'em 'til they die and move on."

"Unfortunately, that's nearly true. Since the massive Ebola outbreak, AIDS research has dwindled dramatically. In spite of what you may have read or heard at the time, the Ebola crisis claimed nearly six-hundred million lives worldwide in less than eighteen months. I was with the World Health Organization during the outbreak. I spent time in Zaire, Somalia, and Bangladesh. It was horrible, devastation beyond description. The WHO threw all its resources at the problem. In only three years it more than doubled in size and tripled in bureaucracy. Less and less went toward the problem, more and more toward sustaining the infrastructure. It was worse than the United Way charity debacle. I couldn't tolerate the politics and the waste, so I left and joined the Proteus Trust."

"And the Proteus Trust deals with AIDS?"

"Exclusively. It's also financially independent. We have no need of public or federal funding. While we have many connections within the government and governmental agencies, we are autonomous. We have our own facilities, our own labs, our own investigators, our own agents, all privately funded. Our agenda is our agenda."

"So, what are your qualifications, if I may ask?"

"I am a doctor, an epidemiologist, to be exact. I spent several years in medical research, then moved into the investigational aspects of the work. I have a medical degree, a masters in statistical analysis, a PhD in epidemiology, and a brother who died of AIDS when I was twelve."

"Ah," Casey said. "The ultimate motivation."

"Yes."

"So, why me?"

She swiveled to face him. "Because you, Joseph Casey, are an anomaly."

Casey felt a tiny thrill of fear trace its way up his spine. "An anomaly?"

For the first time she looked him directly in the eyes. "And you know it, don't you, Joseph?"

Casey shifted his gaze and felt his mouth go dry. He squinted past her into the sunlight and tried not to fidget. "Lady," he said, "I don't know shit."

Moira pressed the attack. "Well then, let me inform you," she said. "You work in the AIDS ward of the prison infirmary. You have worked there since shortly after you came to Macon almost eleven years ago. It seems that your ability as a healer has earned you the nickname 'Doc' among the population. The protocol for treating AIDS has changed very little in the past few years, yet, since you have been working with the patients, the survival time of the prison's acute AIDS victims has increased by over forty percent. I want to know what you do, Mr. Casey."

He looked at her, cursing himself for agreeing to a second meeting. "Here's a piece of very old, very wise advice," Casey said. "Why don't you want in one hand and shit in the other and see which one gets full the quickest."

She ignored his rudeness. "Furthermore," Moira said, "about four years ago you took a patient, one Theotus Lark, outside in a wheelchair for some air. Mr. Lark, a known associate of yours, was terminal. By all estimations he had only a few weeks, possibly even just a few days left to live. While you were wheeling Mr. Lark in the yard, he was stung by a bee. In a few moments he began to go into seizure, followed by anaphylactic shock and cardiac arrest. You threw him to the ground and resuscitated him, mouth to mouth. Incredibly, in his severely weakened physical condition, Mister Lark survived the shock and heart attack. Not only that, two weeks later he was out of the AIDS ward and back in the general population, without any trace of the disease! I want to know what you did, Mr. Casey."

Oh, Jesus. He'd known it was the wrong thing to try when he'd done it, but he just couldn't stand there and watch the big man die. "Ask Theotus," Casey said.

"You know that's not possible. You know he was stabbed in the yard a few months later by a man named Jesus Martinez, the same man who stabbed him some years before, and bled to death before help could reach him. Unless I miss my guess, you'll be relieved to know that his family had the body cremated so it cannot even be exhumed for examination."

"Sorry."

"In addition to that," she said, "birth records indicate that Joseph Edward Casey was born in a suburb of Albuquerque, New Mexico on June 2nd, 1952."

Goosebumps rose on Casey's arms. Aw shit. "That's true," he said.

"Further investigation reveals that Joseph Edward Casey died in the hospital of his birth on June 3rd, 1952. You seem to be remarkably healthy and large for a one-day-old infant that's been dead for over fifty years."

"I watch what I eat," he said.

"Also," she said, fiddling with her clipboard and extracting two pieces of photographic paper, "here are your mug-shots taken the day you arrived at Macon, and your updated mug-shots taken just last year. I see no change in your physical appearance. None. You should be ten years older, and yet you don't appear to have aged a day. I want to know what you are, Mr. Casey."

"Just your all-American boy, gone bad," he said.

Moira glared at him and shook her head. "Bullshit," she said. "Look, I'm not trying to expose anything. I'm not looking for new material so I can get published again. I have no desire to spread your secrets, whatever they are. Goddammit Casey, you are an enigma. You are more than an enigma! In the entire time you've been here, working with critical cases of an infectious disease, you've never even had a cold! You've never seen a dentist, never had an abnormal physical, never broken a bone, never chipped a nail! With no change in treatment protocol, people you care for live a year and a half longer than the national statistical norm! You were born and died one day apart, and yet here you are! You should be in your fifties, and you are not, are you, Mr. Casey?"

Casey leaned back against the bench, crossed his legs, and smiled. "And you, Miss Flynn? Exactly what are you? Some kinda cop?"

"I am an investigator, a damn good one," Moira said. "I have a large infrastructure for data at my disposal, and I am well connected in the intelligence community. I look for patterns, and when something disrupts them, I get curious. I'm curious about you."

Her tone softened.

"Look, I have resources, Mr. Casey, resources that can accomplish a great deal. I also know how to keep secrets. I want to know about you, why you don't get ill, why your patients live longer, why Mr. Lark recovered, why you don't age, and why you were only one day old at the time of your death in1952. I have passed none of this information over to the authorities, nor will I. It is not my desire to coerce you into complicity, but to motivate you into cooperation. Your secrets are safe with me, whether you help me or not."

She leaned back, just a bit out of breath.

Casey knew she meant it. He looked at her.

"Lady, believe me," he said, shaking his head, "you don't wanna know my secrets."

"Yes, I do. I'm totally sincere."

He chuckled. "Oh, I know that. You may or may not be telling me the entire truth, but you are definitely not lying."

He removed a pack of Camels from his pocket and lit one with book matches. "Relax a little," he said, offering her the pack and stalling for some time to think.

She took a Virginia Slim from her purse. They sat in silence for a moment or two.

"How did you know I smoke?" she said. "Better yet, how did you know I needed a cigarette?"

"The same way I know you're telling the truth when you say you're good at keeping secrets."

"How's that?"

"You'll keep my secrets?" he said, testing the water, as it were, with his toe.

"Absolutely."

Casey stared at the ground for a few seconds, then sighed.

"Alright, Miss Flynn. Okay. I'll give you a little secret to keep. I smell you."

Moira blinked. "You smell me?"

"Yep."

"Oh. The odor of smoke on my clothes. Very good, especially outside like this."

What the hell. He was going to have to leave the prison now anyway. "Lady, I know you use mint-flavored toothpaste, I know you ate an Altoid when you saw me walking across the lawn, I know your make-up is cornstarch based, I know you're just getting over a cold, I know you had meat and dairy products in your most recent meal, and I know that you just finished your period."

Stunned, she looked at him.

Angry with himself for exposing so much and unable to curb his recklessness, Casey pressed on. "I also see you, Miss Flynn. I know that you're wearing contact lenses, you've had corrective surgery on your nose, you use a rinse to slow down the arrival of a few gray hairs on your right, sorry, left temple, that your watch is a few minutes fast, that the star sapphire in your pinky ring is real, not man-made, and that the nail on the ring finger of your right hand is false."

She sagged and gaped at him. "Jesus."

"Those are a couple of my tiny secrets, Lady. The big ones would scare the panties off you! Your panties, by the way, are cotton."

He finished his cigarette and flipped the butt into the pond while she stared. Hers burned out between her fingers. Eventually she noticed, lit another, and peered at him.

"That's amazing!" she said.

"Just part of my charm. Nothing the average owl and dog couldn't do."

She took a breath. "How can you do that?"

"That's one of the big secrets."

"I want to know."

"Fat chance."

"Mr. Casey. Joseph. This is all tied into everything else I have learned. You have a tremendous opportunity here! What you know, what you are, is astounding! With your assistance, so much could be learned. Please consider what we might accomplish!"

She was losing him.

"I'm not a lab rat."

"I know that! That is not a factor."

"Not to you maybe, but a lot of other people in your line of work would love to get a hold of someone like me."

"Someone like you? There are other people with your abilities?"

Casey cursed himself for the slip. "I have enjoyed our little chat, Miss Flynn," he said, rising to his feet, "but it is over. You do not want to get involved with me, any more than I need to get involved with you."

"Mr. Casey, I assure you …"

"You can't assure me of anything, Miss Flynn. There are no assurances. There are only promises, and promises are dust in the wind."

"But, your ability to help others, your healing skills, the things you won't tell me! Surely these are things that could be of great benefit to mankind!"

"You are an attractive, dedicated, bright, committed woman, Miss Flynn. That's why I will put this to you in the most gentle of terms," Casey said, backing away from her. "Fuck mankind."

She watched him walk slowly back toward the detention area. "I'll keep your secrets, Casey," she murmured. "But I'm not done with you yet."

Unable to resist, from fifty yards away, he stopped and turned. "Thank you," he said, raising his voice so she could hear him. "And yes, you are."

"You heard that?"

Casey grinned, the distance between them restoring his edge. "The panties?" he said. "Cotton was a guess. For all I know, you aren't wearing any."

Butler escorted him back to the yard. Casey knocked around there for a while, then returned to his cell and tried to relax on the bottom bunk. Jesus. The days were catching up with him, and the situation, too. The years he'd spent at Macon had been relatively enjoyable, actually. Regular meals, place to sleep, work to do, time to pass, the blood bank. The endless sameness of the days stretching out before him had been given shape and meaning by his routine. Now this. Dammit. Moira Flynn had shattered his reverie. It had to happen. For some time, in the back of his mind, he'd realized that he was going to have to alter things. The battle with the years had become an annoyance, now that he was living among humans. He knew he should change locations and relationships every ten years or so to keep his secrets and not give himself away. But Moira Flynn had introduced an element he hadn't given much thought. Even the tightly knit, closed-mouthed security of the prison had been breeched. If she could find him and recognize the discrepancies, so could somebody else. Somebody who wouldn't keep secrets, somebody who wanted recognition or fame, somebody who could be a real threat. Moira, with all her good intentions, was threat enough. She wouldn't give up. That was one determined lady, and she was determined to find out about him. Christ. He had to do something, and he had to do it very soon.

"Doc?"

He opened his eyes and came back. Butler stood in the doorway of the open cell. "What? You wanna follow me around with a gun some more?"

"That was fun, huh? I kept wondering what the hell I'd do if that gal attacked you. Shoot her in the foot, I guess. Nice lookin'."

"Very attractive. You just stop by for a visit, Butler, or is there a purpose to this harassment?"

"You are the most ungrateful sumbitch on the whole block, you crotchety old bastard. That lady left you this." Butler lifted a business card out of his jacket pocket and tossed it on the floor. "Said that if you changed your mind, here's where she was and here's where she worked. Feel free to call. Like you'd get any phone privileges from me, you grouch."

"Kiss my ass, Butler."

"Eat my shorts, Doc."

After Butler left, Casey looked at the card. Proteus Trust, Chicago, Atlanta, and Dallas. Her name, one phone number. The back of the card contained a message.

*Mr. Casey, I'll be at the Southoak Inn, on Clayton Blvd through 8am tomorrow.*
*Change your mind.*
*Room 334, 317-951-9514. Moira*

He flushed the card down the toilet and lay back on the bunk to think. It was time to move on, no doubt about that. Move on where? Other than his daughter, he had no family, and he hadn't seen Catherine in years. He had no idea where she was. Once it had been his mission to find her, but in the years since he'd dried out, he'd given up any thought of trying. She hadn't wanted anything to do with him years ago; she certainly wouldn't want to see him again now. Besides, he had no idea how to go about locating the girl. She could be literally anywhere on the planet.

In addition to that, he had no place to go, no money to get there, no plans, not even any hopes. He had no ID card, no birth certificate, no driver's license, and no credit cards. He did not exist outside the prison. Casey ran his fingers through his hair and got to his feet. He was the man who wasn't there, and he had not been there for a long, long time.

Stepping out onto the catwalk, Casey sighted Butler at the far end and walked to his location.

The guard smiled. "'Sup, Doc?"

"I need to use the phone, Butler."

"You got a call pass, Doc?"

"Nope. Never made a call before."

"Fixin' to talk to that green-eyed gal?"

"Gonna ask her over for dinner."

"Doan blame ya. Far be it from me to stand in the way of true love. Get some change. It's long distance to Indianapolis."

"Don't have any," Casey said.

"Christ," Butler said, reaching in his pocket. "Here. Use my cell phone, for God's sake."

"Show me how," Casey said. "I've never made a call on one."

"What? Where the hell you been for the last twenty years, the fuckin' jungle?"

"More or less," Casey said. "This call's important, Butler. Whatdaya say?"

"I say we go back to your place, I'll show ya how to use it and give ya ten minutes. No point in lettin' every con in the joint see what's going on."

"My hero."

"You owe me, Doc. Big time."


"Moira Flynn." Her voice sounded deep and rich, even over the phone.

"Joseph Casey, Miss Flynn."

"Mr. Casey. You called!"

"Surprised?"

"Yes, I am, actually. I thought I'd have to badger you several more times. You've decided to help?"

"Possibly. First there are some things I'd like to know."

"Certainly."

"You said that you specialized in information."

"More or less."

"You have access to ways to find out things?"

"What kind of things?"

"Locating a missing person, for instance."

"My company has a huge database. In addition to that I have contacts within several governmental and police agencies. Information is my business."

"Can I assume you have access to medical facilities?"

"From hamsters to humans, gerbils to gorillas. Who are you looking for?"

"Nobody at the moment," Casey said. "Are you telling the truth?"

"Of course, unless I'm lying about it. Are we in business?"

"Possibly."

26

"When can I see you again, Mr. Casey?"

"I'm not sure," Casey said. "I'll let you know."

"You'll let me know! What do you mean, you'll let me know?"

"Don't call me, Moira," Casey said. "I'll call you."

"Wait a minute, Buster! I wanna know wha—"

He pushed the button Butler had shown him, and the phone disconnected.

Casey stayed on the bunk for nearly another two hours, trying not to be excessively impulsive about the course he'd already decided to take. He'd need clothes, at least a little money, and some heavy-duty nourishment to get himself out and on the road. It was time to leave Macon behind. Reaching up into the slit on the underside of his mattress, he pulled out the shank that he'd kept hidden for over five years. It was made from a fork, the two center tines missing, the outside tines sharpened to ice pick points. He slid it into his left shoe along the right side of his foot, the handle flat alongside his heel, the tines curving around the ball, then he stood up, and walked out of the cell. At the end of the catwalk he encountered Butler.

"Where you off to, Doc?"

"Back to the infirmary. I forgot to list a couple of med charts. Only take about an hour or so."

"Sure you're not just goin' to pay Evans a visit?"

"I can do without Evans."

"Hell, I'll walk you over so you don't have to deal with the motherfucker. Just be back by lockdown."

"Thanks, Butler."

Once inside the building Casey went directly to the small civilian lounge and locker room and turned the doorknob in spite of the lock. Going through the lockers, he found a pair of brown slacks, a red sport shirt that fit reasonably well, and a light blue windbreaker that was a bit too large. He wrapped the pants and shirt inside the jacket and hustled down to the supply room. Next, he took several minutes to trim his hair with surgical scissors, getting it up off his collar and ears. He went through the personal belongings lockers and lifted over sixty dollars in cash, put the money and the clothes in a pillowcase, sat on a box of paper towels, and thought about Moira Flynn as he waited for dusk.

It was a little after eight when Casey left the building, pillowcase in hand, and sauntered to the first checkpoint. He could see Evans inside the booth and bent over to tie his shoe, palming the shank as he stood up.

"Well, well, well, if it ain't the good doctor," Evans said. "Gittin' close to lockdown, Doc. What you doin' out this late? Tryin' ta git a little before bedtime?"

"No. Thought I'd just drop by, kill you, and leave. Gotta problem with that?"

"What's in the fuckin' bag, convict?"

"The clothes I'm gonna wear when I go. I can't wear these, they'll have blood on them. Yours."

"That's it, you faggot sumbitch! Hands against the wall, feet back, and spread 'em. Assume the position, asshole!"

"I don't think so, Evans."

"What?" Evans bellowed, his eyes registering uncertainty as he reached for his baton.

Dropping the pillowcase, Casey easily caught the guard's wrist and dislocated his elbow. The scream was stifled in his mouth as Casey clamped his left hand around Evans' face and squeezed. The man had never felt anything like it. The pressure was mechanical, as if his face were in a vise, an unrelenting, brittle force that he could not even struggle against. He could feel his jawbone flex under the pressure. The pain was so immense that he stood frozen, unable to move.

Casey looked into the sweating face and rolling eyes and smiled. "All these years you pushed people around to get your jollies, abused people for the fun of it, and made everybody's life as miserable as possible so yours wouldn't seem so bad. See this?" he held up the shank. "Evans, my boy, I'm gonna slip this into your common carotid and bleed you out a little."

Tears were streaming down the guard's face, but the terrible pressure on his jaw held him immobile.

"You see," Casey said, "all this time that you thought you were at the top of the food chain, you were wrong. To a real predator you are nothing more than an after dinner snack."

Casey pushed the shank slowly in until he felt the carotid wall pop. He then dropped the weapon to the floor, placed his mouth over the wounds, and began to suck. The guard's pounding heart made the process easier and, in only moments, Casey had swallowed nearly two pints.

The blood hit his system like a hammer of light, surging white-hot through his belly and veins. Jesus Christ! It had been years since he'd last fed on fresh blood, years since he'd felt the rush. Nothing was like this, no drug, no potion, no fantasy even came near what he felt. Power gushed through bone, muscle, and tendon. He felt Evans' jaw snap in his hand and pulled away from the wound, panting with excitement. The guard's eyes rolled in his head above the dangling jaw, and Casey held him upright by the throat. Blood seeped from the holes, swelling Evan's neck as it saturated the tissue. Casey looked at him.

"It's over, Sweetcakes," he grinned around bloody teeth. "See ya in hell."

He pulled Evans toward him six inches, then pushed him away the same distance so quickly, so violently, the guard's neck snapped from the whiplash effect. Electric with power, Casey ripped the prison clothing from his body, wadded it up in a ball, and screamed with joy pressing the bundle into his face to stifle the noise. He urinated on the guard's body to rid himself of excess moisture and forced control back into his actions. Slipping into the stolen clothing and jacket, he put the cash he'd ripped off in a front pocket. From Evans he removed another twenty-six dollars, ignoring the man's baton, handcuffs, and pepper spray.

It was nearly full dark. Casey stepped out of the checkpoint shack and looked toward the prison's double row of perimeter fencing over two hundred yards away, easily visible from two guard towers. He could see each diamond of chain link. Shit. Even if they saw him, they wouldn't know what he was. Nothing in their experience could move that fast. In less than five seconds he was closing with the fence. Its sixteen-foot height was nothing. He sailed over both fences and the twenty yards between them, laughing as he did. A quarter mile to the highway. Nine seconds flat and he was crouched by the road, looking for his ride, his jacket with a broken zipper from the air resistance to his speed.

It wasn't long before a pick-up truck towing a large gooseneck camping trailer came lumbering down the road at about sixty miles an hour, no vehicles close behind it. Perfect. As it went by his position, Casey gave chase, leapt to the top, and grabbed the air-conditioner unit. No one inside to hear him land, no one behind to see him jump. Forty miles to Indianapolis. He could have made it faster on foot, but why waste the energy? Besides, it felt really good to lay back and let the miles slide by.

He left the trailer on the outskirts of the city and went to a 7-11 to ask for directions. Blind luck. The motel was less than a mile away. He bought two Hershey bars for the sugar, thanked the clerk, and headed out on foot, walking slowly so as not to attract attention to himself.

The South Oak Inn was an upscale, three-story motor hotel, as they liked to call themselves. He arrived about midnight and stood at the side door, fumbling in his pocket as if for keys until an obliging tenant, on the way out, let him in. 334 was at the rear corner of the top floor with a card-keyed door lock. He walked to the front desk. The little girl behind the counter looked at him. He could see the pulse in her throat throb.

"Hi," she said. "Help you?"

"Yes," he said, lisping slightly. "My friend has cut his thumb on a shard of glass. It's not serious, but he's so afraid of scarring. I can't get him to go to the hospital and, really, he doesn't need to. I was wondering if you have a first aid kit? I can just butterfly his thumb and wrap it in gauze, if you do. He'll feel so much better if he has some sort of nasty old bandage, and I'll feel better if he'll just settle down and let me go to sleep!"

"Well, I'm not supposed to provide guests with any sort of medical supplies."

"Of course you're not, Darling. But you do have the opportunity to help a guest get some peace of mind and another to get some rest, for gosh sake. He's such a baby! Last year he ran a toothpick under his thumbnail about a thirty-second of an inch, and he screamed as if he'd been impaled upon a lance! Carried on for hours and bitched for days! Please help us. Please, please, please?"

"Well, we do have a kit."

"You are precious and a love! An angel of mercy! That shade of blue eye shadow really isn't your color, you know. Go a little darker in value, and you'll be stunning!"

"Just a minute," she giggled, and turned toward the back.

Before she made the three steps to the door, Casey was over the counter and in the drawer. She passed through the doorway as he found the duplicate card for Moira's room and returned to his starting position.

"Never mind, Darling," he warbled. She stopped and turned. "I could never forgive myself if I were to put your job in danger. I'll just run to the drug store and get something. There's one just down the street, isn't there?"

"About two blocks."

"Wonderful. I'll just check on him and tell him where I'm going, and be off and back in a flash."

"Okay. What room are you in?"

"Four-fifteen," Casey replied, heading up the stairs. "Ta!"

By the time the young woman realized there was no four-fifteen, Casey was in Moira's suite, reclining on her couch, and grinning at the ceiling. Her scent cobwebbed the room with its intensity. He couldn't wait to see what she looked like in the early morning.

# THREE

Introduction to a Vampire

AT AROUND FOUR A.M. Moira walked out of the bedroom and into the bath. Sleepy, she didn't notice Casey on the couch. He lay quietly until he heard her use the john. Before she could flush, he spoke up.

"Good morning."

A strangled shriek issued from the bathroom and the door slammed, the lock rattling vigorously.

Casey laughed. "Don't panic," he said. "You're in no danger. You might want to put on a towel or something before you come out. I've been in prison a long time. I could forget my manners."

"Casey?" she said, her voice muffled by the door.

"That would be me."

"Casey!"

"Right again."

"What the hell are you doing here? How did you get in my room? Why aren't you in prison?"

"Need something to put on?"

"Jesus Christ! You scared me half to death!"

"I'm a scary guy," he said, smelling her adrenalin sweat. "Need something to put on?"

"You're supposed to be locked up! How'd you get loose?"

"I don't like talking through doors. If you'd like to come out, may I bring you clothing of some type?"

"Ah, there are some sweats on the chair in the bedroom."

Casey collected the clothes and stood outside the bath. "Here you go."

She took the pants and shirt through the slightly opened door. Five minutes later, her hair partially brushed, she walked out into the living area and looked at him. Casey sat at a small table. He'd turned on a light.

"You have some explaining to do," Moira said. "Lemme start the coffee pot and get some shoes." She walked into the bedroom. When she came out, she was holding a handgun.

31

"You stay right in that fucking chair, Goddammit," she growled, pointing the gun at Casey, "and don't you move a muscle." Never taking her eyes off him, she backed toward the room phone.

"You don't have to call the cops," Casey said. "They're probably on the way here already." He glanced at the pistol. "When I smelled the gun oil, I expected a nine. That's a .45."

"If I wanna shoot poodles, I use a nine," she said. "If I wanna shoot people, I use a .45."

"Para-Ordnance, double action only. Nice gun."

"It works," she said, reaching for the phone.

"No calls, please," Casey said.

"Shut up and don't move," she said, lifting the receiver. Casey moved.

He covered the eighteen feet to where she stood in less than a quarter of a second. In the next quarter second he removed the cord from the back of the phone and grabbed the pistol with his thumb against the hammer so it couldn't accidentally discharge. He grasped Moira lightly by the back of the neck and locked eyes with her from a distance of three inches.

"Don't be brave," he whispered. "It won't help."

She passed out.

When she came back, Moira was lying on the couch, and Casey was wiping her face with a wet washcloth.

"Hello," he said. "How ya been?"

"You're not a dream," she stated.

"Nope. Nice of you to think so, though. You okay?"

"This is all real."

"So far. Can you sit up?"

He eased her to a sitting position. She put her elbows on her knees and leaned into her hands.

"How'd you get in here?"

He peeled back the paper on a Hershey bar and handed it to her. "Eat that. Your blood sugar is shot. It'll keep ya going 'til we can get you some real food."

"How'd you get out of prison? What in the hell is all this? What in the hell are you?"

Moira looked at him, tears gathering in the bottom of her eyes, a bit of chocolate clinging to her lip.

"Okay," he said. "Here's the deal. I don't have time to be nice. I don't have time for long explanations. You're in or you're out. You wanted to know my secrets? For a price I'll let you in on them, some of 'em at least, but only on my terms. I'll let you test me, examine me, learn what you can from me. Just to whet your scientific appetite: I don't get colds, I don't get ill, I can't get AIDS, my teeth don't decay, and I was forty-two years old long before your great great-grandfather was born."

Moira looked at him for a moment, then swallowed.

"You're serious."

"Lady, I am the most serious sonofabitch you ever met."

"God."

Resisting the urge to comfort her, Casey went on.

"What I need from you is a yes or a no to the deal. If you say no, I'm gone. When the cops show up, you can tell them anything you want. They won't believe you anyway. If you say yes, then you are in it. You are in it all the way. If you ever attempt to give me up or betray me, I'll be gone, and you'll be dead."

Moira fell back into the couch. "You're not kidding, are you?"

"Not one little bit."

"Okay," she said, running a hand through her hair and regaining some composure. "We know some of what's in it for me. What's in it for you, Casey?"

"Company, cover, a little security, and …"

"And? C'mon," she said, turning to face him. "Don't stop now. What else?"

He looked past her for a few seconds, pleased by the courage behind her quick recovery, and then he caught her eyes. "I want you to help me find my daughter."

"Your daughter?"

"You said you've got all these contacts, all this information. I don't know a thing about computers or anybody, except you, who does. Let's just say that you move in circles that I can't. I need your help; you need my help. Quid pro quo."

"A trade?"

"A trade. Deal?"

"Maybe," Moira said. "How old is she?"

"Fourteen."

"Where'd you see her last?"

"Chicago."

"When?"

"1852."

Moira leaned back on the couch and stared at Casey.

"You're nuts," she said.

"Nope."

"Certifiably ga-ga."

"Not me," he said.

"Then I am."

"Wrong again. I am not what I appear to be, and neither is my daughter. Where's your purse?"

"On the table."

Casey rummaged in her bag for a moment and retrieved a metal nail file.

"Watch carefully," he said, and plunged the file into his left forearm.

"Casey, Jesus!" Moira cried, sitting up.

Casey withdrew the file and held out his arm. In a matter of just seconds, the wound closed and disappeared.

"My God," Moira gasped.

"That's the tip of my iceberg, Miss Flynn."

"I'm in," she said.

"Just like that?"

"Just like that."

"Good. I hope you won't regret it."

She smiled. "I don't have many regrets. What's all this about the police?"

"I talked to you today, Butler brought me your card with this motel written on it, I left the prison. You're the best lead they have. I'm surprised they haven't shown up already."

"I'll just tell them I haven't seen you, I don't know where you are, you told me to leave you alone."

"You're harboring an escaped convicted murderer, Miss Flynn," Casey said. "That's a class A felony. You wouldn't like prison."

"Probably not."

"Plus, I killed a guard when I left Macon."

"What?"

"Graveyard dead. I did it on purpose with malice and forethought. He deserved to die, and I needed his life more than he did."

She studied his face. "You don't seem overly remorseful."

"I'm not. Now, here comes a big secret. It's the only one you get for nothing. You, by you I mean homo sapiens, you don't quite measure up to people like me."

"People like you?"

"People like me."

Her eyes flashed. "Then, there are more of you."

"Yes. While I am unique in your experience, I am not unique in my own."

"And you can do things the rest of us can't."

"Like you can't believe. Most of my kind considers your kind to be little more than cattle."

"Cattle?" she said, and Casey could see her pupils dilate with anger. "You mean like some kind of slow-witted herd?"

"No, Miss Flynn. I mean like livestock. To the Nosferati you are little more than food and recreation."

"What!"

"Prey, if you will."

She shuddered and wrapped her arms about herself. "That's horrible!"

"It is if you're one of the cows."

There was a sharp knock on the door. Moira jumped.

"Do whatever you think is best," Casey whispered. "You can still back out. Last chance."

"Who is it?" she shouted at the door.

"Police, Ma'am. Open up please."

"Just a minute. I've got to put something on." She turned back to Casey.

He was gone.

After the two policemen left, Moira sat on the couch for a while. They seemed to have believed her story. Casey didn't want anything to do with her. He had told her to leave him alone. She'd had no contact with him. He had not called again; he had not come by. How would she know where he was? If the prison couldn't keep track of their inmates, it wasn't her problem. She was leaving in the morning, driving back to Chicago. It had been a wasted trip. She'd talked to him about the survival rate of AIDS patients at Macon. Tracking AIDS data was her profession. Of course, she appreciated their concern for her safety. Yes, she was grateful they stopped by. Certainly, she'd be careful. This whole episode would get her started sooner than she'd planned. Just a quick shower and she'd be on her way. Once she was on the road, she'd be out of their hair and out of Casey's range.

She ate the last half of the Hershey bar, walked out on the balcony, and stared at the other wing of the motel. A blur appeared over the railing and flashed by her. She turned to see Casey sitting on the couch.

"Dammit," she blurted. "Stop that!"

He grinned at her as she walked into the room. "In another day or so. Pretty soon, I won't be able to do it. Good job with the cops, by the way."

"I told them …"

"I know what you told them. I was listening."

"From where?"

"The roof of the next building."

He pulled her .45 from the waistband of his slacks and held it out to her.

"Here. I took this with me when I left in case they shook the place down. Don't want you to get in trouble."

She accepted the gun. "At least they're gone," Moira said, checking the chamber for a live round.

"Silly girl," he said. "They have six men in three unmarked cars triangulated on the parking lot. It'll be getting light soon. Forget the quick shower. Get dressed and we'll hit the road."

"We? You just said they were watching."

"Get dressed. Everything's fine."

In keeping with Casey's instructions, Moira pulled her car under the office over-hang, put her two bags on a cart, and wheeled them out to the Taurus. She opened the rear passenger door and then put her luggage in the trunk. Walking back by the open door, she closed it and noticed Casey grinning at her from the rear floor. She bit her lip to keep from grinning back. Twenty minutes later, she was westbound on I-74, and Casey was in the front seat. They had yet to speak, and she attempted to digest what had happened. When Moira lit a cigarette, Casey knew she was ready to talk. He lit one of his own and partially turned to face her.

"So?" he said.

"So, what are you, some kinda superhero?"

"Superhero?"

"Yeah. You came over that railing like Spiderman or somebody."

Casey grinned. "No superhero. I'm what is often called a Nosferati."

"Nosferati? What does that mean, like Nosferatu?"

"Just like that."

"Vampires? You're telling me that you're a vampire?!"

"That's exactly what I'm telling you."

"Bed rest," Moira muttered, trying to keep her eyes on the road. "Lots of bed rest, extensive therapy, warm baths, long walks, maybe a puppy to play with a little while every day. You are fruitier than a nutcake!" She took a long drag on her Virginia Slim. "Vampire my ass!"

"Take it easy, Miss Flynn …"

"Stop calling me that!" Moira shouted, waving her cigarette dangerously close to the headliner. "I just lied to the cops for you, smuggled you out of a city where they'd just as soon shoot you as look at you, and now I'm aiding and abetting your escape. Thanks to you, I am a fleeing felon! This fleeing felon's name is Moira, goddammit! Call me by my fucking name!"

"Moira," Casey said quietly, "you're driving over ninety miles an hour. We don't need to be stopped by some highway cop. Slow down. Be calm. We just passed a rest area sign. Pull in and let's talk."

She almost missed the exit, braking violently and shooting up the ramp much too fast. She slid into a space in the nearly empty pet-walking section of the parking area and slammed the front tires violently into the concrete retainer. The car rocked on its springs. Moira stared blankly at the dashboard and trembled.

"Jesus Christ," she muttered. "Vampires? Gimme a break!"

"I need one too," Casey said, opening his door. "C'mon. Grab your purse and let's take a stroll before somebody pulls in to walk their dog."

"What's that got to do with anything?"

"Dogs, as a rule, don't like me."

"And I do?" Moira asked.

Casey chuckled. "C'mon. You need movement."

"Stop telling me what I need! Stop telling me what I should do!" She stabbed the dead cigarette into the ashtray. "And for God's sake, don't tell me there are Vampires! That's bullshit! There are no such things as Vampires! No tooth fairy, no Easter bunny, no Santa Claus, no Great Pumpkin, no Loch Ness Monster, no fucking Bigfoot, okay?"

She was pounding on the steering wheel, with tears in the corners of her eyes. She turned to him. "There are no fucking Vampires, goddammit! There are no fucking Vampires!"

Moira sagged back in the seat, head down, her arms dropping to her sides. She sat that way for a moment, sniffling, then glanced sideways at Casey.

"Are there?" she whispered.

"I'm gonna walk around for a while," he said. "Wanna join me?"

"Why the hell not?" she said, and blew her nose into a Kleenex. "I've come this far."

They walked slowly to the concession area, and Casey got her a cup of black coffee from a machine. He then purchased a can of orange juice, two packages of cashews, and some Hostess cupcakes. He led her to a picnic table, and they sat down.

"When you've finished all that stuff," he said, "I'll get you some bottled water, and we can drive on 'til we find a restaurant."

Moira opened the cupcakes with trembling fingers. "So, tell me, Casey," she said. "You a Vampire, big guy?"

"Depends on who you ask," he said. "We, my kind, owe a real debt to Bram Stoker, Anne Rice, Bela Lugosi, Gary Oldman, Wesley Snipes, and all the others who have perpetuated the myth over the years. I have no fangs, I don't sleep in a box, I love garlic, I use a mirror from time to time, and, as you can see, I have a tan."

36

"What about crucifixes? Scared of those?"

"Another myth, presented to ignorant masses by the Catholic Church to help maintain control through fear."

"This is just too weird," Moira said. "You actually believe that you're a vampire?"

"You're missing the point. I actually am a vampire."

"Okay," she said, fingering the filling out of the center of a Hostess cupcake. "I'll play along. Stake through your heart kill you?"

"It might, if you could find somebody good enough to put it there."

"Can you come into my house if I don't invite you?"

"I already did."

"Oh, yeah. The motel room. Can you change yourself into a bat?"

"No, but I can walk down the street and turn into a bar."

"Thank you, ladies and gentlemen," Moira snorted. "Isn't he wonderful? Count Dracula will be here all week. Be sure and catch tomorrow night's show with special guest, The Mummy!"

She finished her cupcakes in silence. Casey waited patiently. Finally, she turned to him.

"You gotta have blood?"

"Yep."

"Really?"

"Really. That's why I worked in the hospital. Lots of blood. I'd syringe ten or twenty cc's out of a fresh bag every day. Nobody noticed; nobody got hurt. Good deal all around. Drink your orange juice and eat some nuts. Make you big and strong."

"And what can I get for you, Sir?" she said. "A pancreas? Some nice liver? A spleen or two?"

"That's enough."

"A warm glass of AB negative?"

"Stop it."

"You wanna straw with that, or just straight from the neck?"

"Stop it!"

"How 'bout a snack?" Moira spat. "I found a four-year-old wandering in the parking lot who looks plump!"

"I said stop it!"

"Fuck you, Casey, and the broom you rode in on!" she snarled.

He looked at her, and something flickered behind his eyes that instantly brought goose flesh to Moira's arms and neck. "Got a chill, little human?" he hissed. A sparrow before his cobra, she froze. "You pompous, judgmental, narrow-minded, ignorant cunt! For centuries I've watched you good, God-fearing fools kill and rape and burn and sacrifice your own kind on a hundred battlefields. In a thousand alleys I've seen you use each other for selfish purpose and then just walk away. Your religion has killed untold millions, your patriotism equally as many. Your kind, Miss Flynn, kills for land or money. Your kind kills for hate or jealousy. Your kind kills for God or Allah. Your kind kills for poison to pump into your own fucking veins! Your kind has blood on your collective hands so rank, fetid, and congealed that no amount of washing could ever remove it, and you call me names because I have a drop or two on my chin?

"You kill more people every day in family disputes than I could slay in a hundred years with a thousand swords! You drop bombs, you fire missiles, you drink your blood from miles away by pushing a button. You commit unspeakable acts against your fellows and even beseech God to help you! And you judge me?"

Casey got to his feet and began to pace.

"I'll tell you who we are, little human Moira. We are the thing that goes bump in the night. We are the tickle on the back of your neck when there is no breeze. We are the gurgle at the bottom of a well, the new creak in an old house, the bare branches scraping against the bedroom window at night. We are the unexplained disappearance, the empty bed, the shadow in the corner of your eye, the empty chair that rocks."

He paused long enough to smile at her. Moira's head spun.

"We are what makes the lonely dog bark and what makes the alley cat hiss. We are the snapping twig in the dark. We are what roams outside the circle of firelight. We live in the closet. We lurk under the bed. We are the werewolf, the shape-shifter, the zombie, the evil spirit, the moan in the woods, and the cry on the wind. We are your worst nightmare, and we may just be your salvation. When the herd is diseased, the wise stockman culls out the sick animals. We are the wolves to your buffalo! Be goddammed careful you don't come up lame!"

He was looking down at her. Energy crackled and sung around him like leaves in a whirlwind. Weak and fighting to breathe, Moira watched him sit down. During the entire tirade, he had not raised his voice, but her ears ached and rang. She clutched at the edge of the table and waited for the world to right itself. After some time, she licked her trembling lips and spoke.

"Jesus Christ," she said.

Casey smiled. "Drink your orange juice, Miss Flynn," he said. "It's good for you."

# FOUR

## Road Trip

THEY STOPPED OUTSIDE DANVILLE, ILLINOIS, for lunch at a Bob Evans. Moira ate like she had three stomachs and said almost nothing. As they got back on the road, Casey could smell some of the fear leave her. He could also sense her struggle with what was left.

"So ask," he said.

"What?"

"Ask. You have questions. Ask."

"Okay," Moira replied, shifting to a more upright posture and taking a deep breath. "Why don't you wear a cape?"

"Jesus! Straight to the hard stuff."

"Forgive me," she said. "This is really scary. If I take it all seriously, I'll explode. This is obviously more than Count Dracula or some old Wesley Snipes movie. I'm just trying to get my mind around it. I don't know what to call you."

"How 'bout Casey?"

"No, I mean your, ah, kind. Nosferati, you said?"

"Yeah. If they had the same mindset and were just human, they'd be Hell's Angels, or white separatists, or black militants, or radical Muslims, or some such. They're vampires and they like it. They want to be vampires. The killing is a recreational drug to them. They're addicted to it."

"Addicted to it?"

"That's the best way I can explain it. You know how some people have addictive personalities. Well, so do Nosferati. Lots of drug addiction, alcohol addiction, sex addiction, blood addiction, killing addiction. They are not nice. The predators that kill for pleasure are almost always human. In the case of the Nosferati, they are more than human."

"What about you?"

"I'm a sweetheart."

She smiled. "I bet."

"A Nosferati might have killed you for your car. Hell, a Nosferati might have killed those cops that came to the motel, all six of them, just for the fun of it."

"Wouldn't that attract a lot of attention?"

"That's about the only thing that contains them. All of us need secrecy."

"Are all vampires Nosferati?"

"Every one I've ever known."

"Including you?"

"Including me," Casey said. He felt her fear rise. "But, I'm more what you could call Nosferati emeritus."

Moira glanced at him from the corner of her eye. "But you can come out of retirement, can't you?"

"In a blink," Casey replied.

He noticed her hands tighten on the wheel and smelled her adrenal response. Casey listened to the faint whistle of breath through her nostrils and let her struggle with her fear. She was, after all, human. The only human on the planet who knew what he was, and she really didn't know everything. No other human who had ever known had been allowed to live. Not one. A trail of corpses followed Casey across the years. And now, on I-74, in glorious summer sunshine, he rode in a Ford Taurus with a woman—a human woman to whom he had told some of his secrets and would possibly tell more on the off chance he might actually find Cat—who probably wouldn't want anything to do with him anyway. Emotions flickered past him at such speed, he could only catch glimpses of them as they darted by. The whole thing was insane, and it frightened him to the marrow.

Moira drove for several miles until she settled down, then spoke up again. "Can bullets kill you?"

"Sure. How many it would take would depend on how long it had been since I'd fed. Almost any trauma that can kill you, can kill me. It would just take a lot more of it to kill me."

"How can you move so fast?"

"I work out."

"C'mon," she said.

"I don't really know. I'm not a scientist. I read once that Ted Williams …"

"Ted Williams?"

"Major League ball player back in the fifties. Hell of an eye. Knock the shit outta the ball. Anyway, I read someplace that he could read the label on a spinning, old fashioned, seventy-eight RPM record."

"Really?"

"Yeah. Most people can't do that, I guess."

"Nobody I've ever heard of. Could you?"

"Sure, but we're not talking about me. Anyway, the article went on to say that Ted Williams had nerve responses about twenty percent faster than the average human. That's why he hit so consistently. He could see better and act on what he saw faster than most people. The information traveled the neural pathways through his body more quickly than normally. I suspect that's sorta what I do. Everything works faster, a lot faster. I'm also much stronger than you are, speaking in generalities. Probably something like sustainable surge energy. A limitless adrenalin rush, although I have no idea if adrenalin is involved. I do know that I'm at my best a few minutes after I feed. It wears off in a couple of days."

"So what if you don't get to, ah, feed? Do you get weak?"

"Compared to you, no. At my worst, I'm still much better than humans. Compared to my best, I'm pretty screwed up."

"So that's why you stole blood from the medical supply. To stay at your best."

He chuckled. "God, no. I wasn't close to my best. Let's see, if an exceptional human is a one, and fresh after feeding is a ten, I never get lower than a four. The hospital munchies kept me around a six."

She looked at him from the corner of her eye. "So how fast are you?"

"Right now, in my present condition?"

"Yes."

"I could run with a cheetah."

"What about right after you fed?"

"He'd barely see me as I went by."

"Really?"

"Really."

"How 'bout your senses. Sight?"

"Like a hawk and an owl combined."

"Smell?"

"Bloodhounds send me fan mail."

"Hearing?"

"What?"

"Heari—asshole."

"I heard that."

"So you're pretty much super-human."

"I can't fly, I don't have x-ray vision, and bullets don't bounce off me, but I'm not afraid of Kryptonite."

"So, when do you need to, ah, feed again?"

"That's not what you want to know," he said, slipping into a bad Baltic accent. "*You vant to know when I em going to keel somevone unt dreenk dere blut.*"

"You think this is funny?" Moira glared at him. "You think that killing people so you can ingest their blood is some kind of joke?"

"No. I take that very seriously. What amuses me is that you're still waiting for me to grow fangs, hiss, and launch myself at your neck. You find the prospect dreadful, but stimulating as long as it's not in the front seat with you. Dracula's biggest fans have always been women. It's the ultimate, totally overwhelming, submission fantasy. Past assault, past rape, past death. The growl in the ear, the breath on the neck, the fangs in the throat, the sucking of the old life, and the licking of the new."

Casey paused for a moment, surprised at what he heard himself saying, and feeling Moira's blood pressure rise as she shifted in her seat.

"The fact that I'm actually here," he continued, "takes a bit of the romance out of it."

"Romance!"

"Sure."

"You got a pretty high opinion of yourself! What if I stopped the car and told you to get the hell out?"

"Moot point," Casey said. "You won't do that."

"Oh, yeah?"

"Yeah."

"Why not?"

"Too much attraction," Casey said, feeling her anger rise. "Too much curiosity. Too much myth. Dracula was quite a ladies' man, you know. It wasn't because he was pretty."

"What?" Moira said, rising to the bait. "Look, Buster! If you think that ..."

"Besides," Casey interrupted, "you're doing much better. You are not nearly as afraid of me as you were a few hours ago."

"What difference does that make?" she said, adjusting her position and taking the wheel in both hands. "I'm still your prisoner."

He raised his eyebrows and looked at her. "Is that what you think?"

"You're here, aren't you? You can kill me with your pinky, can't you? You already threatened my life."

"What?"

"You said that if I betrayed you, you'd be gone and I'd be dead!"

Casey smiled. "Oh, that."

"Oh, that? Oh, that! My life may not be very important to you, you sonofabitch, but it's all I have!"

"Please, forgive me," Casey said. "I had to get your attention. Believable death threats work well. I have no intention of ever causing you harm."

Her sarcasm was thick. "Even if I betray you?"

"You can't betray me."

Moira caught him with the corner of her eye. "Oh yeah?" she said. "You don't get out much, do you?"

"How much do you weigh?"

"Huh?"

"How much do you weigh?"

She glanced at him. "One-eighteen."

"Liar."

"What?"

"You just lied."

"I did not!"

"Again she lies," he said. "Is there no end to her deception? Can there never be honesty between us?"

Moira stared straight ahead and drove. A flush spread up her neck and onto her face.

Casey smiled. "Take it easy. It's not like you can't have secrets from me. You can have them by the carload. You just can't lie to me about them. All I have to do is ask you if you're going to betray me or if you're plotting against me. If you say no, and you're lying, I'm gone. You're left with a story that will have you staying in Hoo-Hah Acres, getting lotsa needles in your lovely ass, and I'll be a speck in the distance."

Still she looked straight ahead and said nothing.

"So, Miss Flynn," he said. "Whatdaya weigh?"

She ignored him and continued to drive.

They passed through Champaign-Urbana and turned southwest toward St. Louis. Moira still wouldn't look at him, but her body posture had relaxed a bit.

"I just love road trips," Casey said. "Unknown destinations, new people to meet. What better way to spend a day or two than getting to know each other, finding common interests, building a bond, sharing an experience."

"Oh, shut up," she said, stifling a smile.

"All better now?" Casey said.

"I'm over it."

"Speaking of being somebody's prisoner," Casey said, changing the subject. "Where are you taking me?"

"Kansas City."

"Nothing on your business card said Kansas City."

She shook her head. "The card lists our offices. Kansas City is not one of our offices. It's a research facility. Provenance Center. From there I can access all the resources Proteus has to offer. We can get started on finding your daughter. Do you have any idea where she might be?"

"None. The last time I thought I knew was in Indianapolis over twelve years ago."

"When you killed those people?"

"Yeah. Nosferati people. Heavy dopers, too."

"They were vampires?"

"Yep."

"Let me get this straight," she said, slowing down and looking at him. "Vampires can get addicted to drugs?"

"Not exactly."

"That clears it up."

Casey smiled. "Physical addiction is minor because our bodies, for the most part, don't become dependant on substances. They work too well to allow that to happen. Almost all illness comes from an imbalance in the function of the physical body. The reasons for the imbalance can be wide and varied, but if the balance goes, sickness results. If a Nosferati is a crackhead, he can be a crackhead for years and years without doing himself any significant harm. His body won't allow it. He does, however, get high, just like anybody else. It may take more of the drug to accomplish the desired effect, but the effect happens.

"The addiction is psychological and emotional. If you don't think that's powerful stuff, try taking a toddler's favorite blanket away. As I said before, Nosferati are addictive personalities. They love the rush. That's why they kill for sport. That, and to feed their habit."

"What habit?"

"Blood. All of us are addicted to that."

Dusk caught up with them as they neared Effingham, Illinois.

"I need a room, a shower, fresh clothes, and a lot of food," Moira said. "How 'bout you?"

"All of the above," Casey said, "but I have no clothes or toiletries."

"There's a Wal-Mart sign," she said, slowing for an exit. "Let's buy you some."

"I don't have much money."

"Relax. I do."

"Real money?"

"Credit cards."

"No good. If the police have happened to put two and two together, they can trace you by the cards. Cash only. There's a grocery across from the Wal-Mart. Park there. I won't be a minute."

She pulled into the parking lot of an IGA, and Casey was out the door. Less than thirty seconds later, she saw him walk out of the building and grin as he approached the car. He got in and held up a wad of bills.

"Jesus," she said. "How much?"

"Couple of grand or so. Stores like this have that elevated office with a swinging door, and they never lock the safe. Simple. A little misdirection and cash in hand."

"Misdirection?"

"Yeah. In this case it was a collapsed pyramid of canned peaches and a broken lobster tank. Let's go to Wal-Mart and spend some of our ill-gotten booty."

"You just walked into that store and stole a bunch of money."

"We needed it. We're fleeing felons. What's a fleeing felon without a crime spree?"

She grinned at him and shook her head. "Jesus Christ," Moira said. "Shades of Bonnie and Clyde."

At a Days Inn, Casey got out of the car on the street and let Moira check in. After she got the small suite, he hurried in before she could close the door.

"You shower first," he said, ignoring the small start she gave when she saw him. "I'll be faster and you can dress while I'm in the john. Less chance of violating your modest upbringing."

"That's exactly why I got a suite. The living room is yours."

"You mean I'm gonna have to sleep out here on some lumpy pull-out couch thing?"

Moira grinned. "I thought you guys hung upside down by your toes when you snoozed," she said, and closed the bedroom door.

Casey took the tags off his new clothes and laid out underwear, a dark blue sport shirt, black jeans, white socks, and a pair of white running shoes. The rest of the clothing he put in his new suitcase. He then quietly entered the bedroom and, under the cover of the shower noise, searched Moira's luggage for any contraband. Nothing of interest except the pistol and an appointment reminder for a biopsy scheduled at a Kansas City hospital in three days. He made it back to the living area with time to spare.

In a few minutes, wrapped neck to toes in the suite's spare blanket, Moira walked barefoot into the living room.

Casey eyed her up and down. "That blanket looks a little heavy. Should have picked you up some suitable intimate wear when we bought my Jockey shorts."

"Like what?" Moira said. "Sweat socks?"

"Okay by me," Casey said.

Moira straightened the blanket as it fell off her shoulder.

"Oh, good. Am I gonna have trouble with you, Casey?" she said.

"What do you think?"

Moira pondered him rather seriously as she struggled with the slipping blanket. "I think, despite your perverse taste for hemoglobin, plasma, and the like, that you are an honorable man. I'm a little afraid of you, Casey, for a variety of reasons, but the sanctity of my virtue is not one of them."

"Damn. How 'bout if I just sit here until the blanket falls off? I love a cheap thrill."

"Be still my beating heart. Take your shower and let's go eat. I'm hungry."

As he entered the bathroom, Casey noticed her heart rate was a little high.

The restaurant, Neimerg's Steak House, was just across the parking lot. They seated themselves at a corner table and were almost immediately set upon by a young woman in uniform asking if they wanted coffee. Moira had two center cut pork chops, green beans, sweet corn, a side salad, and coffee. Casey had a large salad, a twenty-four ounce, extra rare T-bone, a double order of mashed potatoes, onion rings, five dinner rolls, three large glasses of milk, and two pieces of cocoanut cream pie with eight inches of meringue. Moira gaped at him over her cup.

"Jesus!"

"I need lotsa calories. It's one of the prices I pay for my abilities. It gets worse after I feed. I'll be hungry again in a couple of hours."

"Getting tired?" she said.

"Yeah. I need to rest. I can go without a lot of sleep, but I have to have rest. If we go back to the motel now, can I trust you not to try to take advantage of me and spoil what has otherwise been a perfect evening?"

"Me?"

"Don't get all indignant. Just answer the question."

"I suppose I can restrain myself," she said.

"In that case, I'll let you hold my hand when we walk back."

In the parking lot he took her hand and held it securely until he opened the door of the suite. Halfway back to the room she began to weave, even stumbling as she crossed the threshold. He steadied her.

Struggling to keep her eyes open, Moira looked at him.

"God. I'm sorry, Casey, I'm just beat all of a sudden. I gotta go to bed. Can hardly keep my eyes open. You need the john?"

"If I do, I'll sneak in. Go to bed."

She held on to the doorframe, weaving a bit.

"'Kay. Goo'nite Case."

He held the door handle and smiled at her. "By the way," he said. "That biopsy that's coming up?"

Confused, she stared at him quizzically, fighting with her eyelids.

"My biopsy?"

"Yeah."

"How ... how'd you ... wha' 'bout it?"

"It'll be negative now. You're fine."

Casey closed the door and went to pull out the lumpy couch.

Casey lay down and stared at the ceiling. The sound and scent of Moira took him back, back before the blood to a time when God had blessed him with work and family. When his forearms were constantly scarred from shards of hot metal escaped from the blows of the smithy's hammer. When life was hard and good and began in the morn and sometimes did not finish until the morrow. When he lay with fair Elizabeth out of affection more than need, out of love more than want, and when his daughter was still just his daughter.

Umbaylay

NG'MUTU UMBAYLAY had never been so frightened in his life. Awakened from sleep by the screams, he ran out of his mother's house without even taking a weapon. The village was awash with running figures. He saw his sister's husband bolt from his hut and be struck down by several men with clubs. They were everywhere, dozens of them. He ducked back inside, but three followed him. His mother rose shrieking from her pallet and was clubbed into silence. He fought, barehanded, with all his might and courage, but it did no good. Ng'mutu was also laid low.

When he came to himself, he was bound by thongs and lying amid his own urine in undergrowth beneath a tree. Near him were several others he did not know, also in bonds. Nowhere did he see his mother, or anyone from his village. He did not recognize even where he was. His hands and feet were numb and horribly swollen, he was very thirsty and hungry, and dried blood was flaking from the side of his head. A man approached him and began to shout in a language he didn't understand and poke him with a sharp stick. Ng'mutu swayed to his feet and was tied by the neck to several other prisoners. Two or three that could not stand were lifted on poles, and the procession began to walk. On the second day of their journey, a man walking behind him in line spoke.

"You are an Igbo man?" he said.

"Yes. I am Ng'mutu Umbaylay."

"I am Oyo. I am called Huna Toati. These that have taken us from our homes and families are Bevin. They are no better than the Bantu."

"Where are we?" Ng'mutu said.

"I do not know. I have never been to this country. You were carried for three days until your spirit returned to your body. I think you would have been better off if it had not come back."

"We must escape," Ng'mutu said.

"They are many, we are tied."

"I swear to you, Oyo man Huna Toati, that I will find a way to run away, and I will take you with me."

"I swear to you, Igbo man Ng'mutu Umbaylay, that I will go with you if you find a way to leave these Bevin pieces of monkey shit."

They walked for eleven more days, the prisoners kept weak and disoriented, until they stopped on the bank of the biggest body of water Ng'mutu had ever seen. The opposite shore was so far away, it was invisible. He tried to drink from it, but the water was brackish, and he soon threw up most of what he swallowed. He and his fellows were integrated into a group of several hundred other prisoners, all chained together at the ankles. They were given a vegetable stew to eat and water to drink, and allowed to lie down. At dusk, they were surrounded by dozens of Bevin and many fires.

Late that night Ng'mutu finally fell asleep. A severe pain in his upper thigh flung him awake. He struck at the thing biting him, screaming from fear. Shouting erupted from the ring of guards and, suddenly, he was under a pile of thrashing bodies. The fight raged over him for a few seconds, then exploded, several men thrown from atop him by one small man. In the firelight, Ng'mutu could see the man's eyes shining from his blood-covered face. He snapped and snarled at the group that surrounded him, nearly laughing at them. A great noise slapped out of the darkness like quick thunder, and the bloody man grunted and clutched at his throat. Blood welled from between his fingers. Another big noise sounded, and Ng'mutu saw the man's right eye disappear in a splash of blood. He sank to one knee, snarling like a beast, and the group swarmed over him again. The fight lasted only a short time, and when the men got up, one of them held a severed head aloft. The rest cheered.

Then Ng'mutu saw the most frightening sight he'd ever seen. Another man approached the group. His body was covered by strange clothing, and his feet were encased and kept separate from the earth. He approached the corpse and gave it a kick, then turned and looked down at Ng'mutu. The man had hair growing from his jaw, and his face was almost as light in color as the belly of a fish.

For two more days Ng'mutu and the others were held by the water until a house floated up to near the shore. Living in the house were even more white men. They came ashore in small boats with long paddles, and took all the prisoners into their house. Poked and prodded with iron sticks and knives, Ng'mutu went with all of them down into the house even below the surface of the water. There, in a dimly lit room, he and the others were arranged on shelves, shoulder to shoulder, lying on their backs, heads toward a passage down the center of the long room, and secured to metal rings by the iron bindings on their ankles. There were many more people in that floating house than lived in his entire village, and Ng'mutu was afraid for all of them. Many cried and shouted, but he kept silent. Even when the house began to move and sway, he held his tongue. His thigh ached horribly where the man had bitten him, and he felt sick, but he did not want to attract attention to himself.

As the days wore on, Ng'mutu became more and more ill. He sweated and cried, had terrible dreams, chilled and wept, and— at length unable to eat or drink, covered with sores from lying on the bare wood, poisoned by infection in the huge and swollen wound on his leg—became sure he was going to die. He wanted to die, he needed to die, and finally, on the nineteenth day, he did.

On the twenty-third day, Ng'mutu Umbaylay—still shackled in his place and four days dead—opened his eyes and smiled. He was hungry.

The seas were running nearly due west. Van Zant, the pilot, stood at the wheel. It had been like this for nearly two days, and he didn't like it. Even if the seas had been perfect, he wouldn't have liked it. It was his third trip on a slaver and each time he'd promised himself he'd never make another one. The smell was awful, the occasional shrieks and moans struck him as if he stood above the pits of hell. He thought of the wretches below decks and shuddered. It paid well if money alone could justify the trip. Jane was home in London with the children. Two more voyages such as this and he could leave that crush of humanity and live well in one of the shires—perhaps even buy a small title, be a landholder, never to sail again.

The wind shifted a bit to south of east and he turned a point or two into it, tacking, taking the following sea on the port stern. The Wren began to wallow slightly and he shouted to the mate to trim sail and slow her pitching. Truth be told, he didn't like the ship. She was too wide of beam for his taste and short-keeled. Instead of bridging the narrow troughs, she had a tendency to slide into them, bucking as she recovered, moving more like a pony than a horse. Still, she was game and knew her rudder. She could run a bit too, even with her beam. Right now, she was under reduced sail and still had a bone in her teeth. Van Zant felt the wind freshen and eased her off a point, changing her course slightly. The first mate felt it and came up on deck.

"Strange wind, strange sea, Pilot," he said as he scanned the horizon behind them.

"Aye, Mister Blake, it feels less than right to me, too. If this old piss-pot will hold together, we'll give it a run though," Van Zant said. "Have you seen the captain today?"

"He's in his cabin up to his ears in grog, the old sot," Blake grimaced. "When I knew I'd be sailing with Captain Pieterzoon himself, I was cheered, Pilot. I didn't know that he'd outlived his reputation and let the drink have him. He's as useless as a white dress on a pox-ridden whore!"

Van Zant grinned. "You still get your tenth, First, and I still get my fifth. All we have to do is his job. You should just about be in line for a ship of your own."

"That's right enough, Pilot. Two more trips as good as this, and me purse will hold enough to buy into a company or get me a boat of me own. Then I can lay up in me own cabin, soak up all the grog I can drink, and have some poor fools like us bring me a bit of fleshy entertainment from below decks from time to time."

Van Zant laughed. "Live the good life, right, First?"

"What's good for that drunken old croak ain't necessarily good for me. I still got to wiggle under God's almighty eye. It's a sin to be layin' with them darkies and spillin' yer seed into a heathen's cleft. It's the Devil's work, Pilot, and no good will come of it!"

"The Captain doesn't seem to mind."

"Mind? Mind! That rum-soaked sot had Kinnick bring him two last night. Two! For all I know they're still laid up in there with him. I don't know what kind of shape they're in though. I heard him slappin' one or both of 'em around at watch change. He will have what he wants, old pus-bag!"

"Fed and watered 'em yet today, First?"

"Aye. Sent boys below at end of watch. They claim we got seven or eight dead. I thought we'd overboard 'em when the sea settles a bit. I don't want to get no one hurt draggin' no corpses up out of the hold."

"At your pleasure. Whenever you like."

"This wind ever lays, we need to get the rest of 'em up on deck a few at a time and dance 'em some. Scrape 'em down good and bucket 'em off with seawater. Pike says some of 'em has got sores. We don't want to lose too many head."

"That's your end of the business, First," Van Zant said. "I just aim the boat."

The mate let his eyes drift slowly back toward the stern horizon. "Aye," he said. "We all got our ... God in heaven, Pilot! Mind your wheel and stay your course!"

Van Zant followed the mate's line of sight. Three times as tall as the Wren's deck, a wave was rushing at them from the port stern. Both men braced themselves against the wheel as the monster struck.

The mountain slapped the Wren's stern around with casual grace, instantly changing the ship's course by nearly ninety degrees. Water cascaded over the deck, soaking both men and lifting the pilot off his feet. Only his hands on the spokes of the wheel saved him from being washed overboard. Foam sluiced through the scuppers as the Wren shook herself, heeling mightily to starboard, then slowly coming aright. Van Zant stayed with the wheel as the mate rang the helm's bell and called for all hands on deck.

# FIVE

## Breakfast

CASEY WAS LYING AWAKE AT AROUND SIX A.M. when Moira came sneaking toward the kitchenette of the suite. He waited until she was walking beside his position on the couch before he spoke.

"Fair morn."

"Jesus! Goddammit, Casey! Don't do that!"

Casey grinned, enjoying the sight and scent of her and opening his arms where he lay. "My but you're beautiful early in the day," he said. "C'mon, Sweetheart, give us a kiss." He puckered his lips and produced a series of smacking sounds.

She stared at him through the gloom and tried not to smile. "What the hell is the matter with you?"

"Just glad to be alive, sweet Moira," he said, "and trying to catch you off guard in a moment of weakness. You know, you're really lovely with your hair sticking up like that. Been sleeping on the left side of your face I see."

"Bite me."

Casey raised an eyebrow. "I beg your pardon?"

Moira looked at him for a moment before her brain kicked in. "Oops."

"Not that I don't appreciate the offer, but it could have a very negative effect on our working relationship. How you feeling?"

She stared blankly into the distance for a moment. "It's weird. I slept like a log. I don't think I even rolled over. But I'm still beat, or loopy, or something, and I'm so hungry, I'm cramping!"

Casey swung his feet to the floor and sat up. "You should be," he said. "Your body has been working very hard. We should consider staying here for the day. It'll give you a chance to sleep and rest."

"I don't wanna waste time. We need to get back on the road."

"Let's talk about it after breakfast."

Breakfast had the waitress checking under the table to see where the food went. Moira ate an order of pigs n' blankets with hash browns, biscuits and gravy, two over easy, corned beef hash, a ham steak, grits, toast and a side of apple butter. Casey had two breakfast steaks, very rare, a three-egg omelet, home fries, two biscuits with blueberry jam, and a short stack with strawberries. When they finally finished, even some of the farmers were staring.

"God, Casey!" Moira blushed. "I usually don't eat that much in two days! This is embarrassing. Let's get out of here."

"You go on," he said. "I'll be along shortly."

Moira had been back in the room for about five minutes, sitting on the pullout couch and staring numbly at the floor when Casey walked in carrying a paper bag.

"More food?" she yawned, her eyes tearing. "Sorry. I feel like I haven't slept in a week."

"Yep. A turkey sandwich, a club sandwich, and chips for you, two more un-cooked breakfast steaks for me, and four pieces of pie for the two of us. We'll both need something to tide us over until lunch."

She looked at him. "You're not kidding, are you?"

"Nope. If I can't get blood, I eat a lot. I have to."

"I'm just glad you brought something for the room. I don't dare go back in that restaurant again. I'm developing a reputation. I never eat like that! Okay. You need a lot of calories if you can't get blood, I can accept that. What's my excuse?"

"You're healing."

"Healing?"

"Do you remember what I said to you last night?"

"The last thing I remember was you holding my hand as we walked across the parking lot. I don't even remember going to bed." She thought a moment. "That's strange. Did I pass out or something?"

"Yes, you did. I had to take off all your clothes and tuck you in. It was a dirty job …"

"Bullshit."

"Okay. It wasn't a dirty job."

"Bullshit again."

He smiled. "No, you didn't pass out. Yes, you did get real flaky. No, you don't need to get that biopsy you're scheduled for. You're fine."

"My biopsy! How did you know I was scheduled for a biopsy?"

Casey grinned sheepishly. "I, ah, went through your purse."

She stared at him. "You went through my purse."

"Yep."

"Goddammit! Who the hell do you think you are?"

"Aw, our first fight."

"My ass! The next time you get curious about something, just …" She stopped, mouth open, and gaped at him. "I'm fine? Whattaya mean, I'm fine?"

Casey smiled at the shock on her face.

"I don't know what was wrong with you," he said, "but something was, or you wouldn't be this hungry and tired. Whatever it was, it's not wrong anymore."

"What?"

"You are healed," Casey said. He moved to the other side of the room for space and sat at a small table. "Well, healing at least. Whatever was ailing you, Miss Flynn, within twenty-four hours or so, will probably ail you no more."

"Really?"

"Really."

Moira peered around the room for a moment, trying to collect her thoughts and focus. "That's why you held my hand."

"That's one of the reasons," Casey said.

"Oh, yeah? What's the other one?"

"I was hoping you'd pass out, and I'd get to take off all your clothes and tuck you in."

"Didn't work out for you, huh?"

"Naw. Had to settle for a healing. What was wrong with you anyway, if that's not too personal?"

She looked steadily at him. "The biopsy was to double check a positive one I had last week for ovarian cancer."

"Well, you don't need it now."

"No kidding?"

"No kidding," he said, ignoring the tears he saw gathering in her eyes.

Again she paused for control, then looked across the room to where Casey sat. "That's what you did for Theotus Lark."

"I guess."

"Have you always been able to heal people?"

"I don't think so. Nosferati can heal themselves, but healing another person isn't a consideration. As a rule, they don't give a damn what happens to anyone else. I think the healing thing began after I dried out."

"Dried out?"

"Overcame my addiction to blood. I noticed it after I got my job in the hospital. Guys I worked on and actually touched seemed to feel better. I didn't deliberately try to heal anybody until Theotus got stung and went into shock. In retrospect, it was a foolish thing to do as far as my welfare was concerned, but I couldn't stand by and do nothing. Theotus was my friend. I hadn't had a friend in a very long time."

"So you healed him."

"Evidently," Casey said. "I gave him mouth to mouth. Standard protocol. I was as surprised as anybody else when he recovered and was free of AIDS."

Moira sniffed and squared her shoulders. "How do you do that?"

"I don't have the faintest idea."

"Want to find out?"

"Not particularly."

"Well, I do," she said. "Want a piece of pie?"

"Not particularly."

"Well, I do," she said. "Pass me the bag, Casey, and thank you. Now I'm free to show my gratitude and have your children."

"Not mine," he said. "I'm sterile. We all are."

"That been proven medically?"

Casey looked at her. "Nosferati don't go to doctors much."

"Impotence?"

He smiled. "Not hardly."

"Physician heal thyself?"

"Not so far."

"We can look into that," Moira said. "Besides, it doesn't make you a bad person."

Moira lurched into the bedroom while still chewing her last bite of pie and curled up on top the covers. She was snoring softly as Casey covered her with the bedspread and closed the door. Three hours later, running her fingers through rumpled hair, she padded into the main room in search of the sandwiches. Casey was at the small table finishing the last of the two raw steaks. She peered at him.

"Yuk!"

"I know," he said. "I feel the same way about cauliflower."

She rummaged in the small fridge, pulled out a turkey on whole wheat, and sat with him at the table.

"Need blood?" she said.

"No, thanks. Just had some."

"You know what I mean."

"It's a craving, like some people have for chocolate, or lemon drops, or peanuts."

"You said before that it's an addiction, that you were all addicted to blood. An addiction is more than just a craving, Casey."

He stared out the window for a moment feeling slightly uncomfortable. "You're right. In my case, it's more than a craving in that the results of using it are more profound and widespread. But if I don't get it, I don't fall apart, or get the shakes, or the D.T.'s, or something like that. I used to be addicted. I broke the addiction. Sort of like a reformed alcoholic who can drink a little socially, but not fall off the deep end. Seems impossible, but it's true."

"If you don't have to have it, why ingest blood at all?"

Casey chuckled. "Okay, that's a valid question. Imagine that I stuffed your nose and ears with tissue, put you in a three-hundred pound suit of thick quilted cotton from the top of your head to the bottom of your ankles, put heavy gloves on your hands, dark glasses over your eyes, swim fins on your feet, and sent you out into the world."

"Quite a fashion statement."

"How would you like that?"

"I wouldn't like that."

"Why not? Be literal."

"I couldn't see or hear well, I couldn't smell anything, breathing would be difficult. I'd be awkward and slow, I'd have no dexterity, and very little activity would wear me out. It would be terrible!"

"Why?"

"Because of all that stuff."

"Nope. Why?"

"Because I'd be so slow and awkward?"

"So's a tree sloth. They do okay. Think."

She considered his question carefully.

"Because I would be so far removed from my natural condition."

"Exactly. Would you want to spend the rest of your life like that?"

"Absolutely not."

"Okay. Now try to appreciate this. Compared to me, right now, that *is* your natural condition."

"Wow."

"Not only that, compared to one of us who has fed in the last few hours, that's *my* natural condition."

"Jesus."

"I can sustain the level I am at right now on ten to fifteen thousand calories a day and a couple of pounds of animal protein, preferably raw animal protein, or on a regular diet and ten to twenty cc's of viable human blood."

"What level are you at now? I mean, what could you do?"

"I could track you through this shire on scent alone, I could see someone's eye color at a distance where you couldn't make out their face, I could read a playing card by touching the thickness of the ink, I could sit in that restaurant you can't go back to and eavesdrop on every conversation in the room or, with my nose alone, tell you how many people were there, their genders, approximate ages, and relative states of health. I am faster than any other land mammal, I could arm wrestle a gorilla and win, and I could pick a fly out of the air with my thumb and index finger."

"God!"

"See why I'd hate to lose that?"

"What about if you'd just, ah, fed?"

Casey smiled at her and his eyes chilled. "I could tear the gorilla's head off and catch that fly in my lips with my eyes closed."

"Shit. Quite a temptation, huh?"

"It is if you like flies."

"C'mon," she said.

"You can't imagine the rush. That's why the Nosferati are so caught up in it. The psychological dependency is immense! The power, the joy, the surge, the sensation, the sex, the exultation! The basic, back-brain, reptile response is massive. The jaw snapping, bone crunching, sweaty-backed, slick-toothed, grasping, clutching, orgasmic, hissing grin of it is monstrously compelling! And that's just the mental involvement. The physical addiction that comes with feeding two or three times a week is just as bad."

"So, how much do you take in when you feed?" she asked, unwrapping a piece of coconut cream pie.

"A quart, quart and a half maybe. Contrary to popular opinion, we don't leave an empty husk behind."

"That's not that much. I mean, many people could survive losing that amount blood."

"True, but most don't survive the encounter. The rush of feeding almost always leads to murder, unless it's a true frenzy with multiple victims suffering bites and slashes. The resulting infection kills them, however. As near as I can figure, it's always fatal.

Another wives' tale is that being bitten by a vampire makes you a vampire. Almost never happens."

"Wait a minute. You said that a bite is always fatal."

"No. I said that the resulting infection is always fatal. Now and then a bite doesn't transfer infection. We have no fangs. Some feed through cuts made with an instrument of some type. That type of feeding doesn't always lead to infection. I assume victims would recover and battle nightmares for the rest of their lives. Hell, if I could keep fifty or so hostages to bleed for a pint each every five or six weeks, I could feed like a Nosferati and never kill anybody."

"Like a herd of cattle."

"Yeah. Sorry."

"So people that are fed upon don't always get the infection."

"True, but because of the frenzy and the need for secrecy, they rarely survive the encounter."

"And those that get infected die."

"To the best of my knowledge, always."

"You also told me that the same traumas that can kill me, can kill you."

"Also true, if the trauma is large enough. Two bullet wounds to kill you, twenty or more to kill me, depending on when I'd last fed. I go down in a plane crash, that's it. A car wreck takes my head off; I'm gone. Of course, if I'd just fed, I could easily vacate the car before the accident, but you get my drift."

"What if you didn't get any food at all?"

"I'd starve to death."

"And you're sterile."

"Never heard of one of us who wasn't."

"Then how come we don't run out of vampires? I mean, if nobody's making new ones, how come, sooner or later, you guys don't just die out?"

"Simple. Every now and then, maybe one in a thousand or one in ten thousand, I don't know, one of the people who has died of the infection, comes back."

"What!"

Casey smiled at her. "Miss Flynn," he said, "they don't call us The Undead for nothing." He saw her face pale.

"Oh, God," she blurted, clutching the table and lowering her head. Casey watched as her blood pressure dropped and her heart accelerated.

"Deep breaths, Moira," he said. "You're in a fear reaction and you have nothing to be afraid of. Slow, deep breaths. The tingling in your hands and feet will stop in a minute. Hang in there and keep breathing."

She did as instructed, and in a few moments color returned to her face and she relaxed a little. Raising her head, she scowled at him.

"You asshole! I just find myself getting comfortable with you, relating to you, relaxing around you, and you come up with some kind of horror movie crap! The Undead. Goddamn it, and goddamn you!"

"Anger is good," he said quietly. "It's a normal reaction to fear or shock, and it gets the system functioning again. Try and relax, and minimize the adrenalin rush, or you'll get the shakes in a while. They're no fun."

"Stop being so goddammed logical and controlled!" she snapped. "You just tell me you came back from the fucking dead, and then go on to discuss my reaction like you're talking about the fucking weather! What's next? A carriage ride through the park while wolves run with us? Igor drops by for tea?"

"That's Frankenstein. You're thinking of Renfield."

"I'm thinking about kicking your ass! I don't like being scared and I don't like being patronized, and you seem to be good at both of those."

"Everybody needs a hobby."

"Jesus Christ, Casey! I'm a fucking wreck, and you sit there like the Sphinx! You got any emotions at all?"

He stared blankly at the wall for a few beats, then turned to her. "For a long time, Miss Flynn," he said quietly, "my existence was ruled almost totally by my emotions. Then I dried out. Then I went to prison. Prison is not conducive to developing a sound emotional balance. I was beginning to think that my addiction and recovery had pretty much beaten them out of me, and I was okay with that. Emotions lead to hope, and desire, and frustration, and a lot of other things that are not much fun in prison, even if you're there by choice. I thought they were mostly gone, but now I'm not so sure."

Moira dropped her chin and looked up at him. "Really?" she said.

"Really." Casey smiled, his eyes gently holding her. "And I'm afraid it could be your fault."

She looked at him and sighed. "And I'm afraid I need coffee. Go get some willya? Cream, no sugar. And try to keep your emotions under control."

When Casey returned, Moira had brushed her hair and teeth and added a little makeup. She appeared to be collected and businesslike. He could smell her fear had abated. Casey sat at the table with her and passed over a large coffee.

"Thanks. Sorry I freaked."

"You're welcome. Sorry I freaked you."

They sat quietly for a moment. Moira spoke.

"The Undead, huh?"

Casey smiled. "Yeah. We're one of the reasons graveyards are so scary. It's a myth. Should I go on?"

"Why not?

"During the sixteen and seventeen hundreds, there were documented cases all over Europe of vampires being slain in their graves. A wooden stake through the heart or beheading was the usual method. We were around, to be sure, but none was ever killed in his grave to my knowledge."

"How'd all that get started then?"

"Being buried alive was not unheard of in those days, even into the eighteen-hundreds. It happened often enough that special caskets were constructed with bells above ground and a cord tied around the corpse's hand, just in case. The term 'dead ringer' stems from that practice. Embalming was not a factor. Occasionally, for whatever reason, a new corpse would be unearthed. The teeth would often be long and exposed, the fingernails more prominent, the mouth grinning. It was all because of a reduction in the body's natural water. Gums receded making the teeth appear longer, the flesh on the fingers retracted doing the same for the nails. The grinning mouth came from, of course, rictus and shrinking muscles pulling the lips back from the teeth. The church, partly to discourage the robbing of graves and partly to maintain control through fear, did little to dispel rumor and legend. Vampires and werewolves lurked behind trees and rocks everywhere and, of course, only at night. As you know, werewolves appear with the phase of the moon, and sunlight kills us."

"How'd that get started?"

"It's easier to sneak around at night, for one reason, and we're a pretty sneaky bunch, but that may not be all. Years ago, I was fairly sensitive to sunlight. I couldn't see well in bright light. It hurt my eyes. As time has gone on, I've gotten used to it, or the condition has changed. I don't know which."

"How'd all the other myths get started? Mirrors, garlic, having to be invited in, things like that?"

"Beats me. Probably a way to explain how—with vamps running around all over the place—not everybody got gobbled up. There was a time when most houses had a cross on the door to keep us out. We gave the church some great leverage, no doubt about that. I expect that, for a while at least, we were responsible for more conversions than any other factor."

Moira yawned. "Jesus. Ignorance and fear. How many millions have been killed because of those two?"

Casey smiled at her. "Take a nap, you're beat."

"We need to get on the road."

"You need to rest. You'll feel a lot better and have more energy tomorrow. Then we'll take off. Go sleep. I'll knock around for a while and wake you up for dinner."

"You'll be okay?"

Casey smiled and took her hand. "I'll be fine," he said, "and so will everybody else."

Moira flushed and slowly drew her hand back. "Sorry. I just, ah, sorry."

"Don't worry about it. I'm a vampire for God's sake."

# SIX
## Westport

THEY HAD JUST CROSSED THE MISSISSIPPI and were on the north bypass around St. Louis, heading for St. Charles and I-70 west, when Moira glanced at Casey.

"You don't look like a vampire," she said.

Casey grinned. "Gramercy."

"What?"

"Ah, thank you, I think."

"I mean, you're just an average looking guy."

"Thud went the strings of my heart!"

"I'm not doing this well, am I?"

"Not very."

"What I'm trying to say is that you appear to be a normal man. Medium size, medium build, olive complexion, dark hair, a little gray at the temples. Nothing striking or unusual. Another face in the crowd."

Casey was still grinning, and Moira could feel herself getting in deeper. She struggled on.

"It's just that there's nothing unusual about you, dammit! You don't stand out."

"You should see me in a party dress."

"No, I shouldn't. I mean, you don't appear any different than anybody else. There's nothing about you that would give you away."

"Not since I stopped wearing my 'Vamps Need Love Too' t-shirt," Casey said. "What'd you expect? Dark eye shadow, a widow's peak to my eyebrows, long fingernails and dripping pointy teeth?"

"No, it's just that you have all these amazing physical abilities, but they don't show. Weightlifters look like weightlifters, football players look like football players, marathon runners look like marathon runners, boxers look like boxers. You don't look like anything."

"My God, the compliments! Stop, or you will turn my head," Casey said. He began to fan himself with an open hand.

Moira chuckled. "Asshole," she said.

"The reason that boxers look like boxers, weightlifters look like weightlifters, and all the rest of that," Casey said, "is because they are not naturally those things. They force their bodies into an unnatural condition to accomplish unnatural acts. It is not normal for a human being to bench press four hundred fifty pounds. Those people that can press that much weight have worked long and hard to create a body that is not normal. They look different than other people because they have developed abnormal abilities. Gorillas have been estimated to be twenty to thirty times stronger than human beings. They're big, heavy shouldered, thick thighed, but they all look basically alike because they do not spend a large portion of their lives trying to be stronger or faster or quicker than all the other gorillas. They stay in their natural condition. I am in my natural condition."

"Yes, but there's still a difference. You're as strong as a gorilla and as fast as a cheetah, but you're not big and bulky, or skinny and lithe. You appear to be just like everybody else. How do you explain that?"

"I don't know. How can some little Chinese guy take a sword strike to the chest and not get cut? How can Eskimos survive cold that would be fatal to anybody else? How can some Buddhist monks go for weeks without eating and not starve?"

"So you can't explain it."

"Nope."

"Don't you care?"

"Not very much."

"Jesus! I just can't believe that! All these extraordinary abilities, and you don't care how you do it, ah, them?"

"No."

"You're not even curious?"

"Try to get this through your scientifically enquiring mind, Miss Flynn. These 'abilities' as you call them, are not extraordinary to me! The gorilla doesn't give a shit how he got so strong, and the cheetah doesn't wonder why he's so fast, any more than you get all excited about trying to figure out how it is that you can pick up a goddam telephone! They, you, me, all do it because it takes no particular effort or desire, and because we can."

"That's too simplistic."

"No, it isn't. It's just simple."

They traveled in silence for a while. Finally, Moira lit a cigarette and cleared her throat.

"Oh-oh," said Casey.

"Question," replied Moira.

"Here we go."

Undaunted she pressed on. "How old are you?"

"Forty-two."

"Right. When were you born?"

"Ah. Well now, that's different. 1593."

"1593?"

"1593."

"That would make you …"

"Over four hundred years old."

"I just can't imagine that."

"Try and imagine the birthday cake. You could stir-fry over a blaze that size!"

"Jesus, Casey. You're in a rare mood today."

"I feel good," he said. "In some ways, better than I have in years."

"You're telling me the truth, aren't you?"

"Yeah. With that many candles you could bar-b-que a Mongolian."

"I mean about your age, Dummy."

"Oh! Sure. That too."

"Where were you born?"

"Just outside London. My mother died when I was small. My father was a wood-cutter. He sold me to a blacksmith when I was about eight or so."

"Sold you?"

"Aye. I started as a huffer, and then became a striker when I got closer to man-hood.

"A what?"

"A huffer pumped the bellows to feed the forge. A striker used the hammer and anvil to strike the metal into shape. It was called an apprenticeship, but it was little more than slavery. My father got a small sum of money and one less mouth to feed, and Miles Herriott got free labor."

"So you were trained to shoe horses and things like that."

Casey smiled. "Horse shoeing was a small part of it. In those days, smiths made the hardware needed around the home. Hinges, locks, andirons, nails, utensils, dishes, pots, tools, almost anything made of metal, we created. The fine stuff was done by craftsmen. Silversmiths, glass blowers, people like that. We did the more mundane work. Herriott wasn't a bad man. He couldn't read or write, but he made sure I knew how. He also made sure I knew a trade. Because of him, I became a cooper."

"A cooper?"

"I specialized in making buckets and barrels. You know, the old oaken bucket? I cut and dried the oak, shaped the slats, banded them with iron, all by eye and feel. It's an art."

Moira saw the gentle light of pride in his eyes, the comfortable pleasure of an ar-tisan appreciating his work. "Sounds like it," she said.

"A few years ago I actually found a couple of my pieces in use at Colonial Wil-liamsburg," Casey said.

"Really? After all these years?"

"A bucket and a small keg. There was my mark, right on the banding."

"Your mark?"

"Yeah. MH. It was customary for the smithy to sign his work. Helped drum up business."

"MH?"

"Mathew Herriott. I took the blacksmith's last name when he took me."

"So you worked for him."

"Until I was eighteen, then I worked with him and got a share of his business and profit. Seven or eight years later, I married his daughter Elizabeth and became his partner."

"The old boss's daughter trick, huh?"

Casey smiled. "You betcha. He died the same year our daughter Catherine was born. 1621."

"So that left you with the whole business?"

"We took his house and cared for Elizabeth's mother until she died three years later."

"Why did you leave England?"

"A man named Edward Winslow. Winslow was an agent for the Plymouth Colony. Slick fella, politician, almost an ambassador. He came by my smith during one of his visits to London and recruited me to go to the colony. Normally that would have been too expensive or required some sort of indentured servitude, but the colony needed qualified tradesmen. Even my advanced age, I was nearly forty at the time, didn't dissuade him. It also helped that Elizabeth was a fine seamstress and lace maker, and that Catherine was nearly grown. There was a shortage of women in Plymouth, too. So, we loaded up everything we couldn't get or build in the colony and shipped over in 1632. All that was required of me was to give thirty percent of my gross to the colony for seven years and to keep at least three apprentices in training for ten years."

Casey sipped from a Styrofoam coffee cup.

"When we got to Plymouth, Winslow basically just handed us over to his younger brother, Josiah. Josiah, who was the accountant for the colony, set us up with a small cabin in Duxbury, I built a forge, and we were doing business again in the wild western lands. The very next year, Edward Winslow became governor of the colony and plague struck. It killed many people, but we escaped it and so did the entire settlement of Duxbury. We took it as a good omen and the new governor did what he could to spread our name around. Josiah also tossed some colony business my way. We did well. By the time Catherine turned fourteen, we were nicely settled."

"God! You are living history."

"What?"

"You lived through what the rest of us can only know from books. You were there, an actual observer, a participant! You were in early colonial New England!"

"Don't romanticize it. It wasn't that terrific."

"But you were there."

"So were lots of other people. People who starved to death, who died of measles, scarlet fever, simple infection, chicken pox. Imagine a diet without bananas or oranges or pears. Without pasta, or white bread, or ice cream, or sugar, or tomatoes, or a thousand other things you take for granted. Imagine never drinking anything really cold if it wasn't winter. Houses with no insulation, no air-conditioning, no toilets, no running water, no vacuum cleaners, no chocolate, no zippers, no aspirin, no toilet paper, no Novocain, no paperclips, no deodorant, no post-it notes, no direct communication outside shouting distance, no Velcro, no hairspray, no safety pins, no hospitals or emergency rooms or maternity wards. Imagine a place where barbers treated sickness with leeches, diabetics almost always died, a simple broken arm could mean a lifetime of deformity, and many illnesses were credited to demonic possession."

"Pretty bad, huh?"

"Yeah," he said. "But nice."

"Then what?"

"Then came the hurricane of 1635," Casey whispered. "And then it all ended."

He turned from her, staring out the window at the passing farmland.

"And then it all began," he murmured.

An hour later they ate, fueled, and were back on the road.

"What's this place we're going to?" Casey asked.

"Provenance Center. It's the main research facility for Proteus Trust. It's also a business. Its public function is the manufacture and sale of blood test kits for employee drug testing, AIDS clinics, and things like that. The consumer buys the kits from us, uses them according to instructions, then ships the sample back to us for testing."

"So you get 'em coming and going."

"Very lucrative. It accounts for nearly thirty percent of the income Proteus needs to function. It also is a good cover for the research branch. That particular portion of Provenance we don't publicize."

"Secret stuff, huh?"

"More private than secret. The minute a secret company like that becomes even a tiny bit compromised, our friendly neighborhood government starts sticking its nose in. When that happens, progress becomes very difficult."

"So you guys actually accomplish things?"

"We've been responsible for virtually every new drug or protocol to combat the AIDS virus in the past six years."

"That's not very much," Casey said.

"No, it isn't. But there would have been absolutely nothing at all achieved without us. Since the big Ebola outbreak, Acquired Immune Deficiency Syndrome has become rather passé, I'm afraid."

"So what do you do for these people?"

"I'm the big cheese," Moira said. "I run the joint."

"The boss lady?"

"More or less. Technically I work for Proteus, but my job is loosely titled as director of Provenance Center. We have over three hundred employees. The vast majority of them assemble the blood test kits, or ship them, or receive them, or test them, or contact the clients with results. Mundane stuff that I have nothing to do with."

"So, what do you really do?"

"I control money and resources for research that's done by just a few of those three hundred employees. During the past few years, I have moved out of the lab almost entirely, and into administration. Each year Proteus hands me a big wad of dollars. Every couple of years, I give them a new drug or protocol with which, if all goes well, they can make much more money than they gave me. Five years ago, I convinced Melvin Foltz to join the company. Melvin is the premier guy in his field. When you've got Melvin, everybody wants to hand you cash. I spend it pretty much any way I please. As long as I get results, nobody asks questions. So far, the results have been good, and I have a great deal of autonomy. Melvin oversees the lab for me while I run the business. Not only is he responsible for the main research facility, Melvin has a private lab of his own on the third sub-level. In addition to what I let the company know about, I have other interests, too. That's why I came looking for you."

Casey grinned. "And all this time, I thought it was my boyish charm."

"Not to mention your girlish figure," she said. "Sorry, just money. I went digging through our computer monitoring of AIDS treatment centers around the world and happened to run across your statistics from the prison. Really, it was an accident that I even noticed it. It was tacked on, almost as a footnote, to an obscure report on penal facilities. I never concern myself with government programs. They invariably lag behind the private sector. That's what made the prison stand out. Dumb luck I even found it."

"And then you found me."

"And then I found you."

"Well, if all this stuff is so secret, what are you going to do? Smuggle me in through the sewer system?"

"Nope. Right in through the door just like a real person. I'll hang a nebulous title on you and spirit you off to the secure area. There'll be a certain amount of curiosity about you, but there's always a lot of that in a business like ours. Everybody in the place knows we have a lab in the basement, but just a handful of people know what's being done there. That handful knows Melvin has his own lab, but nobody knows what he is personally working on except me. Melvin and I keep each other's secrets. And now we will keep yours."

"So you and this Melvin work very closely, huh?"

"Very," she said. "He's a wonderful man."

"And I'll stay at the lab?"

"You and I will both stay at Provenance. We have living quarters there for visiting researchers and transient staff, sort of halfway between motel rooms and efficiency apartments. We'll use two of those."

"Two?"

"Melvin is there. If you determine him to be trustworthy, I would like you to consider telling as much of your story as you are comfortable disclosing. He will be the only individual, other than myself, who will have any accurate knowledge as to who and what you really are. I assure you that I have known Melvin for considerable time and have complete confidence in his discretion."

"Who is this guy you want me to trust?" Casey said, feeling another ripple of jealousy and putting a little emotional distance between them.

"The staff calls him Doctor Blood. He's a researcher. He has several PhD's. Biomechanics, Physiology, Neurology, stuff like that. He will originate all your blood work so you can remain anonymous. He knows nothing of your abilities. My suggestion would be to go slowly and let him discover your talents on his own. How much he is told will be strictly up to you. If and when you feel comfortable with it, I'm sure he'll want to do some additional physiological testing on you. Speed, strength, endurance, that kind of thing. To the best of my knowledge, Melvin does not suspect anyone like you exists. He'll be excited. You are very much his holy grail."

"And what are you going to do while I'm being a lab rat?"

"I'll assist Melvin and also start procedures on locating your daughter."

Casey looked intrigued. "How?"

"Among other things, through contacts to which I have access in the arena of law enforcement. I'll look over data on unsolved serial killings, suspicious deaths, unexplained disappearances, dumped corpses, and things of that nature. We'll see if some kind of pattern develops. If your daughter and her friends are out there, they've left tracks. A girl's gotta eat."

They arrived in Kansas City late in the afternoon, connected with I-35 as they passed beneath Bartle Hall, and took it to the Kansas side.

"Welcome to Kaycee," Moira said. "Ever been here?"

"Yeah, but it was a lot smaller," Casey said. "They called it Westport back then."

Moira flinched. "Jesus, Casey. That kind of stuff just scares the hell outta me! I can't get used to the fact you've been around so long."

"No cars in those days," he said. "Mud streets, lots of mules."

"Times change," she said. "This is Olathe, Kansas."

She drove through a suburban area for a while, finally turning off of Blackbob and into a chain link fenced parking lot beside a low, light gray, featureless building that fronted an entire block. Stopping at a guard shack, she flashed a badge and was admitted to the parking area.

"Damn," Casey said. "This place makes the prison look scenic."

Moira drove across the lot to the rear of the building and approached a large bay door. The door sensed her car and opened to reveal a box about the size of a two-car garage. Moira rolled inside and stopped. The door closed and the walls began to rise.

"Trapped like a rat," Casey said.

Moira smiled. "Yep," she said. "But a very special rat."

The garage lift stopped shortly, and they exited it through a doorway on the driver's side of the vehicle that opened onto what appeared to be a small lobby area. An elevator carried them another floor deeper and opened into a reception room complete with comfortable seating, live plants, and a counter attended by an attractive older brunette.

"Moira!" she said.

"Elesia!" Moira said. "Nice to see you."

"Good to have you back, Hon." Elesia's eyes flickered over Casey. "And who is this?"

"Elesia, this is Joseph. He'll be with us for a while from the Chicago Circle campus. Everything ready?"

"All set up."

"Thanks. Sorry about the short notice."

Elesia shook her head. "We live to serve." She turned her attention to Casey and raised an eyebrow. "Welcome, Joseph. Very nice to have you."

Casey smiled, his nostrils full of her interest. "Ah, Elesia," he said, "what could be better than a warm welcome from a handsome woman? Thank you." He turned and followed Moira as she headed off down a hall.

They walked for around fifty yards between white walls and on white tile, finally proceeding through a set of swinging doors into an area labeled "Security." There, with the help of a casually uniformed young man named Ted, Casey's left palm print and his right retina pattern were entered into a computer. His photo was taken, a plastic and metal bracelet was affixed to his left wrist, and he was handed an ID card on a clip. From there, Moira took him to a closet and fitted both of them with white lab coats. She produced her own ID card and clipped it to the lapel. Casey did the same.

"Never leave your room without your lab coat," she said. "And never wear your lab coat without the card clipped to it."

"Yes, Ma'am. Do I get a stethoscope or anything?"

"If you're good," she said, "I'll get you a whole box of tongue depressors, too."

Another walk and several more swinging doors led them to an area with thickly carpeted floors, pastel walls, textured ceilings, and warm ambient lighting.

"I'm lost," Casey said.

Beside a wood paneled door was a small digital screen built into the wall.

"Place your palm on that," Moira said.

Casey did as instructed, and the door clicked.

"Home, sweet home," Moira said, and pushed it open.

The living area was about twenty feet square and done in comfortable pastels. A couch, two deep chairs, and several small tables were set about on the rich pile carpeting, and a picture window let light into the room through a scene of the Rocky Mountains. The adjoining kitchenette was small but serviceable, and there was even a gas fireplace.

"Bedroom and bath through there," Moira said, pointing to a partially open door, "TV and stereo behind those louvered doors across from the couch."

Casey wandered around looking things over. "Where you gonna stay?" he said.

"In the apartment next door."

He stopped at a door set into the living room wall and turned the knob. Nothing happened. "What's through here," he said.

"The apartment next door."

Casey looked through the cabinets and checked the fridge.

"All stocked up. I don't see much red meat, though. I'm gonna need some soon."

"We can do better than that."

"We can?"

"You forget where you are, Casey. We have blood. Lots of blood."

# SEVEN
## Doctor Blood

A LITTLE AFTER SEVEN THE NEXT MORNING, a knock sounded on the door to Moira's apartment as Casey, wearing jeans and sweat socks, rummaged in the kitchen for some breakfast.

"Who iiis iiit?" he sang.

"Who the hell do you think it is?" came the muffled reply. "Open up!"

"Go away. I gave at the office."

The door swung open and Moira, attired in white walking shoes, black gabardine slacks, a plain white shirt, and her lab coat, swept into the room. Her hair was pulled back, and she was wearing oversize glasses with thin silver rims.

Casey attempted to cover his torso with a paper towel. "Eek," he said.

She grinned. "Knock off the theatrics and let's go eat."

"I thought that connecting door was locked."

"It only opens from my side, Casey."

"Perhaps a wager, M'Lady?" He walked into the bedroom and left the door open.

"Don't get any big ideas," she said, feeling a tiny tingle in exactly the right place. "You're not invited, and I have a case and a half of minced garlic in there."

Casey entered the living area, buttoning his shirt, immediately noticing the slight shift in her scent. "The garlic and crucifixes don't work. The 'not invited' does. Fair morn, Miss Flynn. You're looking quite scientific today."

"And you look positively human," she said. "Grab your lab coat, and let's go to the cafeteria. I'm hungry."

Five minutes walking through various white hallways had Casey totally turned around by the time they finally reached the cafeteria. "Jesus," he said. "How the hell do you know where you're going?"

"Lost?"

"No, I just don't know where I am."

"What's the difference?"

"Well ... I have no idea where my room is, but I could walk directly to it."

"How?"

"Backtrack our scent."

"Jesus! That shit is so weird!"

66

"Nothing the average poodle couldn't do."

"Yeah. Just don't start peeing on the carpet, okay?"

"I'm housebroken. I like to growl and wrestle, sometimes I sit on command, and if you rub my tummy, I'll give you a great big lick."

Moira colored. "And hump my leg if you get the chance?"

Casey laughed. "Sure," he said. "But only to establish dominance."

At five feet seven and one hundred thirty-five pounds, Melvin Foltz was not an imposing figure. His watery blue eyes, wispy mustache, and wiry red hair sprouting in continual disarray from behind a severely receding hairline, was somewhat less than macho. That, coupled with a sudden darting walk and quick, bird-like movements, augmented by a voice that still seemed to be thrashing its way through puberty, made being near Melvin a scattering experience. The truth was, Melvin's mind ricocheted along at such reckless speed and in so many different directions that he was in a constant hurry to keep up with it. It affected him physically to the point that he seldom seemed to have focus or, when watched, to even be in focus.

Moira saw him flapping his way down the far side of the cafeteria, spilling the milk on his tray as he bobbed along. She waved and caught his fleeting attention. He changed course several times before settling on the correct route, then fluttered his way to their table. His pale eyes fixed on her with something akin to adoration.

"Well, Moira! Gosh, I haven't seen you in days! May I join you? I'm so glad you're back. Do you mind if I sit? I hope I'm not interrupting anything."

"It's good to see you too, Melvin," Moira said. "Join us."

Melvin perched on the edge of a chair, completely ignoring his food and Casey.

"Goodness, it's good to see you. I thought you left us for good, taking care of the company the way you do. What have you been up to? It's a pleasure to have you back. How long will you stay? I have some new figures you might be interested in. I could have them sent by. The protocols on the eicosapentaenoic acid balancing look extremely promising."

"I'm here, Melvin, because of the gentleman sitting on my left."

For the first time the little man seemed to realize there was someone else at the table. His eyes darted to Casey, then settled back on Moira. She continued. "Melvin Foltz, let me present Joseph Casey."

Melvin extended a thin limp hand and looked intently at Casey for about a half second, then returned his attention to Moira.

"Nice to meet you, Mr. Foltz," Casey said, enjoying Melvin's fixation.

"Mr. Casey has consented to work with us for a time. I believe you might be interested in him," Moira said. "He has some very unusual abilities."

Reluctantly, Melvin turned his attention to back to Casey. "Such as?"

Moira caught Casey's eye and nodded.

Casey paused for a moment and looked at the little man. "You wash your hair with the same soap you use on your body," he said. "Irish Spring, I believe. You used nasal spray this morning, your two front teeth are capped, you're fond of garlic, you have Odor Eaters in your shoes, you're currently having a problem with constipation, and your heart rate and blood pressure are both climbing a bit."

Melvin blinked and looked at Casey. Moira ceased to exist. "Be in my office in thirty minutes," he said. "We have to talk."

He stood and left them, nearly trotting from the room. His tray, untouched, remained on the table.

"That went well," Casey said.

"You accomplished the nearly impossible," Moira said. "You got his attention."

"An even greater accomplishment with you at the table," Casey said. "He worships you, you know."

"Yes, I know," she sighed. "Thankfully from afar."

Resting his chin in his hand, Casey gazed at her. "I know just how he feels," he said.

"Oh, shit," growled Moira, shifting her weight in the slick plastic chair. The tingle was back.

Melvin answered the knock and peered at Casey nearsightedly.

"Yes?"

"Here I am," Casey said.

"I beg your pardon?"

"As you requested at lunch."

"At lunch?"

"Melvin, it's me, Joseph Casey, Moira's friend. You asked me to come by and chat?"

"Oh? Oh!" Recognition registered in his watery blue eyes. "Mr. Casey! Of course. Come in, sit down."

The small office was stacked with books, periodicals, correspondence, and files to such an extent that there was no place, other than behind the desk, to sit. Melvin flitted about, scattering materials even further, until the seat of a chair was uncovered. Casey took it. Melvin sat at his desk.

"Interesting what you did at lunch today, Mr. Casey. Are you psychic?"

Casey smiled. "No."

"I thought not. What intrigues me most about your little display, is your correctly assessing the constipation problem. How did you know?"

"Your liver and kidneys are working overtime," Casey said. "They cannot keep your system as pollution free as it should be. You give off an odor."

Melvin blushed. "Do I?"

"Relax, nobody else can scent it. You don't smell bad or anything like that. The average person will never know."

"You smell it, this odor."

"Yes."

"How do you account for that?"

"I don't. I have no need to account for it."

"Alright, Mr. Casey. Nearby I have some gum. I wonder ..."

"Juicy Fruit," Casey said. "In the desk somewhere. It's very stale."

"I assume this acuteness of sense is not confined to smell alone. You certainly didn't smell the caps on my teeth."

"No, I saw those."

"Smell and sight. Interesting. Hearing?"

"Yep."

"Touch?"

"Yes."

"How good is your sense of smell?"

"Right now, about as good as a hound."

"Sight?"

"A hawk in the daytime, an owl at night, and probably a touch of infrared. I can read a newspaper at a hundred feet, run when you'd need a flashlight to walk, and see the general shape of your body in total darkness."

"Extraordinary! Hearing?"

"Acute. Somewhere between a kit fox and a bat, I suppose. I don't really know."

"Wonderful. May I examine you?"

"Maybe. Moira said you were absolutely trustworthy."

The little man waved a hand and cleared his throat. Casey went on.

"She also said that you would find me to be more than just interesting. I am here as a favor to her in return for a favor she is attempting to do for me. You may examine me, Doctor Foltz, on one condition."

"Name it."

"I must impress upon you that I am totally serious when I state the condition, and that I am completely capable of enforcing it."

Melvin's eyes shone as he leaned forward over his desk. "Name the condition," he said.

"If, through deliberate action or negligence on your part, harm comes to either me or Miss Flynn, I will kill you."

"Define harm."

"Physical injury, loss of faculties, curtailment of freedom, restriction of movement. I am prepared to allow you liberties I have never allowed another human being, because Moira has asked me to. I will not let myself be restrained or compromised in any way. What you and I do, must remain secret. I am not to be personally connected with any tests, findings, or results. My identity must be protected at all times. Let me state it as clearly as possible, and please accept my apology for being so direct. If you fuck with me or Moira in any way other than exactly what I agree to, I will bleed you like a pig. I will slit your throat and hold you up by the ankles until you stop quivering. Clear?"

"Quite," Melvin said.

The smell of the doctor's fear wafted over Casey. He smiled. "Relax. It had to be said. Just one more thing and then we'll forget all about this. You cannot lie to me. Don't bother to try. I can smell it. One lie, no matter how small, and I'm gone. Okay?"

"Certainly," Melvin said, clearing his throat and holding a pencil in both hands to stop from shaking. "It all seems very reasonable to me, in a gothic sort of way."

"Fine," Casey said. "Now what can I do for you?"

"I want some blood," Foltz said.

"Melvin," Casey said, "you have no idea how much I can empathize with that."

69

Casey was stretched out on the couch in his living room an hour or so later when Moira knocked on the connecting door.

"Are you decent?" he shouted.

She came in. "I'm supposed to ask you that," Moira said, handing him twenty cc's of blood in a small beaker.

"It's a question I don't care to answer. Coffee's fresh."

"Thanks," she said, walking toward the pot and avoiding watching him drink the blood. "How'd it go with Melvin?"

Rinsing the beaker in the sink, Casey laughed. "He drew some blood. Had a little problem. My blood's pretty dense. He thought his equipment was malfunctioning. He finally had to do it with a larger needle."

"I bet that got him going," she said.

"He excused himself and fairly jogged out of the room. I guess he went to the lab to …"

There was a knock on the door.

"Mister Casey. Mister Casey! Are you in?"

"Speak of the devil," Casey said.

He opened the door, and Melvin stalked into the room.

"This is amazing!" the little man blurted. "I just finished the preliminary on your blood workup. Your hemoglobin is off the charts, your red blood cell count is four or five times normal. Your white cells are tigers, Mr. Casey. Absolute tigers! Your blood clots in record time, it has antibodies everywhere and almost no free radicals. The oxygen content is huge! You must have the heart of a racehorse and the lungs of a dolphin! How far can you run? How long can you hold your breath?"

Casey took a cigarette from his pack and lit it. "I don't know, Melvin."

"You smoke! Impossible. There's no carbon monoxide. There are no pollutants of any kind to speak of. Have you ever had a cold? Do you ever get sick? Do you have any allergies? Where have you been living, the South Pole?"

"Melvin, where are you manners? Say hello to Moira!"

"W—what?" he stammered, looking about. "Oh. Hello, Moira. Mister Casey, to say this is unusual may be the understatement of the century! Your blood is not possible. It's just not possible! I mean, I drew it from you, that would make it possible."

He lowered his voice. "That is to say, Mister Casey, it's not, uh, it's not, oh dear." He gulped a breath and forged ahead. "I mean, it almost is, but, then again it really isn't at all. Your blood, Mr. Casey, is just not human!"

Casey looked at him for a moment, and smiled.

"Melvin, my boy," he said, putting his arm loosely around the smaller man's shoulders, "take it easy and I'll tell you a secret."

"W—what?"

"Neither am I."

Melvin was shaking his way through a second cup of coffee before he could look directly at Casey. Eyes darting and hands quivering, he cleared his throat.

"Wha … what are you?"

"Well, I'm not from Mars, I don't want to rule the world, and I'm not going to eat your face or anything like that. What I *do* want is to assist Miss Flynn in discovering as much about why I am what I am as possible. She recommended that you would be best able to assist in that process."

"Melvin," Moira said, "Joseph has an extraordinary power to both stay well and heal others. I firmly believe he could be directly injected with the AIDS virus and the Ebola virus, and suffer no ill effects. We want to know why this is so. There was a time in Mr. Casey's life that he did not have this ability. Now he does. As much as you need answers about him, we need answers about that. If we can find those answers, it is entirely possible that we could do a great deal toward eradicating infectious disease. I know you have a lot of questions, but you're just going to have to live with them for now. You have some of Casey's blood. I suggest you direct your attention toward that. We'll get more into his background later. Okay?"

"Well, certainly. You're the boss, Moira, and I do have a lot of work to do. I'm just so excited at the very prospect of what I've found so far!"

Moira smiled. "Go find more."

"Mum's the word, Melvin," Casey said.

"What? Oh, absolutely! I won't mention a thing to anyone. Something like this could have very serious repercussions! I'll do all the lab work myself, no one else will even see the results. You have my word!"

"Good," Casey said. "I'm not going anywhere. You and I will have plenty of time to get together. You help me, I'll help you. Fair enough?"

The little man rose to his feet. "Certainly. I must go. I have found this extraordinary blood sample in my private lab. I have no idea where it came from. Very unusual. Very unusual, indeed. Perhaps we'll talk about it later." He went out the door.

"Melvin is gonna love this," Moira said. "In a few days, he'll be wearing a trench coat and skulking around corners."

"He controls his fear well," Casey said. "The poor little guy is scared to death."

Over the next few days, Casey was pretty much on his own, giving him ample time to think. Melvin saw him twice to draw more blood and do blood gasses. Moira, between her regular responsibilities to The Proteus Trust and digging for information to possibly locate Casey's daughter, was only seldom available. Casey read, avoided the room's computer, and watched TV. He was slouched in front of the tube one evening when Moira knocked and came in.

"Hi."

Casey grinned. "Hi, yourself. How ya been?"

"Busy. Taking some time off. Thought I'd, ah, invite you to dinner at my place."

Casey felt a tingle in the pit of his stomach. "Sure," he said, "but the commute is terrible."

"Fresh salmon broiled in butter and lemon. New potatoes steamed in dill and chives. Pea pods sautéed with water chestnuts and bacon bits. Melon and blueberries for dessert."

"I'll call a cab. What time?"

Moira forged ahead before she lost her nerve. "How 'bout now? You can watch me cook and we'll make small talk."

"Great. Gimme me fifteen minutes to shower and change and I'll be over. Leave the—"

A knock came through Casey's door. He opened it to find Melvin Foltz standing in the hall.

"Melvin! Come in. Join the reunion."

Melvin walked in, looking tired and worn.

"Oh. Hi Moira," he said. "I hope I'm not interrupting anything?"

"No, of course not. Have a seat." She shot Casey a quick glance. Melvin flopped into a chair.

"You look beat," Casey said. "Everything alright?"

"Yes and no," Melvin said. "Four or five days ago I cultured some of your blood and, on a whim, injected a few cc's into Alice and Andy."

"What! Who are Alice and Andy?"

"Just two rhesus monkeys. They've been part of our program here for over four years. Both terminal with AIDS."

"Rhesus monkeys? Oh, shit! Where are they now?"

"Dead. They both died yesterday."

"What happened to the bodies?"

"They're burned."

Casey sagged against the arm of the couch. "That's a relief," he said.

"Eventually."

"Eventually? What the hell does that mean?"

"It means that we don't fire up the incinerator for just one or two monkeys. We wait until we have enough corpses to justify the expense."

"Goddammit, Melvin! Right now, right this minute, where are the bodies?"

"I don't see what you're getting so upset about."

"*Where are the fucking bodies*!!?"

Melvin paled and took a step back. Moira moved to stand beside him.

"In a cooler in the primate lab," he said.

"Any people in that lab?"

"No. It was empty when I left."

Casey grabbed his lab coat. "Take me there," he said.

"It's alright," Melvin protested, following Casey out the door. "They're dead!"

"You better fucking hope they are. Move!"

It took the three of them less than two minutes to jog to the lab. Melvin reached for the heavy door. From behind it came the sound of simian screaming.

"Don't!" ordered Casey. "How can we see in there without opening anything?"

Moira headed for another door. "In here," she said. "Closed circuit monitors."

She went inside and switched on the array. The central screen told the story.

The cooler door was open. Inside lay the still body of a monkey. On the floor directly in front of the camera, a chimpanzee was curled in a puddle of blood. Red splashes were scattered across the walls and tile. Moira panned to the left. A row of cages, their wire ripped apart, stood tumbled and mute. Small bodies lay sprawled all over the room. Blood was everywhere. A blur, little more than a flicker, flashed across the screen.

"What was that?" Melvin asked in a small stunned voice.

"Alice or Andy," Casey said.

"But they're dead!

A resigned weariness crept into Casey's tone.

"I have no doubt they both were," he said, "but one of them isn't now. I'd rather have a rhino loose in the halls."

A flicker moved past the monitor again, then returned and stopped. A monkey's face appeared close to the lens.

"Alice," murmured Melvin.

Alice opened her mouth and crunched the lens between her teeth. The screen went blank.

"I'll get the tranquilizer gun," Melvin said.

"You go in there with an air rifle and she'll kill you, Melvin."

"Nonsense."

"She killed a chimp. You faster or stronger than a chimp?"

Melvin looked at Casey and swallowed. "What'll we do?"

"I need a weapon. A short piece of pipe, a big butcher knife, a, pardon the pun, monkey wrench. Go get something." Melvin scuttled off. Casey turned to Moira.

"Blood," he said. "As fresh as possible. At least a quart. Go."

"Gone," she said, and was.

Casey stripped to his jeans, tossing his lab coat, shirt, shoes and socks on the floor beside the door to the lab and waited, listening to the screams and thumps on the other side of the wall. Melvin came trotting down the hall. He was carrying a meat cleaver and a marble rolling pin.

"Great, Melvin. Just perfect. Put 'em on the floor by my clothes please."

In a moment Moira came trotting up with two IV bags of whole blood.

Casey took one from her. "Good work," Casey said. "This will not be pleasant for either of you to watch. Melvin, Moira knows why I am going to do this. I'll explain it to you later." He turned the bag upside down, ripped out the tubing, put his lips to the stem, lifted it like a water bladder, and began to drink.

The rush started half way through the second bag. Casey trembled with it, and some of the blood spilled down across his chin and chest. He dropped the bag to the floor and let it take him, fire coursing through his veins, electricity through his nerves, joy through his brain. Panting, he grinned at his compatriots with bloody teeth and smoldering eyes, shaking with the surge of power. Moira stared back solemnly. Melvin recoiled from him to the other side of the hall.

Casey chuckled. "Bathroom?" he said.

"Around the corner and three doors down," blurted Moira.

"Too fucking far," he said and turned his back, voiding his urine against the wall. When he finished, he shook himself like a dog.

"I'm going to go in there now and kill that monkey. We do not want her to get out of the room. She is just as fast as I am, maybe faster, and amazingly strong. If she escapes, there is nothing here that could catch her. When it's over I'm going to need a shower in a contamination containment area. Moira, you will take me there. Under no circumstances will you touch me, or allow any blood or fluid that may be on me to get on you. When I leave the area, Melvin, you will clean up. Consider this a full-blown Haz-Mat alert. This is as serious as Ebola. You will disinfect the entire lab and wherever I go when I leave the room. You will burn every body left in the lab, including mine if for some reason I don't make it out. Are we clear?" They both nodded. "Is there negative air pressure in the room?" They nodded again.

"Alright. I'm going to count to three, then open the door and go inside. When you hear me say three, the two of you slam the door as hard as you can and make sure it locks. Before I come out, I want both of you in full suits."

"But the door won't be open when you say three," Melvin said.

Casey scowled at him. "Just do as you are told, human, and you may live through this," he hissed. "Now is a very bad time to argue with me, Melvin. Just fucking do it!"

Casey picked up the cleaver and stood next to the entrance. When he said three, the door was ajar about fifteen inches and Casey just winked out of sight. Melvin stood frozen with his mouth open.

Frightened for herself, Melvin, and Casey, Moira slammed the door.

### Sugar Coveted

For two more days the wind blew from the wrong quarter. For two more days the Wren showed her tail feathers to it and ran before following seas. For two more days Van Zant was almost constantly at the wheel, occasionally lashing himself into the pilot's chair for an unsettled nap, while Blake, the mate, spelled him. For two more days Ng'mutu Umbaylay tossed in his chains on the wooden platform deep in the hold of the lurching ship and hungered. Then, the wind stopped. The Wren was becalmed.

"A pox on this bleedin' weather, Pilot!" Blake said. "A pox on this ship, and a pox on her captain, the grog swillin' sot!"

VanZant smiled, scanning the flaccid canvas overhead as the Wren slowly rolled on an oily sea. "Mister Blake" he said, "you seem less than pleased with our current situation."

"You can joke if ye like, Pilot, but this don't seem right to me. I was with Jursten on his first voyage to the Japans, and we come becalmed for thirty-one days off the east coast of Africa. Thirty-one days, Pilot! Three of our good lads throwed themselves into the sea to escape it! It's not right for a sailin' ship to set still over long on the open sea. It steals the soul out of her and the heart out of them what serves aboard her."

"Perhaps we need a sacrifice to Neptune before he rolls us over and feeds us to the Kraken, First," Van Zant said. "Do you volunteer for the good of the ship and crew?"

"Go ahead, Pilot. Laugh at me if ye like, but sure as Judas gave up God's only son to the cross, this calm is a foul omen, right enough."

"Why don't you get some sleep, Blake. Use my cabin if you like."

"That's a kind offer, and fair too, but I can't sleep on no ship that's settin' still."

"Very well, work then. Assemble a party to remove the dead from below and cast them overside."

Blake looked at him with large eyes. "Why Pilot, why would you want to do that? They'll just float along side us on this sea. We won't be able to get away from 'em."

"We can't get away from them if they're below decks either. I'd rather have them stinking up the sea than stinking up the Wren. Heave to, Mister Blake."

"Aye, Pilot, but it's bad business ye set us on. Bad business."

Ng'mutu Umbaylay stayed as still as he could when he heard the white devils coming down into the bottom of the floating house where he lay. They jabbered nonsense among themselves and pulled several of his fellows from their places and piled them in a heap on the floor. They even took him, so still he lay, holding his breath, and cast two or three others on top of him, one of them barely alive, his ankle against Ng'mutu Umbaylay's face, dripping blood on Ng'mutu's cheek from the wound the iron restraints had made. Ng'mutu Umbaylay kept still, even though the blood ran down his jaw and across his lips.

Wah! This was almost too much. True, many tribes ate the members of other tribes, but the Igbo and Oyo did not do such things. They were not Bevin or Bantu. They did not eat their fellow men, or capture them and sell them into the bottom of the white man's floating house! Still, Ng'mutu Umbaylay had had nothing to eat or drink for a long time and, as the blood ran across his cracked lips, they soaked it up, becoming once again soft and supple. To stop the tingling he felt, he shifted his tongue across the wet surface.

The blood tasted like salty fire! He licked again. Like scratching an itch, the flavor soared through his mouth. His stomach cramped with the need of it, his throat throbbed with the want of it, and when the white men went again up their ladder into the light above, he shifted his position slightly in the pile of bodies and used his teeth to enlarge the wound on the ankle of his unconscious benefactor.

He felt the blood race through his entire body, bringing light and strength wherever it touched. He felt his muscles respond, his skin flex and shift, his head grow full and urgent. He needed more. Unbound, he pushed his way free of some of the crush atop him and sucked on the ankle, tearing at it with his teeth. Not enough! Not enough! Without conscious thought he shifted to the neck, chewing his way into the throat, sucking, slurping, licking, drinking. With every swallow, power surged through him. With every mouthful, his senses blossomed. He could clearly see everything in the dim light. He could hear every footfall on the decks above him. He could smell every person held in that place with him. He was sucking desperately for more—when the rush hit.

It lifted him to his feet, then dropped him to his knees. Coursing through every cell in his body, it filled him with great thrusts of need and satisfaction. He threw back his head and howled from the joy of it, then fell to his side and quivered with painful pleasure at the cellular orgasm that tore him apart and sealed him back together. When it was over, he urinated on the floor beside his first victim and waited for the white devils to return.

On deck, Van Zant and Blake heard the howl, but paid it little attention. Shrieks and moans from below decks were common. They watched as several men gathered at the hatch to begin a body brigade and pass the corpses, one to another, up the ladder, and out of the hold.

God in Heaven, this had to be his last slave voyage! From England to Africa to pick up these wretched blacks—three hundred forty-six of them laid by and chained in the hold when they started this trip—then to the bloody tropics in Central America with the stifling heat and swamps to trade the black cargo for sweet cargo. Then back to England with the coveted sugar. Home for a few weeks, then back again. He was through with living cargo. Maybe some runs to the colonies. It wouldn't be as profitable, but it wouldn't be as grim either. Blake was right. This was bad business.

A scream pulled him back from his thoughts. He'd seen two stout lads go down the ladder only a moment before that blood-curdling screech. A second one began, but was abruptly cut off an instant after it started.

"Take the wheel, Mister Blake!" he shouted, pulling his pistol and running for the hatch. He was still thirty feet away when the thing rose from the bowels of the ship.

It was one of the blacks, covered in blood, and he came up the ladder as if he were flying, swatting crewmen out of his way as casually as a grown man could slap kittens. Covered in blood and grinning with red teeth, he pulled pieces from some who opposed him, his hands tearing flesh as if it were warm lard.

Van Zant took aim and fired his pistol. The ball struck the apparition in the upper chest, and he flinched when it hit him, rubbing at the wound as if it were no more than a fly bite. He turned his attention to the pilot, and Van Zant attempted to flee, but the bloody black was on him with impossible speed, catching him by the arm and snapping it like a twig. The pilot's last sight on this cruel earth was that dripping red mouth closing with his face.

Ng'mutu Umbaylay, or what he had become, fed five more times that first day. Four of his victims were white. He would save the blacks for later. Restrained the way they were, it would be simple to feed when he chose to. He might have to use a few as caretakers of the others, but food was abundant. He laughed at the simplicity of it. Sooner or later, the floating house would run out of water. Sooner or later he would be on land where there were villages and people. For now, he would float and feed, feed and float, a cruel ruler of his own little world. Never had newly deceased Ng'mutu Umbaylay felt so alive.

Late that night, the wind rose from the south-southeast. A little over three hundred miles from the eastern shore of Cuba, the Wren turned with the erratic light breeze and began to travel north northeast. If the pilot and the mate had been alive, they would have wondered at the curious direction, but they were not and did not. No one knew and no one cared that the strange wind was a harbinger. It was the first indication of an event that would change many things, including the destiny of a cooper in the Plymouth Colony named Mathew Herriott. That errant little breeze was the beginning of the hurricane of 1635.

# EIGHT

Duxbury

THREE HOURS AFTER CASEY WENT INTO THE LAB, he was in Moira's apartment munching Cheetos out of the bag and drinking his second can of Coke. The big dinner had been canceled. She had no appetite. A knock on the door announced Melvin's arrival. He lurched into the room, without waiting to be let in, and sprawled on the couch, throwing an arm over his eyes.

"God!" he said. "I'm exhausted. What a horrible mess!"

Slumped in a chair, Moira gazed numbly at him. "You look terrible, Melvin. Can I get you something?"

"Vodka," he said.

"I didn't know you drank."

"I don't. Rocks. Triple."

"I'll join you," Moira said. She groaned to her feet and walked stiff-legged into the kitchen.

"I just can't believe it," Melvin muttered. His hands fluttered of their own accord. "Five spider monkeys, four rhesus, and a full grown male chimp. All killed. And not just killed, but ripped apart. Ripped apart! By Alice! Alice was old and sick."

"And dead," Casey said.

Melvin appeared not to have heard him.

"Rhesus monkeys don't kill chimps. They can't kill chimps. Sultan was eighteen years old, in his prime. Perhaps ten times stronger than the average man. It's not possible for a healthy rhesus to do what she did to him. It's just not possible!"

"Especially when you consider, she'd been dead for some time," Casey said.

"She shredded those cages," Melvin went on. "Stainless steel. The most secure containment we could buy. Shredded! She even broke out of the cooler!"

"Where you'd put her body after she died," Casey said.

Melvin stared at the ceiling. "I mean," he said, "all of that was impossible. Virtually impossible! But then, one has to consider an even larger conundrum. Not only did Alice actually do all those impossible things, she did them after she had died!"

Moira handed him his drink. Melvin slowly sat up and swung his feet to the floor. He took a sip, placed the glass on a table, propped his elbows on his knees, put his face in his hands, and sat rock still for a moment.

"My mind just can't encompass it," he said. "How could such a thing happen? How could it happen?"

Casey smiled. "About that," he said.

For the next hour or so Casey told Melvin most of what he'd already told Moira. Alternating between euphoria and despair, the slight scientist listened raptly, speaking up only after Casey finished.

"You're a vampire?" he said.

"As much as I hate the term, I guess I am, more or less."

"Then you and Alice are, or rather were, alike."

"Well, I wouldn't go that far. I'm much taller and have less body hair," Casey said. Moira snorted.

"Oh! Excuse me," Melvin said. "It was not my attention, ah, intention to imply you are simian."

"Don't worry about it," Casey said.

Halfway through his second triple vodka, Melvin peered at Casey. "So it's your contention that this, this, vampirism is infectious in nature."

"Aye."

"And that the infection is almost always fatal to the ho, hoist, ah, host."

"I believe so."

"But, it was not fatal to you."

"Not permanently, no."

"Wh … why not?"

"The same reason it was not permanently fatal to my daughter."

"And that would be?"

"I have no idea."

"You have no idea."

"None."

"Interesting," said Melvin. He put his glass on the table and stared blankly at the ice cubes. Moira extended her hand, and Casey passed her the Cheetos.

Melvin blinked his way back from contemplating his drink.

"How did you become infected?"

"I was bitten."

"And your daughter?"

"She was also bitten."

"By what?"

"Whom," Casey said. Sadness sagged into his posture.

Melvin took another drink. "By whom?"

"An African. An escaped slave, I believe."

"An escaped slave? When was this?"

"1635."

Melvin's body twitched. He squinted at Casey. "1635?"

"That's correct."

"Oh, my goodness."

"We, my wife, my daughter, and I were living in a settlement called Duxbury in the Plymouth Colony. It was August. It had been very windy and stormy for several days, but that particular afternoon the weather cleared. Catherine, my daughter, was helping me straighten things up in the forge. On the other side of our cabin, my wife, Elizabeth, was checking on her flowerbeds. We heard her scream. Cat and I ran to see what was wrong and found her in the arms of a naked black man, his teeth fastened to her throat. I closed with him, but was powerless against his strength. He bit into my shoulder and cast me away like so much chaff. Cat did likewise, and he bit through her breast and tossed her aside. When I came to myself, I found sweet Elizabeth with her entire throat torn open and her neck broken. Dear Catherine lay whimpering in the weeds, afraid even of me, bleeding from her left breast. It took me some time to gain her confidence, and then she clung to me as if for life, sobbing desperately into my bloody shoulder, unable or unwilling to give up her grasp on me."

Casey paused for a moment and looked around the room with empty eyes. He rubbed his face and focus returned.

"An hour or so later a group of men and several hounds came by, tracking the wretched African. From them, I learned that a slave ship had beached on the coast during the hurricane. Examination of the slaver had revealed carnage beyond belief. Both black and white rotting bodies littered the deck, and the hold contained over one hundred mutilated corpses still in chains, at least another hundred chained individuals who appeared to have died of thirst or starvation, and less than two dozen pitiful souls left alive. Dogs brought to the scene struck track from the grounded vessel. They had been trailing the murderer of my darling wife for two days."

Casey shook his head with the memory and took a sip of his drink.

"I built a box, and Catherine and I committed her mother to the earth. A few days later, Catherine became ill and her breast swelled terribly. I had her bled twice, but to no avail. I also became sick and feverish. In about two weeks, while I held her in my arms, my dear Catherine, my only child, passed away. I strove to dig her grave, but had not the strength, and collapsed on the floor of our cabin beside her, held her cold hand, and waited for the Reaper."

Casey stopped his narrative for a moment to collect himself. Moira moved behind him and squeezed his shoulder.

"When next I came to myself and opened my eyes, I saw Catherine's lovely face looking down at me. Filled with wonder, I spoke to her. 'You didn't die,' I said. 'Oh, but I did, Father,' she said. 'So did you. As Lazarus, we have returned, but we are not the same. We are more than we ever were.' She held a bowl out to me and bade me drink. Without thought, I did. The liquid flowed through me like fire, bringing energy and vitality to every cell in my body. I was halfway through it before I realized it was blood. By then I was beyond care."

"My Lord," Melvin said.

"Full of hope, we unearthed her mother, but my wife was no more than a festering corpse. We covered her box and spent the night in the forge. The next morning we set off southward, avoiding settlements, searching for travelers on their solitary way, or red natives, reveling in our new abilities and appetites, feeding as we went, more alive after death than we had ever been in life. We didn't return to the shire for nearly a week."

"Vampires," Melvin said, suddenly sober.

"I suppose so."

"So the two of you killed people and drank their blood?"

"Aye," Casey said. "After we departed Duxbury the second time, we avoided civilization as much as we could, preferring to take red natives from their hunt, or people who were traveling alone. And we kept on the move, so as not to attract undue attention to ourselves or one particular area. When no other choice was at hand, we would harvest someone from a village or camp, but we tried to limit contact with groups as much as possible. The screams of war were music to what we had become. The French-Indian conflict was a buffet. Tribal battles were meat on the table. We sought out such conflicts. When men kill each other, we are most free. We fed daily at such times, reveling in our power. Humankind was our sup and cup, and we feasted."

"Are you telling me the truth?" Melvin said.

"Aye, that I am."

"What do you think, Moira?" Melvin continued, shaking his head. "Can all this possibly be true? Can this man have done what he professes to have done? Can he have lived four centuries ago?"

"Listen to the pattern of his speech, Melvin," she said. "Hear how it changed when he spoke of the past? I have no doubts. He's telling the truth."

Melvin rose to his feet and began to pace.

"Unbelievable!" he said.

"More unbelievable than a dead rhesus killing an adult chimpanzee?" Moira said.

Melvin thought for a moment, swaying where he stood. "I suppose not. But I find the entire prospect of being harvested for food disgusting!"

"Said the monkey to the leopard," Casey murmured.

Around midnight Moira made sandwiches, and Casey went to his apartment to retrieve a bag of chips and some bottled tea. When he came back, the scientist in Melvin had returned. The slight man raised an eyebrow.

"So it took you about two weeks to succumb to the infection?"

"About that."

"And it took around four days after your death to come back."

"Around that."

"Your daughter took a little less time for both events."

"That's correct."

"And Alice took only four days to die and around a day to return," Melvin said. "She was directly injected with your blood, which may account for some of the difference in timing for death from infection, but I would suspect the primary reasons are body mass and metabolism. Alice weighed only about twenty-five pounds, and rhesus monkeys function at a much more rapid metabolic rate than humans. Rats might make the entire transition in a very short time. Twenty-four to thirty-six hours, possibly."

"Pretty dangerous injecting the virus into animals," Casey said.

"I can assure you," Melvin said, "that we have the most sophisticated containment facilities available."

"Alice thought so."

"Perhaps you're correct."

"It will be very easy for you to become complacent," Casey said. "To the best of my knowledge, at least with human victims, only a tiny percentage of those infected survive their death. Alice might be one in a thousand, maybe one in ten thousand. The odds against that particular monkey doing what she did are huge."

"And yet you and your daughter both survived."

"Yes, but the odds were very much against us."

"So the total number of vampires is small?"

"Very small. I don't know how many, but I would suspect there are very few of us."

"Have you met others?"

"Yes."

"How many?"

"Less than ten."

"Does your kind, ah, get along?"

"I killed four of them."

"I see. Just how strong are you, Mr. Casey?"

"Right now, just after feeding, pretty strong."

"And your speed?"

"Very fast."

"How fast?"

"I'll indulge you, Melvin. When you care to, close your eyes, say your name and open them again."

Melvin did, and when he looked around, the room was empty. Casey and a disheveled Moira, walked out of the bedroom.

"Remarkable," Melvin said.

Casey smiled and turned to Moira.

"Did I notice a tennis bag in the bedroom?" he asked.

"You did," she said, blinking and finger combing her hair.

Casey stepped into the bedroom and returned with a tennis ball. He held it up between his thumb and forefinger and squeezed. The ball exploded and fine dust filled the air.

"Amazing!" Melvin said. "Tomorrow, with your permission, I'd like to run some physical tests on you. Strength, speed, endurance, things like that."

"I won't be as strong tomorrow as I am now, but I think you'll be pleased."

"You're at your best shortly after you've, ah, fed, is that it?"

"That's it."

"We can always get you more blood."

"That's okay, Melvin," Casey said. "These days I prefer sipping to drinking."

At around eight the next morning, Casey joined Moira in the cafeteria. His tray was piled high with food.

"Good grief," Moira said, "you leave any for the rest of us?"

"Joy of my days," he said, enjoying the sight of her. "My magnificent rippling animal."

"Jesus, Casey, my ass feels like it's been run over by a truck, and you're coming on like a lunatic."

"The next time your ass is threatened by a motor vehicle, let me know. I'll defend it to the death."

"I don't need you to protect my ass."

Casey rested his chin in his hand and bumped his eyebrows.

"How 'bout admire it?"

Moira laughed. "That's different," she said. "You seem to be loosening up quite a bit. How come you're so cheerful?"

"I guess it sorta feels good to have told somebody about how all this began. It's not a story you wanna spread around."

"Wow," she said. "I suppose it must be hard living a secret as long as you have. I'm a little surprised you were so candid with Melvin."

"Melvin doesn't have a devious bone in his body."

They ate in silence until Casey chuckled.

"What's so funny?"

"We are the subject of considerable interest," he said.

"Oh?"

"Across the room behind you and slightly to your right, Elesia and three other women are having a conversation about us."

"You can hear what they're saying?"

"Most of it. If they'd shut off the dishwasher in the kitchen I could get it all. They're talking about you bringing a man back with you and wondering if the Ice Queen is finally thawing out."

Moira jerked upright and narrowed her eyes.

"The Ice Queen?"

Casey leaned back and raised his hands to defend himself.

"Not my words," he said.

"The Ice Queen?" Moira hissed.

"Don't hurt me," Casey said. "The little blond said that."

Moira quickly glanced over her shoulder. "Cheryl," she snorted. "I'm not surprised! I'd expect something like that from that little ..."

"Ah, ah, ah," Casey said. "It's a private conversation. Besides, Elesia is defending you."

"Really?" Moira whispered, leaning forward.

"Relax," Casey said. "They can't hear us."

"What'd she say?"

"Something about how you're too dedicated to the job. You don't have time for men. You're not cold, you're just busy, but she'd sure as hell find the time, if ..." he let the sentence trail off and filled his mouth with food.

"If what?" Moira said.

"Nuffin'," Casey replied around a mouthful of toast.

"If what, Casey?"

Casey took a drink of milk. "If she had me hidden away in one of the apartments," he said.

"Elesia said that?" Moira blurted, dropping her spoon to the tabletop.

"Ah, yeah. The little blond …"

"Cheryl," Moira snapped.

"Cheryl seems to agree that she'd make the time, too."

Moira folded her arms and huffed.

"Now don't get excited," Casey said. "I told you there was some interest coming this way. Ol' Elesia seems to have drawn a bead on yours truly."

"Your superpowers tell you that?"

"A lot of interest from the brunette too," Casey said. He lifted his chin, sniffed two or three times, and grinned. "A lot of interest."

"Bonnie," Moira said.

"If that's her name. More than just interest," Casey said. He shivered in his seat for effect and continued to sniff the air. "Almost unbridled, naked lust. Woof!"

Moira's mouth dropped open. "Bonnie? But that's not, I mean, everybody has always thought, ah, Bonnie's a lesbian!"

Casey's eyes danced. "I didn't say she was hot for me, Sweetie."

Moira looked at him for a moment, then realization struck.

"Oh, no!" she said. "Oh no! Oh, Jesus. I gotta get outa here! Aw, man! Casey, goddammit …"

"Relax, they're leaving. Just sit tight. Eat something and be cool."

It took Moira several minutes to settle down. They ate and made small talk, and Casey could feel her warming toward him again.

"Gonna do some tests with Melvin today?"

"Yep. The stress tests."

"Gonna hold back?"

"Yep again."

She smiled. "Holding back with me?"

"In more ways than you know."

Moira shifted in her seat and leaned toward him a bit. "Going to keep holding back?"

"In more ways than you know."

She studied him for a moment. "Casey, what's wrong?"

He glanced over her shoulder.

"Fair morrow, Melvin," he said.

An hour later, swathed in wire and tubes, Casey ran on a treadmill. Melvin stood beside him, flushed with excitement.

"You've run five sub-four-minute miles in a row, Casey. Your pulse is under eighty, your respirations under twenty-five. This is quite unusual!"

Feeling bored, Casey let it out a little. Melvin's eyes darted back and forth between read-outs, and he started to become agitated. Casey let it out a little more. Melvin began to turn red and hop in place.

"Your sixth mile was under three minutes!" he shouted. "Pulse eighty-six, respirations twenty-nine!"

Grinning, Casey went up to around half speed. The treadmill began to smoke. Laughing, he slowed and stepped off. The acrid smell of the scorched belt permeated the room.

"My Goodness!" shouted Melvin. "Amazing! If the machine had held up, that last mile would have been under a minute! Over sixty miles an hour! Maximum measured pulse: ninety-three, respirations: thirty-four! And look at this! The recovery is unbelievable! Already you're down to under sixty on your pulse and under eighteen breaths a minute. How close were you to full speed?"

"Getting there," Casey said.

Melvin began unhooking him. "Any idea how fast you could run a hundred meter dash?"

"Fast enough they'd lock me up and perform experiments."

Melvin grinned. "How long could you keep up the three minute mile pace?"

"I really don't know. Several hours, I guess. I'd have to rest and feed."

"Outstanding! I don't think there's any point in testing you on any of the strength machines. You'd easily overpower them. They're not constructed for someone like you."

"No, they're not," Casey said.

"Right. You look so normal, I keep losing sight of the fact that, ah, that you're not …"

"Human?"

"Well, yes. That would be the, ah, case, I suppose. I forgot that you are not human."

A small smile swept Casey's lips.

"Don't ever forget it, Melvin," he said. "Not for a minute."

# NINE

Tongues

CASEY WAS PEERING IN HIS FRIDGE for sandwich possibilities when a knock came on the connecting door. Moira walked in without waiting for an answer.

"Hey, Hotshot!" she grinned. "You got poor ol' Melvin running in ever diminishing circles over your performance in the lab this morning."

Casey returned her grin. "You ever wait 'til somebody actually answers the door before you barge in?"

"Not if I might catch 'em nekked."

"Sorry."

"You're sorry? Imagine my disappointment."

"So Melvin is shook up, huh?" Casey said, changing the subject.

Moira laughed. "To the ground. What'd you do to the poor man?"

"I showed him a little."

"Well, it must have been plenty. He thinks you could sprint from here to L.A. while you held your breath."

"Always good to have an enemy overestimate your virtues and underestimate your faults," Casey said.

She looked at him for a moment.

"Is that what you think we are? Enemies? Is that who you think I am?"

"Hard to change old patterns, I guess. Your kind has been the enemy of my kind for so long. Jesus. I'm sorry, Moira. No, I don't think you're my enemy. You've been wonderful. You've taken me in, given me a place of safety. I spoke out of habit. Please don't take an offhand comment personally. Please."

Arms folded, she stared at him. Casey could see a trace of tears gathering along her lower eyelids. He sank into a chair.

"Aw, shit," he said. "I know the fact that it wasn't my intention to hurt you makes no difference. I did hurt you. Try to understand. For a very long time I have not allowed myself to become emotionally close to anyone. Anyone. Human or otherwise. For more years than you can imagine, there has been nobody on the fucking planet that I could trust, no one that I could turn to, no one that I could share with, nobody with whom I could even be remotely honest. And, it was beyond my ability or interest to behave in such a manner with anyone. Then I dry out and spend a few years among several hundred prison inmates, a virtual hotbed of sensitivity and understanding. Then you come along, and you are so goddamn sincere, and so goddamn direct, and so goddamn open. And the next thing I know, I'm out of prison trying to find a motel room in Indianapolis, Indi-fucking-ana for chrissake, to throw myself on the mercy of some woman I've only seen twice in my life! And now, I'm in some goddamn lab someplace, running on treadmills, breathing through tubes with electrodes or whatever glued all over me, giving blood, my blood, to some weird little shit who doesn't even wear socks that are same color!"

Casey got to his feet and began to pace. "This fucking scares me to death! This is worse than stupid, this is insane! This is absolutely the wrong thing for somebody like me to ever do, and I am doing it anyway. And do you want to know why?"

He walked to within three feet of her, fists clenched and trembling. Moira held her ground.

"I'll tell you why," he whispered, his shoulders sagging as if from great weight. "I'll tell you why. It's not to find my daughter, it's not to help mankind. It's much more selfish than that."

He looked her in the eyes, and Moira could see sadness creep across his face. Casey relaxed his fists into open hands and held them at his sides.

"I have nowhere else to go," he said, "and I am *so* tired of going nowhere. And you, Miss Flynn, talking with you, sitting with you, laughing with you, knowing you, just knowing you, makes me want to be more human."

He flopped back into the chair and stared at the floor.

Swallowing the lump that had suddenly appeared in her throat, Moira stepped behind him, leaned down, kissed him on the cheek, walked into the kitchenette, and began to paw through the fridge.

"I'll bet you say that to all the girls," she said. "Hungry?"

They small-talked their way through lunch. After Casey finished his milk, Moira got down to business.

"Any idea where your daughter might be?"

"None."

"But you seem to feel that she's in this country."

"Probably. This continent, at least."

"Why?"

Casey thought for a moment. "There is almost no example of terrain or population density that can't be found in the states. Things like that are important to the Nosferati. They have to hide, yet they need people. They must be very secretive, yet what they do attracts attention. They need access to population but still must be wary of it. A single vamp, or a couple for that matter, can go undetected in a large city. A group, five or more, especially if they feed as often as the Nosferati like to feed, have to be very careful not to foul their nests. While they choose targets of opportunity many times, they also have to be very cautious about who they harvest. They need a fair population base from which to pick their prey. People of violence, those who are homeless, those who are alone, those who are shunned due to illness, people who will not be missed or whose disappearance can easily be explained away—those are the most likely victims."

"Don't attract attention."

"Yep. That also applies to the refuse."

"The refuse?"

"The bodies. Can't leave a bunch of corpses lying about, now can we? Sure way to attract attention is to have a bunch of stiffs in the front yard. People talk. If they're feeding near home, they have to hide the evidence. The obvious answer is go elsewhere, but if I'm a Nosferati, and I want that rush at least couple of times a week, I'm gonna have to feed near home at least some of the time. Disposal problem."

"What's the solution?"

"I have to operate from someplace rural, but near population centers. Someplace remote, but not distant. Plus, most Nosferati use drugs and booze. Gotta be able to get those."

"So what we have are very specific needs that often contradict each other."

"Just like life," Casey said.

"Well, my pal Marley, who is a Fed and works with the disease control people, has stroked a couple of her pals over at NCIC …"

"NCIC?" Casey said.

"National Crime Information Center. Marley sent along a little something you might want to look at."

"What?"

"A map, Casey. A map of disappearances, deaths, diabolical deeds, and dastardly doings."

"Ooooh!"

"Right up your alley, huh, Fang?"

"And where would this map be?"

"On the table next door."

"In your room?"

"If I let you come over, will you promise to behave?"

The map was without terrain or highway and city designation. About six feet square, it delineated the contiguous forty-eight states and was marked with small colored dots. Red for unsolved murders involving mysterious blood loss, yellow for the location of unexplained mutilated corpses, blue for disappearances, green for unsolved serial killings. On each dot was a number. In many cases the colored dots overlapped. The heaviest concentration was in the northeast and far west population centers.

"What are we looking for?" Moira said.

Casey shrugged. "I'm not sure."

"Think about this. If what you said is correct, then maybe we should be looking for donuts."

"What?"

"Donuts," Moira repeated. "Maybe a croissant."

"You still hungry?"

She smiled. "What we want are locations where there are dots that form a circle or a partial circle, but with little activity in the center. See? There's a weak one here in what has to be Oregon, another near the middle of Florida, one in the northern

Midwest near Minneapolis/St. Paul, and another down in what is either southern Missouri or northern Arkansas."

"Gotcha," Casey said. "How far, time wise, does this map go back?"

Moira sat at the computer. "The data is good for twenty years. Pick a number and read it to me."

Casey's eyes were drawn to Southern Missouri. "Twenty-three thirty-five."

Moira used the keyboard and the screen came up. "Cheryl Robinson. Disappeared with her boyfriend David Reynolds on or about June 10th, 1998, while camping in the Mark Twain National Forrest near Doniphan, Missouri. Neither of them was ever found."

"Thirty-one twelve."

"Carson Bailey, white male, 53, found dead in a dumpster in Branson, Missouri on September 3rd, 2003. Cause of death was a severe wound in the throat and the loss of over half the body's blood. Little or no bleeding in the dumpster."

"Double or triple feeding," Casey said.

"What?"

"Thirty-seven fifty-one."

"Cassandra Furlander. Found along a gravel road two miles outside Little Rock, Arkansas, March 19th, 2004. Throat cut, bled to death. Small amount of blood at the scene. When last seen, she was in the company of her daughter Amanda, age 7. The child was never found."

"Fifteen twenty-four."

"Arthur and Louise Lonigan. Found beside their car on a county road near Jonesboro, Arkansas, November 23rd, 1994. The vehicle had a flat tire. Both appeared to have died from blood loss because of wounds. Mrs. Lonigan's tongue had been bitten off. The bodies had been ravaged by what appeared to be feral dogs or coyotes. Yuk!"

"Can you access injuries on that thing?" Casey said, pointing to the computer.

"Sure."

"Ask it for tongues."

"Tongues?"

"Yep. Just locations. I don't need victim data."

"Ick."

Moira used the keyboard for a moment, then peered at the screen. "Ah, near highways 181 and 14 southwest of Willow Springs, Missouri, outside Poplar Bluff, Missouri, near Paragould, Arkansas, south of Springfield, Missouri, near Ozark, Missouri, Fort Smith, Arkansas, Little Rock, Arkansas, Cape Girardeau, Missouri, Branson, Missouri. That's all this shows."

"That's enough. Here's our donut, this section of northern Arkansas and southern Missouri. If she's around, she's probably around here."

"How do you know?"

"Tongues, Miss Flynn. When she can, Cat gets their tongues."

Still a little pale, Moira emerged from the bathroom a few minutes later and glared at Casey.

"What?" he asked, the picture of innocence.

"You know damn well what!"

"Sorry."

"My ass!"

"Don't change the subject," he said, leering at her below the waist.

"Shit," she said. "Just don't drop stuff like that on me."

"You're a doctor. You people are supposed to have strong stomachs."

"Another myth," Moira said.

"Now that we know where my daughter might be, what's next? Road trip?"

"Probably. You need to change your appearance a little so nobody tries to arrest you for breaking out of prison."

"And committing another murder."

"And that. We'll lighten your hair, change your eye color with contacts, and give you some credentials from a government agency. You'll do fine. Got a picture of your daughter?"

"A what?"

"A picture of, oh. Of course you don't."

"Of course I don't. Not a lot of cameras around in 1852."

"Jesus, Casey. Sometimes this shit really freaks me out!"

"Spoken like a true scientist."

"We need a picture of your kid. I'll make a call or two, and get an artist over here tomorrow or the next day. Meantime, we'll work on changing your look. We'll give you a makeover, Casey. My big chance to mold you into something respectable."

"Oh, hell."

"I'll be back in about half an hour."

"Where you going?"

"To the drugstore. Take a shower, wash your hair, and get ready."

"Promises, promises."

"Make no mistake," she replied. "It's a threat."

When Moira returned, Casey was freshly coiffed and waiting. She swept in without knocking and put a bag and a digital camera on the table.

"My victim! All squeaky clean?"

"As pure as the driven snow."

"Great," she said. "Now just put yourself in my hands."

For the next two hours Moira clipped and snipped, tanned and fanned. The intimacy of the close contact told on them both, and several times Moira took a break. Eventually, Casey became a blond with his hair trimmed high and tight on the sides while remaining long on top and parted slightly off center. His already reasonably dark complexion was deepened by two more shades.

"Jesus!" he said, peering at a mirror. "I look like a refugee from a beach party! This almost makes me sorry I can see my reflection!"

"I think you're cute," Moira said. "You look younger."

"Than what?"

Moira laughed. "Than you used to, Dummy. Not a day over thirty-five. Tomorrow we'll get you some blue contacts. Nobody'd recognize you in a hundred years."

"I look weird."

"Only to you. Somebody who's never seen you before will accept your appearance on face value. Relax. The rinse will come out of your hair, and the tan will fade from your face. We need to get you some clothes, too. Blue jeans and sweatpants are not acceptable. You need to be able to look a little more official than that if necessary. We'll also get you some ID."

"You can do that?"

"I have low friends in high places."

"Who am I supposed to be?"

"Anybody except Joseph Casey, or Mathew Herriott for that matter."

"Well, I've changed identities before. As a matter of fact, it's time to do it again anyway."

"Great. Stand over against the wall." Moira picked up the camera and took three shots. "I'm off to work and to start things moving," she said. "Get some rest, whoever you are. Tomorrow you become a new man."

Casey was trying to get a straight part in his hair when Moira breezed in around eight the next morning.

"Aw," she said. "Want me to part your hair for you, little man?"

Stifling his grin, he flipped her off.

"It'll take time to train it. Don't be so macho, Doris. There's hairspray on the shelf. Use it, or learn to enjoy the hayseed look."

While Casey struggled with his hair, she placed some items on the table. At length he left the bathroom and sat with her. She handed him a Virginia driver's license and a new ID for the World Health Organization. He looked at the pictures.

"That's me?"

"Kenneth Charles Mitchell. Born and died thirty-four years ago in Arlington, Virginia. I can still call you Casey. K.C. get it?"

"I look like that?"

"You will when I get done with you." She placed a small box in front of him. "Contacts. The new porous membrane variety. Leave 'em in for a month, toss 'em, put in new ones. Ever use contacts?"

"With my vision?"

"God, do I have to do everything for you? Lean over here and open wide."

In a few moments Casey was looking around the room and blinking. "Feels strange," he said.

"You'll get used to it." She removed a double syringe kit from the bag.

"What's that?"

"A little collagen for each side of your nose and a little more for your lower lip. As we age, the nose drops and the lips shrink. Fatten the nose a touch, make the bottom lip a little rounder, ten years gone in a flash. Especially with this." She held up the second syringe.

"And that would be?"

"Muscle relaxant. Synthetic Botox. A little between the eyebrows and at the corners of your eyes, the creases and crow's feet lighten right up. You'll look sixteen again. Sit in the recliner and kick back. I'll shoot you up."

"Jesus."

"You're gonna be so pretty, Casey, you're gonna have to beat 'em away with a stick."

An hour later, Kenneth Charles Mitchell, dressed in oxblood loafers, brown pleated slacks, a dark blue shirt, and a light brown herringbone jacket, adjusted the band on his stainless steel Rolex knockoff and looked at himself in the mirror.

"Damn," he said.

"Ooo," purred Moira. "I just love younger men, Kenny."

"Sorry, Babe. You're, like, way too old for me. I'm gonna profile through campus in my Beemer with the top down."

"Ungrateful wretch. Lay low around here until we leave. I don't want the staff to see your new hair or blue eyes. When we get back, we'll restore your old hair color and dump the contacts. You can live with the tan, the collagen, and the Botox stuff." She glanced at her watch. "We also have a date with an artist to make a picture of your daughter, who, may I remind you before you get too youthful, is about four hundred years old."

Casey smiled. "You don't have to remind me," he said. "I delivered her."

Moira returned his smile and looked into his new blue eyes. They seemed darker. Just a little.

Less than twenty minutes later, a middle-aged woman named Sylvia arrived at Casey's room with a sketchpad and a computer. After amenities were observed, Sylvia got down to business.

"Sex?" she asked.

"Female."

"Age?"

"Fourteen."

"Face shape? Long, oval, heart, round."

"Oval, I guess, but her chin is a little square."

"Fine. Cheekbones? Wide, narrow, low, high, prominent, strong?"

On it went as Sylvia's pencil flew over the paper. Wide dark eyes, the single dimple on the left side of her mouth, the short nose with the tiny bump at the bridge, the full lower lip, the strong chin and fine jaw line, the close-set ears, and curly hair. Casey watched his daughter take shape on the pad, her face gaining power and substance under Sylvia's talented hands.

"Jesus," Casey said. "That's her. That's absolutely her."

"We're getting there," Sylvia said. She slipped the sketch into a scanner and moved to the computer keyboard. "If you could use one word to describe her appearance, what would that be?"

Casey thought a moment. "Impish," he said.

"Complexion?"

"Medium to fair."

"Teeth?"

"One front tooth slightly crooked. Very white."

"Eye color?"

"Brown. Dark brown."

"Lashes?"

"Quite long."

"The hair is blond, I take it?"

"Especially in the summer."

"Fine," she said. "Now we'll make a picture."

For the next thirty minutes, Moira and Casey sat across the table from Sylvia as she worked on the computer. At length she stopped and struck one key. Her printer began to hum. In a moment she retrieved a piece of photo paper and passed it over to Casey.

"How'd we do?" she said.

There, looking back at him with a lopsided smile and challenging eyes, was his daughter.

"Jesus Christ," he choked. "It's Cat—my sweet kitten."

The two women left the room.

Sweet Thang

CAT SAT IN THE OLD CHEVY PICK-UP and watched the front of the bar. The parking lot contained several ratty trucks and four or five motorcycles. Loud country music blared out the open door punctuated by raucous laughter and shouted swearing. Dummy and Idiot should be along about any time.

She's spotted them two nights before when they'd passed her on I-44 just outside Springfield, Missouri. They'd turned their motorcycles onto PP highway near Republic and she'd followed, headlights off, until they'd pulled into an overgrown lane that wound its way up to a junky little farmhouse. That's when she smelled the meth. Surprised that either of these two Hell's Angels wannabees had enough brain cells to run a meth lab, she lingered for a while, establishing that there were also three women in the house and one more man. Munchies and meth. She was gonna bring home the bacon.

When she left, she told Colin she'd be back in three or four days with goodies for everybody. He knew how often she was overtaken by wanderlust and had to be on the move and didn't bitch at her about it even though she hadn't been home very long. More than any of the rest of them, even Hammond, she needed the movement, the excitement, the hunt, the kill. Fucking around stoned or ripped and sipping on one of the bleeders just wasn't enough for Cat. It never had been.

She took the pick-up with the bed cover and two or three changes of clothes, from saintly to sleazy, and headed west across northern Arkansas through the lakes area, stopping once to feed at a campsite and several times to rip off convenience stores and food marts for cash. When she turned north, she had over four thousand dollars and one aging corpse hidden in the bed of the truck. She left the corpse behind a truck stop near Hollister and headed on into Springfield.

Springfield, Missouri was a sprawling community, well blessed by the bounty of the Branson blight. Just past its heyday and beginning to turn slightly downhill, it offered ample population, ignorance, complacency, and a sufficient supply of lowlife to make it attractive enough that Cat visited there once or twice a year. She avoided the campus and the upscale areas entirely and went straight for the seedy neighborhoods. It was there she hunted. It was there that she'd tracked Dummy and Idiot on their beat-to-shit Honda pseudo-Hogs the night before. It was there she watched Dummy and Idiot roll in again, already gassed, and lurch inside. She sat in the truck for nearly an hour to smoke a couple of chubbies and let them get as lit as possible, then wiggled into her tight stone-washed jeans with the rips across the front of her thighs and just below her butt. She slipped on a snug cotton Harley t-shirt and felt her nipples harden with anticipation. Then Cat added too much lipstick, too much black eyeliner, too much cheap jewelry, and too many sticks of gum in her left cheek. Stepping out of the truck, she put on her black leather jacket, the one that stopped just above her ass, left it unzipped to let her nipples breathe, pulled on her black Justin's with the riding heel, and sauntered toward the front door of the bar, dripping with attitude. She was wet. She was ready.

The main room was thirty-by-forty with a short bar, a dozen tables, a wheezy jukebox, and a stained and empty pool table. Layers of smoke hung in the air, beer signs flickered on the walls, the floor was sticky, and fifteen or so Harley rats and hangers-on slouched on chairs or stood at the bar. Seven or eight women leaned on various men. When Cat stepped through the door the place grew quiet. Even the jukebox stopped. She walked to the center of the room, looked around, shrugged, and headed back for the door.

"Whar yew goin', Sweet Thang?"

Cat stopped and looked at an immense man standing at the bar. Greasy blue jeans, a filthy t-shirt, and a too small black leather vest were highlighted by a wispy mustache, black oily hair, and a huge stomach.

"What?"

"Ah ast yew whar the fuck yew wuz a-goin'?"

She looked at him and smiled. "No place you could ever take me, Pus-Gut," she drawled. "I got standards."

There was a split second of silence, then the bar erupted with heavy laughter. Pus-Gut stayed at the bar and turned red.

Cat turned for the door. At a table beside it were Dummy and Idiot, grinning at her. She stopped. "You guys seen Frankie Faine?"

"Who?" asked Idiot.

"Frankie Faine. Blond dude, Grim Reaper tattoo up his right arm. Rides a dark red knucklehead?"

"Don't know him, ain't seen him," Idiot said.

"Fuck! Now I ain't got no ride an' the motherfucker's got my crank!" She turned again for the door.

"That ain't no problem," Idiot said. "I gotcha ride an' your crank, too."

Cat turned back. "That right?"

"Betcher ass, that's right, ain't it Earl?"

"Betcher ass," Dummy said. "Yer ride an' yer crank. You git ta crankin' on my crank, maybe yer crank doan cost ya shit!" Dazzled by his own sense of humor, Dummy broke up.

"Doan mine Earl," Idiot said. "He's all fucked up."

"He thinks I'm gonna walk in here and trade a blow job for some meth, he's more than fucked up, Motherfucker," Cat snapped. "He's fuckin' crazy!"

"Aw, come on," Idiot said, licking his lips and looking around. "Take it easy. Siddown. I won't let Earl give ya no shit. Hell, I'll buy ya a beer or two."

Cat hesitated for a second, then swung a leg over the back of a chair and sat. Idiot licked his lips again and Earl peered at her through bleary eyes.

"Longneck Bud," she said.

"Goddamn, Virgil," Earl said, staring at Cat's chest. "Lookit them titties."

"Shut the fuck up," Virgil said.

"He always like this?" Cat said.

"He is when he's fucked up, an' he's real fucked up. He's been snortin' meth all day, then got into some Wild Turkey. Mavis was glad for me ta git him out the house."

"Who's Mavis?"

"She's his ol' lady."

"He's actually got one?"

"Yeah. She ain't too fuckin' particular."

"She ain't got no sense a smell either," Cat said. The beer arrived.

Earl, oblivious to the conversation going on around him, spoke up. "I bet yer head a the itty-bitty-titty-committee, aincha Darlin'? Goddamn, I'd like ta git a look at them nipples."

Holding her grin, Cat quickly lifted her t-shirt for an instant.

"Motherfuck!" blurted Earl, reeling back in his chair. "Virgil, did you see that shit? This little bitch flashed my ass!"

"Just wanted you to know what yer missin'," Cat said.

"Shit!" roared Earl. "Goddam, I'd like ta fuck yew!"

"So would half the women and all the men in this bar, Shithead. They ain't got no chance either!" Cat said. She picked up her beer and drained it in long swallows.

"Earl," Virgil said, "why doan you leave her alone. You shut up for a minute, you'll pass out and stop botherin' people. Yer gonner piss her off, an' she's gonner leave, an' I doan want her to."

Earl began to swing his head from side to side, looking down at the table.

"You don't want me to leave, Virgil?" Cat said.

"Naw."

Cat pushed back her shoulders. "Why not?"

Virgil licked his lips. "'Cause I like yer comp'ny," he said.

"My company, huh?"

"Yeah."

"Then buy me another beer."

"Hell, I'll buy ya two more beers!"

"Two it is," Cat said.

Earl was leaning back in his chair, staring at the ceiling, spittle running out of the corner of his mouth.

"Can he ride like that?" Cat said.

"Yeah. I wake him up, he kin ride."

"He's sleeping?"

"Yeah. He sleeps with his eyes open most a the time."

The beer arrived and Cat drained one immediately, then looked at Virgil and smiled.

"Thanks," she said, pushing her shoulders back again. "Tell me how much you like my company."

Virgil's eyes darted back and forth from her chest to her face. "A lot," he said.

Cat stretched. Virgil's tongue had a life of it's own. She gave him a lazy smile and drained the second beer. "You know what I think, Virgil? I think you like my tits. And, I think you'd love my ass, Virgil, that's what I think. I also think that you ain't gonna get a chance to really appreciate my company as long as we stay here. So why don't we wake Earl up and go someplace where I can get some crank to go with all this beer, spit out my gum, and you can get a little more for your tongue than just your lower lip. That sound like a good idea to you, Virgil? Whadaya think? Huh?"

"Earl," Virgil said. "Wake the fuck up!"

The ride to the farm consisted of Virgil pushing back between Cat's legs and pawing her bottom and thigh. She played along, drinking two more beers that she carried in the pockets of her jacket, occasionally rubbing Virgil's bony chest and enjoying the vibration through the hard pillion pad on which she sat. Amazingly, Earl made the trip just fine, falling way behind, then continuing on ahead while she and Virgil stopped as they turned off the super highway.

"Hey, Virgil!" she shouted into his ear. "Pull over for a minute, willya?"

He rolled to a stop on the gravel shoulder of PP highway.

"Too much beer," she laughed. "I gotta pee. Wanna watch?"

"Watch?"

"Yeah. Ya wanna watch me pee? Some guys like that. You one a those guys Virgil? I'll pee again after while, but you won't be around to see that one. This is your only chance."

Cat walked into the glow of the headlight, peeled down her pants, and squatted on the shoulder.

"Sure!" Virgil grinned, weaving her direction and trying to focus. "You don't got on no underwear, Girl!"

"Not with jeans this tight," she said, shaking her butt before rising. Standing, nude from waist to knees she looked at him. "Whatcha think, Virgil. Want some salt with my sugar?"

"Yeah!" he blurted as he advanced on her.

She let him lick for a while for the fun of it, before turning away and pulling up her pants. "Don't rub all the pink off, Hero. Somebody else might want some. Let's go."

She swung a leg over the seat and settled in, tucking Virgil up against her spread legs, then reached around him and lightly scratched his crotch. She felt him squirm, and he missed the shift into second gear. Cat threw back her head and laughed at the stars.

They caught a badly weaving Earl just at the driveway to the farmhouse and rode into the yard together. A pole light came on, and three women and a man came out onto the rickety porch. The acrid scent of a meth lab was evident to her sensitive nostrils.

"What the fuck you got there?" the man shouted from the porch, peering at Cat.

"Got us a damsel in distress," Virgil said, shutting off the Honda. "Got no ride, got no meth, but she's salty and sweet."

The four came down into the dusty yard and gathered around as Earl got tangled up trying to get off his bike and crashed to the ground. He didn't move. The group ignored him.

"By God, she's a looker, ain't she," said the third man. "Young too. Damn, Virgil, ain't you somethin'! Can I take a run at her when yer done?"

"You can fuckin' have her right fuckin' now," roared a tall heavy woman, pushing her way to stand in front. "Virgil wants some fuckin' pussy, it's my fuckin' pussy, or it's no fuckin' pussy!" She loomed over Cat, twice her size and weight. "You scrawny little bitch! You stay the fuck away from him, or I'll kick your ass!"

"You smell bad," Cat said.

Had the blow landed, even Cat would have felt it, but she saw the roundhouse coming as if in slow motion. She slipped the punch easily and, holding back, used an open handed push to the woman's chin that rendered her instantly unconscious. She toppled to her back in the dirt and lay still.

"Jesus," Virgil whispered.

"Next?" Cat said.

The man threw himself at her. She grasped his left arm, dislocating the elbow and the shoulder, then, with two short kicks, broke both his feet. He collapsed, screaming. The other two women, even the one with the knife, were candy. Virgil ran for the house. It took him ten steps to reach the front door. Cat was standing in it, waiting for him.

"Virgil, Virgil, Virgil," she smiled, patting him lightly on the cheek. "Stick out your tongue."

Seven hours later, Cat, driving a newer old Chevy pick-up with a camper shell, arrived home. In the back of the truck was Virgil's dead body and the live bodies of the five others, each securely bound with duct tape and gagged with sweat socks. In the cab was the money she'd taken on the way to Springfield, three bags of canned goods, an extra twenty-three hundred dollars she'd found in the farmhouse, and almost five pounds of powered methamphetamines. Colin grinned at her as she bounced out of the truck.

"Soup's on!" Cat crowed, kissing him on the lips. "Dessert, too. God! These trips to the market just wear me out."

# TEN

## Chez KC

AFTER ABOUT TEN MINUTES, Casey walked sheepishly into the hall. Moira was waiting for him. His chagrined expression and puffy eyes called to her.

She smiled and opened her arms. "C'mere," she said.

The hug lasted nearly a minute and never threatened to become an embrace. When Casey pulled slowly away, she leaned up and kissed his cheek.

"I feel like a fool," he said.

"You have four hundred years of repressed emotions to deal with. Live a little. You okay?"

"More or less," Casey said.

"Aw, shucks," she grinned, warm from the contact of the hug and resisting the urge to touch him. "I really do give a damn about you, Casey. I care how you are. C'mon. I'll buy you a cup a mud, you sentimental old fool."

They sipped stale coffee silently at her kitchen snack bar for a while, both a bit shy. Finally, Moira broke the ice.

"So why do you want to find your daughter?"

"I want to see how she is."

"What's the other reason."

"Other reason?"

"Casey, if you want to find your daughter just to see how she is, you've wasted over a hundred and fifty years. There's more to this than just curiosity or missing your kid. What's the real reason?"

Casey stared at the counter top for a moment, then looked at Moira. "I wanna give her a choice," he said.

"A choice?"

"She's Nosferati. She doesn't have to be, but she probably doesn't know that. I want to break her addiction. Once she's free of it, she can make a decision on how she wants to continue with her life."

"What if she decides to continue as a Nosferati?"

"Her choice. I just want her to make the choice independently, with a clear head."

"Have you been looking for her?"

"Off and on, but not very seriously."

"Why look for her now?"

"Because of you," Casey said.

"Me?"

"Sure. You have the technology. I don't know anything about computers, I have no contacts, I haven't functioned in the real world since I was infected. What would I do, go house to house? Plus, I'm wanted for murder and jailbreak. You've already accomplished more in the short time I've been here than I could have in years. I really am grateful, Moira. Really. Besides, I never knew I had anything to offer her until I got busted about twelve years ago."

"That's when you almost found her?"

"Yep. And when I killed four people."

"In Indianapolis?"

"No. It was summer and I was traveling. I stopped at a state park in Indiana called Turkey Run. Small hotel, campground, lots of trails through some really beautiful country, rocky terrain, hikers, vacationers, things like that. There's a spot there, near the river, called The Devil's Icebox. I was hunting. I hadn't fed for several days. I stopped to sit a while in the cool of the Devil's Icebox and this kid, twenty or so, came along. I took him. I wandered around the park a while getting off on the rush, then headed back toward the parking area near the hotel before anybody found the corpse. In the Rockies or someplace like that, you just drag the body off into the woods a ways. Bears or some other carnivore takes care of it. In Yellowstone for instance, Grizzlies get blamed for a lot of stuff they don't do. Not a lot of eight hundred pound bears in Indiana, so I walked back to the main area. I was really soaring, high as hell. Then I smelled Cat. Just luck. Pure luck. I had no idea she, or any other Nosferati for that matter, were anyplace in the area."

"And you decided to find her."

"Understand that when one of us is in the middle of a intense rush," Casey said, "judgment is heavily impaired. I should have laid back, checked out the area, waited for her to show herself, a dozen other things I didn't do 'cause when you're that high, you just don't give a shit. Instead, I charged into the hotel, tracked Cat's scent to a room, and went through the closed door. She wasn't there, but three male and one female Nosferati were. As I mentioned, I had just fed. They hadn't. The fight and screaming attracted immediate attention in the hotel and in the pavilion across the road. Unfortunately for me, in that pavilion across the road, there was a picnic in progress for the Covington, Indiana Fraternal Order of Police."

"Oh, shit."

"I killed the four in the room, got my shirt ripped off, and suffered significant injury myself. Then I backtracked Cat's scent to the front of the building. Nearly berserk, covered in their blood and mine, I roared out the front door of the hotel and almost straight into thirty or forty armed off-duty cops. I wasn't at my best or they would have never even seen me go by. The fight in the room had used an immense amount of energy, and the wounds had weakened me. I took a bunch of bullets and still made it to a cop car at the curb. The key was in the ignition. I lurched into it and took off, but crashed on a curve trying to get out of the park. Blacked out."

Casey made a face and poured his coffee in the sink.

"I don't remember much after that until I sort of came back to myself in a reinforced rubber room at a detention center for the criminally hoo-hah. I found out later that, when they pulled me out of the car, most of my wounds had reconstituted, but my condition was so depressed I had to have surgery for the four rounds that were still in me. The doctors saved my life. Really. I very nearly died and was closer to being, excuse the expression, *human* than I had been in four hundred years."

He went to the fridge and got ice water.

"After what they called an amazingly rapid recovery from devastating injuries, I basically went nuts for about a month. I can only assume that a portion of that time was recovery from addiction to various controlled substances. Most of it, I believe, was a recovery from what contributes to the behavior of the Nosferati. My addiction to the feeding rush, both physical and psychological, was broken. My mind returned. My judgment returned. Control of my life returned. I pled guilty to all charges to avoid the gas chamber and giving myself away."

Casey grinned.

"While recuperating in The Fortress of Solitude, I resolved to use my powers only for good. All I need now is a suit with a big red 'S' on my chest and a pair of horn-rimmed glasses to use as a disguise."

Moira looked adoringly at him and batted her eyes. "Oh, Clark," she said.

Casey was still chuckling when she returned from the cafeteria with a pot of fresh coffee and two pieces of mediocre coconut-cream pie.

"So why didn't the hospital freak out over your blood?"

"They just cross-matched for type. I was heading into emergency surgery. I test AB positive. That's what they gave me. Plus, they only put it in, they didn't have to take any out. They got what they needed for the cross-match from suction. I probably only needed one bag. I do remember being pissed they had it trickling so slowly into my arm when I could have swallowed it in seconds. Besides, even with a prisoner, they can't just do tests without permission. I was out of my head, but nothing in my physical condition made it necessary for an in-depth blood analysis. Later, when I became lucid, a couple of doctors asked if I would submit to some tests. It seems I'd recovered from my wounds in record time. I told them, no tests, no blood, nothing. I was out of there and in prison fairly quickly. When there's no trial, it doesn't take long."

"And you didn't see Cat?"

"Nope. She'd been there, but was gone when I arrived. I don't know if she even knew I was around. If she didn't get my scent, she may have assumed the Nosferati killed each other in some sort of argument. That's not unknown. They're a very strange bunch."

"How strange?"

"Hell's Angels on PCP is an understatement."

"Jesus."

"Jesus wouldn't be caught dead with those people."

"They must be something."

Casey rubbed his face and looked away, deliberately avoiding eye contact. "Imagine you've seen it all, done it all, and been it all," he said. "For hundreds of years you've never had to worry about disease or infection. You can eat or drink almost anything with no ill effects, cleanliness means nothing, you live to get as high as possible, and drink blood to get even higher. Your main methods of recreation are to kill someone, or fuck someone, or fuck someone and then kill them, then drink their blood, then do more drugs or alcohol."

"God, Casey!" Moira shuddered, rubbing her arms. "Stop. That's awful."

"It's more than awful," Casey went on, feeling slightly sick to his stomach. "It's a vile, filthy, disgusting parody of existence. In some ways the Nosferati are to be pitied, but they would certainly show no pity for you or me."

"How do you know so much about them?"

Casey smiled. "For over four hundred years, Miss Flynn, I was them."

Moira thought for a moment. "So, that's what you want to save your daughter from."

"No. I don't want to save her from anything because I can't save her from anything. I want to give her the opportunity to save herself. To do that, I'm going to have to take her out of that environment and hold her for a period of time."

"You believe she'll be with other Nosferati?"

"Almost certainly. She likes, ah, company. Cat is a very social animal."

"Then you'll have to remove her from the company of others."

"I hope not. That could get really dicey. It'll be tough enough just to get Cat if she doesn't want to come. I can almost guarantee you she won't want to come."

"Then how are we going to capture her?"

"We aren't, little human. I can't fight a cougar with a rabbit in my hands. I will certainly need your help after I get her, but I will get her without your help. You can watch, but you can't play."

"Then how are you gonna do it?"

"I don't have the faintest idea."

"That's nice. I love a good plan."

"Look at the bright side," Casey said. "We may never find her in the first place."

"Yes, we will, Casey, I'll be helping with that. As a matter of fact, I'll start right now," she said, drawing a small pad and pen from her pocket. "Describe Cat."

"Little. Five-one, maybe five-two, around a hundred pounds. Light complexion like her mother, slim athletic build, well muscled. She's very pretty in a tomboyish kind of way. She has delicate ears, really lovely hands, and a very fetching smile that turns into an almost belligerent grin. Her eyes are nearly too large for her face. Her waist is narrow, her hips are slim, and her breasts are relatively small. On the left one there's a scar on the upper swell where she was bitten by the African."

"She sounds beautiful," Moira said.

"Tear your heart out," Casey said, then blushed. "Shit. Sorry. Bad choice of words."

Moira smiled. "Anything else?"

"She's very, ah, sexually confrontational. Very sensual. She told me once that Cat was the perfect name for her. A pussy with claws."

Casey flushed and fidgeted. Moira put a hand on his arm.

"Take it easy."

"Jesus," he muttered, shaking his head as he recalled his and Cat's past relationship. "You've got to understand that among the Nosferati normal rules of conduct and morality don't apply. There are no boundaries, no taboos. Things that you would consider repellent are just …"

"Casey?"

He kept his head down and didn't reply, embarrassed by his memories.

"Casey!"

"What."

"Look at me."

He slowly lifted his head. Moira's eyes shined into his.

"Shut up," she whispered. "What's done is done. What has happened has happened. I make no judgments on past conduct, or the reasons for it. You are a good man. That's all I need to know. That's all anybody needs to know."

Casey lifted her hand from his arm and kissed it.

"You'll do, Miss Flynn," he said.

"And Miss Flynn has things to do. I'm gonna go type up this description in the appropriate manner and get it and copies of the picture out to every cop shop I can find in our donut. We are gonna find your kid. Why don't you go kick back for a while, then decide on what you're going to fix us for dinner."

"Me?"

"Yep. We're dining at Chez K.C. tonight. Don't disappoint me."

He watched her leave the room and sighed. This thing with Moira was heading in exactly the wrong direction. As flattering as it was to him, Casey knew it was not possible.

At about five o'clock, as Casey was removing slices of a butterfly chop from a honey and garlic marinade, the connecting door slammed open and Moira bolted into the room.

"We got a hit!" she crowed.

"Already?"

"Eureka Springs, Arkansas. I just talked with the sheriff down there. It seems a church group from Fort Smith bussed over to Eureka Springs to watch the Passion Play. It's a very big deal in Eureka Springs. Thousands of visitors every year. Anyway, in this church group is a kid, Wes McCoy, 'bout seventeen, high school jock, like that. In one of the exhibition rooms that visitors tour while waiting for the play, a couple of his friends see him talking to this little blond girl. Short shorts, tank top, cute butt, big grin. She's comin' on to Wes, and the other guys are jealous. By the time they get through a few of the displays and start heading for the Passion Play outdoor theatre, Wes and the girl are arm in arm and hanging back so the chaperones won't nail 'em. After the play is over, McCoy doesn't show up for the bus. Nobody can find him or the girl. One of the church people calls the sheriff. The kids are carted off to a motel, and a search is started for the missing kid and the blond girl that was with him. Nothing. Eventually the group goes home without Wes."

"That sounds like Cat," Casey said, removing a rice steamer from the stove and setting it in the sink.

"The interviews by deputies show that eight or nine of the boys got a good look at the blond girl. Their descriptions match. Little, pretty, short hair, big eyes, very sexy and young. They, to a man, thought she was hot. The girls that noticed her were not as kind. Sleazy, trampy, forward, dirty. One of them stated that the blond girl was obviously not a Christian."

Casey added oil to a hot wok. "Well," he snorted, "they got that right."

"The local sheriff is gonna get in touch with the Fort Smith cops and get a couple of the kids to look at the picture. He said he'd get back to me as soon as he knew anything. This could be it, Casey."

"Yeah. Might be her. At least it will tell us where we won't find her and that we probably guessed right on her general, ah, theatre of operations. When did all this happen?"

"About two weeks ago. No trace of either one of them was ever found."

"Probably Cat," he said. "She always was good at that kind of thing."

Casey dropped the sliced pork into the hot oil and fired up another wok. Moira watched as he deftly flipped the pork and added a little cornstarch. The phone rang next door, and she went into her room. He was adding peapods, bean sprouts, water chestnuts, and soy sauce to chopped carrots in the second wok when she returned.

"Got a positive identification from three of the boys and one of the girls. It's her," Moira said. "That smells great."

Feeling both elation and fear, Casey struggled to remain stoic.

"You'll probably get more sightings from other locations," he said. "Cat is not easy to forget. Who are you claiming she is?"

"A runaway and probable witness, maybe even accomplice, to a homicide. I'm requesting that if she is seen, she is not to be detained or molested in any way and that we are to be notified ASAP. I'm also suggesting that unconditional cooperation with us could result in a sizeable grant to the law enforcement agency involved if they do exactly as we say. If they don't cooperate and things get screwed up, heads will roll, badges will burn, and a plague will be visited on their offspring."

Casey grinned. "And who, exactly, is we?"

"A little known arm of the federal government with amazing resources and unlimited funds."

"Ah. Which arm?"

"I haven't decided yet."

"You can really pull this off?"

"I told you that I have low friends in high places."

Casey turned back to the stove and drizzled some sweet and sour sauce onto the sizzling pork. "Hang around," he said. "We'll eat and do some planning. There are things to discuss before we get on the road."

"To the donut?" Moira said.

He piled rice onto two plates and stirred the veggies. "Yeah. The donut surrounds part of an area in northern Arkansas they used to call the Boston Mountains. Ever been there?"

"Nope."

"Old, scenic, remote. You'll love 'em," Casey said, spooning sweet and sour pork onto the steaming rice. "The rednecks are beautiful this time of year."

# ELEVEN

Pineal Envy

AFTER THEY ATE, Moira left to go check on Melvin. Casey was putting dishes in the sink, when the knock came, and she opened the door. Melvin blinked his way into the room and sat heavily at the table. His thin hair was more disheveled than usual; the dark circles under his eyes made his pale and drawn face look ashen and his hands were trembling. He flicked his gaze back and forth between them.

"Melvin, you look awful," Moira said.

"Too much coffee, I suppose."

"Have you eaten?"

"I don't think so," Melvin said.

Casey smiled, took a couple of eggs and a little bacon out of the fridge, and turned on the electric stove.

"How long since you had food?" Moira said.

"When is it now?"

"Thursday evening," she said, glancing at Casey. He winked at her and lifted a skillet out of the cabinet.

"Yesterday morning, I think."

"You think? Melvin!"

"I've been working."

Casey put bacon in the skillet. "On what," he said.

"On you, that is to say, on your blood. I'm going to need some more, by the way."

"My blood is your blood, Melvin, unless, of course, you get so wrapped up in what you're doing you die of exhaustion and malnutrition. You haven't slept since yesterday morning either, have you?"

"I don't think so. It's not important."

"Bacon and eggs coming up," Casey said. He rummaged around in a cabinet and grabbed a partial bag of Oreo cookies. "Eat three or four of these," he said, tossing the bag to Moira. "What's so earthshaking that you don't have time to sleep or eat?"

"You," Melvin said, shoving in an entire Oreo.

"Me?"

"Yesh, you," Melvin went on, spraying crumbs across the table and chewing frantically to clear his mouth. He accepted a glass of milk from Moira and gulped at

103

it, nearly choking in his rush. "You're a myth," he went on. "You don't exist. You can't exist, and yet you do exist. You are an impossibility become possible, an evolutionary theory become fact!"

The little man lurched to his feet, trembling with emotion. Wide-eyed, Moira rose beside him, a hand near his elbow.

"There were rumors of this kind of thing twenty-five years ago," Melvin said. "Rumors, postulations, arguments that someone like you could exist, even did exist. We've known for years that there was a theoretical potential, but it was so far beyond the realm of practicable viability, so far past even slightly rational assumption that it became little more than a parlor game, a scientific *what if* relegated to drunken late night discussions and hypothetical comic book claptrap! Even those of us who took it seriously, didn't take it seriously! Even the evolutionists who could conceive it didn't really believe it."

Melvin began to pace as Moira watched him and took a step backward, a hand to her mouth. "You have said that you are not human," Melvin went on. "You're wrong, Casey. You're more than wrong. You're human, make no mistake about that. You are so human, it makes me dizzy! In some ways you are human arising, human inceptive. But you are more than human Alpha, Casey. It could be that you are also human Omega! Human to the next power! Human concentrated, human expanded, human multiplied."

Melvin stopped walking and gripped the back of his chair with vibrating hands and white knuckles. Pale, Moira sank into a seat. "Even though you have come from our past," he said, "you damn well may be our future!"

Flushed and shaking, Melvin stared at Casey as if waiting for him to explode. Casey smiled. "Take it easy, Melvin, it's only me."

"*Only* does not apply," Melvin said.

A half an hour later Melvin, loaded with Oreos and bacon and eggs, burped, leaned back in his chair, looked at Casey, and tried to explain. "What do you know about viruses?" he said.

"Next to nothing."

"Okay," Melvin replied, a little indulgently. "A good virus is one that can live a long time in its host. Herpes is an example. The virus lives off the host, the host can tolerate and survive the virus. On the other end of the scale we have something like Ebola; it kills the host in a very short time. In doing so, the virus also destroys its environment. The host dies. The virus, unless it is spread, dies. The AIDS virus is someplace in between. It eventually kills the host, but the process is much slower than Ebola, so the virus gets to hang around a lot longer. Follow?"

"Yeah."

"You have a virus. When your family was attacked, all three of you were infected. For some reason both you and your daughter—I assume she got it from you—have a marker that allows the virus to complete part of its mission before the body breaks down to the point it can no longer be, ah, resurrected, as it were."

"And that part of the mission would be?" Casey said.

"What do you know about DNA?"

"Jesus. Nothing."

"DNA forms the basis of the cell and products of the cell. It is the building blocks from which every living thing is constructed. A strand of DNA is a chromosome. Now, DNA is composed of four individual proteins that come in pairs and those pairs can only combine in specific ways. It's kind of like bar coding. Simple components, infinite combinations. The proteins are Guanine and Cytosine, Adenine and—

"C'mon, Melvin," Casey said. "I don't need to know how the engine works to start the car. Get on with it."

"Yes. Well, normal people's DNA consists of two strands assembled sort of like a ladder with a twist. The virus—I have no real idea how, but I assure you that this is more than mere conjecture on my part—somehow the virus added extra strands of DNA to your helix."

"Huh?"

Melvin sighed and shook his head. "I have two strands, Moira has two strands, a rat has two strands, an elephant has two strands. You, Casey, have *twelve*!"

"Oh," Casey said.

"Jesus Christ! This is immense!" Moira said. "The repercussions of twelve strands accounts for ..."

"It accounts," blurted Melvin, "for the ultra aggressive white cells."

"And the high concentration of red cells," Moira said.

"And the abundance of T-cells.

"And chromosomal configurations," she volleyed.

"And the proteins."

"And that's why he needs the blood!"

"And the higher oxygen level!"

"To support the accelerated phagocytosis!"

"And ... Moira?"

"And ... the altered DNA lets him produce extra T-cells from somebody else's blood!"

"To control the virus!"

"To keep the balance!"

"But how can he have both these conflicting immune systems functioning at the same time?" Melvin said, encouraging her.

"He can't!

"He can't?"

"He doesn't!"

"Why not?"

"The goddamn floating brain!"

"So what?" Melvin said, nearly jumping up and down.

"It's gotta be his neurotransmitters!" Moira shouted. "His neurotransmitters allow the alternate system to function by turning down the normal immune system with the influx of outside blood and vice versa when he can't get outside blood, like when he was detoxing!"

"Exactly!" Melvin hooted.

"Exactly!" Moira crowed, offering him a double high five.

They stood grinning at each other, savoring the moment. At length, Melvin raised an eyebrow. "This, of course, brings up another possibly even more repercussive consideration."

"What?"

"The pineal gland," Melvin whispered, his eyes alight.

"The pineal gland!" Understanding slid over Miora's face. "My God," she said slowly turning and gaping at Casey.

"Oh, shit," moaned Casey, catching a glimpse of recognition on Melvin's face, as the small man peered quizzically at him.

Melvin approached within two feet of Casey and squinted. "Did you dye your hair?" he said.

After things settled down, Moira escorted a nearly catatonic Melvin to his room and sent him to bed. She returned to find Casey munching a cookie and drinking coffee. She stood in the doorway and looked at him.

"Stop staring at me like I have two heads."

Moira nodded. "Sorry."

"What the hell is going on? What's all the fuss about?"

"First of all, let me say that I don't have the depth of understanding of all this that Melvin does. They don't call him Doctor Blood for nothing. Secondly, I have not seen the results of what he's been doing and drawn my own conclusions. But, if I understand what he said correctly, you could be the biggest thing since Moon Watcher bumped into the monolith."

"Who?"

"Arthur C. Clarke. An old sci-fi story. What I mean is, it's very possible that you are a missing link, Casey. An evolutionary hiccough, the next step, the new opposable thumb, a *homo-superior* for chrissakes!"

"I'll bet you say that to all the boys."

Moira laughed. "Goddammit, you Transylvanian refugee," she said.

Casey bumped his eyebrows. "You've been peeking in my shower, haven't you?"

"Oh, shit. Casey, you could be the end to infection as we know it. The end to the common cold, the end to cancer, to hay fever, to herpes, to AIDS, to Ebola, to gangrene, to pink eye, to acne, to a thousand other things. You could allow the rest of us to live to our full potential life spans of a hundred and fifty years or more. What's going on inside you is a miracle!"

"Compared to you, I'm a freak."

"I'm not talking about Nosferati and the blood drinking. I'm talking about the anti-bodies your system has developed to keep your virus in check. Your production of T-cells, things like that. You are living with a virus in your body that is more deadly than Ebola. Somehow that virus allows both you and your daughter to manufacture or acquire what you need to keep it in check and not die from it. It's a nearly perfect arrangement. A parasite that helps the host defend itself against the parasite so the parasite can continue to inhabit the host. In the meantime, the host has immunity to everything else that comes along, and the ability to actually heal other infected or damaged organisms!"

She looked at him and said calmly, "I had the biopsy, Casey. My cancer is gone."

"That's good news."

"Good news?" Moira said, tears dwelling in her eyes. "Casey, this thing, this dark thing was hovering over me every minute of every day! Every breath, every thought, every movement was permeated by that cancer. The minute I knew it was there, I swear I could feel it inside me, growing, stealing my life, betraying my body. Then you held my hand and walked me back to the motel. Goddammit! Don't you get it? You took it away. You took that hideous, mind-numbing thing away. You saved my life!"

Casey didn't know what to say. He smiled and looked at the floor while she peered at him.

"Look," Moira went on, "Maybe, because you are what you are, you can't relate to how it feels to be so threatened and lost, but it's awful. Just awful. And then, when it's gone, it's like a rainbow in your heart. Like one of those spring days when you stand in the rain and the sun is still shining. If we can use your blood to create a serum, we could have a cure or preventative for almost anything! The problem is, of course, not killing the patient with the cure."

Casey shook his head. "Wait a minute. I don't think you want to wind up with a big chunk of the population running around that have a Nosferati's physical abilities! Playing God almost always involves playing the devil, too. The fallout from that kind of situation could be devastating. Talk about a caste system! The possibility for abuse is huge. In a world of horses, even very kind and noble horses, being a pony would be terrible."

Moira kissed him on the cheek and he shivered from the touch of her lips and the warmth of her breath.

"You're a good man, Casey," she whispered, her palm resting over his heart. "See you to tomorrow."

"I ain't that good," he said. "Go away."

Moira didn't arrive until nearly ten-thirty the next morning. She schlepped through the door wearing sweats, a disgruntled expression, and a bit of toothpaste in the corner of her mouth. Casey beamed at her. "Good morning, Sunshine. God, but you're lovely."

She sneered at him. "Coffee."

"Black?"

"And thick."

He placed a cup on the table. "Lookin' a little bloodshot there, Cutie."

Moira squinted at him. "You kept me up 'til four a.m."

Casey grinned. "Not me," he said. "I'd remember."

Moira sneered. "I went to Melvin's lab after I left here last night. As nearly as I can figure, he is right."

"About what?"

"About everything he was ranting about. About you possibly being the next step. A pivotal man, as it were."

"What if I don't want to be the next step?"

Moira looked at him and shook her head. "There's the door. Beatfeet."

"I could walk out of here, no questions asked, no authorities alerted. Just quits?"

"Yep. No purpose, no goals, no future. Back to prison or the Nosferati. Either of those appeal to you?"

Casey stared at her. "You're a hard woman, Flynn."

Moira launched to her feet and glared at him. "I'm damn sure not inclined to beg, Buster! You were one of us once, tired, weak, slow. Then, through no fault or effort of your own, you changed. You became strong, fast, powerful, nearly immortal. So what do you owe the rest of us? The way I have it figured, you owe us four hundred years of drinking the blood of our parents and children, of gnashing teeth in the night, of screams in the dark, of treating the rest of us like cattle! You owe us big time, Casey, but with or without your help, we'll go on. For our sake, we have to. For your sake, we have to. Without rabbits, even the wolves die. Everything you are, you owe to us! You'll have to pardon me if I don't get overly involved in your personal angst over being the next step. I'm trying to save lives. Your conscience is your problem. Deal with it or hit the fuckin' bricks!"

Casey looked at the floor for a moment, then raised his head. "Okay, okay. I'm properly chastised. So why is ingesting blood important to me?"

Moira grinned. "Cause you're a vampire, Dummy! Don't you know anything?"

Casey laughed. "All right. I deserved that. Now answer the question."

"Basically because it's food, the same reason the rest of us need cheeseburgers. But your needs are more demanding because your general condition requires more support. Understand that this is all supposition, but it wears well. We won't know for sure until we do a lot more work. Blood is why you get the rush and are more physically capable after a fresh feeding. It kicks up the nutrient level in your body. Digestion, which requires a great deal of energy, is eliminated and you get an oxygen boost because of the content of the blood and extra red cells. You also get a real hit of T-cells and a huge influx of phagocytes."

"Those would be the cytes that wear a lot of velour."

"And watch old Bette Davis movies. Phagocytes, to use correct medical terminology, eat the bad shit in your blood. When eating all that bad shit, they require up to twenty-five times the normal amount of oxygen. You have a huge red cell count; it soars when you ingest blood. The phagocytes respond accordingly. Your whole immune system kicks into hyper-drive. The more blood you get, the better it works. The immune system is called the body's floating brain. Millions of transactions take place there every second, billions of pieces of information are passed back and forth, trillions of events occur, and it all happens without conscious thought. The immune system, for the most part, runs all by itself. There may be more going on in the blood than in the brain. Your blood is very bright, Casey, and your immune system is a five-hundred pound gorilla."

"Medically speaking," he said.

"Medically speaking," she agreed.

"So how does this explain my ability to fix your cancer?"

"I don't know. Maybe when we held hands your floating brain got enough information from my floating brain for my neurotransmitters to allow your expanded DNA to tell my DNA what to do to kick the cancer. I don't have any real conception of what went on, but something sure did. Near as we can figure at this time is that your twelve-strand DNA is what makes it possible for you to do the physical things you do. The virus that gave you the DNA may have done some other things, too."

"Like what?"

"Like juiced up your pineal gland."

"What's the pineal gland do?"

"Nobody knows for sure, but I think it's a safe bet that yours does a lot more of it."

"Oh, yeah?"

"Yeah. The magnetic resonance stuff we did shows yours is four to five times larger than normal."

"What's that mean?"

Warming to her educational task, Moira moved to the snack bar and perched on a stool. "Some years ago the Russians did several studies that showed people with slightly larger than normal—and I'm talking only ten to twenty percent here—slightly larger pineal glands, were more prone to have metaphysical abilities. They also showed that of those people they found to actually be psychic, virtually every one had heightened pineal activity, size, or both."

Casey grinned. "So much for the pineal myth," he said. "Size does make a difference."

Moira laughed.

"C'mon. Tell the truth," Casey said. "Don't you have just a little bit of pineal envy?"

"What all this means is anybody's guess, but I have a theory if you'd care to get your mind out of the gutter and hear it."

"If I must."

"I think that possibly your heightened senses of sight, hearing, smell and such may be augmented by a certain amount of psychic awareness masquerading as augmented senses. After all, your body is going to present you with information in a manner that you can understand and interpret."

Casey looked at her, and recognition flowed over his face; he got to his feet. "Damn! If you're right, do you know what this means?"

"What?"

Casey began to pace. "This makes sense! Think back to our second meeting. When I told you that stuff about you and ..."

"Yeah?"

"And heard you talking when I was walking away ..."

"Yeah?"

"And I told you that the white cotton panties were a guess, for all I knew you weren't wearing any?"

"So?

"You were wearing cotton panties! I was right, wasn't I? It was my engorged, sorry, my enlarged pineal gland talking to me!"

"Asshole! I'm gonna go take a nap so you and your gland can be alone." Shaking her head, Moira headed for the door.

"It's today you're not wearing any!"

Moira slammed the door behind her.

"God, I love this gland!"

The room was large, measuring over six thousand square feet. Its fourteen-foot ceiling seemed low due to the size of the space. Once, the ceiling had soared to forty feet. Once, the walls of the room had displayed heavy native stone, massive blocks fitted by thousands of man-hours of dangerous labor. Once, the building had been a sentinel overlooking the mountain pass and river far below its intimidating height. Many would have called it a castle, but it was not. It was merely a keep: a place where troops were housed, from whence early warning could spring, where delaying actions could be mounted against an opposing army; an outpost that could be sacrificed for the greater good, as a hand might be sacrificed to save a heart.

Long before Casey was born, that had been its purpose, but the keep had outlived its usefulness. For almost two hundred years it kept its vigil with empty silent eyes, an aerie of eagles, abandoned by man. Winter snows covered it, spring storms lashed it, summer sun warmed it, autumn decay littered it, and the keep did what it did best. It waited. In their wildest dreams, the original builders could not have imagined the nature of its rebirth. Vivid hallucinations would not have revealed its eventual purpose. The entire keep was given over to the support and sustenance of that one eighty-foot room and what dwelled within.

Three of the stone walls, the ceiling, and the floor were covered in smooth white polymer. There were no ninety-degree angles, no brittle corners, no sharp edges. A portion of the fourth wall was also polymer, but clear. Behind the crystal section were video screens, televisions, computer monitors, and digital projectors. A computer geek's dying fantasy come to life; the world and its information revealed through transparent plastic.

The room was cold in both appearance and temperature. Air, as sterile as it could be made and conditioned to thirty-five percent relative humidity and fifty-two degrees Fahrenheit, flowed through dozens of concealed vents, replenishing itself five times per hour. Facing the clear section of wall was an immense oval desk, also of white polymer. Panels on each side were festooned with button controls for the media wall, each button carefully curved and recessed. This edgeless theme was present throughout the space. The bed, the restroom, the shower, the sparse furnishings, all were rounded and smooth and white. There were no windows. Manufactured sunlight entered the room through several recessed ceiling grids controlled by panels near the bed and the desk. As sterile as NASA's clean room, the place had all the personality of an operating theater.

The only door was surrounded by a ten-foot square, clear polymer airlock maintained with slightly negative air pressure. One of the three exposed walls of the airlock contained two step-through full-body sterile suits, each with its accordion tether connecting it to the wall like the collapsed carcass of some immense caterpillar. The second wall sported an emergency entrance and rotating carousels to pass items back and forth. The third wall faced directly into the room and was fronted by an armchair in dark green velvet. It was the only positive color to be seen within the area.

In the chair sat a man wearing a dark blue suit, an eggshell shirt with a deeply pointed collar, and a gray silk tie without pattern. His immaculate black wingtips gleamed in the white light. He was forty-one years old, sandy haired, green-eyed, over six feet tall, and slightly under one hundred eighty pounds. A thin white scar bisected his cleft chin. He looked like a Secret Service agent, and he indeed had been, until he came into the employ of the man he awaited. His eyes were steady upon the figure at the desk. He knew him by only one name, Unruh. That was enough.

Elderly, Unruh appeared to be an albino. He was not. A tensely cloistered existence had drained the color from him as it would have drained the will from a normal man. At six-four and less than one hundred fifty pounds, Unruh should have appeared thin, but the white, full-body, padded suit he wore did not reveal his weight. As pale as the rest of the room, his thinning hair was cut clumsily short, his hands were encased in thick gloves, his feet in padded slippers with soft rubber soles. He had no facial hair and nearly invisible eyebrows. As he turned from the desk, swiveling his chair to face the man in the airlock, his gray eyes seemed unnaturally intense. Beside him was a white dinner tray with remnants of softly stewed carrots, thoroughly chopped ground beef, mashed potatoes, and egg custard. Nearby lay a clear plastic spoon. There was no knife or fork. No points, no edges.

When Unruh spoke, the man in the green chair heard the voice through a speaker above his head. He resisted the urge to look up and kept his eyes fixed upon the pale narrow face.

"Voorhees?" The voice was as thin as the body.

"Yessir, Mr. Unruh?"

The gray lips smiled. "Voorhees, I have detected a vibration near the edge of my web."

"Yessir."

"It is a small flutter, but a flutter nonetheless. I require that it be examined."

Voorhees held the steady gaze of those gray eyes. It would not do to look away from a viper. He knew what the man was capable of. He knew what he'd helped him do. He knew the single-minded ruthlessness behind those cold eyes and the utter lack of conscience that supported and sustained his twisted will. Voorhees was as incapable of fear as a man could be, yet Unruh gave him gooseflesh. Resisting the urge to swallow, he replied.

"Yessir?"

"Working as an administrator and epidemiologist for the Proteus Trust is a woman named Moira Flynn. An agent in my employ has reported that she recently visited a correctional institution near Indianapolis, Indiana, in which I maintain an interest. While there, Ms. Flynn met with an inmate named Joseph Casey on two occasions. On the evening of the day of their second visit, it would seem that Mr. Casey killed a guard and left that institution. Three days later, Ms. Flynn arrived at our Kansas City facility, Provenance Center, in the company of a man named Joseph Casey. Outside of his prison record, he does not seem to exist. I find that curious, Voorhees. I need to know who he is."

"Yessir," Voorhees replied. He took no notes.

"Working in her company at Provenance Center is a scientist named Melvin Foltz. Just a few days ago there was what has been described as an accident in his infected primate holding facility that resulted in a great deal of simian bloodshed and a mass burning of the residents of that lab. This was reported to me by one Ted Plank, a security person whose salary I augment. Determine what occurred."

"Yessir."

"Doctor Flynn also acquired a map through an acquaintance in the WHO, named Virginia Marley. This map describes the locations of murders, maimings, suspicious deaths, and suspect disappearances throughout the United States for the past several years. I need to know why she requires information so atypic."

"Yessir."

"As usual, feel free to contact me at any time. The helicopter leaves in thirty minutes to deliver you to Geneva. From there to London, then New York, then Kansas City. You'll be in the 707. Customs offers no problem. Take whatever you might need."

"Handle or report, Sir?"

"Report for now. I'm curious, not vengeful. Of course, if things escalate rapidly, do whatever you feel is necessary to protect yourself and Proteus. You have my complete confidence."

Unless I fuck up, thought Voorhees. Then you'd swat me like a bug, you bloodless freak. "Thank you, Sir," he said.

"Dismissed."

Unruh watched Voorhees depart, resisting the urge to scratch the itch around the shunt in his left forearm. He'd been careful all his life, guarding against the possibility of infection, frightened of the tiniest wound. It was a miracle he'd survived his youth in the backwater civilization of Venezuela. If his mother and father had not fled from Germany at the end of the war with all that Jewish money, he certainly would not have lived through his childhood or the years growing up in South America. He finally returned to Europe in his mid-thirties, getting sicker and sicker as his feeble immunities faded away. Since his birth, there had been the hemophilia. From the beginning, his blood had failed him. Always there had been the fear of the tiniest cut or scratch. It was that fear which motivated him, the desire for a place of safety, the need for answers, the hope of deliverance; the price exacted from anyone else for his desire, need, and hope, was less than inconsequential.

He'd begun rich and the blood of others had made him richer, wealthy beyond avarice. The drugs he'd developed. The epidemics he'd started. The crises he'd created and then controlled. The thousands upon thousands of lives sacrificed for his purpose. Their blood was responsible for his success, and his own blood was the ultimate failure. It always came back to blood. Whatever Moira Flynn was doing, that's why she was doing it. He had no intention of interfering yet. He had never interfered with any of her efforts before, and she, however unknowing, had served him well. He believed in giving the bright ones a free hand. After all, so far, her concerns had paralleled his.

Blood. Always blood.

# TWELVE

Mo-Ark Liquors

SHORTLY AFTER DONATING MORE BLOOD to Melvin Foltz, Casey drifted back to his room for lunch. Moira was waiting with a glass of V-8, a tuna sandwich, and bean salad on a cafeteria tray as he walked through the door.

"Stop by for a panty check?" he said, "or just searching my room for contraband?"

"You wanna check something, check your pulse. And sit down. Besides, I owe you one after the way you went through my purse."

"Oh, that."

"Oh, that. I know you've been isolated from polite society for a long time and, because of that and the fact that you are a thick-headed, insensitive, male of the species, you have little knowledge or awareness in such matters. So pay attention. Here's a short course in male-female etiquette one-o-one. Never, ever, go through a woman's purse without her permission. As a matter of fact, don't even do it with her permission."

"Okay," Casey said, properly castigated.

Moira smiled and put the tray on the counter. "Good. I'm glad we got that cleared up. Eat. I have news."

Casey sat. "Oh?"

"Oh, indeed. On the road again."

"Us?"

"Sure."

"Oh, goodie," Casey said around a bite of bean salad. "Long drives, intimate dinners at intimate diners, relaxing evenings in sleazy motels, and thou. The mind reels."

"How can you stand yourself?"

"Appreciation of the finer things," he said.

"Well, appreciate this. We may have a line on Cat."

Casey's eyes snapped. "Where?"

"A little berg called Thayer in southern Missouri. I just got off the phone with the Oregon County sheriff. He's the local law down there and the one that called. Said a liquor store guy may have spotted her three or four days ago."

"When do we leave?"

"Bring your sandwich. Melvin's loading a cooler with your, ah, essentials as we speak. And I've called for a car."

Casey controlled his disappointment. "Melvin's coming?"

"All three of us."

Casey stroked his chin. "Driving off with two men into the scenic beauty of the Ozarks. Strange behavior for an Ice Queen."

She glared at him. "I thought there might be need for a chaperone."

"Don't trust yourself alone with Melvin, huh?"

The *car* turned out to be a three-quarter ton, black Dodge Van with an extended body, what appeared to be federal tags, and a small World Health Organization logo on the driver's door.

"Why didn't we just commandeer a tank?" Casey said as Moira was backing out of the garage lift.

"Not intimidating enough," she said. "We look so governmental, nobody'll screw with us. You two are my assistants, I'm World Health Organization."

"Who?" Casey asked.

"Exactly," Moira replied. "W.H.O."

Casey glanced at Melvin. "Power trip," he said.

"What?" Melvin said, looking around the Spartan interior of the van.

They drove east on I-70 through the middle of Missouri to Columbia, then south on 63 to Jefferson City. Shortly after they crossed the Missouri River, Route 63 became a two-lane. They passed through Licking around five p.m. and stopped for more fuel and dinner in Cabool, Missouri, just after six. Casey was fidgety. Moira sat beside him in a truck stop booth.

"Stop bopping," she said. "You're shaking the table."

"Sorry."

"What's the matter? You're jumpy. You're not the type to get jumpy."

"I don't know. Tired of riding, I guess."

"Bullshit."

"Maybe I'm just hungry."

"C'mon, Casey. What's going on?"

"It's weird."

"Even for you?"

Casey looked around the room. "This is gonna sound stupid. I think Cat's been here, or through here, or by here, or something."

"What makes you say that?"

"Oh, boy. Okay. It's like I can, smell her, only I can't smell her, y'know? I'm fulla shit."

Melvin looked at Moira. His eyes twinkled. "Linear transference?" he said.

"Or maybe linear translucence."

"Or linear transparency."

Moira grinned. "A tear in the space-time continuum?"

"A ripple in the force!" Melvin said.

"Luke," growled Moira, "I am your father." They both began to giggle.

"What the fuck are you two babbling about?" Casey said.

114

Moira smiled at him. "You said that you can smell Cat, but you can't really smell her, right?"

"Yeah."

"That she's been here."

"Well, not here exactly, but around here, or through here, or near here."

"When?" Melvin said.

"I don't know. How the hell would I know? I don't know anything, all right? It's just a feeling. It's gone away anyhow. This is ridiculous."

"Ah, but it may not be," Melvin said. "It may not be ridiculous at all. It may be pineal."

"Aw, geeze."

"There has long been the theory that if twelve-stranders like you did exist and that supercharged DNA was responsible for hyper-activity in, or enlargement of, the pineal gland, those of you so endowed might have the ability to function in other dimensions, as it were."

"What!"

"Remember the Russian studies on the pineal-psychic relationship."

"Metaphysical clap trap!" Casey snorted.

Melvin looked at him with serious eyes. "Carl Sagan once said that there was no metaphysics. Only physics we have yet to come to understand."

"Okay, fine," Casey said. "Now all I need is a crystal ball, some Tarot cards, and some Gypsy robes, and I can call myself Madam Zola. Sees all, knows all. I'll get a séance parlor above the barber shop."

"It's just a theory, Casey," Moira said. "A lot of theories have turned out to be fact, though."

"You expect me to believe that shit?"

"I don't expect you to believe or disbelieve anything," she snapped. "All I want from you is an open mind. An open mind from a four-hundred year old Vampire, for chrissakes, who has reformed and is looking for his daughter, a teen-ager that's addicted to blood, sex, and rock n' roll, has a tongue fetish, and hasn't been seen since before Lincoln was shot! Who the fuck would believe that shit?"

Casey stared at the table for a moment, then raised his head.

"Yeah, well …"

"My ass!" Moira said. "An open mind. That's all! Just an open mind. Go ahead, Casey. Open it up. There's not much in there to fall out!"

They spent the night in Cabool and breakfasted that next morning at the Stateline Truck Stop a mile south of Thayer, Missouri, while they waited for the liquor store to open. Casey was a little chagrined. He looked across the booth at the other two. "Okay. Let's go ahead and talk about this. Let's say, just for the sake of argument, that this pineal theory is right. What happens?"

"Nobody knows," Melvin said. "That's why it's just a theory. Do you, ah, smell your daughter now?"

"A little. Like she's been near here or something. I don't know what to call it."

"Why should you?" Melvin said. "The first time somebody saw a zebra, unless somebody else was there to call it a zebra, he wouldn't know what to call it either.

This is new ground for you, Casey. It's new ground for all of us. What you do may not involve smell at all. It just may be the point of reference your brain picked out. The same could be true with a lot of what you hear and see. You once said you thought you saw a bit in infrared."

"Yeah."

"Maybe it's a visual sense, not just visual sight."

"To be honest, this is kind of scary."

Melvin smiled. "So are you, Casey," he said.

Mo-Ark Liquors sat atop a small bluff east of Highway 63, overlooking the Arkansas State line from the Missouri side. The big black Dodge van was the first vehicle in its pot-holed lot after the place opened at ten a.m. Moira led the procession through the wide glass door and up the center aisle to the counter. Behind it stood a beefy fifty-year-old man with thinning reddish gray hair, a florid complexion, and tiny eyes. He looked Moira over.

"Hep ya'll?"

"I'm looking for a man called Mutt Colton," Moira said. "That you?"

"Yew ain't from aroun' hyar, air ye?"

"No. You Mutt?"

"Who wonts ta know?"

Moira put her leather ID folder on the counter.

"I'm with the World Health Organization. My name is Moira Flynn. These two men are my associates. The county sheriff is aware that I'm here. The federal government is aware that I am here. They both know that it is necessary that I speak to Mutt Colton. You Mutt?"

"I reckon," he said. His eyes roamed over her body.

Moira produced a picture of Cat and held it in front of her chest. "When you get around to it," she said, "look at this picture, too. Seen her before?"

Mutt flushed a slightly brighter shade of red. "Yep. I seen her. I seen this pitcher before, too. One a Hoot's boys come by with it a couple a days ago."

"Hoot?"

"The sheriff. Marvel Gibson, 'cept nobody doan call him Marvel. Everbody calls him Hoot."

"She was in your store?"

"Whachew wont her for?"

"Was she in your store?"

"Yer a pushy li'l thang, aincha?" Mutt said.

Casey stepped up beside Moira and smiled at the man for a moment. "You can answer Ms. Flynn's questions," he said, "or you and I can have a private discussion. Your choice."

Mutt flicked his gaze between Casey and Moira a few times and licked his lips. "Yes Ma'm," he said. "She was here in the store 'bout a week, ten days ago. Wonted ta buy a couple bottles a mescal. Only 'bout half dressed, 'an not too particular about it, neither. Cute l'il shit."

"You sell her the mescal?" Moira said.

"Hell no! She waren't but about thirteen 'er fourteen year ol'. Showed me some I.D. with her pitcher on it. A Arkansas driver's license outta Yellville. Thet's over not too far from Flippin, jest south a Bull Shoals Lake. I tole her thet I didn't give a shit 'bout no license, I wadden gonna sell her ass no booze. Little bitch called me all kindsa names. Got mad as hell! Even hissed at me!"

"Hissed at you?"

"Yeah."

"Like a snake?"

"Naw. Kindly more like a cat. She was drivin' a ol' Ford pick-up. I got the plate number an' gave it to one a Hoot's boys. Next morning I come down ta work an' the door's ripped plum off'n the hinges, an' ever bottle a mescal in the place is busted on the floor! Ever one!"

"Do you remember the plate number?"

"Naw. The dep'ty got it, though."

"Did you have any physical contact with her?"

"Huh?"

"Did you touch the girl?"

"Touch her?"

"Yes. She may be contagious."

Mutt looked puzzled.

"She may have a disease, Mr. Colton. Since you didn't touch her, you should be fine." Some of the color drained from his face.

"I wouldn't worry," Moira went on. "Thanks for your time." As she walked past Casey on the way out, she winked.

"Scared that sonofabitch," Moira said after they were back in the van.

"That sonofabitch has no idea how scared he should be," Casey said. "He's lucky Cat didn't tear him apart. She doesn't deal real well with stupid. She was there. It was her, alright."

"Are you sure?" Melvin asked.

"Without a doubt."

"How do you know?"

Casey paused for a moment. "I could feel her, Melvin. If I could have really concentrated in there, I probably could have walked her path through the store."

"Progress," Melvin said.

"Can't learn to fly 'til you learn to flap," Moira said.

Casey laughed. "Can't learn to fly 'til you learn to flap? What the hell is that?"

"Something my grandmother used to say, if you must know."

"Jesus. The old broad had a firm grasp on the obvious!"

"Who you calling old, you relic?"

"And where was Grandma from?"

"New York City."

"Now there's a source for folk wisdom! Must have had a lot of pigeon friends."

"Let's go see the sheriff," Moira said.

"Yeah," Casey snorted. "Let's flap on over that way."

About fifteen miles northwest of Thayer, Missouri is the Oregon County seat, Dalton. The county sheriff was a relatively short man with little neck, massive shoulders, broad stubby hands, and tobacco juice stains at the corners of his mouth, Marvel "Hoot" Gibson had been Oregon County sheriff for nearly twenty years. Not to say that Hoot was in law enforcement, he was not. Hoot was the law. Barely literate, he believed himself to be highly respected. In truth, he was highly despised and greatly feared. The effect was nearly the same when viewed through Hoot's diminished IQ.

When the three strangers walked into the dusty lobby of his office in the ancient county courthouse, Hoot tried vainly to pull his greasy uniform pants over his colon enlarged stomach, spat his plug into the spittoon by the corner of his desk, broke wind, and strutted out to greet them, his badge askew and hanging by only the top of the pin. The clasp had broken again.

"Howdy folks," he said, stifling a belch. "Canna do for ya?"

"Sheriff Gibson?" Moira said.

"That's me."

"Sheriff, my name is Moira Flynn. I spoke with you on the phone yesterday morning."

"Well now, little lady, it doan take you long ta git whar you're a goin'! I didn't speck you for another day er two. Who're these fellas?"

"Mr. Foltz and Mr. Mitchell," Moira said. "They are my assistants, both specialists in their respective fields."

Hoot eyeballed Casey and Melvin and seemed to swell up a little. "And what would those be?"

Moira released a thin smile. "Of no consequence to this conversation, Sheriff."

"Hawl!" he laughed without smiling. "You are a feisty thing, ain'tcha, Honey?"

"My name is Moira. You may call me Miss Flynn."

He grinned around heavily stained teeth and rubbed his hands together. "Aw now, doan git yer nose all outta joint, Darlin'. I'm just a ol' country boy. Doan got no big education like you city folks. My ways is kinda rough, I guess."

Moira smiled. "Here's the deal, Hoot. I wanna know who that vehicle was registered to that the young girl was driving at the liquor store, and I want to know that information as soon as possible."

Hoot leaned on his counter. "Wouldn't that be nice? Yessir, I'd shore love ta hep ya, but my dep'ty, Darrel Brantly, has all that stuff with him, an' he's plum up in Texas County."

"He's lying," Casey said.

Hoot moved onto the balls of his feet. "What you say?"

Casey smelled Hoot's anger grow through the sour odor of the sheriff's three day old sweat. "You're lying," he said.

A flush began to spread up the sheriff's neck. "You come in my office an' call me a liar, Boy?"

"Pretty much."

Hoot took a step forward. "Now jest a gawddam minute, Bub!"

"That license check paperwork here in your office?" Casey said.

"Hell no! I tole you that it's …"

"It's here," Casey said. "In your desk?"

"Naw, gawddammit, it ain't …"

"It's in his desk. Top right drawer? Center Drawer? Lower right drawer? Top left drawer? It's in the center drawer, Moira. I'd be more than happy to go get it."

Moira smiled. "Please."

"What the fuck do y'all think yer a-doin?" roared Hoot, turning on Moira.

"Just take a minute, Sheriff," Moira said.

When Hoot looked at Moira, Casey moved. He was in and out of Hoot's office, paperwork in hand, in well under two seconds.

At the sound of the copier firing up, Hoot whirled, first looking at his office door, then at Casey where he stood across the room at the copy machine. "Hey!" he bellowed. "Git the fuck away from that!"

"Just finishing up," Casey said, removing a copy and the report from the machine. He crossed to the confused sheriff and handed him the original. "Thanks a lot."

Moira laughed and turned toward the door. "Take care, Hoot," she said. "Write if you find a steady job."

Staring at the paper in his hand, Sheriff Gibson never noticed them leave.

# THIRTEEN

Honey Pie

"SAYS HERE THAT PLATE WAS REGISTERED on a 1991 Ford half-ton pickup to Flavel and Aleen Potts. The address is given only as rural route, Newton County, Arkansas," Casey said.

From his position in the rear seat, Melvin looked over an Arkansas map. "According to this we could go south on Route 63 about a mile to Mammoth Spring, Arkansas, and then go west on Nine, I suppose.

"It appears that after about twenty miles or so on Nine, we'll arrive at Salem," Melvin said. "From there it's about 80 miles to Highway 65, then ten miles to Harrison, Arkansas, then south, out of Harrison on Route 7, twenty miles or so to Jasper."

"Jasper?"

"Newton County seat. That would seem to be our most advantageous destination. Sheriff's office and all that."

"Oh, good," Moira said. "Another county sheriff."

"We'll pass through Gassville, Flippin, and Yellville, too," Melvin said, "but we'll miss Monkey Run and Eros."

"Damn," Casey said. "I hate to miss Monkey Run. I especially hate to miss Eros. How 'bout you, Moira?"

"The gutter. Your tiny mind is in the gutter. Melvin, don't tell him when we get close to Eros. I don't want him getting too excited. A man his age could hurt himself."

"Actually, there is what appears to be an attractive alternative," Melvin said, oblivious to the conversation and pulling away from the map. "When we get to Yellville we could take Fourteen up to Seven, then Seven down through Harrison, across the Buffalo National River area, and on into Jasper. It's marked as a scenic route on the map."

"Now we're tourists?" Moira said.

Casey shrugged. "Why not? We're not in hot pursuit here. Besides, this area of the Ozarks is one of the most beautiful places. Some people call where we're going the Boston Mountains. Ancient range. Much older than the Rockies. Nothing over a mile or so high."

"You're not the one that has to pilot this whale through a bunch of twisty roads," Moira said.

"I'll drive," Casey said.

"So will I," Melvin said.

"Like hell! I'm not gonna put my life in the hands of the four-hundred-year-old man or the absent minded professor! When I go, I wanna die in my sleep, not screaming down a three-hundred-foot drop off 'cause some idiot at the wheel was watching a little birdie instead of the road."

Casey shook his head. "Control freak."

"Always has been," Melvin said.

"Christ! Driving into the backside of civilization on roads two feet wide, and I'm locked in a van the size of the space shuttle with two testosterone-propelled ass-holes!"

Casey grinned. "Some girls have all the luck."

It was nearly dark before they reached Harrison and found a motel. Moira had stopped several times to get out and look at the scenery.

Dinner in a small log-cabin-style restaurant was filling; around nine they gathered in Casey's room. Melvin perched on the edge of the bed. Moira and Casey sat at the small table.

"So," Melvin said, "when we find your daughter, what are we going to do with her?"

"Take her back to Provenance Center if that's okay with the two of you," Casey said. "We need to dry her out. I don't know how long that'll take. I was screwed up for over a month."

"We can do that at Provenance," Moira said. "Melvin, you'll need to make a couple of calls and get a containment area set up. I'd suggest, as hokey as it seems, a padded cell."

"I really don't want to have to keep her restrained, unless she's completely hysterical," Casey said. "Besides, unless we used log chains, I don't know what would hold her. A room with a partition we can close, so we can clean the side she isn't in, would be good. I know wall pads seem humane, but they're a bad idea. She'll just tear 'em up. Don't worry about bathroom facilities or anything like that. We need a space strong enough to contain a pissed-off gorilla. An area that we can literally hose out when it gets filthy."

Melvin thought for a moment. "There's the adult chimp facility on sub-level four."

"It's not in use," Moira said. "I've only been down there once."

"Reinforced cement walls," Melvin said, "lined in sheet steel. Three rooms, actually, two separated by a sliding steel partition, the third by a heavy door. From the third room we can look into the other two through Plexiglas windows."

"How thick?"

"Four inches, I believe. Quite secure. Before I came here, I believe some rather bizarre behavioral experiments were conducted there. I put a stop to that type of thing—too much entertainment, too little science. I'll phone tomorrow and have it cleaned up."

121

"Thanks, Melvin."

"How do you intend to transport your daughter?"

"I'm not sure. If we could find a Rhinos R Us, we could buy a cage. I'm working on it. I'll come up with something."

Melvin yawned. "I'm sure you will," he said. "Just as I am sure that sleep is calling." He rose to his feet. "I'll see the two of you in the morning. Bright and early?"

"Dark and early," Moira said. "I want to be on the road at dawn."

"Dark and early it is. Rest well."

They watched him go and sat quietly for a while, each feeling the presence of the other. Sensing his sorrow, Moira reached across the table and took Casey's hand.

"How you doin'?" she said.

"Me? I'm okay." Casey's shoulders sagged and he stared blankly at the tabletop.

"Gramercy, Moira," he said, tears gathering in his eyes. "I fear we won't find her and fear we shall. I have no idea what kind of shape she'll be in, where her mind will be, if she'll know me. And even if all this works out, what she'll have to go through just breaks my heart."

The tears overflowed and began to run down his face. Moira swung her chair around to his side of the table and opened her arms. Against his better judgment, but unable to resist, Casey fell into them and buried his face in her shoulder, his body racked with sobs. "It doesn't make any difference how old we are, or how long since we've seen each other," he choked. "She remains my child. Fair, sweet, Catherine."

Moira held him while he cried.

After a few moments, Casey's sobs slowed. She stroked his back and kissed his salty cheek. He pulled away, red-eyed and puffy, smiling that quivering, lopsided smile that emerges only after long tears and deep sorrow. Moira thumbed tears away from under his left eye.

Embarrassed by the intimacy and resisting several kinds of urges, Moira stood up.

"Well, you look like hell," she said. "Go sit on the bed."

As Casey complied, Moira went into the bathroom and dampened a washcloth. Walking back to the bed and finding him leaning against the headboard, she was shocked to see how small he appeared. With Casey the man, his presence was such that it was easy to assume he was larger than he actually was. With Casey the worried father, all that went away. He had never looked or felt so frail and human to her, and Moira's heart went out to him. Without reservation, she knelt beside him on the mattress and began to wipe his face. The cool cloth felt wonderful and Casey luxuriated in it, giving himself over to her ministrations and tenderness.

After her second trip to re-wet the cloth, he said, "Thank you."

"I'm just a sucker for tearful vampires, I guess," Moira said, running the washcloth gently across his chin and tossing it on the nightstand.

She picked up matches and a pack of cigarettes from beside her on the mattress and lit two. Feeling himself respond as he scented her condition and surmised her intentions, he couldn't help going along. She placed one of the cigarettes between his lips. "I've always thought that to be one of the most intimate of gestures," Casey said.

Moira smiled. "How 'bout this one?" she said.

Tenderly, she removed the cigarette from his mouth, leaned forward, and kissed him gently on the lips. Tentative and hesitant, the kiss lingered, becoming curious and probing, then necessary and needed.

Breath was inhaled sharply through noses, tongues touched, weight and substance came to their mouths, will flowed through the kiss, demanding and expecting, searching and anticipating. Touching nowhere but their faces, they leaned into each other, discovering, realizing, meeting and joining. They finally separated.

Casey's head thudded back into the headboard. "Prithee, Moira, forgive me," he said.

Moira struggled to focus. "For what?"

"We cannot do this."

"Sure, we can," she said, leaning forward. He gently held her biceps and kept her away.

"Nay, we cannot."

"Look. I know you're a little old for me. If that's the factor, there are drugs. You'll do fine. I'll help."

Casey smiled. "Age has nothing to do with it."

"You're not gay."

"Not recently."

"War wound?"

"No."

"Maybe you don't get it, Casey. This is it. The time is now. The moment has arrived. You're emotionally vulnerable, and I'm feeling all motherly and warm. Your hormones are growling, my hormones are grinning, our collective juices are flowing right where they should be flowing. Blood pressure is up, heart rate, respiration. We are ready. That kiss was a midnight swim in a warm pool. It's time for the two of us to skinny dip in the surf. You won't need your suit."

He stroked her cheek. "You mean too much to me. I won't risk it."

"Risk it? Risk what?"

"Killing you."

Moira sat up straight and looked at him. "That's a factor?"

"It is."

"You gotta work on your control, Big Guy," she said.

Casey laughed sadly and shook his head.

"Look," Moira said, "if I don't go for humor here, I'm gonna feel rejected and my feelings are gonna get real hurt. I don't like it when my feelings get real hurt, Casey. That's why I haven't had any kind of relationship in four years. Now I let myself get all gooey and misty, and you turn me down. Miss Flynn is willin' and you ain't. Explain."

"I'm contagious."

"Oh. Shit," Moira blurted, sitting straight up. "Yeah. Of course. I forgot."

"You and I exchange bodily fluids, it's a hell of a risk. We accidentally get blood involved, and you've got two weeks to live. And if you did get infected, and did happen to survive, I don't want to have to be looking for you in another hundred and fifty years. Moira the Nosferati. You want to risk that?"

"Yes. But I won't," Moira said. She swiveled on her knees and fell to her back beside him, embraced his arm, and buried her face in his shoulder.

"This isn't fair," she said.

"No. But it is amazing."

"Amazing?"

"That somebody like you would want to get involved with someone like me."

Moira rose up on her elbow to look at him.

"What?"

"Jesus, Moira! I'm barely literate! Sometimes I feel so stupid. When I went into the prison, I hadn't done any reading or writing to speak of for nearly four hundred years. People like you and Melvin are educated and smart. You're aware of what's going on in the world. You know about medicine and computers and cell phones and laboratories and business and ..."

"Shut up."

"And I'm just this dumbass that ..."

"Shut up!" Moira hissed, adjusting her position to look down at him. "If that's what you think, you are a dumbass! Jesus Christ! So Melvin and I know about medicine. You think either one of us could have healed my cancer?"

"Well, that doesn't mean ..."

"Shut up! Don't you dare pull this 'poor little me, I don't deserve you' crap! And don't you dare confuse education with intelligence, either. Some of the most stupid people on the planet have doctorates falling out of their asses. What? You think I was born with three degrees? I worked for those fuckers. That is something that almost anybody can do. You included, Dumbass!"

"Sure, but ..."

"*Shut up*! And I'll tell you something else. When you were telling me about putting me in that three hundred pound suit with my ears and nose plugged up and the swimfins on my feet, I was blown away by how your mind went directly to the problem of me being so uncomfortable because I was not in my natural condition. I didn't get it until you led me there! My fine mind and exceptional education was smoked by your tiny illiterate brain, Dumbass! And once, when I called your assessment of a physical process too simplistic, you told me that it wasn't. It was just simple. Holy shit, Casey! You've got some non-linear thinking going on here that is outstanding!"

She paused in her tirade and looked at him expectantly.

"Ah ..."

"Shut up." Moira smiled and kissed him gently on the lips. "Everybody on the planet is ignorant," she said. "Everybody. Some of those people are stupid. Ignorance we can fix. Stupid is way beyond repair. I don't hang around stupid people. It's bad for my image."

"Okay," Casey grinned. "It's just that I ..."

"Shut up, Dumbass," she whispered and snuggled into his neck.

They lay that way for some time, each absorbed in the other and in their own private thoughts, until Moira flopped onto her back beside Casey and lit a cigarette.

"Fuck!" she said. "You get involved with a really nice guy and just when you're ready to take him home to meet the family, you find out he's twelve or thirteen times your age, drinks blood, and is contagious. Every maiden's dream."

"Bitch, huh?"

"And it all looked so good for you, Casey. You wash behind your ears, you pick up after yourself, your breath doesn't stink, your back isn't hairy, you cook, and you've got all your fingers and toes. The perfect man except for one little thing—you're a goddamn vampire! Why couldn't you have had big ears, or been short, or had a fat ass, or been bald, or had buckteeth, or something I could have dealt with, that wouldn't kill me? But no, I had to pick the perfect man with the fatal flaw."

"You picked me?" Casey said.

"Of course I picked you."

He reached for her hand. "Really?"

"Really"

"Wow."

They lay side by side for a few moments, holding hands and smiling at the ceiling.

"God," Moira said. "I feel like I'm in junior high."

"You picked me," Casey said.

"You deaf? Yes, Casey, I picked you."

"When. When did you pick me?"

She thought for a moment. "When I finally realized the huge risk you were willing to take on the off chance you might be able to help a daughter from whom you've been estranged for two normal lifetimes. That's also when I knew, I wasn't afraid of you anymore. Why all the questions? You never been picked before?"

"*No*, not by my wife," Casey said, "and certainly not by someone like you that I'd already chosen."

Moira jerked to a sitting position and looked down at him.

"You chose me?"

"Yep."

"When?"

"When I realized you weren't afraid of me, and when I knew I didn't have to be afraid of you."

Moira peered at him. "So love is the absence of fear?"

Casey smiled. "No, but it's a hell of a bonus when you've been afraid for four hundred years," he said.

They spent the night together, holding each other until Moira slipped out an hour before dawn.

The sky was just beginning to show light in the east when Casey walked out to the van. Moira sat blearily behind the wheel. He eased into the passenger seat.

"Mornin' Pookie," he grinned, and kissed her on the cheek.

She jerked as if slapped with a wet towel. "Good morning, who?"

"Pookie?"

"No. Not now, not ever."

"Cumquat?"

"Nope."

"Sweet cheeks?"

"Absolutely not. What the hell is the matter with you?"

"Well, now that we've picked each other, I thought a pet name would be nice, Babycakes."

"Now you listen to me, Buster," Moira growled. "If you start calling me idiotic names just because you think I like you a little bit, I can positively guarantee you a place in the Vienna Boy's Choir. I know where and when you sleep. Keep it up, and you'll be carrying those things of yours around in a fucking jar while you try out for the soprano section!"

Casey grinned at her. "Any lasting relationship begins with threats of neutering," he said.

Moira smiled at him. "Thanks for getting me through our first post-admission encounter," she said. "I was really nervous about our meeting this morning."

"Me, too," Casey said. "Now I'm just scared shitless. What a relief."

Melvin walked to the van carrying his bag and a large aluminum briefcase. He opened a back door, put them inside, and took his place in the rear seat.

"Morning, all," he said.

"Fair morn, good Melvin," Casey said.

"Breakfast, Melvin?" Moira said.

"Yes. Actually, I'm famished."

Moira looked at Casey. "How 'bout you, Snookums?"

"Love some, Honey Pie," he said.

As they drove from the lot, Melvin looked out his window and sighed.

# FOURTEEN

A Tisket, a Casket

AFTER BREAKFAST AT BOB EVANS—where Moira tried to get a preoccupied Casey to ask for the senior's menu—they motored through the outskirts of Harrison in search of Highway 7. Casey stared blankly at the passing scenery.

"God, Casey," Moira said, "I wish you'd settle down and shut up. You're driving the rest of us crazy."

"We can't just handcuff her to the roof rack," he said.

"What?"

"Cat. She'd just tear the rack off anyway. I'm trying to figure out how, if we find her, we're going to transport her."

He continued to stare out the window for a moment. Then, as they passed an immense white house with a sign by the drive that read *Beeler and Sons*, he began to chuckle.

"Stop at a gas station or somewhere," Casey said. "We need a phone book."

"What for?"

"We're going to have to rent another van."

Two hours later, after leaving Melvin parked at a Wal-Mart in the Provenance truck, Casey and Moira walked from a Budget cargo van to the front door of Beeler and Sons Funeral Home. Casey rang the bell.

"God," Moira said. "Could this be more stereotypical?"

"Shut up," Casey said.

The door opened to reveal an elderly, blue-haired woman, wearing a black dress with a white Peter Pan collar, black sensible shoes, rimless glasses, clip-on silver earrings, and too much rouge. She folded liver-spotted hands in front of her, peered up at them from posture twisted by a widow's hump, and pursed her lips in an expression of sad disapproval.

"Yessss?" she intoned.

"Good morning," Casey said, his voice somber and hushed. "I'm afraid I need to purchase a casket for my daughter."

"Pleeease, come in," she said, stepping back from the doorway.

It was like walking into a velvet-lined cave. With the exception of a slight creaking of ancient floor joists beneath ponderous maroon carpet, the reception area seemed to suck sound from the air. Heavy, dark green drapes covered the windows, antique brass sconces wasted light that was absorbed by greedy flocked wallpaper, the musty scent of dead roses assaulted their nostrils, and a twelve foot ceiling weighed on them like the roof of an underground cavern.

"Take a ssseat, if you like," the woman said, indicating a narrow, overstuffed couch in deep gray velour. "Milo will be with you shortly. I'm sssorry for your losss." She glided away into unknown dark recesses as if on wheels. Moira avoided the couch as if it were a snake.

"Jesus!" she said. "Where's the pipe organ?"

"You don't find this cozy?" Casey said.

"I'd rather be upside down in a sleeping bag! I could breathe better."

"I kinda like it."

Moira grimaced. "Sure you do. Somebody like you could spend the weekend here with their pet bat!"

Stifling a laugh, Casey put his finger to his lips. Three seconds later they were approached by Milo. Around fifty, he was impeccably dressed in a dark gray double breasted suit with a delicate blue pinstripe, a pale blue silk shirt with French cuffs, a discretely patterned dark blue tie, and rimless glasses. His five-foot six-inch frame was trim, his black hair brushed back severely from a pronounced widow's peak, his nails expertly manicured, and his small feet encased in black pumps with an amazing shine. He pursed his lips and peered at them for a moment.

"You met my mother," he said. "I'm Milo Beeler. Shall we go someplace less ominous?"

Milo's office was bright, airy, and comfortable. Casey introduced himself and his "wife." Milo poured coffee, served lemon cookies, and got down to business.

"How may I be of service to you?"

"I need a casket for my daughter."

"Oh, my. How tragic, Mr. Mitchell. A child?"

"Fourteen."

"Dear me. I'm so sorry. We have a number of models on display. Perhaps you'd care to view them and determine where your taste might lie, and what would be appropriate for your child."

Casey smiled at him. "Appearance is not important, nor is the lining, ticking, or cosmetics. What I require is the utmost security and strength."

"Of course, all of our internment vessels are well constructed. Much of the security, however, comes from the vault in which the casket is placed."

"No vault."

Milo raised an eyebrow. "No vault?"

"No vault."

"If I may enquire," Milo went on, "where is the body, and when did you plan to have the service?"

"No service."

"Unusual," Milo said, pursing his lips.

"Yes," Casey smiled. "Your funeral home will have no contact with the body and none of the customary jobs to do. All I want is a very strong, very secure casket. Cash and carry, so to speak."

"Cash and carry?"

128

"I have a rental van waiting outside."

"Unusual," Milo repeated.

Moira spoke up. "Is there a law against selling just a casket, Mr. Beeler?"

"Well, no. There are, of course, a myriad of rules and regulations involved in my business, but no law against the selling of just a casket, I suppose."

"Then we'd like your strongest, most secure casket. To go. How much?"

"Well, our Eternal model is of aluminum alloy construction with an enameled stainless steel laminate shell, a double compressed baffle, eight uniform tension screw-lock closures, and fully welded seams. It is absolutely air and water tight and weighs almost six hundred pounds."

"How much?"

"It's lined in padded silk, stuffed with goose down, and trimmed in velvet. Really quite lovely."

"How much?" Moira asked again.

"Well, ordinarily, it's eighty-eight hundred dollars, but that price applies with our full service for the departed."

Moira leaned forward. "Look, Milo," she said, "you keep the pillows and lining to dress up one of your cheaper models. Drop a pad in the bottom, drag it out the door, throw it in the van, and we are out of here. For that, I'll give you six grand. Cash. You make at least a four thousand dollar profit for thirty minutes work, pay no taxes, and don't even have to put on a lab coverall or clean an instrument. You in business, or what?"

Milo smiled. "Oh, I'm in business," he said.

"Great," Moira said, rising to her feet. "Let's go look at the thing."

Less than an hour later Casey slammed the rear doors on the Budget van, and Moira handed Milo six thousand dollars cash.

"Thank you very much, Mrs. Mitchell," Milo said. "You may rest assured that you have made a wise choice. I personally guarantee the security of that vessel. Nothing will get in."

"Thank you very much, Mr. Beeler," Moira said, unable to contain a wicked little grin. "Something getting in was never our concern."

Melvin was sitting in the Wal-Mart parking lot when Casey and Moira arrived.

"Everything go okay?" he asked.

"Moira took charge," Casey said. "I still have a little chill."

"We got the box," Moira said. "How 'bout you?"

"I have the cordless drill, the bits, and the tarp."

"Great. Break out the tarp and let's transfer the casket."

Moira backed the rental van up to the rear of the Provenance van as Casey opened both sets of rear doors. With the trucks less than a foot apart, he slid the casket into the black van and covered it with the tarp, securing the cargo with bungee cords. He then headed back to Budget to return his truck; Moira and Melvin followed him.

"Will it hold her?" Moira asked as the three of them drove out of the Budget parking lot and headed south on Highway 7.

"I think so," Casey said. "I'll charge up the battery pack on the drill at the motel tonight and make four or five small holes in the casket. I want her to be able to get a little air. She can go without oxygen for several hours. I want to keep her weak, but I don't want to stress her completely. A few quarter-inch holes will allow some gas exchange and yet not be large enough she can get a finger in any of them."

"It sounds like we're caging a wild animal," Melvin said, obviously distressed.

"Worse, Melvin," Casey said. "Much worse."

"But, she's your daughter," Melvin said. "She's just a child. I find the thought of locking her away in a casket horrifying!"

Casey shook his head. "Aw, Melvin," he said, "don't let her picture fool you. You have got to understand that there is nothing in your experience to compare her to. Nothing. She has killed thousands of people. Thousands! Ruthlessly, eagerly, joyfully, with her teeth! Men, women, children. Babies, for God's sake! She has eaten their flesh, she has swallowed their blood, then opened her legs for the nearest men and women available, and giggled the entire time. Things that would make you vomit on your shoes are the highest recreation to her! She is as smart as anybody you know and as ruthless as a tiger after a goat. Melvin, she would use you, she would kill you, and she would discard you, just for the fun of it, with no more thought than you'd give a Kleenex. You have got to come to terms with this, God-dammit! You'd have a much better chance of surviving an encounter with a leopard in a fucking phone booth, than if she came after you."

Melvin appeared a little pale. "You've seen her do those things?" he said.

Casey looked at him and swallowed. "Oh, hell," he said. "I've helped her do those things."

The drive was silent until they entered the Buffalo River valley and stopped at a scenic overlook near Pruitt, Arkansas. They all got out to stretch their legs. Melvin wandered a short way off.

"Don't be too hard on Melvin," Moira said. "He's spent his whole life between the covers of books. The real world is distant from him."

Casey shook his head. "The world we're going to be dealing with could literally eat him alive," he said. "One moment of misplaced compassion at the wrong time, and he could screw this whole thing up. We do not want that to happen. None of us."

"Try to get a grip on the fact that he just cannot believe anyone could be as ruthless as the way you describe your daughter."

Casey looked out over the rolling expanse of valley below them and sighed.

"How 'bout you? Do you believe it?"

Moira touched his arm. "No," she said, "but I don't have to. I believe you."

Mid-afternoon they arrived in Jasper and went to a "Mom and Pop" motel. As Casey was settling in his room, Melvin dropped by.

"May I speak with you for a moment, Casey?"

"Sure! Grab a seat."

Melvin collapsed into an orange plastic chair.

"I'm not sure I'm cut out for this," he said. "I'm not much of an adventurer. I mean, beneath this suave and manly exterior beats the heart of a scarecrow, I'm afraid."

Casey chuckled and sat on the bed. "Scared?" he said.

"Yes. I suppose I rather am."

"Good," Casey said. "So am I."

"Yes, but I'm not a brave person. I have never had to be."

"Bullshit."

"I beg your pardon?"

"Bull. Shit. Bullshit," Casey said. "Every week, sometimes every day, you deal with substances in the lab that could be fatal to you. You assume the responsibility for findings that can save or take life. You work tirelessly for the sake of your fellow man. Those are very brave things to do, Melvin. Rare courage indeed."

"Well …"

"The whole concept of bravery is badly distorted. Being brave is just doing it anyway."

"I don't, ah …"

"Doing it anyway. In spite of the fact you're exhausted, in spite of the fact you're frightened, in spite of the fact it's dangerous, just doing it anyway. The kind of stuff you do all the time. You're brave enough, Melvin."

"Thank you," Melvin said.

"I'm asking you to do something that is very difficult for you. Ignore your rational mind. You must, Melvin. You absolutely must."

Casey rose from the bed and began to pace. "Logic does not apply to all this. And rationality is not a factor. What we are doing defies rationality and logic. If you try to deal with this situation and Cat in those parameters, you stand a good chance of becoming very dead. Moira too. Fail to believe me and you could easily kill yourself and her. You must, at least for a time, release a couple of the most basic tenets of your life. That is a very brave thing to do."

Melvin spoke up. "I just find it hard to believe that a young woman, a child really, could be as brutal as you claim. Please don't misunderstand, Casey. I am not implying that I think you are lying. That is not the case."

Casey changed tactics. "Look," he said, "when you were a freshman in high school, how large were you?"

"I never was a freshman, actually."

"Alright then, how 'bout when you were thirteen? C'mon, Melvin. 'Fess up.'"

"About five-three and a hundred pounds."

"Almost everybody your age was bigger and stronger, right?"

"Yes."

"Tough to take, huh?"

Melvin's eyes flickered about the room. "Not so bad," he said. "I had my books and studies."

Casey stared at him for a moment. "Tough to take, huh?"

Melvin colored. "Well, yes," he said. "I … I suppose I found it to be quite dreadful."

"Now suppose, all of a sudden, you could have turned school buses over on their sides with your bare hands. Would you have done it?"

"I don't know."

"You are a thirteen year old wimp, Melvin! Everybody calls you a nerd."

"Sure. Of course I would."

"Would you, now? Today?"

"No."

"Why not? What's the difference?"

"Age. Maturity."

"Cat, in spite of her age, has never had a chance to mature emotionally. She's still as self-centered and immortal as she was when she was a child. Emotional stability is not a strong point of the average Nosferati personality anyway. Cat likes turning over busses, Melvin. She'd turn over several a day if she could. In her world—a world populated by absolutely ruthless predators—most of them fear her."

Casey returned to his seat on the edge of the bed.

"Listen to me, Melvin," he continued, drawing the slight man's gaze with his intensity. "Cat is one of the baddest in the entire Nosferati valley. She could be the worst of the bunch, and she has been from day one. It's a game to her. She fears no consequences, she fears no reprisal, she fears no judgment. She has no more feeling for her victim's angst than a boa has for a rat. Unlike the boa, however, she enjoys her prey's struggles. She likes the screams and the terror. In her way, she is probably the most dangerous predator on the planet. She is also probably the most intelligent. She, if we can catch her, will use your emotions and intellect against you. She will play you like a banjo. I guarantee it. You are going to have to be one hard sonofabitch, Melvin. That is what I want you to understand."

Melvin swallowed. "So, how are you going to catch her?" he said.

"I don't know. Wait for opportunity to present itself, then gas up big time. How are our supplies? Am I gonna have to visit a blood bank or hospital?"

"We're good for now, I think. Perhaps we'll get lucky and she won't have fed recently."

Casey smiled. "False hope," he said. "Believe me, Melvin. Cat has always fed recently. Always."

# FIFTEEN

## Bobbalee

BOBBY LEE SHARP had never been a man to overlook possibilities. When he'd come back to Jasper in '02 after eight years in the service, he'd taken a job with the sheriff's department and waited for opportunity to knock. In less than a year, it was beating on his door. The High Sheriff's daughter, Florence Beechum, graduated high school. Flo Beechum wasn't the sharpest axe in the shed, but Bobby Lee had seen the power her daddy, Floyd, had in the county, and he wanted a piece of that action. After all, Floyd was nearing sixty, had blood pressure almost off the charts, and coughed so hard now and then he couldn't get his breath. It was just a matter of time. Bobby Lee put that time to good use. He courted Florence with dogged determination, sloe gin, and a stiff dick, and he sucked up to her daddy every way he could.

Floyd, on the other hand, was also no stranger to opportunity, and he saw his daughter through realistic eyes. That girl was going to be a carbon copy of her mama. Unless he wanted to support another whining dumbass until he rotted in the cold hard ground, he had to get her married off, and he couldn't be too goddam choosy. Flo sure wasn't. She'd fuck a snake if somebody'd hold its head, then puke booze on the back walk comin' home and not brush her teeth for three days if nobody reminded her to. Hell, she was gonna be worse than her mother! So when Bobby Lee showed up sniffin' after his daughter, Floyd Beechum was more than happy to dangle the head deputy's job out there on the end of Flo's stick. Bobby Lee wasn't half as smart as he thought he was, but he was damn sure smart enough for Flo. Floyd's gratitude for getting her out of his house and off of his back got Bobby Lee the head deputy's slot. Floyd's gasping death in the monstrous August heat of '04 got Bobby Lee the job he craved: Sheriff of Newton County.

Bobby Lee became the tall hog at the trough. He liked it. He took care of the county, accepted favors and repaid them, picked up an extra piece of change whenever he could, stretched the law when he wanted to, broke it when he needed to, never forgot the near invincibility of a southern High Sheriff, accepted payoffs, sold protection, and carried on the tradition of his exalted office.

Bobby Lee noticed the big Dodge van in the parking lot as he drove by the Maple Motel and, just for fun, ran the tags. No wants, no warrants, no restrictions, no other information. Access to registration information limited. Well, fuck! He'd seen

133

that kinda thing once before. Didn't make no difference if you were a High Sheriff or not. Unless somebody was gonna wake up the goddam president or somethin', you didn't get any information on who the vehicle belonged to. Now, what the hell would somebody like that be doin' in Jasper? He called Darlene at the motel desk.

"Maple Motel."

"Hey, Darlene."

"Oh, hi, Bobbalee. Whachew doin?"

"Settin' out here cross the street a watchin' you through the glass."

"Zat right?" Darlene asked, leaning against the counter and fidgeting with the buttons on her blouse.

"That's right. Just lookin' at ya."

"Justa lookin', Bobbalee?"

"Just lookin'."

"See anythin' ya like?"

"Yeah, but not enough of it. Maybe I'll do a little more lookin' later tonight."

"Harmon's home."

"I doan give a flyin' fuck if Harmon's home. I can still look!"

"If he sees you out there by the shed, Bobbalee, he'll beat my ass!"

"Maybe you need your ass beat."

"Mebbe I do, but not by him."

"Who's driving that big black van?"

"Three folks, two men and a woman. Three rooms."

"Where they from?"

"Doan know. Paid cash, just give they names. I gonna see ya tonight?"

"How late you workin'?"

"Seven."

"Them folks git stirrin' around, you call me."

"I gonna see ya tonight?"

"Well, not if Harmon's home."

"You gonna see me?"

"Maybe. You just be damn sure to call me if them people go anywheres!"

"I'll be in the winda, Bobbalee."

Casey walked into Moira's room through the open door to find Melvin sitting on the edge of the bed, watching her dust.

"This place is filthy," she grimaced, flailing away with a washcloth from the bathroom.

"Somebody's curious about us," Casey said.

"Oh, yeah?"

"Yep. The gal at the front desk was horsing around on the phone with someone who asked about us. I couldn't hear the other end of the conversation, but this end was pretty juicy."

"Juicy?"

"Yeah," Casey grinned. "If Harmon don't beat her ass, she's gonna be in the winda tonight for Bobbalee!"

"What?" Moira said.

"Sounds like my kind of girl. Let's go check her out, Melvin. Whaddaya say?"

Ears red, Melvin fidgeted. "Ah …"

Moira rescued him. "I need food," she said. "It's time for dinner."

Fifteen minutes later they were in Peggy's Restaurant, directly across the street from the motel, giving their orders to a young woman in a t-shirt that proclaimed she was a graduate of the Mid-South Cheerleading Camp.

"That's the meatloaf special, a quarter fried chicken special, a dinner salad with ranch, and a grilled cheese, a coffee, a ice tea, a coke, an' no grits for anybody, right?"

"Perfect," Casey said.

She grinned, popped her gum, and bounced away.

"Your kinda girl, too?" Moira said.

"Oh, yeah. I've had a cheerleader fantasy for years."

"Sis boom bah," Moira said.

The bell over the door tinkled and Casey looked up.

"Cheeze it," he muttered. "The cops."

Bobby Lee Sharp watched the three walk across the street to Peggy's. One blond-headed fella 'bout average size, one little herky-jerky guy with hair that stuck up all over the place, and a good lookin' woman with dark red hair and nice tits. He eased his Ford cruiser up the road half a block and stopped next to the restaurant, then he lifted his hat out of the back seat and cocked it on his head. He made sure his single-action, western-style Ruger magnum was strapped securely in its low-ride holster, stepped out of the car, stamped some dust from his new Tony Llama's, and headed for the door. City folks. Shit. Stifling his grin, he pushed open the door, expanded his chest, and ambled inside. Bobby Lee ambled real good.

Rawboned and freckled, wearing a brown uniform and a tan Resistol pulled low over his forehead, he slowly crossed the room and slid back the empty chair at the city folk's table. He sat in it backwards, tilted the Resistol to the back of his head, and smiled.

"Howdy, folks," he said. "I'm Bobby Lee Sharp, Newton County sheriff. How y'all doin'?"

Casey looked at him for a moment. "Sheriff," he said. "My name's Mitchell. This is Miss Flynn and Mr. Foltz. You alright this evenin'?"

"Fine, Sir. Thanks for askin'. Welcome to Jasper. How long y'all gonna be with us?"

"Not very long, Sheriff. We're just passing through. You probably get a lot of that in these parts, huh?"

"Noticed your van," Bobby Lee said, leaning forward, his arms crossed on the back of the chair. "You folks guvmint?"

"The people we work for sort of are," Casey said. "We're just peons with an official vehicle."

"Somethin' goin' on I need to know about?"

"I don't think so, but thanks for taking an interest. It's nice to know the law's so watchful."

Bobby Lee grinned at Casey and shook his head. "This ain't the first time you talked to no laws, is it, Mister ..."

"Mitchell," Casey said.

"Is it, Mr. Mitchell?"

"You want some coffee or a piece of pie, Sheriff? On me."

"Naw, thanks. Nice of you to offer."

"Then what is it you do want, Sheriff?" Casey said, holding on to his smile.

"Aw, I guess I'm jest a curious kind a feller," Bobby Lee drawled, standing up and turning his chair around. He sat and placed an elbow on the table, edging closer to Casey. "Whatcha all doin' here?"

Casey held his position. "Nothin' illegal," he said. "We'll be gone in a day or two."

"Who's that van ya'll are drivin' belong to?" Bobby Lee said, nodding toward the motel across the street.

"People we work for."

"The people you work for."

"Yessir," Casey said.

Bobby Lee brought his gaze back from the motel and looked Casey in the eye from less than two feet.

"And who would that be?"

"I don't believe I'm authorized to tell you that," Casey said. "Lemme check and get back to you."

Bobby Lee pulled his hat forward. "Who you folks work for?"

Casey scented anger and frustration. He put his smile away.

"I forget," he said.

"You forget."

"Yep."

Bobby Lee slid his chair back. "You got a terrible memory, Mister," he said.

Casey's smile returned, cold and brittle. "Just slipped my mind, Sheriff. Must be all the pressure. Maybe if you go away, it'll come back to me."

"Ya know," Bobby Lee said, "I doan like it much when folks doan answer my questions."

"Then this must be very difficult for you," Casey said.

"Now lookee here," Bobby Lee went on, leaning toward him a bit. "You keep this up an' mebbe I'll jest take you down to my office for a talk."

Casey's tone was flat and emotionless. "Maybe you'll try," he said.

He smelled fear drift from the sheriff.

"Now, Boys," Moira said, leaning in on the other side of Bobby Lee and turning on the charm. "Let's not get into a pissing contest here. Sheriff, I think I can clear this up. The fact is, unless you have reasonable grounds to believe we are committing a crime, planning to commit a crime, or are in violation of something, you have no right to question us about anything. None. I know this upsets you because you're used to exploiting your countywide authority, but I'm not in any way abusing your rights as a law enforcement officer. You are. If, for any reason, we need you or your services, we will not hesitate to call. Until such time as we do call, however, please exercise your ego somewhere else."

Bobby Lee looked at her blankly, attempting to process what he'd just heard. He felt he'd been insulted, but he wasn't exactly sure how.

"What we got here, is a failure to communicate," Moira said. "Okay, Bobby Lee, here's the deal. We need you, we'll call. Otherwise, stay the hell out of our way. This is over your head. Leave us alone. If you choose not to, you will be in shit to your earlobes. Do what you're told, and there might be a nice donation to your retirement fund. You have a decision to make. Make it someplace else. The cheerleader is gonna bring our food soon, and I wanna eat in peace. See you later."

Bobby Lee looked at her and began to redden, his knuckles white where he gripped the edge of the table. Casey casually put his hand on Bobby Lee's arm. The sheriff winced and the color drained from his face.

"No," Casey said. "Absolutely not. You are not going to do anything, Sheriff. You are not going to hassle this woman or anyone else at this table. You are way out of line, and if you push it, I'll have enough writs and warrants in here by tomorrow morning to wallpaper your office. I absolutely guarantee you my dog is bigger than yours. Smile, nod, and leave, and I'll let you take your arm with you."

"Just a goddam min …"

Casey increased the pressure slightly and Bobby Lee choked off his words behind bloodless lips. The sheriff sagged in his chair and the fight leaked out of him. Smiling, Casey released the arm, and Bobby Lee stood up and shuffled to the door, willing himself not to grab his numb forearm.

"Dammit!" Moira said, after Bobby Lee went outside. "Well, we screwed that up! So much for a low profile."

"What an obnoxious man," Melvin said.

"And he'll be watching us like a hawk," Casey said.

Moira grinned. "God, that was great!" she said. "Hey, Casey, wanna swap your meatloaf for my grilled cheese? All of a sudden I'm feeling carnivorous!"

Out in the cruiser, Bobby Lee rolled the shirtsleeve up above his tingling and sluggish left hand. There was a four-inch bruise blooming on his forearm.

"Sonofabitch!" he grunted as he tried to rotate his left wrist and the pain shot to his shoulder.

The more Bobby Lee thought, the more he realized that those strangers had just thrown him out of a restaurant in his own county seat. He picked up his phone and dialed. "Junior? Bobby Lee … I know it's your fuckin' night off … I make up the schedule, Dipshit. Git up off the fuckin' couch and get in here. I got some assholes I want ya to watch. By God, you'll fuckin' work if I need ya to work! I'll git Luther or Dwayne in to relieve ya before dawn. Meet me at the Chevy lot in fifteen minutes. One a these fuckers takes a shit, I wanna know what color it is, an' I don't want them ta know yer a peekin' in the toilet! Git your ass down here, Junior, and I mean right goddam now!"

After dinner, Casey returned to his room. Thirty minutes later he stepped out into the night for some fresh air. Moira walked up beside him.

"Just on my way to see you," she said.

Casey smiled. "My pleasure," he said, opening his door. They went back inside.

"I just got off the phone with my pal Marley," Moira said. "She tapped into a database with global positioning. I got directions to Flavel and Aleen Potts' place. It's only ten or twelve miles from here. We can drop by there tomorrow and ask them what happened to their truck and if they've seen Cat."

"Good old Marley," Casey said. "Where do you know Marley from?"

"She and I went to grad school together. She's a doll. Got a couple of kids. Works her ass off. The only friend from school I have. Actually, we shared an apartment before she got married. Her husband's dead. You'll meet her someday."

"We got a shadow," Casey said.

"A shadow?"

"A deputy is parked about a block down the street under the overhang of a big willow tree. He doesn't think we can see him."

Moira peered out of the window into the darkness. "Well, I can't," she said.

"I can. We have been staked out, Pookie."

Moira returned his grin. "No Pookie. Never Pookie."

Casey tried to look innocent. "Not even when we're alone?"

"Especially then."

"Well, maybe we should discuss my cheerleader fantasy. Would you say 'sis boom bah' again?"

"I'll say 'sis' and 'bah'," Moira said. "You want some 'boom' from me, you lecherous old fart, you're gonna have to work for it. What are we gonna do about the shadow?"

"I think we might consider dropping by the Potts place later tonight. I'll go visit Melvin for a little pick-me-up, then say hello to the nice policeman. Perhaps he'll take a well-deserved nap."

An hour later, while High Sheriff Bobby Lee Sharp masturbated in the darkness beside Harmon's shed as he watched Darlene fondle her breasts through the bathroom window, Casey approached Junior Seaton where he slept in his squad car in the shadow of the willow tree. Almost gently, Casey placed his hand around the top of the deputy's head and gave it a quick shake. Junior sighed and slumped to the passenger side of the seat. Casey moved him upright and patted his cheek.

"Sorry 'bout the headache, Son," he whispered. "A concussion'll sure do that to you. Rest well."

Ten minutes later, Casey and Moira, leaving Melvin behind to sleep, eased the van out of the parking lot and down Highway 7 in search of County Road 9.

# SIXTEEN

### Deer Coming

MOIRA AND CASEY picked up County Road 9 a couple of miles south of Jasper and turned east as Marley's instructions indicated. An overcast sky sucked the pale moonlight away and Moira struggled a bit with the big van on the switchbacks and tight curves of the narrow Arkansas gravel road.

"Jesus!" she bitched, slowing to a crawl as she negotiated an off-camber plunge into a narrow valley. The gloomy pines and ragged post oaks seemed to absorb the light and reduce the headlights to a dull glow. "Who the hell is the head of the highway department in this state, Salvador Dali?"

She wrenched the van onto a flat stretch and accelerated to twenty miles an hour, displaced gravel rattling on the undercarriage in the still night.

"Deer coming," Casey said.

"What?"

"Deer coming. Brake."

"Deer coming? Wha ...?"

A large tawny blur flashed across the windshield.

"*Shit!*"

Moira stood on the brake pedal, and the van slewed to a gravel-crunching halt, sliding on the high-crowned road and stopping almost in the ditch.

"Why the hell didn't you say something?" Moira shouted, panting behind the wheel and jamming the transmission into park.

Casey grinned. "I did," he said. "I said there was a deer coming."

"Deer coming," she snorted. "What the fuck does that mean? Deer coming."

"What would you preferred me to have said?"

"How 'bout, 'stop the fucking van, or some huge animal is going to crash through the windshield and cut your pathetic little life short on a Goddam cow trail way the hell down in Bumfuck Arkansas!' Deer coming, my ass!"

Casey laughed. "Let's see. Stop the fucking van or some, uh, could you repeat that? I didn't get it all."

"Oh, shut up."

Casey grinned at her, remaining silent while she collected herself. At length, Moira put the van in gear and eased away from the ditch toward the center of the road.

"Deer coming," Casey said.

"Jesus Christ!" Moira blurted, jamming the brake pedal to the floor and lurching to a halt.

Two does delicately picked their way across the road twenty feet in front of the van, toe dancing on flinty hooves. The second one took flight, soaring into the clover on the left side of the lane, passing through a thin shaft of moonlight just as it broke through the clouds.

"Oh, my," Moira whispered.

"Yeah," Casey said.

"We ought to find their driveway in another one-point-two miles," Moira said.

She eased the van off Nine and onto a rutted single-lane path. Weeds grew in the center of the road and overhanging trees reduced their world to a gloomy tunnel that the headlights could barely penetrate. A fox stood in the glow for a moment, watching them come, then slithered off into the black. The darkness leaned on them, nearly pushing the van downward into the road with its weight. Moira shivered.

"God! This is awful," she muttered, chewing on her lip. "Casey, I'm scared."

"I'm here," he said, most of his attention directed outside the van.

"I know. Think how freaked I'd be if you weren't."

She flinched as something with wings flitted across the headlight beams. Locusts started up, their *Kree-ree-ree* coming from all directions, loud in the stillness of the Ozark night.

"About a hundred yards," Casey said. "Mailbox on the right."

"How can you see that?" Moira asked, her voice tight and thin.

"I had a snack just before we left. Nearly a pint. I'm in pretty good shape."

As predicted, the mailbox appeared.

"Stop here," Casey said.

He climbed out of the truck. Moira stayed where she was, chewing her lip and trying to get her hands to relax on the wheel.

Casey looked in the mailbox, then examined an open pipe gate at the front of a weedy drive. Up a lightly wooded slope about fifty yards distant crouched the silhouette of a small house. Behind it loomed the dark mass of a barn. The locusts went silent as if someone had thrown a switch. Crickets chirped and insects whirred in the headlights. Moira rubbed gooseflesh on the back of her arms, brought on by the moment and a nighttime chill, and kept a careful eye on Casey. He stood looking up the drive for a little while, then walked to her side of the truck.

"This is not good," he said.

An inhuman shriek cut the still air, a soulless, high-pitched scream that seemed to come from everywhere at once. Moira lurched in her seat and battled for bladder control.

"*Whatthefuckwasthat!*"

Casey, smiling, put his hand on her arm through the open window.

"Take it easy, we're fine. Screech owl."

"A what?"

140

"A screech owl. 'Bout as big as your fist, weighs three or four ounces. Eats mice, shrews, and bugs."

"A fucking bird?"

Casey laughed. "A little fucking bird."

"Jesus Christ! I gotta pee."

Casey opened the door for her and Moira moved to the rear of the van for a little privacy. When she came back to the headlights, Casey was standing near the gate. Walking over, holding her crossed arms and trembling, she sidled up next to him. He put a hand on the small of her back for comfort.

"Okay," she shivered. "What's not good?"

"Some of the mail in the box is over two weeks old and the gate is open. Country people never leave a gate open. It's almost a cellular imperative. Even if there is nothing to be kept in, gates are always closed."

"Jesus," she said, peering through the darkness toward the house. "Now what?"

"Back to the motel before anybody notices we left."

"Aren't we going up to the house?"

"Not necessary. I already went."

"When?"

"When you were answering the call of nature behind the van."

Moira gaped at him as this new information soaked in. "You left me here?" she said.

"For a little while."

"You left me here!" she spat.

"For less than a minute."

"You sonofabitch!" Moira whispered, trying to control her volume in the quiet country night. "You left me all by myself in this background for a Tarzan movie while you went traipsing off up to the house, without even telling me you were going?"

"Let me ask you a question."

"Goddammit, Casey!"

"Let me ask you a question."

"Goddammit, Casey," she hissed, punching him on the arm.

"Let me ask you a question," he repeated.

"What?"

"Would you have preferred knowing you were alone?"

"What?"

"Would you have pre …?"

"That's not the point!"

"That is exactly the point. Would you have preferred knowing you were alone?"

Moira stared at him for a moment. "Probably not."

"Okay," Casey said.

"Get in the truck, Asshole," she grumbled.

In spite of the fact that Moira never said a word all the way back to the motel, the ride seemed significantly shorter. When they arrived in the parking lot, she went directly to her room and slammed the door. Casey sat on the edge of his bed in the dark, having too recently fed to sleep. About thirty minutes passed before the knock came.

"Whooo isss iiiiiit?" he trilled.

"Open the door, Shithead," came the muffled reply.

Chuckling, he turned on a lamp and did as he was asked. Moira, wearing a short robe and what appeared to be little else, came stomping into the room.

"Okay," she said, "I'm over it. What'd you find up at the house?"

"Bodies," he said, sitting on the bed. She sat beside him.

"Oh, shit. Whose?"

"Three feeder calves and two pigs outside, two cats and one parakeet inside. There was some dog sign, but only one dog. His skull was crushed. I figure the other dogs must have taken off. The outside animals had been gone over by foxes or coyotes pretty thoroughly, the inside animals were unmarked except for bugs. I figure all of them, except the dog, died from the same cause."

"What?"

"Thirst. There was nobody around to water them. No sign of Mr. or Mrs. Potts. Food spoiling in the fridge, bags in the hall closet, toiletries in the bathroom. A lot of the house had been gone through or ransacked. The folks that lived there didn't leave. They were taken."

"Christ. You're sure?"

"Oh, yeah."

"Cat?"

"There was dried urine on the kitchen floor. It was hers. No doubt about it."

"Jesus."

"Jesus wouldn't have anything to do with my daughter," Casey muttered and sagged back against the headboard.

Moira slid up beside him and took his hand.

He looked at her, and the pain in his eyes hit her like liquid lead. "Sometimes I think I'd be doing her, the world, and myself a favor if I just killed her on sight. She's the worst of them, Moira. The worst of them. Cat is the most horrific serial killer to ever draw a breath or claim a victim. She is a monster. Nosferatu himself would retch at some of the things she's done."

"And she's still your daughter."

"God save us both, she's my baby." He turned onto his side, curled into the fetal position, and was still.

Moira snuggled up behind him and hung on until deep sleep claimed him. Stretching the kinks from her back, she rose and sat by the window looking out at the night. Her lips curled into a snarl.

"You bitch," she whispered. "You screw this up and I swear, I'll find some way to kill you myself."

Unable to sleep because of his wife's burbling snores and anger over being thrown out of a restaurant in his own Goddam county, Bobbie Lee Sharp crawled out of bed around three a.m. slipped into a soiled uniform, and stumbled out to his cruiser. He dropped by the IGA and pounded on the back door until one of the stock boys opened it. Inside before store hours, he helped himself to a bag of donuts off the shelf and two large coffees from the break room urn. Back in the car, he headed for the Maple Motel. He'd been too hard on Junior. Coffee and donuts might fix things up.

Approaching the motel, he noticed Junior's car in the willow shadow. Good spot. He pulled up beside the other vehicle. Junior was asleep. Furious, Bobby Lee reached across the foot or so of space between the cars and slapped the side of Junior's head. The deputy leaned to his right and fell over in the seat.

"Goddammit, Junior!" Bobby Lee hissed, "Wake the fuck up! What the hell is the matter with you?"

No response.

"Junior! Junior! Wake up!"

No response. Bobby Lee pulled his car forward and got out. When even opening Junior's door and shaking him had no effect, it began to dawn on Bobby Lee that Junior might not be asleep. He could be unconscious. Abandoning his own squad car and driving Junior's, he rushed the deputy to the county hospital on the southwest edge of Jasper. A little after dawn, the doctor came out of the emergency room.

"He has a concussion, Sheriff, and a couple of badly subluxated vertebrae in his neck."

"What?"

"Yessir. Some real trauma. He'll be semi-conscious for a while. We're gonna keep him for a day or two. He's hurt."

"What ya figure done it?" asked Bobby Lee.

"I have no idea. To produce injuries of this type requires a significant event. I couldn't find a bruise or indication of contact anywhere on him. Due to the extent of the trauma, I wouldn't have been surprised to find he'd been hit with an axe handle, but that's not the case. I can see no reason for the injuries, but the injuries are real. Count on it."

"Can I see him?"

"Certainly, but he can't talk. We have him sedated. Any conversation would most likely be gibberish. Perhaps late this afternoon."

Disgusted, Bobby Lee drove back to the motel and parked Junior's car near the office. He then retrieved his own car and circled through the parking lot heading back toward the street. As he passed Moira's room, she came out and turned to lock her door. Bobby Lee stopped.

"Mornin', ma'am," he said, squinting at her in the glare of the sunrise reflecting off her window.

Moira smiled at him. "Morning, Sheriff. Up early or out late?"

"Just wanted to drop by and wish you folks a good mornin'," he said.

"You shouldn't lie, Bobby Lee. You don't do it well."

"You're about a mouthy little bitch, aincha?" Bobby Lee said. "Somebody ought to teach you some manners."

"Gotta have 'em to teach 'em," Moira smiled. "Guess that lets you off the hook, huh? I'm on the way to breakfast. Buy you a cup of coffee?"

"I want anything from you, girl, I'll wear it offa ya!"

Casey walked out of his room next door. Ignoring Bobby Lee, he turned to Moira. "Everything okay?" he said.

"Fine. The Sheriff here was just trying to intimidate me with sexual innuendo."

"Did it work?"

"Not very well."

Casey looked at the sheriff. "Long night, Bobby Lee? Guess things get a little tense when Harmon's home, huh?"

Melvin came out of his room and the three of them crossed the street. Bobby Lee watched them go, not quite able to close his mouth.

In the restaurant, Moira and Casey brought Melvin up to speed on the events of the night.

"So what is our proposed course of action?" he said.

"I guess the county hospital," Moira said. "I'll use my credentials to talk with some of the staff about unusual deaths, suspicious homicides and such in the area over the past few years. It's for sure we won't get any cooperation from the local law."

"The local law is dirty," Casey said.

Moira grinned. "Ya think?"

"No, not just southern sheriff dirty, but slimy. I got a real bad feeling about this guy. He's a lot more danger to us than just a shitty sheriff."

He paused and thought for a moment. "Okay. Here's the set-up. While we remain here in Deliverance City, if at any time you guys look around and I am gone, give me thirty minutes to contact you. If I do not, get the hell out of town. If you're in the motel, leave immediately. If you are not in the motel, don't go back. Get on Seven and head north. Do not waste time, do not dally. Your lives could depend on it. You remember that scenic overlook we stopped at near Pruitt in the Buffalo River Valley?"

Moira and Melvin both nodded.

"Go there. Do not stop. For the next twelve hours, stay with the van and keep on the move. At the top of every hour, drive through that scenic overlook. If I'm okay, I will be there sometime during those twelve hours. Do not look for me. I'll find you. If I don't show up, head back for Provenance and Kansas City. Don't stop for anything but gas. Keep moving. Eat in the truck. I'll find you there within three days. If I don't show up, the fat lady has sung. Got it?"

"Jesus," Moira breathed.

"Has it come to this?" Melvin said.

"Maybe."

"I'm not totally sure that I'm comfortable with abandoning you here, Joseph, ah, sorry, Casey. That would not seem to me to be the appropriate thing for us to do."

Casey smiled. "You are fine and true, fair Melvin, and I appreciate your loyalty, but if things go so far that I must leave you two, you are not safe. You must get away. You are not running out on anybody. You are attempting to save your life and Moira's as well."

"Ah. Well, of course, I will do as you ask."

"You're a good man, Melvin."

Melvin peered at him thoughtfully for a moment.

"Perhaps I am," he said.

Sitting in his cruiser a block down the street, Sheriff Sharp punched a number up on his phone.

"Colin?" he said. "Bobby Lee Sharp here. Somethin' might be up. We got some official type folks in from outta town, an' they just might be too smart for they own good. I doan know yet, but I got my eye on 'em, just tryin' ta keep ya posted on anythin' unusual, like we agreed. Naw I doan need no help or nothin' yet, but it could be that y'all might wanna take a personal hand in this'un. ... That's fine, just leave it out by that low water bridge like last time. ... I 'preciate it. Cat there? Well, when she gits back, if this goes down big, you tell that slick little shit she is gonna owe me somethin' really special. Yeah, I bet she can, Godamighty! ... Naw, just lay low for now. I'll keep ya posted. These assholes could be real trouble. If it looks like y'all need to jump in, I'll come out."

It always scared Bobby Lee a little even to talk to Colin. That was a strange bunch in the middle of all them sinkholes and shit south of Polk Ridge. He'd only been out there three or four times, but it gave him the creeps to think about it. Some kinda commune or somethin'. Only five or six of 'em. No plumbing, just that big spring. No electricity, just a generator. No refrigeration, no central heat or air. Damn! But they kept to theyselves, and their money spent just like everbody else's. And that Cat. Jesus God! Couldn't be more'n fourteen or fifteen, and wring a fella out like a dirty rag. Just the thought a her'd git him hard as a three cell Kel-lite. Somethin' big come a all this, maybe he'd git Cat for a whole night. Wear some a the shine off a that slick little shit. Damn!

Deceased

There was very little light in the massive room, only a quiet blue glow radiating from panels above the translucent ceiling. If a fixture were to break, no debris could drop into the containment area. The single occupant would never have to fear falling shards of glass. The bed had not been slept in. It almost never was. The sterile life that spent its minutes and hours in that hell of safety needed little sleep, indeed feared the outcome of slumber as others feared deep anesthesia, regarding it as temporary death from which he might never emerge. He sat at his desk, not quite dozing, skirting the edge of meditation, his mind too active for release. The room was completely silent save for the ever-present hiss of the air conditioning. When the pale blue light on the arm of his chair began to blink, it caught his attention immediately. There was no ring or tone. He was never to be startled. A heavily gloved hand extended a finger and touched a recessed button beside the light.

"Unruh." His voice was as raspy and thin as the cry of a starling.

"Hello, Sir. It's Voorhees."

"Well, Voorhees. Have you anything to report?"

"Not as much as I'd like, Sir. You were correct. Joseph Casey does not exist. The individual in question may be a recent escapee from a private prison outside of Indianapolis, Indiana. If it is the same man, he had been incarcerated at that facility for over a decade as a multiple murderer. Model prisoner. Worked in the hospital. Dealt with terminal AIDS patients by choice. An individual fitting his general description came to Provenance with Moira Flynn. He, she, and Melvin Foltz recently left Provenance in a company van. The incident in the primate lab is sketchy, but I have been able to determine that some sort of accident resulted in a total of eleven primates having to be incinerated in the AIDS blood study program."

"Indeed?"

"Yessir. The entire area was declared off limits to all personnel and dealt with exclusively by Doctor Foltz."

"Go on, Voorhees."

"Yessir. Only today I learned that the three subjects are in Arkansas near or in a small town named Jasper."

"How Twainish."

"Jasper is the county seat of Newton County, Sir, just south of the Buffalo River Valley. Ms. Flynn requested that Mrs. Marley secure an address and directions for her to a residence in that area. The rural home of Flavel and Aleen Potts."

"Do we know these people, Voorhees?"

"Nossir. We do not. As you know, on prior occasion, Mrs. Marley also provided Ms. Flynn with information on unexplained deaths across the country. It would seem that the visit to Arkansas was motivated, at least to some degree, by that information."

"Does this suggest anything to you, Voorhees?"

"Nossir, not at this time. I do believe that it requires further investigation."

"As do I, Voorhees. It is possible that the unraveling of this tangle could be vital to my overall enterprise. I assume you have been conducting yourself with your usual thoroughness and dedication?"

"Yessir."

"Could Mrs. Marley provide you with any additional insight?"

"I'm sorry, Sir, she could not. I questioned her at some length with varying methods."

"I am sure you did. And how is Mrs. Marley?"

"Deceased, Sir."

"How sad. Natural causes?"

"Yessir, by what will appear to be a massive stroke. Unusual in a woman of her age, but not unheard of."

"Ah. A tragedy no doubt. I will see to it that her two daughters are amply rewarded for the inconvenience of their mother's demise."

"Yessir," Voorhees replied, hearing just a trace of amusement in his master's voice.

"What now, Voorhees?"

"I'm off to Arkansas this evening, Sir. It's not quite six p.m. here."

"Perhaps you should question Mr. and Mrs. Potts."

"That is my intention, Sir."

"Very good, Voorhees. I am in accordance with whatever methods you deem necessary."

"Yessir. Thank you, Sir."

"And, Voorhees?"

"Yessir?"

"Follow the blood, Sir. Always the blood."

# SEVENTEEN

### Effemininity

"I'VE BEEN THINKING ABOUT FEAR," Melvin commented, spreading butter on his waffle. Moira and Casey glanced at each other then turned their attention to him.

"What brought this on?" Casey said.

"The chat you and I had," Melvin said. "It's really just a chemical reaction, you know. The physiology of fear is no great mystery, although it differs somewhat from the physiology of fright."

Moira smiled into her corned beef hash and let Casey have it. He looked at Melvin and took the plunge.

"How so?"

"Fright," Melvin went on, "is sudden and short-lived. Someone jumping out at you from a darkened doorway, a near miss while in traffic, a bee flying near your ear. Adrenalin rush, et cetera. An almost violent response to sudden stimuli. Fright cannot be sustained very long. The reaction is too intense. People do not faint from fear. They faint from fright. Physically it cannot be sustained. Fear is different."

Casey turned from his eggs and gave the little man his attention.

"Go on," he said.

"Fear," Melvin continued, "can be sustained for a very long time. Even active fear."

"Active fear?"

"As opposed to passive fear. Suppose I am deathly afraid of snakes. There is no snake in my proximity, nor do I expect there to be. I am passively afraid. I leave my living room and go outside into the yard where several snakes have been seen in the last few days. My passive fear puts me on alert. Fifty feet away, I see a snake in the driveway. Now I am afraid. Now I feel active fear. My eyes open wider, my heart rate and blood pressure rise, I may begin to perspire, feel anxious, get nervous. Even though I know that I can get back into the house before that snake can possibly get to me, the active fear is there. Follow?"

"Sure."

"I turn around to go back inside, and there, right in front of me, is a snake! At my feet! I scream and launch myself into the air before my conscious mind even realizes the threat. I am over that snake and into the house so fast that I don't even remember opening the door and going inside. Frightened and leaning against the wall, I pant and begin to feel sick at my stomach. A few minutes later I'm sitting on the couch, trembling with adrenalin shock. If one combines fear and fright together long enough, as in war, it can profoundly affect the organism. Extended exposure to the changes in blood sugar, peptides, adrenalin, and such, as well as performance in the pancreas, liver, kidneys, and the like, plus the accelerated stimulus to the nervous system, the hippocampus, the pituitary, the pineal and more, can have profound effects on an individual. Delayed stress syndrome is a prime example. Unexplainable physical illness is another. Mental illness is, of course, a common effect. Follow?"

"So far."

"Eliminate the fright, and the results are, in many ways, far more insidious. Extended fear can slowly devour the personality. It can become so much a part of our lives that we no longer recognize it. We distrust others, we have difficulty communicating with people, we cannot maintain a relationship, we are paranoid, we either give up on life, or we constantly try to prove our superiority over the herd. We often become brutal or abusive, and care little for the needs or wants of others. What is essentially a completely physical reaction that can be measured quite accurately by instrumentation becomes a mental and emotional ailment that is far more destructive to the organism and those with whom the organism associates."

"You definitely have been thinking," Casey said.

"Oh, yes."

"And has all this thought done anything to help with your fear of not being brave?"

Melvin smiled. "No. But it has possibly shed some light on your kind, and on you."

Casey looked at him.

"What?" Moira said.

"You have given me the impression that Nosferati neither give nor receive love," Melvin said.

"That's true," Casey said.

"And yet, you never really stopped loving your daughter."

"Also true," Casey said.

"Then that could be one of the major reasons you are no longer an active Nosferati, and the rest of them are."

"Love?" Casey said, his eyebrows rising.

"Love," Melvin stated. "And what is the opposite of love?"

"Hate."

"No," Melvin said. "Fear. And extended fear, as I described before, produces symptoms similar to the Nosferati personality, wouldn't you say?"

Casey stared at him.

Melvin smiled. "Just a thought," he said as he returned to his waffle.

After breakfast, Moira and Casey walked out of the restaurant. Melvin tagged along behind. Casey paused and looked up the deserted street.

"Huh. Now that's strange," he mused.

"What's strange?" asked Moira.

"Our shadow's gone. I don't see Bobby Lee watching us from his cruiser anywhere."

"Maybe he went home."

"Maybe, but … *shit!*" Casey vanished across the street in a blur.

Moira looked at Melvin.

"I wish he wouldn't do that," Melvin said. They began to trot toward the motel.

The door to Casey's room was standing open. Nobody inside. They found Melvin's door pulled from the hinges. The blood cooler was lying on its side, ice and blood bags scattered across the floor.

"How much blood was in that thing?" Moira asked.

"Six pint bags, but not now. Two are gone. He must have needed them." The color drained from Melvin's face. "Oh, my," he said.

Moira's nostrils flared. "Grab your stuff, Foltz! We've got to run."

When Casey entered his room and noticed the computerized picture of Cat he'd left on his table had been moved, he knew the situation had changed. *Shit! Stupid!* Bobby Lee had been there. Casey could smell him. A locked motel room door would have meant nothing.

Back outside, he saw Bobby Lee's car exit the far motel drive and accelerate down the street. Casey ripped Melvin's door out of the way, grabbed two bags of blood from the cooler and set off in pursuit, sucking down the contents of the first bag as he ran.

Clotheslines, fences, above ground pools, bar-b-que grills, dogs, it made no difference. Casey sailed past, over, or around all of them, streaking through back yards to catch up with Bobby Lee's car, pausing only long enough to empty his bladder behind an immense oak after the feeding kicked in. So what if somebody saw him? Damn! It felt really good to move again, to feel the power and the purpose and the pulse.

Bobby Lee turned north on Seven and let it out to nearly 80 miles an hour. Casey stayed well away from the road and a quarter of a mile behind, flickering through the fields and across the ditches, keeping pace, watching, waiting, grinning. About halfway to Pruitt, on the edge of the Buffalo River Reserve, the car slowed to a near halt, eased onto an old rutted logging road, and began a slow eastward grind through clawing post oaks and heavy weeds. Casey went on ahead a few miles and encountered a rock and stump studded clearing, its back to a ragged ridge. The three or four acres of hardscrabble sprouted a rundown old house and a couple of weathered outbuildings. Five or six cars and pickups and three motorcycles sat about in various stages of repair. There were no electric lines, no TV satellite dishes, no livestock, no farm implements save one ancient Case tractor rusting away in the weeds, still attached to a harrow. A half dozen buzzards loafed overhead. There appeared to be no dogs.

Staying well back in cover, Casey circled the place, skittering to the top of the ridge behind it and moving a couple of hundred yards to the east to stay downwind and out of sight. He drank the second pint, let the rush take him for a moment, and leaped to an overhanging branch of an ancient seed pine, thirty feet off the ground. Getting comfortable, he watched Bobby Lee's car wallow its way toward the house.

A gust of wind wafted in his direction and he caught a familiar stench. Nosferati! Well … now. Smiling, he settled back to watch and listen. He hadn't felt this good in years.

Colin stepped out onto the porch as Bobby Lee closed the car door. Appearing as if he were in his early twenties, Colin was a slight man of average height with nearly delicate features, shaggy black hair to the middle of his ears, pale gray eyes, and dark Cupid's bow lips. While he was not effeminate, his manner was slightly feminine. He stood on one leg with a fist resting on his outthrust hip. In spite of the cool air, he was barefoot, wearing only jeans and a soiled t-shirt. His thin arms were a ropy collection of sinew and veins. He cocked his head to one side and squinted into the morning light. A tolerant smile teased his lips.

"Now then, fair mornin' to you, Sheriff." His voice was a condescending crisp alto.

"You got trouble," Bobby Lee replied, advancing on the porch.

"Do we now? And what type of difficulty might that be, Love?"

"Those folks I told ya about? They got a picture of Cat."

"A photograph?"

"Naw. One of them computerized drawin' things. Looks just like her. I slipped into one a their motel rooms and found it. Left it right where it was so they wouldn't know I'd been looking at their stuff."

"I see."

"Thought you'd want to know. Maybe go deal with these folks yourself. This might be more than I can handle alone. I think these people is guvmint."

"The constabulary?"

"What?"

"The police? FBI, BATF, U.S. Marshals?"

"I doan know. I tried to trace the plates on their van, but they won't trace."

"Right. Go back to town and keep an eye on these folks like a good lad. Apprise me regularly."

"Sure. Cat around?"

Colin grinned. "It would seem that you have a bit of a thing for our little Pussy. When she returns, I'll be sure and tell her what a good boy you've been. Off with you then, Constable."

As Bobby Lee drove away, Hammond joined Colin on the porch. A head taller, fifty pounds heavier, fair, blond, and appearing to be a couple of years younger, he watched the car make dust on the ragged gravel lane.

"Bloody hell!" Colin spat. "If Cat has fucked this up, I'm going to pull her claws! Off she goes with Michael on one of her little jaunts, muckin' about for some fun and games, and now this!"

Hammond grinned and sucked a tooth. "I'd think twice, if I was you, before I tried to de-claw that one," he said. "She just might suck out your eyeballs. I'd hate to tangle with her."

"We got us a prime set-up here! Constable in our pocket, unknowin' natives, lots a caves and sinkholes for the bleeders and the trash, freedom of movement. God's holy trousers, I hope she hasn't spoiled it all!"

Still grinning, Hammond shrugged. "She'll do whatever she's done and not worry about nothin'. You know Cat."

"Yes I do, Love," Colin replied. "And I have since you was suckin' on human tit, and that been a fair piece of time, what? So don't try to give me lessons on our fair little Pussy, Mate. It won't wash!"

Hammond's grin got wider. "Take it easy, Old Man. Remember your blood pressure. You pop a vein, I might not be able to help myself. Want me to tag along and keep an eye on Bobby Lee?"

"Right. It's a wonder how he can stay on his feet, not havin' no brain an' all. Bit a brunch before you leave?" Colin smiled.

"I could eat."

"Why don't you fetch us a bleeder then, Love? Better yet, somethin' fresh. Mrs. Potts is in the second hole and she seems lively. Let's have a go at the old girl, shall we? Then it's off to town with you, Hammond me lad, and a close eye on our friend Mister Sharp."

Bobby Lee stormed into the Maple Motel office a little after noon. Darlene smiled and leaned against the counter.

"Hi, Bobbalee."

He glared at her. "Where's that fuckin' van?"

"Huh?"

"The van. That big fuckin' black van and them three assholes that was in it. Where'd they go?"

Shrinking a bit and biting her lower lip, Darlene backed up a step.

"They checked out, I guess, Bobbalee. They was gone when I come in at eleven. Doan yell at me. I ain't done nothing."

"*Shit!*" he shouted, turning in a small circle, trying to think.

"Bobbalee ... Bobbalee?"

"What!"

"Harmon's outta town agin'. Be gone ta Tuesday a next week."

He stared at her blankly, his mind struggling with the absence of the van. "What?"

"I said, Harmon's outta town."

"Harmon's outta town? Why the hell do I care? Jesus Christ, Darlene. I got a fuckin' problem here!" Bobby Lee raged. "Why don't you just go in the back room and fuckin' jerk off, or somethin'?" He stomped out the door and back to his cruiser.

Darlene sank to her knees behind the counter and began to cry.

Bobby Lee hit every restaurant and motel in town. Nothing. Goddammit! Now he'd have to get aholt of Colin and give him the bad news. God, he hated to even be around Colin. There was somethin' really wrong with that kid, somethin' kinda girly. And those eyes! Jesus! Chill a fella to the bone. And now that fuckin' van was gone. Colin would be pissed off. There'd go his thousand bucks a month and his occasional shot at Cat. It was a sweet deal. All he had to do was let Colin and them roust all the restaurant and grocery store dumpsters they wanted to, protect them from any local law, and let 'em know if anybody was askin' about 'em. They didn't keep any pigs that he ever saw, and he didn't know where the hell all that shit from the dumpsters went, but who cared? A thousand bucks was a thousand bucks. And Cat. Goddam! Fuck. Tellin' Colin he'd lost the van wasn't high on his list of things he wanted to do. Colin was a little shit, not more'n twenty, twenty two-years old, but there was somethin' about that kid that was scary. Then there was his sidekick, Hambone or something. He was even younger than Colin, but he was a big sono-fabitch! And, there was two or three other fellas he'd glimpsed, but never met. The whole damn set-up gave him the willies. Them folks wasn't normal, livin' the way they did. And the smell! He caught a whiff of sometin' real nasty out there a time or two. Hell, *they* smelled bad! Even Cat, unless she was comin' to visit him, was kinda dirty most of the time. It was like none of 'em ever washed unless they had a real good reason. Fuckin', flabby-ass Florence let herself git pretty rank now and then, but she wasn't never as bad as them folks. He didn't know what went on out there and didn't want to know what went on out there, but he sure was gonna miss that extra cash if the whole deal went south, and he sure hated to tell Colin that that van was gone.

A little after one p.m. Bobby Lee was sitting near the street in the bowling alley parking lot, contemplating his next move, when a black Lincoln passed by, committed an illegal U-turn, and returned to his location. The car pulled in beside his cruiser and the driver's window hummed down. The face that looked out was male, thin, and had a white scar on its chin.

"What the fuck you want?" snarled Bobby Lee.

Green eyes crinkled a bit. "Afternoon, Officer," the man said. "My name is Voorhees. I wonder if I might have a moment of your time?"

At almost that instant, Melvin and Moira were exiting the Buffalo River Scenic Overlook near Pruitt, Arkansas for the fifth time that day. There was a rush of wind when the sliding door opened and closed, and Casey bounced into the rear of the van. Moira screamed and swerved, and Melvin fell back into his seat, gasping.

"Hello, Boys and Girls!" boomed Casey, crackling with energy, his eyes alight and shining. "Are we having a fun day at camp?"

"Jesus H. Christ!" thundered Moira, struggling with control of the van. "What are you trying to do, prove Melvin's fright theory? Why can't you just step out beside the road like a normal person, you idiot! Are you alright? Is everything okay?"

"Food, you toothsome wench! Water for my horses, grog for my men, and then, perhaps, a bit of crumpet for you and me to share as we satisfy more basic appetites!" Casey continued, giving Moira a wet cartoon kiss on the back of her neck. He turned to the passenger seat. "And you, sweet Valiant. Doest thee fair well?"

"I, uh, I'm fine," stammered Melvin, looking at Casey with owlish eyes.

"It is good to find you both well! An inn, Moira m'Lady. We shall eat, and I will apprise you of the events of this day!"

"Christ, Casey!" Moira said, flicking her eyes back and forth between the road and the rearview mirror. "Are you okay?"

Casey grinned. "Just a little too much to drink," he growled.

The hair on her forearms stood up.

They bypassed Pruitt and went north another three or four miles to Marble Falls, stopping, at Casey's insistence, at a Sonic drive-in.

"C'mon, Casey," Moira complained, "I can't eat this junk."

"Terribly unhealthy," Melvin added.

"I need to stay in the truck," Casey said.

After Moira and Melvin each had a grilled cheese and a Coke, and after Casey had consumed three Coney Dogs, three orders of Tater Tots, two helpings of onion rings, a cheeseburger, and something that resembled a purple milkshake, he leaned back in the rear seat and belched.

"That's better," he said. "Drive. Melvin, I want to travel a circular route, twenty to thirty miles across, as close as the existing roads will allow, around the Jasper-Pruitt area. Cat is not here at this time, but I have located from where she left and to where she will return. If I can get a sense of which way she went, perhaps we can make an educated guess as to how she'll come back."

"You know where she lives?" Moira asked.

"Yeah. A miserable little country dump not five miles from where you picked me up. I followed the sheriff there. He'd been in my room and saw Cat's picture. He lit a shuck for the countryside, so I tagged along. Sorry about just running off like that, but I didn't have time to explain. The place has no running water, no electricity except for a generator. I saw two men and scented two or three more. They're all Nosferati. They stink. The place stinks. It's a real hell-hole in more ways than one."

"Whatta ya mean, 'more ways than one?'" Moira asked, afraid of the answer.

"Ah, they keep bleeders there."

"Bleeders?"

"Yeah. People they've taken and not killed. The area is riddled with caves and sinkholes. Great for disposing of bodies. Put a few people in one of the sinkholes where they can't climb out, throw 'em some scraps of food, keep 'em watered, and you've got a permanent blood supply. From what I could tell by circling the place as much as possible without getting upwind, they've got sixty, maybe seventy-five head on hand. The way the ..."

"Head on hand?" Moira said. "*Head on hand?*"

"Yeah. People used for food."

"Christ, Casey, these are human beings! We've got to get them out of there!"

He looked at her for a moment. "Alright, fine. We'll go tomorrow. We'll walk right in there and say, 'C'mon, Guys, these are people, human beings, they have the right to life, liberty, and the pursuit of happiness!' And then I'll be dead and, if you and Melvin aren't, you two will be down in some filthy hole, standing in shit and rotting food, waiting for some foul-smelling kid to drag you out of that mess every couple of weeks, suck a pint or so of your blood out of anywhere, and I mean *any-where* he cares to bite or cut or lacerate, abuse you sexually for a while, then drop you back in that hole again. Chances are overwhelming that you will be terminally diseased within the first couple of hours you're in the place. You might live as long as a month, maybe two, but you will surely die and there is not a goddamned thing medical science can fucking do about it! And, if you don't die, you'll be one of the lucky ones who'll get to drink somebody else's blood for the next few hundred years and create even more misery from the hideous misery we already have on hand. Those poor wretches cannot be saved, Moira. They are absolutely doomed! If I could, I'd shoot 'em all just to get it over with, but I can't. What I can do is use my head and maybe do something that has never, ever been done before. Save one person from life as a Nosferati. One. Just one. What I will not do is get emotionally stupid and charge in there to right a disgusting wrong. I will surely be killed! If I am dead, everybody loses."

Casey ran his hand through his hair. "And excuse the hell out of me if I happen to prefer to think about them as 'head' instead of people. It's a four hundred year habit, a defense mechanism, and the truth. They are not people anymore. They are lost, Moira. They are simply livestock that happens to have once been human and will soon be dead, God rest their souls."

"How is it," she snapped, "that you have this level of understanding and the Nosferati don't?"

"I don't know. I've asked myself that same question a thousand times. Maybe because I worked with the AIDS patients, maybe because I saw it for so many years that it sickened me, maybe because I was human for over forty years to begin with. Nosferati are young. I've never known one older than his mid-twenties who survived when infected."

She glared at him. "Maybe you're just above it all, Casey," she snarled.

A sad smile swept his lips. "Ever known an alcoholic that was above alcohol? A cocaine addict that was above cocaine? It's with me all the time. Sometimes it's not so bad, sometimes it's awful, but it's always there, every minute of every day. Also with me, every minute of every day, are the things I've done because of it. That's the difference between me and the Nosferati, Moira. Not the addiction, not the need.
…

"Regret. Simple regret. And I'm trying to give that to my daughter. Unsatisfied craving and heart tearing regret, in exchange for a life of unparalleled sensation and unrivaled ecstasy. Sound like a fair trade to you? How 'bout to a fourteen-year-old who has done exactly as she has pleased for four hundred years? Seem like a good deal?"

He shook his head and smiled. "Well, it is. It's the best possible deal. If I can work it with her, maybe I can work it with some others. Maybe the stuff Melvin is doing with my blood can help even more people. Maybe some of this will be enough to bring me a little peace when stacked up against all the wrongs I've done in my life, I don't know. But I definitely do know that storming into that camp trying to save a bunch of livestock already irrevocably condemned, and getting myself and you and Melvin killed or worse, ain't the way to go about it. You wanna call the National Guard and have a go at it, be my guest. I'm sure they'll believe you and rush right over. You got that big of a problem with how things are, hit the bricks. Melvin and I have a job to do."

There was dead silence in the truck for a moment as Moira and Casey stared at each other.

"He's right, Moira," Melvin said. "Be quiet."

Casey broke the ensuing quietness. "Melvin! My man!"

155

"You be quiet, too, Casey," Melvin said. "You keep asking us to understand, well you need to understand that you have no conception of how horrible all this is to us. This shakes our world and our faith and our stomachs. You just shut up, too. Now, Moira, drive north on Seven almost to Harrison. We'll take Forty-three southwest through Compton to Ponca, then Boxley, then Twenty-one south. Let's get this circle started. While we travel, Casey, you work on your understanding while Moira works on hers. Then prepare your apologies. And not just to each other. You both owe me one for your atrocious behavior. I'm in this too, you know."

# EIGHTEEN

Feral Joy

THE VAN WAS SILENT almost all the way to the south side of Harrison. When Casey and Moira suddenly began to speak at the same time, Melvin took control.

"I suppose you two are going to argue about who gets to apologize first. That's appropriate, considering your personalities," he said, unsuccessfully attempting to stifle a grin. "Casey, do you freely admit to being an insensitive bastard?"

"I do."

"Fine. Moira do you freely admit to being a boring bitch?"

"Who's boring?" she snapped.

"Good. I pronounce both of you to be suitably contrite and chagrined. Being the single sane occupant of this van, only I am qualified to make that judgment. Our turn onto Highway 43 is coming up, Moira."

"It's almost four o'clock now," Casey said. "Why don't we stop in Harrison for the night? You guys can get some rest, we can charge the cell phones, I can drill some holes, we can re-ice the cooler, and I can pay a midnight visit to the local hospital to replenish our blood supply. This is no time to get caught short."

Late that night, unable to sleep, Melvin heard Casey leave his room. My God. Had things actually come to this? He was a man of science, a doctor, a researcher, a person who valued logic and learning above all else, and here he lay in an Arkansas motel room while his traveling companion, a vampire, went out to steal blood. How could this be? How could he be immersed in such an impossible scenario? To compound the lunacy, he was soon to be a partner in a kidnapping, a flight across state lines, and the incarceration of another human being!

And what if it was not what it seemed? What if Casey was not what he seemed? Melvin had seen the effect that drinking blood had on the man, the light in his eyes, the energy in his body, the change in his personality. It was a frightening transformation. Casey became nearly feral—explainable as a surge of influence from the reptile brain and an emotional response to the rush of power and energy—but the explanation in no way softened the effect. What if Casey was using him and Moira, just availing himself of their resources to find his daughter, so the two of them could be reunited in some disgusting way to re-kindle their relationship as Nosferati? Was it all just pretext?

No. Trusting facts and formula was fine, but sometimes it was necessary to trust a human being, too, even if he was a vampire. Maybe because he was. Besides, their lives were in Casey's hands, just as his was in theirs. He had shown tremendous confidence in both of them, exposing at least some of his abilities and history. Casey would do what he said he would do, or he would die trying. What could be humanly more trustworthy than that?

Casey awakened an hour before sunrise and smelled Moira on his sheets. She'd come in during his deep sleep and spent some time spooning him. Smiling, he luxuriated in the thought for a while before rising.

Dawn came clear and crisp. Some of the trees were beginning to turn with the season and the fifty-degree air was a welcome splash of life. He was standing beside the van when Moira came out of her room. She walked directly to him, put her arms around his neck, and kissed him wonderfully on the lips.

"Good morning," he said when it was over and she'd stepped back a little.

"Good morning," she replied, smiling at him. "I love you," she continued, tears collecting in the bottoms of her eyes. "I just wanted you to know." She turned away and went back into her room. Casey followed.

"Wait a minute," he said. "You can't walk up and lay something like that on me and then just go away!"

"I can't?" she replied, wiping her face with the heel of her hand.

"Hell, no! You're supposed to gaze longingly into my eyes and wait for my reply."

"And that would be?"

"I love you, too," he whispered, his throat closing with emotion.

"Aw, Casey," Moira said, her face twisting and tears running down her cheeks. "Do ya? Do ya, really?"

"Oh, yeah. Really."

She came into his arms then and clung to him for support. He held her and let his own tears run into her hair. They stood that way for some time until she pushed against his chest.

"Lemme go," she snorted, and crossed to a box of tissues on the table. Not looking at him, she blew her nose with gusto.

"Well, that'll call every moose in the county," he said.

She glared at him. "You love me, huh?"

"Yep."

"Casey," Moira said, "we are so fucked."

"One day at a time."

"Oh, shit," she replied, dropping her tissue into the wastebasket and reaching for another.

Lunchtime found them eating pre-packaged sandwiches in the van just south of Mossville, southbound on Highway 21 in yet another Ozark National Forest. Turning left onto Highway 16, a two-lane secondary road, they wound their way surrounded by dense pine and oak woods, passing through Swain, Nail, and Deer, before again encountering Seven, about twenty miles south of Jasper.

"Turn right," Melvin said. "We'll go south to Lurton, and catch One-twenty-three north to Mount Judea."

"No," Casey said. "Pull over and stop."

Melvin and Moira watched as he got out of the van and walked to the edge of the road. Head back, he turned in all directions for a few moments, and then squatted on the shoulder for a time. At length, Casey returned to the van. His face was rigid, his body tense.

"We're right behind her," he said. "She passed through here not more than twenty minutes ago, heading north." Casey reached into the cooler and removed a bag of blood, then checked to make sure he had a cell phone. "Here's the hard part," he continued. "Wait here. When I've got her located, I'll call. If you don't hear from me by dark, head north. Hit the scenic overlook up by Pruitt just like before. I'll find you."

Then he was simply not there anymore.

When Hammond stepped onto the porch, Colin, nude, walked out the door and sat in an old overstuffed chair. "Well?" he said.

"We got us a new player," Hammond replied, making sure not to let his gaze fall anywhere near Colin's gently protruding breasts. There was no point in getting anything started. "He showed up yesterday while I was watchin' Bobby Lee. Introduced himself as Voorhees. Him and Bobby Lee had quite a conversation. Voorhees is lookin' for the people Bobby Lee warned us about. He claims not to know what they're up to, but wants to find out. The two of them had dinner together at Peggy's last night. Bobby Lee talks too much."

"A bit free with his tongue, then?"

"The van is gone. No trace. Bobby Lee's scared. Figures he fucked up. Figures you'll be pissed. Figures he's safer sidin' with Voorhees than tryin' to make up with you," Hammond said.

Colin smiled. "He's a bit balmy."

"He told Voorhees everything he knows about us, where we are, the fact that we were payin' him off, that the van people had a picture of Cat. It's a good thing he didn't know much. Voorhees is familiar with the people in the van, he just doesn't know what they're doing. Guy is slick. Very professional. If he isn't government, he's real close. Got access to a lot of information. Bobby Lee is suckin' up to him like a dirty-kneed whore."

"Gone over, has he?"

"Looks like it to me."

"Can't allow that."

Hammond grinned. "That's what I thought."

"Where's the lad now?"

"That's the interesting part. On the way to the Potts' place."

Colin's eyebrows rose. "Indeed?"

"Voorhees is takin' him out there. The guy is good. We're probably gonna have to deal with him, too."

"One way or another, Love," Colin said, picking up a pair of dirty jeans from the porch floor and slipping his legs into them. "One way or another." He rose and stepped off the porch. "We can be there in less than ten minutes overland. You up for it?"

"Sure. I had a snack before I came to the house."

"Who?"

"Mrs. Potts again. I like the way she squeals."

Colin laughed. "Hammond, Boy-o," he said, "you're a sentimental fool."

"You know these people?" Voorhees asked as he and Bobby Lee stood in the empty kitchen.

"Yeah. Flavel and Aleen Potts. Mid-forties, no kids, keep to themselves. Been livin' out here eight or ten years. Just gone." He looked around. "Wonder what happened to 'em?"

"Something drastic," Voorhees said.

The back door opened. Colin and Hammond stepped into the room. A Beretta appeared in Voorhees' hand. "Hello," he smiled. "And who would you two be?"

"Shit," croaked Bobby Lee, the color draining from his face.

"We'd be the lads that Sheriff Sharp has been tellin' you about," Colin said, ignoring the pistol. "Constable, why don't you wait outside while I speak with Mr. Voorhees, Love. Break his feet, Hammond. He abused my trust."

Very quickly and with casual indifference, Hammond kicked Bobby Lee in both insteps. The sheriff screamed and fell thrashing to the floor. The big man picked him up by the belt and tossed him through the screen into the backyard. The screaming stopped when he hit the ground.

A veteran of violence, Voorhees was stunned. He backed up a step and tightened his grip on the Beretta. The world seemed to be rushing by him at breakneck speed.

Colin smiled. "I'll have your weapon now," he said. "This is a friendly conversation."

There was a flicker of movement and Colin was holding the gun while Voorhees clutched at a broken finger.

"Christ!" Voorhees shouted, leaning back against the wall, waiting for his blood pressure to rise.

"I'm your savior now, Bucko," Colin said, "if ya want one. I can give ya more than you can imagine, or take away everything ya have. It'll be a decision of your own makin'. Sorry about your lovely finger. Let me offer amends."

He raised the Beretta and, laughing, shot himself through the back of his left hand. The shock of the explosion reverberated off the walls, the bullet and pieces of bloody bone splattered on the floor. Voorhees flinched but held his ground. Colin crossed to him and held the ruined hand in front of his face.

"Look at it," he said.

Holding on to his composure, Voorhees peered at the hand. Over the space of forty-five seconds, he watched the wound repair itself.

"My God," he breathed.

"Very nearly," Colin said leaning back against a kitchen counter top. "I am two-hundred and thirty-seven years old," he said. "I don't get sick, I don't catch cold, and major wounds are a minor inconvenience. I can run faster than your car. I can see in the dark, I have the nose of a bloodhound, and can hear a pocket watch tick two hundred yards away. So can Hammond. So can others in my group. You have information and contacts that I need. For your help, I am prepared to be your friend. Could you use a friend like me?"

"Certainly," Voorhees said, as Bobby Lee began to moan and swear in the rear yard.

"Right. Then we'll have a nice long chat and establish some rules for our relationship. But first," he continued, handing Voorhees back his Beretta, "go put a stop to that noise."

"With pleasure," Voorhees smiled, his broken finger all but forgotten.

"I thought so," said Colin.

As soon as he was safely out of sight of the van, Casey stopped and drank most of the blood in the bag. He gave himself over to it for a moment, then urinated and began to move rapidly north, parallel to the road. In only about two miles, he encountered the pick-up truck on a logging road. Leaning against the front bumper was a longhaired young man. Damn! In the distance Casey could hear conversation and laughing. Fading back farther into the woods, he moved in that direction. Another mile brought him to a picnic area that was deserted except for a small group of four or five young college age men, drinking beer and giggling around an open fire near one of the pavilions. Again, he pulled well back into the trees and began moving south toward the location of the truck. He pulled out the cell phone.

"Hello?"

"I found her partner and I found her prey. She's got to be someplace between them." Casey's voice was hard and edgy.

"Okay," came Moira's nervous reply.

"North of you four or five miles, on Seven, right at the edge of the woods, is one of those Government supported picnic areas. That's where she's headed. I'm on the way to deal with the guy she's left by her vehicle. Then I'll try to intercept her before she gets to the kids."

"I understand."

"In thirty minutes, head for that picnic area. No sooner. I've got to get there before you do."

"Okay."

"I'll leave my cell phone and most of my clothes by the edge of the road at the entrance to the park. Pick them up, willya?"

"Will do. You be careful, Casey."

"Yeah."

"No … wait," Moira said. "Screw careful! You do what you have to do, the way you have to do it, whatever it is. I love you and I want you back."

"Hell of a woman, Flynn. I love you, too. See ya in a half an hour."

Shit. She had a kid with her, and he had to be another Nosferati. That complicated matters. Without question, Casey had to take him out, and he had to give the boy no chance at all. Casey might have some use for him, actually. He needed a real jump on Cat. The young man could provide that edge, but it was dangerous. Hell, it would probably be fatal. But he needed it to confront Cat.

Retracing his path through the woods, Casey encountered an abandoned area that had been fenced in five foot steel posts and electric wire. Carrying a post pulled from the ground and a coiled length of thin wire, he moved silently through the trees. A few moments brought him again in sight of the pickup truck and the young Nosferati pacing beside it.

In spite of the acuteness of their senses, because they are predator and not prey, Nosferati are prone to be a bit complacent. A human could not have approached Cat's companion without being discovered, but Casey was another matter. He was no more than thirty yards away as he watched the man step in front of a Red Oak to urinate. Carefully and quietly, Casey moved to within twenty feet of the young man and raised the fencepost to hold it beside his ear as a lance. When the boy was zipping his fly, Casey's arm flashed forward.

The fence post entered the Nosferati's back just to the left of his spine, passed through his body, and buried itself nearly twelve inches into the tree. Directly behind it, the length of wire in his hands, came Casey. Once over the head with the wire in crossed hands and pull. Casey's strength forced the wire deeply into the flesh of both his fists, blood flowing down his forearms. The young man's severed head bounced to the ground, his body still held erect by the fencepost stuck in the tree. It was over in less than five seconds. Somewhere between revulsion and elation, and throwing caution completely to the winds, Casey plunged his face into the severed neck and drank.

He soared. Nothing had ever been like this. The blood of a Nosferati so far surpassed that of a human that Casey was transported into a world of sensory appreciation unlike anything he had ever dreamed. He drank the blood to give himself an edge over Cat, so that he might be able to restrain her without either of them suffering severe injury, but this, *this* was Nirvana! For long moments, it held him in its grasp, suspending him somewhere between heaven and earth. When it released him, he lay on his side soaked in his own urine, his hands healed, his heart full. Urgently he clambered to his feet. Cat! He had to get to Cat. Instantly he knew exactly where she was, sauntering down the drive in that picnic area, still two hundred yards from her intended victims. Repressing a howl of feral joy, feeling the world in crystalline colors and flint-sharp scents, Casey laid back his ears and ran.

"Well, howdy there, Ma'am," the young man said when he saw Cat walking toward their fire. "Just how can we help you?"

Standing, arms akimbo, in Levi short shorts and a black t-shirt, Cat let a slow grin drip on the men for a moment.

"I though maybe you boys would share your fire. Just look at all my goose bumps. Think you guys could warm me up?"

A slightly embarrassed chuckle spread through the group as Cat walked to the fire and stood next to it, feet spread, rubbing her thighs.

"Ooo," she said. "Now doesn't that feel good?"

She turned and presented her backside to the blaze.

"Damn!" one of the young men exclaimed.

Cat spread her legs apart, slowly caressed her bottom, and chuckled.

"Anybody wanna help restore my circulation?"

Taking the initiative, the first young man spoke again.

"My," he said. "Just whose little girl are you?"

"Mine," came a growl from behind them, and Casey, his nostrils full of the succulent odor of human flesh and wearing only urine soaked blue jeans, stepped out of the trees.

Cat stared for a moment, her mouth open, then laughed.

"Hello, *Father*," she sneered. "My goodness it's just been ages! How ya been?"

# NINETEEN

CASEY COULD BARELY TAKE HIS EYES OFF HIS DAUGHTER. The familiar scent of her washed over him like liquid flame. Physically, she looked exactly the same, as if weeks had passed instead of over a hundred-and-fifty years. The Nosferati blood sang in his system, and from the edges of his eyes he saw multiple overlaid images of her surging up from his memory, glimpses of Cat as a baby, a child, a girl. Other scenes of times they had not spent together—seen through different eyes—scrolled before him, all wrapped in flickering ribbons of emotional and spiritual color.

Sensing his conflicting emotions, Cat licked her lips and smiled. "What do you see, *Father?*"

His heart pounded. "I see you, Cat. As you are, as you have been, and as you might come to be."

"What brings you to the wilds of Arkansas, little old me?" She pouted coquettishly, the tip of her index finger against her chin.

"You," Casey replied through clenched teeth, struggling to stay in the current reality. "I needed to see you. I want to talk to you."

Casey's blood roared in his ears. The smell of humans was distracting and the van was coming. He could feel it.

Amused by his discomfort, Cat went on. "Ah. Is it finally time for the important daddy-daughter chat, *Father?* Gonna tell me about the birds and the bees, *Father?* Gonna make sure I'm a good girl, *Father?* Gonna do your daddy duty, *Father?* Isn't that sweet? Fuck you." She laughed. "I was about to have a snack. You're in the way."

"We need to talk, Cat," Casey said, holding his elbows to quell the trembling in his arms.

"No, *you* need to talk," she snorted. "I don't need to talk. I've gotten along fine without you for a long time. Why should I clutter up my life with some sentimental old fool?"

"Hey!" one of the kids spoke up. "She doesn't want anything to do with you, Mister. Fuck off!"

Cat laughed. "Oh, save me, please!" she said, grasping at a potential diversion. "Help! Help!"

The entire group of students got to their feet. They looked confused. Casey singled out the one who had spoken. He could see the boy's veins pulsing beneath his skin, smell his fear, almost taste him. Reality returned with an audible rush. Food was right there. *Right there!*

"You are about to make the mistake of your life, Son," Casey hissed, red flickering through his vision as he sought to maintain control.

"Oh yeah? Just who the fuck do you think you are?"

"I'm the Boogey Man," Casey rumbled, walking slowly toward the lad, "and I am about to de-bone a couple of you stupid shits."

Cat yawned. "Help. Save me."

"Goddammit, Cat," Casey spat, fighting to rein himself in, "let it go! There's no reason for these kids to get hurt."

"How 'bout fun, *Father?* Fun's a good reason. A little blood on the moon? C'mon guys," she pleaded, turning her attention back to the boys and giggling. "There's five of you and only one of him. Kick his ass and we'll party. I'll blow every one of ya! Save me, oh, save me."

The group drew together, the young men seeking strength and purpose from each other, and began to move in Casey's direction.

"Aw, shit," Casey said, resisting his need to shred a few of them. Trembling from the scent of so many humans, he crossed to the fire, reached into the flames, and picked up two handfuls of coals.

"Yeah, c'mon you snot-nosed little pussies," he said, his fingers and palms sizzling. "Kick my ass."

The entire group pulled back.

"C'mon, *Boys*," he continued, rubbing the red-hot coals across his chest and stomach, the scent of his scorching flesh wafting through the air, "let's play!"

"Jesus!" yelled one of the kids. All five of the young men bolted, running from the pavilion and across a gravel parking lot to their waiting vehicles. Curses and slamming doors echoed across the clearing, and their cars tore off down the road leaving Casey and Cat alone.

"You win, *Father!*" Cat teased, pursing her lips. "Want your blow job now?"

"Cat, stop it."

"Maybe some lickety-split?" she asked, scratching her crotch.

"Cat!"

"Hungry? How 'bout we split a three-year-old for old time's sake?"

"Catherine, listen to me."

"*Catherine, listen to me*," she whined. "Kiss my ass, *Father*. I listened to you for over two hundred years! You left *me*, remember? You ran out on *me*, remember? Maybe I looked for *you!* Maybe I missed *you!*"

"Did you?"

Cat grinned. "Naw. I'm just fuckin' with ya," she said sinking to her backside by the fire. "Speaking of fuckin' with ya, want some pussy, *Father?* Piece a ass just like the good old days?" She leaned back and spread her knees.

Trembling with the effort of controlling the Nosferati within him, Casey looked down at her. "Would you really like to know what I want, Catherine?"

165

"God, yes!" she said. "What you want means more to me than anything in the whole wide world!"

"I want you to come with me. I want you to come with me to a place where you can get your mind back, where you can come to understand what has happened to you, where you can break your addiction and see your life for what it is, and for what it can become."

"Ha."

"I mean it, Cat," Casey nearly moaned, empathy clawing its way through his blood rush. "Whether I am in it or not, I want your life to be yours. I want you to be able to make choices based on understanding instead of addiction. I want you to know what you are and what you can be."

She looked at him for a moment and the mocking grin fell away.

"Christ. You're serious aren't you?" she said.

He knelt in front of her, tears welling in his eyes.

"Aye, Kitten. I really am. I know what it's like. I'll help you through it."

Cat stared into the fire for a moment, then raised her eyes to his, reaching out and touching his cheek with her finger.

"Suck my dick, *Father*!" she laughed. The van came crunching up the gravel drive.

Casey turned toward the truck and extended a hand, palm out. The van stopped about sixty feet away.

"Oh goodie," Cat said, clapping her hands. "You brought dinner!"

"They're friends of mine."

"Human friends?"

"Human friends."

Cat laughed. "How low you have fallen," she said, rising to her feet. "Fucking the livestock now, *Father*? Humping the sheep? A little lip, a little dip, a little sip? Let me have a look at these piggies."

Suddenly she was past him. Casey caught her arm as she reached the van door and pulled her away.

"Oooh! Fast! You haven't lost a step, have ya? Pretty quick for an old man. By the way, where's Michael?"

Casey looked at her.

"I see," she said. "Just as well. He wasn't much. Had performance anxiety even when he'd just fed. Loyal though. A lot like a dog. Shit!" She looked at him and grinned through her revelation. "You *drank* him, didn't you? You drank Michael!"

Casey continued to stare at her.

"*Wheeee*! I bet that's a rush! You're just breaking all kinds of rules, aren't you? God! I can't believe this! Hey, Michael!" She laughed and peered at Casey. "You in there, limp dick? Hello?"

Cat looked at the ground for a moment, slowly shaking her head.

"Jesus Christ," she muttered, then raised her eyes back to Casey. "Talk about split personality! You have got to be *so* cranked!" she grinned. "Wow. *Father*, can I ask you a question?"

"What?"

"Can Mikey come out and play?"

Casey clenched his fists. "Stop it, Cat," he hissed.

"And who have we got here in this truck?" she went on, peering in the side window. "Ooh, look! Real live human beans! Do they know what you are, Father? Ha! I bet you don't even know for sure right now, do ya?"

"Jesus, Cat," Casey whispered, shaking his head.

"And you even brought a lady friend! Nice tits. Fucking the redhead, *Father?* Moo! Get her out here and let me have a look at her nipples. Maybe she could be my brand new mommy!"

Casey fought the serrated edge of anger that tore through him.

"Cat, please!"

"*Cat, please ... Cat, please!* Eat shit, you pathetic Motherfucker!" she snarled. "Eat *her* shit, for all I care, but just stay the fuck away from me!"

She darted toward the tree line, Casey in pursuit.

Casey was at a disadvantage, in spite of his intake of Nosferati blood. Even though he was faster and stronger than Cat, he had to expend a great deal of energy to hold his temper in check. Plus, it was not his desire to maim his own child. He also had to exercise a certain amount of physical restraint. Cat suffered no such inhibitions. He closed with her several times, from the earth to the treetops, each time withdrawing, wounded and bleeding, rather than cause her permanent injury. She bit, she clawed, she kicked, and all he could do was attempt to restrain her. She could not escape, he could not win. The battle raged.

Moira and Melvin, now standing outside the van, saw bits and pieces of the fight, especially the running engagement up in the trees. Cat's shrieks and curses occasionally reached their ears, and Moira trembled as she leaned against the truck. Melvin opened the rear doors, raised the lid on the casket, and began fussing in his big silver briefcase. Suddenly, the noise stopped. From the far side of the picnic grounds, Casey came jogging toward the truck, a limp Cat under his arm. Panting and covered in blood from a dozen or more wounds, he was no more than thirty feet from the van when Cat struck.

She whirled from under his arm, wrapped her legs about his torso and her arms about his neck, sank her teeth deep into the flesh below the left side of his jaw, and began to chew. The assault drove Casey to his knees, his head thrown back, his teeth clenched in pain. He tried to peel her off, but she wouldn't come, locked as she was about him. He struggled briefly, then fell to his back, Cat still attached and gnawing at his neck. As Moira watched in horror, a third party joined the battle.

With a keening cry, Melvin launched himself at the pair, landing on Cat's back and plunging a massive hypodermic into the rear of her upper left thigh. Cat screeched and swung an arm backwards, catching Melvin in the right side of his ribcage. He inscribed a tumbling arc in the air, landed ten feet from the truck, and lay still. Panting, the girl raised herself from the still form of her father. She saw Melvin where he lay and lurched toward his broken body. Moira reached into the driver's floorboard, lifted out her .45, and pointed it at Cat.

"No," she said.

Cat smiled, turning toward Moira and wiping blood from her chin and throat. "What the fuck do you think you're going to do with that?"

"This," Moira said, and fired three shots into Cat's chest.

The girl staggered backward a step, lost her balance, and sat heavily on the ground. A confused expression crossed her face and she picked at one of the wounds for a moment.

"Fucking cow," she muttered to herself, shaking her head. "Shoot the daughter, fuck the father. Not when I'm done. Not when I'm finished." Her unfocused eyes searched for Moira and found her. "You fucking twat!" Cat hissed, rising to one knee. "Time for a little lesson, Sweetie!"

Moira shot her twice more.

Cat fell back on one elbow and ran her hand over the blood on her chest. "Goddammit! Quit it!" she shouted, rocking forward and getting to one knee, spitting red saliva onto the dirt. She glowered at Moira from under tensed brows. "I'm gonna turn you inside out, Bitch. Split you like a fucking *chicken*!"

Weaving from side to side, she placed a hand on the ground for balance. "I'm gonna eat your liver, you miserable cunt! I'm gonna ..." A quizzical expression crossed her face, and Cat fell to her side, eyes open, quivered, and then lay still.

Moira approached her body and prodded it with a toe. There was no reaction. She turned to Melvin and found Casey kneeling beside him. Blood bubbled from Melvin's nose and his lips were blue.

"Deep shock," she said, dropping to the ground and taking Melvin's wrist. "Cyanotic. Probably got a badly punctured lung." She turned to Casey. "How are you?"

"Healing. Put Cat in the casket. Lock it tight. Leave Melvin to me."

"Cat's dead."

"Do as you're told!" Casey snarled, "and keep the hell away from me. Don't give up your gun. You may still need it."

Startled, Moira took a backward step as she rose and nearly fell. Casey leaned over Melvin, put his hands on the smaller man's chest, and concentrated. Trembling from what she'd seen in Casey's eyes, Moira dragged Cat to the rear of the van and boosted her body into the casket, closing the lid over the small form and securing all eight screw locks as tightly as she could. When she returned to the front of the van, she saw Melvin lying on his back and rubbing his right side. Casey was gone.

She kneeled beside Melvin and put a hand on his cheek. "How ya doin'?"

"Just had the wind knocked out of me, I guess," Melvin said, struggling into a sitting position. "That young woman is very strong!"

"Melvin," Moira said, shaking her head, "you were as good as dead. You were respirating and aspirating blood, cyanotic, and in deep shock. A trauma unit couldn't have helped you. You very probably saved Casey's life tonight. He certainly saved yours."

"Oh, my!"

"What was in the syringe?"

"Animal tranquilizer," he replied, dusting off his clothes as Moira helped him to his feet. "Enough to knock down about three rhinos. I have an old classmate that works at the zoo. Where's Casey's daughter?"

"In the box. Locked tight. I shot her five times after you injected her. She's dead, I'm afraid. Casey made me put her in the casket anyway while he worked on you."

"Where's Casey?" Melvin asked, creaking around in small circles.

"Out here, more or less," came a rasp from the trees. "I can't come in right now. I can't get too close to either of you. I'm too far gone to be trustworthy. You've got a fire, you've got wood, you've even got abandoned beer. It'll be dusk soon. Spend the night. I'm going away until I settle down a little. Keep the casket closed."

Moira put some wood on the fire and got a couple of extra layers of clothing out of their bags. She and Melvin sat by the blaze until after moonset, saying very little and staring into the flames. Finally, Melvin curled up on the rear seat of the van as Moira stretched out on a picnic table and covered up with the tarp that had been over the casket.

Just before dawn, Melvin awoke with a start. He listened carefully but heard nothing. His bladder, straining under the load of the three beers he'd consumed, demanded release. He stepped around behind the van. Sheltered from a sleeping Moira by its shadow and the open rear doors, he relieved himself. After zipping up, he sat on the bumper for a moment and yawned.

*"Help!"*

The cry was so muffled and muted that, at first, he wasn't sure he'd heard anything.

*"Please ... help. I can't breathe!"*

A chill ran down his back, and Melvin whirled to stare at the casket. He leaned into the rear of the van and listened intently. In a moment the voice came again.

*"For the love of God, I'm suffocating! I can't breathe. Help me, please! There's no air! Please help! I can't breathe, I can't breathe!"*

"Oh, my!" Melvin whispered, and began to struggle with the nearest screw lock. "Hold on!" he said. "Hold on!"

The world spun as his shirt tightened about his neck and he was lifted off his feet through the van's rear doors. His glasses came loose and he was looking into Casey's blurred face, six inches from his own.

"Now you listen to me, little man," Casey growled, his breath rank and feted from the Nosferati's blood. "If you do not do exactly as you are told, I will hang you by your feet from the nearest tree. This is a very bad time to hassle me, Melvin. Do you understand?"

Pedaling in the air, Melvin attempted to nod against the choking collar.

"You will *not* open that box for any reason. You will *not* tamper with the latches. You will *not* attempt to give its occupant additional air. You will *not* do these things because I am telling you *not* to do these things. Are we absolutely clear on all this, human?"

Again, still pedaling, Melvin attempted to nod.

"Good," hissed Casey, lowering the struggling man to the earth. He took a deep breath and shook his head. His face softened. "I can't be near humans right now. I'll be back in a couple of hours. Then we'll leave." In a blink, he was gone.

Rubbing his neck and wheezing, Melvin pawed around on the ground until he found his glasses.

"Melvin?" said a sleepy Moira from over on the table. "I thought I heard something. Everything alright?"

"J-just fine, Moira," he stammered. "Uh, Casey came by. He says we'll leave in a couple of hours. You can go back to sl-sleep."

"Okay," came the muffled reply.

Melvin, still rubbing his neck and breathing raggedly through his mouth, sat back down on the bumper and tried to collect himself. Again the muted voice came from the casket.

*"Help!"*

"My ass," Melvin muttered and closed the doors.

# TWENTY

### Woman's Wasted Wit

WHEN MOIRA AWOKE AGAIN, it was a couple of hours after daybreak. Groaning her way out from under the tarp and off the cold picnic table, she limped off toward a public restroom. Walking back, attempting to pluck the tangles from her thick auburn hair, she noticed Melvin squatting as he poked at the nearly dead fire.

"Morning, Melvin," she smiled, stepping to him and rubbing his left shoulder. "How are you?"

"Fine," he said. "Actually, more than fine. I haven't felt this good in years. I feel very rested and alert. I have no aches and pains at all."

"That makes one of us," Moira grumbled. "I need coffee."

"We have beer," Melvin said.

"Great. I'll use it to brush my teeth. Seen Casey?"

"Not since he stopped by early this morning."

Casey, shirtless and covered in dried blood and wood ash, walked up from the trees in their direction. Moira started to go to him, but something in his carriage and body language stopped her. Puzzled and apprehensive, she watched him come. He stopped about twenty feet away and looked at her. His eyes smoldered.

"You look like shit," she said, tossing a t-shirt at him. "Use this for a rag and clean up at the water fountain over there."

Casey didn't seem to notice the shirt when it hit him in the chest and fell to the ground. He blinked and looked around for a moment, as if seeing his surroundings through a fog, then bent over and retrieved the shirt. His face flickered with various emotions while he silently walked to the fountain and began to wash. His bitter laugh bounced off the distant trees.

Casey had spent the night with memories of Cat. Playing with her as a child, teaching her about the forge, watching her run through the English grass and flowers, holding her squirming, warm little body, and kissing her dirty face. He laughed with her as a youth, worried about her impetuousness and lack of fear.

He watched her bloom and blossom, after they came to the new world, struggling with his concern as she approached womanhood. He watched her die after the attack and willed himself to join her, for there was nothing left for which to live.

He was there again as she brought him fresh blood to drink for three days after his re-birth—teasing him, toying with him, finally luring him out into the world—teaching him to kill and then to feed on his victims. He watched her welcome the bloody life and find her joy in it, her passion, her need. Even when he tore himself away from her and returned to the village in a futile attempt to live a normal existence, she wouldn't leave him. Again he saw her blatant walk as she approached the smith, again he felt her warm breath coaxing him to return to the blood, again he saw the villagers massed at his forge, demanding he turn his daughter over to them, hearing their screams of accusation. Again, he saw Cat leap into a tree, stand on a swaying branch, spit on the mob, and laugh at their calls of "Witch!" Then he fled with her—back to the blood—and it was she who led, she who controlled. It was her body holding him, her tongue caressing him, her hands comforting him. Cat lost herself to the blood, and he lost himself to her.

Through the night, Casey traveled with Cat back to the Virginias and the Carolinas, to the Indian wars and the war of Revolution, to the expanding frontier and back again, feeding as they went, wrapped up in the life, caught up in the blood. He and she returned to Chicago during the night and the buffet of victims, finding other Nosferati, kindred lost souls who understood the need and the joy.

Recollections other than his own swirled about him as swallows in the wind. Submerged in Michael's memory, he remained immersed in Cat. Cat laughing at him when he couldn't perform. Cat teasing him with her hands as they rode a motorcycle. Cat throwing the bloody body of a young boy out a window at him as he stood beside a house. Cat rubbing him and licking him and slapping him and cursing him and exciting him and humiliating him. Cat touching herself as he watched afraid to move and break the spell. Cat telling him to wait with the truck while she collected dinner. Cat, not there when the horrific pain seared through his back and chest, when he was nailed to a tree, when darkness closed in as a wire tightened about his neck.

All that with thousands of repetitions flowed and raged and twisted and ripped through Casey during the night. All that writhed inside him as he stood, washing the blood and grit from his body. A cacophony of images surrounded him as he walked to the fire and gazed down at Moira.

Feeling a chill, she looked up at him. "Casey?"

His eyes actually seemed to glow. "Your wit is wasted on me, woman!" he spat. "You are the cause of this abomination! You are the author of this travesty! Because of you, *she* is dead. You will not survive her long!"

He grasped Moira by the front of her sweatshirt and yanked her to her feet. She gasped and struck at him, but the blows were as butterfly wings and he didn't notice. He clutched at her hair and forced her head back, exposing her neck.

"*Casey!*" she screamed, uselessly flailing at him. "*Casey!*"

His teeth touched her throat.

In desperation, Melvin swung a piece of firewood across Casey's back. "*Michael!*" he roared.

The figure dropped Moira to the ground and swung to face the little man.

"Cat is alive, Michael," Melvin said, taking a step backwards and dropping his club. "She's alive!"

172

Confusion flickered over Casey's face.

"Michael, listen to me," Melvin begged. "Listen to me! Cat is alive, but you are not. You are the one who is dead. You! You're dead, Michael. Dead! You're free now. For God's sake, just let go! Let go, Michael," Melvin pleaded. "Let go."

Casey's shoulders dropped, and he placed both hands to his head.

"Oh, Jesus," he said. "Did I hurt anybody?"

"Not quite," Melvin replied.

Moira got to her feet. "Casey?" she said reaching for his cheek.

"Touch me not!" he choked. "Spare me your hands or suffer at mine!"

"No," said Melvin, "absolutely not. I am going to give you an injection, Casey. It is going to allow you to sleep for a while."

"Keep your needles away from me, Human," Casey threatened.

"I am going to give you this injection so Moira and I can return to Kansas City with your daughter and be safe from you," Melvin went on, pressing to keep the momentum as he held out a syringe. "And you have two options. You can take this shot, or you can kill me. Do you want to kill me, Casey?"

Tears leapt to Casey's eyes.

"Hold on to that thought," Melvin said, slipping the needle into Casey's bicep. "Sorry, no alcohol. Infection isn't a major concern, though, is it?"

Ten minutes later they'd loaded Casey's inert body in the back of the van, laying him carefully down beside his daughter's casket. When they sat down in the front seats, Moira stared blankly out the dusty windshield. "He nearly killed me, Melvin," she whispered.

"No," Melvin sighed. "That other Nosferati, Michael, nearly killed you. The one that Cat said Casey drank. He's the one. Not Casey. Never Casey."

"Melvin, this is crazy!"

"In many ways."

"I mean we have two fucking vampires in the back of this truck! One that I shot five times, and another that just tried to kill me! And I got you involved. ... Why? Why am I here?"

"Because you are the nexus of all this," Melvin replied. "Because you are the only one who could have pulled this together. You're the only one dedicated enough, strong enough to make all this happen and see it through. You are a person of tremendous strength, Moira, a person of *real* power."

They sat in silence. At length Moira seemed to pull back from the edge of the abyss. "Oh, Lord," she sighed, rubbing her dirty face with both hands. "What am I doing in this mess?"

Melvin reached out and put a hand on her arm. Moira jerked at his touch, then turned to face him. "You are doing what you promised you would," he said. "In spite of the fact that it is hard, in spite of the fact that it is dangerous. You are doing it anyway. You are being brave, Moira, brave for the purest of all reasons."

She raised an eyebrow in inquiry.

"Love," Melvin said. "Now start the truck."

THE BUMBLEBEE SETTLED ON HER ARM and waddled around. She stared at it, feeling the press of its tiny feet, not afraid of its sting. The greatest fear of her young life had come to pass the evening before, and she had survived it. She was fresh out of fear, standing on that grassy hillside, the aspen rattling on the slope high above her, wildflowers splashing at her feet. Bobby. Sean Robert Flynn—her brother, her friend, her teaser, her tormenter and teacher, the single biggest influence in her life and the person she most dearly loved above all others—was dead. She could not weep, she could not rage, she could not scream. All she could do was endure. Moira Marie Flynn was twelve years old, and life had dealt her the cruelest blow possible. Never again would she see his eyes, or feel his smile, or hear his laugh. Bobby was gone, and she couldn't go with him.

She sat beside him when he died, and it wasn't like the movies. There was no moment of truth or heart rending declaration, no shining instant when he'd received clarity or been blessed with peace. Her mother had gone to the kitchen to get some more chipped ice for his parched mouth; her father had stepped outside to make sure the front gate was latched. Bobby, eyes closed and breathing shallowly, had waited for the instant they were alone. His breath stopped, his already emaciated body seemed to sink into the bed and grow smaller, and he was gone. For the first time in her life, there wasn't a Bobby. She didn't know what to do with that.

On her way through the kitchen to the back door—to go sit on the tire swing and think about it all—she turned to her mother, chipping ice in the sink. "It's over," she said, and went outside.

Cars came and went, an ambulance arrived and departed, but she didn't go back in the house. Later, well after it got dark, her father came out and stood beside her. He rubbed her back for a moment. They didn't speak. Moira Marie Flynn stayed on that tire swing for the rest of the long night, imagining a world without Bobby. The next morning, she climbed the hill partway to see if things looked any different. Down in the valley, Glenwood Springs appeared to be the same, but it wasn't. Bobby wasn't around anymore.

She couldn't help him. Nobody could help him. Bobby was so smart. When he graduated from high school at age seventeen and decided to take a year off before college, nobody suspected what would happen. He wanted to be out in the world a little, he said. He'd work and live in Denver for a year. The scholarships would still be waiting. He just needed to be on his own for a while. He moved, got a job, came home every weekend for the first month or two. Then he stopped coming home, only called every couple of weeks. When he finally did come back for Christmas, he'd lost weight and seemed nervous and jumpy, then he'd just go sleep for a few hours and be fine. It went like that the whole five days he was home. Something was wrong with Bobby. She knew it. He wasn't the same. He never would be.

The addiction almost killed him. For a year and a half, he stayed in Denver, finally living on the streets and stealing to support his habit. That's how her mom and dad found out about the drugs. Bobby was arrested. They paid his bail and got him in a treatment clinic to dry out. There they found out he had AIDS. Thanks to Moira's efforts on the Internet and the education she gave her parents, Bobby came home.

For almost two years, Moira watched Sean Robert Flynn die. AIDS became her passion. She studied more at home than she ever did at school. She found out how it worked, why it worked. She dedicated herself to her brother and the disease that was killing him. Tirelessly, she went to school, she cared for Bobby, and she studied. A realist, even in her pre-teen years, she knew she could do nothing for Bobby but love him. People were people; they did what they did. Bobby didn't have to take drugs and share needles, but he chose to. That was fact. People did stupid things. She worked for all the little sisters so they wouldn't have to watch their brothers die. She worked for the children, so they would not have to go through what she was going through. Without a formal declaration or even a passing realization, her life's path was charted by the time Moira Marie Flynn was eleven years old. She had dedicated herself without even knowing what that meant.

She was twelve when Bobby died. On the day of the funeral, when everyone was stopping by the house after the burial, Moira was in her room on the computer, learning. When she graduated from high school, she already had over thirty hours of college credit in courses relating to communicable disease and epidemiology. College itself was a blur. She worked constantly, took little time for a social life and, despite an abundance of offers, dated seldom. Nobody measured up to Bobby. She knew Bobby was just an excuse, but she drew him like a gun and kept entanglement at bay.

After college, medical school. After medical school, even more graduate studies and classes. She was twenty-eight when she went to work for the World Health Organization. Twenty-nine when the big Ebola outbreak hit, thirty-one when she left the WHO and was snapped up by the Proteus Trust. Her time in Zaire and Somalia put her on an intimate basis with pain and suffering and made her aware of her own limitations. She didn't scare, she didn't give up, and she didn't back down. Moira knew what she was doing, knew where she was going, and had never been sidetracked for an instant. Then she met Casey.

Here was a man who had survived an infection much more deadly than that which had killed Bobby, deadlier even than Ebola. Here was a man with an addictive condition under conscious control. Here was a man who was—because of his very addiction and the survival of its cause—immune to communicable disease. Here was a man with twelve strands of DNA who was over four hundred years old. Here was a man who—with everything to lose—trusted her to not betray him, who saw something in her that she had never seen in anyone besides her brother. Here was a man who was ready to trust her with the life of his addicted daughter, a child she had attempted to kill. Here was a man who professed to love her and who could—but would not—endanger her life with that love.

Moira Marie Flynn knew what to do with that: love him back and ask Melvin Foltz for help.

# TWENTY-ONE

Grizzly

MELVIN AND MOIRA HAD BEEN DRIVING for nearly twelve hours when Casey opened his eyes and felt the movement of the van. For a moment, he didn't realize where he was. Conversation from the front seats cleared the drug fog from his brain.

"We're going to have to try and wake him up in a little while," Moira said. "I hope he's okay."

"It's a miracle he's even alive," Melvin confessed. "While you were in the building at the last rest stop, I checked. Respirations shallow and normal, at least for him. Around twelve a minute. Heart a little under forty."

"That's low."

"Not for Casey it isn't. God, Moira. I gave him well over twice the amount of tranquilizer I gave the girl. It would have literally killed a couple of elephants. Amazing. I just hope Michael is gone."

"Maybe we should check him again," Moira said.

Casey smiled into the dimness for a moment as the van grew silent, then sat up in his position beside Cat's casket and looked toward the front seats. It was not quite full dark. Moira and Melvin were silhouetted against the horizon and the headlights of oncoming cars. "Are we there yet?" he asked.

Moira squeaked and the van swerved. "Goddammit, Casey!" she shouted.

"Just passing Independence," Melvin gulped, turning to look at him. "You okay?"

"I think so. I'm sure better." He yawned. "Geeze," he went on, "Sorry about everything. I feel like a ..."

"Jesus Christ, Casey!" Moira blurted, struggling to keep her eyes on the road and the van straight. "I shot your daughter! Did my level best to kill her. Would've if I could've."

"And I hit you with a chunk of firewood and injected you with a fatal dose of animal tranquilizer," Melvin said.

"God, what a couple of assholes!" Casey said. "You two are off my Christmas card list."

"I'm Jewish," Melvin replied.

176

"I worship Satan," Moira said, relaxing with Casey's acceptance of her confession. "That's why I get along with you."

"Thanks," Casey replied.

"Yeah, yeah, yeah," Moira muttered. Melvin smiled. Casey could smell their relief.

They were quiet for a few miles. Then Melvin spoke up. "About releasing your daughter into the facility," he said. "That could be a bit awkward. We're going to have to subdue her somehow."

"Another injection would be difficult," Casey said. "She'll be on her guard and very pissed. If she got loose, there'd be hell to pay."

"We have a gas system in place in that lab," Melvin said. "It, however, is not designed to tranquilize. It is designed to kill."

"What is it?"

"It's similar to Halon gas. It replaces oxygen, and the victim has nothing to breathe. Very effective, pretty fast, easy to work with. The techs would just use small tanks of air and masks until the blowers had dissipated the gas. Not poisonous by itself."

"So if Cat didn't know it was coming …"

"It would be too late. After she'd inhaled it, holding her breath would be moot. The oxygen in her lungs would be gone, and since the natural instinct is to gasp, the oxygen in the blood stream is removed. An adult chimp is unconscious in less than twenty seconds, brain-dead in a minute. Could she survive such a thing?"

"Oh, yeah. We can go without oxygen for hours. Our bodies hoard it in times of stress."

"No. Let me clarify," said Melvin. "There would be no oxygen to hoard. The gas would replace it, right down to the red cells in the blood stream. Would that kill her?"

"Not for a while. She'd go into stasis. Just shut down. No respiration, no heartbeat, nothing. I imagine that she could handle such a thing for at least an hour or two. Of course, less time, less risk."

"Good," Melvin replied. "When necessary to control her for tests or cleaning her facility, we can use the gas, then sedate her. The hypo I gave her lasted for about three hours. We should never need more than an hour to do what is necessary. Most of the time, a lot less. Do you agree to that, Casey?"

"Sure. Whatever it takes. Everyone of us I have ever known goes into a very deep sleep for an hour or two out of every twenty-four. During that time, you should be able to approached and inject her without resistance also."

"Could you recognize this condition as genuine?"

"If I'm awake," Casey said.

Moira passed under Bartle Hall and wrestled the van onto I-35.

"We'll be there in about twenty minutes or so," she said. "I called in while you were sleeping and let Provenance know we were coming. The gate security guy is expecting us. The floor we're going to and two floors above it are clear. Melvin and I are the only staff members with keys to that level of the sub-basement, and only the three of us are cleared by the monitoring system to get into the floor or the lab facility there. Nothing is foolproof, but we are damn close."

"Heard from Cat?" Casey asked.

"It's hard to hear anything from inside the casket at all, but she complained and shouted for the first few hours. Not a peep since Springfield," Melvin answered. "I hope she's alright."

"That's what she hopes you'll hope," Casey said, shaking his head. "She'd like nothing better than for you to become concerned enough to try to check on her. She'd kill you and Moira in a heartbeat. She was trying to kill me when you injected her. Damn near got it done. Thanks, Melvin."

Melvin waived his hand in dismissal. "The child needs help," he said.

"Yes, she does," Casey agreed, "but what has to happen for her to get help is going to make tough love look like a weekend in the country. There are some very rough times ahead, for both Cat and the rest of us. Empathy? Sure. But pity or compassion is worse than a waste of time. They're dangerous. It won't be easy, Melvin, but try and keep that in mind. And Moira. She's already jealous of you. You shot her, you're holding her captive, you're only a human, and you have my affection. That's almost unbearable for her. When she realizes the depth of our relationship, it will get worse. Melvin she'd kill. You, well, killing would be the least of it. We need heavy drugs close at hand and the gas system fully charged all the time. We'd need that for any Nosferati, but for her …"

"Whadaya mean, for her?" Moira asked.

"Years ago, Cat stepped over the line that I crossed yesterday. She fed on one of her own kind. That is forbidden among the Nosferati and for more than just the obvious reason of personal security. There is no taboo on killing one another. That happens occasionally. I know of only two or three other times when Nosferati fed on Nosferati. In one instance, the woman went insane and took her own life less than twelve hours later. In the other, the man just vibrated apart. He went through such a surge of energy, his body could not contain it. When I fed on Michael, I took a risk. I needed the physical edge to subdue my daughter, and since she'd survived a forbidden feeding, I figured I might also."

"You fed on Michael knowing that kind of thing kills Nosferati?" Moira asked.

"I fed on Michael knowing Cat had survived such a thing."

"Jesus, Casey!"

"Now, Pookie," he said, "don't be cross."

"Pookie?" asked Melvin.

"Shut up, Foltz," Moira growled.

"I'll find a heavy cart we can slide it onto," Melvin said, opening the rear doors of the van and looking at the casket.

Casey laid the tarp on the floor behind the van, lifted the coffin down onto it, and looked at him. "Where to?" he asked.

When the elevator doors to the fourth sub-level opened, Cat began to stir. They could hear faint shouts of rage coming from inside the box as Casey pulled it and the tarp down the hallway. Melvin held open a door for him and he dragged his burden into a room about twenty by thirty feet. Constructed of concrete blocks and painted pale yellow, it embodied institutionalism at its loveliest. A folding table, a few plastic chairs, a corner restroom, a rolled fire hose, a kitchenette, and a control console only magnified its bleakness. Two large windows looked into the containment area.

Slightly smaller than the observation space because of extra thickness in the walls and ceiling, it made the first room look luxurious. Pale gray, it was featureless, without furnishing or appliance of any kind. The walls and ceiling were perfectly smooth, save for an inch thick piece of steel that projected from overhead the full depth of the room. The floor, also gray and smooth, contained two heavy grates recessed slightly below the surface. Lighting came only from fixtures in the observation area, directed through the two windows. Casey inspected them.

"Four inch polymer," Melvin said. "Unbreakable. The polymer is actually the entire wall. The block on this side and the steel on the other side were applied over it. The steel itself is a titanium alloy, three-quarters of an inch thick and completely seamless. Behind it are poured concrete and resin walls eighteen inches thick. Overhead in the center is a dividing wall to keep the animals contained as needed on one side or the other. It is one inch thick, of the same composite as the walls, and weighs over eighteen thousand pounds. The drains were cast into the cement of the floor before it was covered with steel. They also act as vents for the heating and cooling as well as …"

Casey held his finger to his lips, and Melvin stopped, looking at him quizzically. Recognition came over his face and he nodded.

"As well as air filtration and gas exchange to keep the lab as fresh and odor free as possible," he continued. "The connecting door between the rooms is of the same variety that services safes, locks with six horizontal pins, is of solid stainless steel, and has no method of opening from the containment side. No one ever opens it without someone else in attendance. Due to the thickness of the walls and the depth of the basement, no sound will escape the area. Only very low frequency might, but we have no elephants on hand, so the point is moot. This area is secure."

"Power failure?" Casey asked.

"Also moot. The entire building has its own plant. Should the public power fail, we would go down for less than ten seconds. In addition, this level has a separate generating system should the main generating system fail, and we have four hours at full consumption battery back-up."

"It's a small place, but we love it," Moira said.

Casey slid the casket into the containment area and returned. Melvin closed and secured the heavy door. "Sorry about almost mentioning the gas," he said. "She could have heard me?"

"Sure," Casey replied. "She may or may not have been able to actually understand what you said, but she would have certainly heard your voice."

"But we talked about it in the van."

"The van had a lot of ambient road noise and stuff. We're a lot like dogs. Low rumbles and such greatly effect how we hear. That's one of the reasons dogs don't like thunderstorms. They have trouble hearing through them."

"The floor grates also contain a communication system," Melvin said. "When it's shut down, very little passes between the rooms. You can hear someone pounding on the window, but that's about all."

"Great. Unless we screw up, that should hold her just fine. If you're ready, so am I. Gas her."

"Wait a minute," Moira said. "What about food and water?"

"None," Casey said. "No food, no water, nothing for at least three days. It will help wear her down. I want to get her system flushed as quickly as possible and it will still probably take a month. After the first few days feed her what you fed the chimps or gorillas. Raw fruit and veggies, things like that. I know it seems cruel, but if it can shorten the time of her confinement it's worth it."

"Jesus."

"I need blood," Melvin said. "Some of hers, some of yours. I'll have to sedate her for that and clear the room of gas, so her blood gasses won't be affected."

"Fine," Casey said, appearing impatient. "Let's rock and roll."

They left the gas in the room for a full thirty minutes before going in. Moira and Melvin both wore small air supplies dangling from respirator masks. Casey held his breath.

He unscrewed the locks on the casket and opened the lid. In the fetal position and still, lay his daughter. She looked tiny and ten years old. Casey felt hot tears leap to his eyes as Melvin injected her thigh. She never moved. Moira took both radial and carotid pulses and used a stethoscope. "I'd swear this girl is dead," she said from behind her mask. "Her body is even cooling. Amazing."

They returned to the observation area and Melvin began to evacuate the gas. Moira looked at Casey. "Rough, huh?" she asked, touching his arm.

Melvin looked over the control board. "Gas is clear of both rooms," he said.

Casey inhaled, and Moira and Melvin removed their masks.

Thirty minutes later, the three of them were in Casey's room upstairs. Melvin had taken the blood to the lab, the casket was in the observation area, and Cat was stretched out on the containment room floor.

"Three days?" Moira asked.

"No food, no water, no contact, nothing."

"But surely some light."

"No light.

"Casey, the darkness is total there."

"She'll know where she is. From the moment she wakes up, her proximity sense will tell her the dimensions of the room as clearly as if she could see. We did not leave a fourteen-year-old girl down there. We left a Nosferati down there. For the next three days, she does not exist. In some respects, she needs the break. We certainly do."

"How are you holding up?" asked Melvin.

Casey smiled. "I feel okay physically. Emotionally, I'm a basket case. This whole thing about being reunited with your daughter after over a hundred-and-fifty years is very taxing. I'm just glad it wasn't a long time."

"Why'd you two split up?" Moira asked, "If that question isn't too personal."

"I left her. Walked out."

"Why?"

Casey sat on the couch and dropped his gaze to his feet for a moment, then leaned back and regarded Moira with cold eyes. "Don't ask if you don't want to know," he said.

She looked at him and remained silent.

"Okay," he said. "While we were in Chicago, Cat met Gunnar and Felene, a Nosferati couple living under the docks by the lake. She was overjoyed to find others like us and brought them home to where we stayed. I'd like to say we became friends, but that is not really the case with most Nosferati. We became tolerant competitors who enjoyed each other's, ah, company from time to time. Please remember that Cat had not matured with her years. Still hasn't, for that matter. Regardless of the nature of our relationship, she was still, in many ways, a fourteen-year-old living with her father, and had been for a very long time. She began to crave independence from me. Gunnar and Felene encouraged this. The more Cat was independent from me, the better opportunity they had to impose their will on her. Cat decided to get her own place and be more on her own."

Casey paused for a moment and took a deep breath.

"Money was never a problem, she could get whatever she needed. She actually cleaned up, got respectable looking, and rented a small house. Quite proud of herself. I didn't see her for about two weeks. Then she dropped by and invited me over for dinner. When I arrived, Gunnar and Felene were there. He was in his late teens, she in her mid-twenties, and, as is the case today, someone like me was too old for them to be taken seriously. The emotional gulf between us was really too wide to overcome. I was jealous of their influence over Cat."

Again he paused

"Cat seated us with great ceremony, announcing that the meal was sort of a christening of her home and independence. Then she retrieved the roast from the oven in a covered pan. She placed it on the table and lifted off the lid. Served on a nest of carrots and potatoes was a human infant, about a year old, baked with a crabapple in her mouth. I walked out."

"Oh, my God," whispered Moira, her hand over her lips.

Melvin bolted for the bathroom.

Casey went to the sink for a glass of water.

Melvin's retching echoed through the silent space. Even after he returned to the living area, no one spoke for nearly ten minutes. Casey returned to the couch. "Now you know," he said. "I just couldn't deal with her anymore. Now I have an opportunity to allow her to save her from herself. I have the two of you to thank for that."

Melvin cleared his throat. "So," he said, "you stated before that you wanted to give her the opportunity to choose her way of life with a rational mind; that the choice was up to her."

"It is."

"What if she chooses to return to the Nosferati?"

"I've been thinking about that, Melvin. I did say the choice was hers to make, and it is. But if she chooses to return to her old life, I'll have to kill her. I know Cat. She'll come after you and Moira. I won't allow that to happen. I won't let her harm the two of you."

Again the room was silent. At length, Melvin stood up.

181

"I'm off," he said, and headed for the door. "See you tomorrow. I'll need some blood, Casey." He closed the door and was gone.

Moira stared numbly at Casey.

"Jesus Christ," she murmured, "what you have had to live with."

He smiled at her. "My bear to cross," he said.

"Been a grizzly, huh?"

"It hasn't killed me."

She crossed to him and knelt by his knee. "Want me to stay?"

"No. Not tonight."

"Okay, Bub," Moira replied, getting to her feet. "I can handle rejection, but only for so long. Tomorrow evening, salad, spaghetti, garlic bread, and spumoni at my place. Wear a tie." She went to the door.

"Deal," he said.

"Tomorrow morning, basted eggs, corned beef hash, pancakes and maple syrup at your place. Wear pants."

"You'll get corn flakes and like it," Casey said. "Pants are optional."

"Deal," Moira replied, and was gone.

# TWENTY-TWO

## Down at the Old Corral

CASEY WAS STANDING AT THE STOVE, wearing a dark blue sport shirt, khaki Dockers shorts complete with a braided belt, white crew socks, and tasseled loafers when Moira came breezing into his room at about eight the next morning. She flipped her eyebrows at him.

"Not exactly what I had in mind when I agreed to the pants optional thing last night," she complained.

"Harlot," he said, blowing her an air kiss. "Blueberry pancakes, corned beef hash, and scrambled eggs. I couldn't baste an egg if my life depended on it. I know it's a disappointment. Please stay."

"Well, you do exhibit naked limbs …"

"I also don't have any maple syrup. Is Mrs. Butterworth's a deal breaker?"

"God, Casey. You're making this awfully hard for me."

"That's my line," he said.

"Oh, fine! Now I'm subjected to lewd conversation. These pancakes better be pretty special."

He opened the oven and removed the warm cakes, put two on a plate along with a spatula of hash and eggs scrambled with sour cream and chives, and placed it on the table before her. A small pitcher of hot syrup followed, along with a liberal pancake dousing of aerosol whipped cream.

"Shut up and eat," he growled, returning to the stove for his breakfast.

Moira shoveled in a forkful or two, and regarded him with whipped cream on her lip.

"Jesush, Casey, thish ish wunnafoo!" she chewed. "Be my food slave!"

"Thank you."

"Where'd you learn to cook like this?"

"I was a full-time cook and part time corpsman on the Arizona just before World War Two."

"What?"

"Yep."

"The battleship? The one at Pearl Harbor?"

"That's the one."

"Were you on it when it sank?"

183

"No. I was on the island. The Navy believes I was on it. Great way to lose an identity. Supposedly, I was one of the sailors that never made it off the boat."

"God! How many identities have you had?"

"Not that many. It's only been in relatively recent years that a solid identity was even needed. During the seventeenth, eighteenth, and nineteenth centuries, there was very little way to trace who somebody was. You just moved, called yourself whatever you wanted, and that was that."

"Ever meet anybody famous?"

"I held Ben Franklin's kite."

"Really?"

"You're too easy, Flynn. No."

"Asshole. Lucky for you these pancakes are from heaven."

"I did meet Kit Carson, once."

"Oh, yeah?" Moira replied skeptically.

"Uh-huh. Right up the road a ways in St. Joe. Mouthy little shit. Didn't like him at all."

"Zat right?"

Casey grinned. "You don't believe me."

"I'm not sure."

"Then finish your breakfast."

"Okay," Moira replied. "We have work to do, anyway."

"Work?"

"Yep we gotta make you look like Casey again so you don't have to stay cooped up." She peered at him critically. "You're aging."

"What?"

"You're aging. All that work I did with the collagen and the synthetic Botox is almost gone. It should have lasted for months."

"Sure," Casey said. "My body won't allow foreign substances to hang around very long."

"That's convenient," Moira smiled. "I have a rinse next door to darken your hair. We'll do that, pop out those contacts, and you'll look just like the old Casey with a new haircut. Then I can be seen with you, not only in the cafeteria, but in public."

"In public?" Casey asked. "We going out?"

"Yep, like real people do. You and I are taking the day off, as soon as we fix your hair and I stop by and see Melvin."

Casey looked at her, puzzled. "What's up with Melvin?"

"That would be none of your business at this time," Moira answered, remembering she couldn't lie to him.

"What do you mean, at this time?"

"That also would be none of your business," she said.

"You won't tell me."

"Nope," she beamed.

Casey looked at her and grinned in spite of himself. "I assume by your attitude that's its nothing serious."

"Stop probing and change the subject."

"All right," Casey said, shaking his head. "So if we're going out, where we going?"

"Where would you like to go?"

"I dunno," Casey said. "The mall, a movie, shopping. Any or all of the above. It's your town, you tell me. Any place but a museum. I want to stay in this moment."

"Great!" Moira said. "Gimme five minutes to finish breakfast, then we'll do your hair, and while you're drying and stuff, I'll go visit Doctor Blood. Then I'll squirt on some foo-foo water and change clothes. We'll give Westport a walk-through, grab lunch at someplace laughable, catch a movie, and cruise Overland Park. Back in time for dinner and a restful evening sitting by the fire and whispering sweet nothings in each other's shell-like ears."

"Perfect," Casey said. "Let's go soak my head."

It was a silly day. Casey tried on women's hats in a Westport shop, and he and Moira got so rowdy the salesgirl asked them to leave. They created a scene on the second level of the Cheesecake Factory where lunch disintegrated into a low level food fight of airborne shrimp and straw wrappers. The tension and fear of the past few days washed out of them and they became giddy and childlike with the release. Not wanting to sit still long enough for a movie, they headed for Independence and raced go-carts and played miniature golf instead, leaving havoc in their laughing wake. Late afternoon they stopped by Galyan's Sporting Goods to look around on their way back to Provenance. Casey eyeballed the two-and-a-half-story climbing wall.

"No," said Moira, looking at the wall and the two climbers hanging from it on belay.

"Why not?" Casey teased.

"No."

"Aw, c'mon."

"Dammit, Casey," she giggled, "no!"

"I gotta!"

"You're on your own," Moira laughed, moving off.

Casey stepped to the bottom of the wall and, before either of the officially dressed young men on hand could stop him, sailed up it like a fly and sat on top. He looked around for a moment, then came down the wall at the same speed he'd gone up. The seven or eight people on hand were stunned, gaping at him. He looked at one of the official young men.

"Thanks," he said, "but, what are the ropes for?"

Moira joined him as he inspected camping lanterns.

"Let's get out of here before somebody realizes what you did was not possible," she said.

"Yes, Dear," he replied, and headed for the parking lot.

They arrived back at Provenance a little after six.

"My place, eight o'clock sharp," said Moira, rising to her toes and kissing Casey on the lips. "Bring your appetite."

"This is really good," he said.

"What?"

"Feeling human. I could get used to this."

"You ain't felt nothin' yet," she said.

Casey showered and shaved, surprised by the tingle of excitement he felt. He put on a suit and tie, as requested and, at eight promptly, rapped on Moira's door. She opened it, and he stepped into candlelight and the scent of roses.

Moira was wearing her little black dress, except, in her case, it was very dark green. A slightly scooped neckline was held in place with spaghetti straps, the skirt, slit up the back, stopped three inches above her knees. Her shoes were three-inch pumps in dark green velvet, her only jewelry a diamond ankle bracelet over neutral hose. Her hair was loose and shining auburn, her eyes lightly made up with green eye shadow, her lips carefully penciled in wet red, her nearly translucent Irish skin touched with freckles and shining in the light of the candles. The dress clung to her as she moved. Nylon brushed nylon.

"Oh, my," Casey breathed.

Moira gave him a lazy smile. "Wanna give up now, or should we eat first?"

"Doesn't the condemned man get a hearty meal?"

"You're not condemned. The verdict isn't in yet. Open the wine."

The salad was a romaine wedge with Parmesan, pine nuts, and garlic olive oil. The pasta—fresh angel hair dressed with a dusting of Romano cheese, basil, and oregano, drizzled with sesame oil containing bits of seared salmon—was complimented by sautéed peppers and baked garlic. A rich Pinot Noir meshed with everything perfectly. After dinner, they laughed and talked over spumoni and dry champagne. When the bottle was empty and the ashtray was full, Moira rose to her feet.

"Go home," she said. "Start the authentic gas log, and relax. I'm going to slip into something more comfortable, as it is said, and be over in about ten minutes. Take the rest of the Pinot Noir with you. I'll bring fresh glasses."

Casey did as he was asked, starting the log, and slipping out of his jacket, tie and shoes. He felt a bit nervous. Literally smelling what was coming, he was attempting to arrive at a graceful solution to the problem of rejecting Moira's advances without rejecting Moira. As much as he wanted her, he would not risk it. As much as he needed her, he could not.

She came walking in wearing a silk robe the same color as her dress. She placed the glasses on the coffee table and sat beside him on the couch, swiveling to face him. It was reasonably evident she was wearing nothing beneath the robe.

"Ah," he said.

She kissed him.

"Uh," he said.

She kissed him.

"Look," he said.

She kissed him.

"Moira, we can't do this …"

Again, she kissed him.

"Dammit, Moira, stop!"

"No."

"Yes."

"No," she chuckled, backing him across the couch and into the arm.

"Yes!" he said, trying not to laugh.

Moira giggled. "Too much fun," she said, her voice muffled by his neck as she scooted up on top of him.

"Christ!" Casey blurted, writhing as her tongue found his ear. "Quit!"

"Oh, all right!" she snapped, pulling away, gathering up her robe and sitting primly in the center of the couch. "Now what do you think is so important that you have to resist my advances?"

"You know," Casey said. "We talked about it in the motel."

"Oh, that," she said, dismissing it all with a wave of her hand.

She poured two glasses of wine and handed one to Casey.

"Drink that, and shut up," she continued.

Casey took a sip.

"No," Moira said with exaggerated patience. "Drink all of it. Be a good boy."

Casey downed the wine and looked at her.

"Now," she said. "Try to keep up. We can do anything we like, Casey, for as long as we like, Casey, anywhere we like, Casey, and you don't have to worry about a thing. I've had my shots."

"Your shots."

"My shots.

"What shots?"

"The ones Melvin has been giving me for two weeks. Just like the shot he gave me before we went out today."

"What shots?"

"Oh, just the ones that have made me immune to the vampire virus."

Casey stared at her. "What?"

"I'm immune, Casey," she said, leaning toward him and smiling. "I'm immune. Melvin isolated the antibodies in your blood, cultured them with some of my blood, and found them to be compatible. I've been taking shots almost daily. Soon I'll be down to one a week, then one a month, then a booster every six months or so. I'll never have another cold. I can, however, have you."

"You're immune?"

"I asked you to try and keep up," she said. "Yes. No more infections. My immune system is as good as yours. No AIDS, no herpes, no tonsillitis, no Ebola. Probably no cancer or anything like that either, we don't know for sure yet."

"My, God!" shouted Casey, springing to his feet. "That's wonderful! You've probably added a hundred years to your life! Most likely more! So many of the things you'd have to worry about, especially in your line of work, make no difference anymore!" He began to pace. "This is incredible! The ramifications are just incredible!"

Moira stood up and walked to him. She placed her arms about his neck and kissed him into silence. When they parted, she smiled her slow smile and looked up at him.

"I got your ramifications right here," she said, and began to lead him toward the bedroom. "Let's go see if it's true what they say about the saddles down at the old corral, Cowboy. And don't, for any reason, call me Pookie."

# TWENTY-THREE

## Multidimensional Movement

THERE WERE TIMES DURING THE NIGHT WITH MOIRA when Casey felt as if he would never return to the day to day world of doors and windows, ceilings and floors, but would remain suspended elsewhere, peacefully and joyously adrift in a four dimensional sea the color of love attained and the texture of need fulfilled. She seeped into his pores, splashed behind his eyes, entwined herself so thoroughly in his senses, and melded so totally in his marrow that he came to realize they could never completely extricate themselves from one another.

He awoke before dawn and lay with her, listening to her gentle, and sometimes not so gentle, snoring. Luxuriating in the feel of her against him, the whisper of her breath on his skin, and the scent of her morning body, he grinned until his cheeks protested. Nature yammered at him without mercy, and eventually he eased away from her amazing comfort and made his barefoot way to the bath. Twenty minutes later, showered, shaved, and draped in a robe, he padded into the kitchen.

He attempted to muffle the noise of the coffee grinder with a pillow as the scent of a Kenya dark roast permeated the apartment. The cabinet yielded a jar of English Blueberry preserves. Half a pound of thin sliced bacon was in the freezer and he popped it in the microwave to thaw, dug out a griddle that covered two burners, found some Half & Half in the fridge, put everything on the counter, lit a Camel, and sat on a kitchen chair to wait for the coffee, grinning like a collie pup. When the grin escalated to an out and out chuckle, Casey arrived at a startling revelation. He was happy. His daughter lay in the dark on a cold steel floor three or four stories below him, his need for blood yipped and yowled in the blackness somewhere behind him, but it made no difference. It really made no difference. At this time, in this place, during this moment, he was *happy*. He, despite times of joy and jubilance, excitement and exaltation, had not been happy in nearly four hundred years. Tears filled his eyes at the thought. The complex simplicity of being happy covered him like a blanket, and he shivered from its warmth.

When the coffee finished, he drank half a cup as he put the bacon on the griddle over low heat. Feeling Moira nearing wakefulness, he poured another cup and padded into the bedroom. As he walked through the door, she modestly raised to one elbow and squinted at him.

"Eek," she said. "There's a man in my room."

"Good morning."

Moira peered at the walls for a moment. "Eek," she said. "I'm in a *man's* room. How could I have been brought so low?"

"I love you," he said.

"Now that I see you have coffee," Moira replied, "I love you, too."

He sat. She drank. They smiled at one another.

When she finished the coffee, Casey took her cup into the kitchen and raised the heat under the bacon. He looked up as Moira creaked by, bent slightly forward at the waist, her hair sticking out in all directions, pressing her left hand against her low back, taking short stilted steps.

"Jesus," she muttered, casting him a short sideways glance. "I think I'm ruined. I'm going home to die. Be back in fifteen. Food."

She was back in thirty, freshly scrubbed, wearing institutional gray sweat clothes, white socks and no makeup, with a large blue towel turbaned about her head. Casey turned the oven off from keeping the bacon warm and pushed two sliced bagels down in the four-slot toaster. Moira walked around the counter and pushed up against him, her arms around his waist, her face pressed into the hollow of his neck.

"Hold me up," she said.

"For a minute," he said, slipping his arms around her low back and patting her bottom. "Gotta take care of the food."

"Insensitive bastard," she bitched, groping behind her for a stool.

"You didn't seem to think so last night."

"Wine. I wasn't thinking clearly." She winced her way onto a stool and accepted another cup of coffee. "Sore," she said, munching a piece of bacon as Casey put jam on the bagels.

"Sore?" he grinned.

"My knees are sore, my ass is sore, my shoulders are sore, my low back is sore, my … yes, I'm sore. Why wouldn't I be sore, locked up all night with the wild man of Borneo?"

Moira grabbed a slice of bagel and began to munch.

"Complaining?"

Jam on her face, Moira bumped her eyebrows and grinned.

"Speaking from my extensive personal knowledge of such matters," Casey said, "I would recommend a very specific protocol of treatment for your condition."

"Oh, yeah?"

"Indeed. A deep and thorough massage, followed by a course of stimulating exercise."

"Uh-huh," she said, crunching another piece of bacon. "And just who would supervise this protocol?"

"Unselfish me."

"You'd do that?"

"Yes, I would."

"With no thought of yourself."

"Not one."

"Okay," she said, walking toward the bedroom. "Bring the last bagel in case I get bored."

Chuckling, Casey left the bagel on the counter.

After Moira went to sleep, Casey rose, dressed, and walked to Melvin's lab. He found the slight scientist sitting on a stool and peering into a microscope.

"Her red cell count is even higher than yours," Melvin said, glancing at Casey and returning his attention to the instrument.

"Whose? Cat?"

"Of course, I haven't checked your latest sample yet. Since you, ah, fed on Michael, there could be some changes in your blood that I am not aware of."

"Melvin," Casey said.

"Interesting," the little man murmured. "Her red cells actually seem to be larger than yours, too."

"Melvin," Casey repeated.

"Her white cells definitely are, and their count seems elevated."

"Melvin," Casey said again.

"Of course, that could be a response to the sedative."

"Melvin," Casey grinned, tapping him on the shoulder.

Melvin looked up, blinking. "I'm sorry," he said. "Did you speak?"

"Yes, I did," Casey replied. "I came by to thank you for what you did for Moira and me."

"For Moira and you?" Melvin asked, appearing confused.

"The serum you developed so she wouldn't catch the virus. You've lengthened her life and made our relationship possible."

"Oh. Well, uh, that is to say …"

"I have some idea of what it took for you to do that," Casey said.

"Actually, it wasn't overly difficult," Melvin replied. "Fairly standard procedures, really. The trick is going to be synthesizing enough serum to …"

"That's not what I'm talking about, Melvin."

Melvin blushed and looked away.

"I know that you are extremely fond of Moira," Casey went on, choosing his words carefully. "That was a very unselfish thing to do. I just wanted you to know that I appreciate what you did, especially under the circumstances. The man I once viewed as a threat has turned out to be a superb and selfless friend."

Melvin fidgeted for a moment, then turned his eyes to Casey. "I suffered no delusions about Moira," he said, "because I suffer few illusions about myself. Look at me. I am somewhat less than the accepted conception of masculine pulchritude. In my youth, rejection by members of the opposite sex was a common occurrence for me. Perhaps in compensation for that, I do not seek feminine companionship on an intimate level. Experience has taught me the folly and pain of such action. I know many of the women in this very building laugh at me. Moira never did. I found that fact very encouraging and I did have my fantasies. She is a wonderful woman, Casey. And I am no fool. She came to me, as a friend, seeking help. What else could I, as a friend, do? My personal wants and desires did not enter into it then, and they do not now. I am more than happy for the two of you."

Casey swallowed. "Those women that rejected you, Melvin," he said, his voice thick in his throat, "and those that laugh at you. None of them truly know Melvin

Foltz. If they did, there'd be a line. I just hope I live long enough that someday I can be as much of a man as you are right now." He patted Melvin on the shoulder and turned for the door.

Melvin sat for a moment, digesting the conversation, then turned his attention to the microscope and smiled. "A threat," he said, and returned to his work.

Moira awoke again mid-afternoon and grinched, damp-headed, out into the living room. Casey bustled in the kitchen.

"Now what?" she asked.

"Late lunch, early dinner," he replied. "Teriyaki pork, rice noodles with asparagus, water chestnuts, bean sprouts, and egg. Still sore?"

"I can live with it," she said, "at least until its time for another massage."

"What courage."

"Ah," she said, "the simple life. Eat, physical therapy, sleep, wake up, eat, physical therapy, sleep, wake up. How long can this go on?"

"How long is there?"

"Not long enough. Sometime we're going to have to return to the world."

"Not yet."

"Oh, no," she said, loosing her slow grin and moving around the counter. "Not yet."

It was three days before they came back.

"Casey," Melvin said, looking at him across breakfast in Moira's apartment on the fourth morning after Cat came to the lab, "your pineal activity seems to be increasing."

Moira snorted. "Ya think?"

"Pineal, floozy," Casey said.

"That too?" Moira asked, wide-eyed and innocent.

Melvin looked confused. "It still, however, is not as strong as your daughter's."

"Really?"

"Her pineal activity, as least as far as I can tell with the limited data available, is very high. This is just supposition, but it would not surprise me to find out that the increased level has something to do with the fact that both you and she have consumed blood from another Nosferati."

"Interesting," said Moira.

"It also seems that while Cat has this accelerated pineal output, the output itself has little direction, that is to say, it lacks focus. Yours, Casey, although smaller and less productive at this point, seems to have a rhythm or an integration that hers lacks."

"I'm not sure I understand."

Melvin thought for a moment. "Imagine a table covered with a thousand candles," he said. "Lots of golden light, a significant amount of heat. Lay a newspaper atop it and it would immediately catch fire. Do the same with a sheet of plywood, and the candles would be extinguished. Follow?"

"So far," Casey replied.

191

"Now, take the same energy required for those thousand candles, condense it and sharply focus the output, and you have a torch that will burn through steel. Cat has the fuel, she just doesn't have the focus. You have the focus, but not the fuel. At least not yet."

"Jesus," whispered Moira.

Melvin looked at her and his eyes began to shine.

"Yes?" he said, grinning. "You have something?"

She stared at him. "It's just theory," she said.

"Mere supposition. Go with it."

"There are no facts to support anything."

"No applicable data whatsoever. Follow it."

"But if the body's natural rhythm is in tune…"

"The music of the spheres."

"If the harmonics are in place…"

"The power of vibration."

"Then the twelve-strander could be free of two strand physics!"

"Theoretically true," Melvin agreed.

"Which could open up a bunch of impossible possibilities!" Moira said.

"Telekinesis!" Melvin blurted.

"Teleportation!" Moira replied.

"Physical astral projection!" Melvin countered.

"Time displacement!" Moira crowed.

"Speed without velocity!"

"Travel without distance!"

"Distance without travel!"

"Irrelevant time!" Moira shouted.

"Irrelevant *space*!" Melvin roared.

"*Multidimensional movement*!" they yelled in unison.

"That's not a moon," Moira howled, "that's a space station!"

"Aw, geeze," Casey moaned, dropping his head to the tabletop. "Here we go again."

Grinning, Moira looked at Casey. "Don't panic," she said. "Nobody's getting ready to send you to Alpha Centauri for the weekend. Look on this as when we first realized that if we could build a rocket big enough, it could actually lift a man. The possibilities of what Melvin may have discovered are amazing, but not immediate. This is all theoretical. Warp drive is a long way off."

"And possibly unnecessary," Melvin said.

"Christ," Casey muttered.

"Anything unusual happen since you, ah, encountered Michael?" asked Moira.

"Like what?"

"You tell me."

Casey thought for a moment. "I saw Cat walking down the road to where those college kids were drinking beer and partying. I knew how many boys there were, what they looked like, and what Cat was wearing before I got there."

"Uh-huh," Melvin said.

"I knew you guys were getting close in the van before I saw or heard you. Several times in the past few days I've known when Moira was getting ready to wake up, even when I wasn't near her."

"How do you explain that?" asked Melvin.

"I dunno."

"But things are at least a little different since Michael."

"Now that I think about it, yeah. I guess they are," Casey said. "More blood and tests, Melvin?"

"Oh, yes. Cat, too, I should think. Perhaps we should go check on her."

"Perhaps we should," Casey agreed, finishing his coffee.

They all stood and headed toward the hall, each fearful of what they might find. In the elevator, Moira briefly rubbed Casey's back. He was rigid as a statue.

When Melvin switched on the lights in the lab, they saw Cat sitting cross-legged against the back wall of her cell. She opened her eyes and smirked.

"Hello, *Father*. Come to let the poor little humans get a look at the wolf-girl?"

"Hello, Catherine," Casey answered.

"When do the crowds start? Hurry, hurry, *hurry*. Step right up! She walks, she talks, she bites babies' heads off!" Cat grinned. "Ten bucks a gape, and you'll be rich in no time."

"I'm sorry to have to do this to you, Sweetheart. But it's necessary we keep you here for a while."

"Tell ya what," she said. "You let me go, right now, and I'll disappear. You'll never see me again. One time offer, *Father*. Last chance, *Father*."

"I can't do that."

"You won't do that."

"Alright. I won't do that."

"My, my, my. Honesty between parent and child," she smirked. "A rare thing in today's world, don't you think?"

"Cat, you have to break your addiction so you can think clearly about your life. That's why you're here. That's why you'll remain here."

"Will I? You actually think that you can keep me in this cage? You better pray you can, *Father*. You've got as much chance of kissing your own ass as you have of keeping me in here!"

She shifted her position, crossing her legs out in front of her and grinning at them. Casey could see the tiny trembling of her body, feel the thick hunger concentrating in the rear of her throat, the dripping need of it sliding downward from her nasal passages. She shifted her attention to Moira.

"Hey, Cow," Cat purred. "Nice shootin', podnuh! It'll take a lot more than a gun next time. Next time, I'll piss in your mouth after I eat your tongue. Won't that be fun?" She giggled and shook her head. "You little humans have no idea what you're fucking with here. I almost feel sorry for you. Oh! The poor little girl! She's confused, she's lost! Let's give her a chance to be a good girl. We can help!" Cat laughed. "Jesus Christ, can even humans be that stupid?"

Cat yawned, eased back on one elbow, scratched her crotch, and turned her gaze on Melvin. Casey felt him tense.

"And you," she said. "You're the little shit that stuck that needle in my ass. You get off on sticking things in peoples asses, little man? Got a thing for *Father*? Is that why you're in this? Wanna stick something in his ass?" Cat smirked, then sat up. "No," she said. "That's not it, is it? You followed the cow into all this, didn't you? Must really piss you off that the cow's doin' him, and not you, huh? Makes it a lot tougher to concentrate when you're chokin' your chicken into those sweaty midnight sheets, knowin' she's fuckin' and suckin' him instead of you, huh?"

Melvin turned and left the room.

"Well," Cat said, "that's one down. He's your weak link, *Father*. Better watch him. Now get the fuck outta here. It's time for my nap. Shut the light off when you leave."

"God, she's brutal," whispered Moira after she and Casey walked into the hallway. "Poor Melvin."

"Nobody pushes buttons better than Cat," Casey said.

They found Melvin waiting for them in the hall outside Casey's apartment. "I'm really sorry about all that, Melvin," Casey said, as he opened the door and they went inside.

"Her adrenal output must be terribly erratic," Melvin replied, moving to sit on the couch. He blinked, as if noticing the room for the first time. "In some respects, she was quite correct," he went on. "Your daughter is very insightful. She is also very intelligent. She is also quite brave. I find that I admire her."

"Jesus, Melvin," Moira said, fussing with the coffee maker, "you are something else."

"That girl is in the most horrific situation of her life," Melvin continued. "She is in an acute state of both fear and fright. She, who believed herself to be invincible, who thought herself so superior to the rest of us, who has done exactly what she pleased when she pleased for centuries, is a captive! She is in her enemy's hands and at her enemy's mercy! The monkeys have captured the leopard! She is being denied a substance that she believes is absolutely essential to her survival, she is caged, and she is at the mercy of the very creatures that she fears and who have been at her mercy for hundreds of years! Her entire life, and all she could imagine as her life, has undergone a complete reversal. Yet, she spits in our eye! What courage! If we can assist her in directing her power correctly, she will be amazing."

He cleared his throat and accepted a cup of coffee from Casey.

"She's a compound," Melvin continued, "like water. It's a gross simplification, I know, but look at water. Hydrogen and oxygen. Neither one of them has the properties of water. Hydrogen is volatile, explosive. Oxygen is corrosive, but absolutely vital to life. One 'bad', one 'good'. Combined together, in the proper amounts, they make water, a completely different substance, a careful balance of the two. Cat cannot be totally evil. She is also a compound. Within her, there must be the substances necessary for balance. If there were not, she, like water, could not exist. We cannot reform her, she must reform herself. The best we can do is seek the balance that will allow that reform to happen. A bit simplistic I know, but true. She won't scare me off again. Actually, I find her quite fascinating."

Moira and Casey looked at each other and smiled. Melvin didn't notice.

# TWENTY-FOUR

Peach Juice

LATE THAT NIGHT, when a sleepy Casey deemed it feasible, they entered Cat's enclosure. Melvin injected her with a sedative, and he and Moira drew blood and performed various tests and measurements while Casey hosed out the area and brought in bottled water and a basket of fresh fruits and vegetables. With a damp cloth, Casey washed Cat's face and smoothed her hair back from her forehead. She appeared peaceful and calm and looked her age. Leaning over, he kissed her cheek, and Moira thought she saw the faintest trace of a smile flicker on the child's lips. Back in the observation room, Casey leaned against the wall and sighed.

"Are you alright?" Melvin asked.

"Sleep," Casey replied. "Gotta have it."

"I'll get him upstairs to bed," Moira said, taking Casey by the arm. "You going to the lab?"

"Yes," Melvin said. "I want to start work on these samples right away."

Thirty minutes later, carrying a thermos of fresh coffee, Moira entered the lab. Melvin crouched in front of a computer, peering at the screen.

"How's it going?" Moira asked.

"Interesting," Melvin replied. "Very frustrating as well. We have discovered an entirely new virus, isolated it, determined a tiny amount of its capabilities and parameters, and we can't tell anyone. We can't publish, we can't even announce it to our fellows."

Moira grinned. "Why you blatant publicity hound! Melvin, I thought better of you."

"A brand new living entity, and we can't even whisper its name," Melvin said.

"It has a name?" Moira asked.

"Of course."

"And that would be?"

"Nosferatum Robustus," Melvin beamed.

"Nosferatum Robustus?" Moira said.

Melvin smiled. "Yes."

Moira chuckled. "Have you strictly attended to the International Code of Virus Classification and Nomenclature in choosing this particular name, Melvin?"

"I have not."

"I didn't think so."

"What?" Melvin asked innocently. "Perhaps something more like Saccharomyces Cerevisiae Ty 3? Nomenclature more in line with the standard set forth by our stogy peers?"

"Far be it from me, Melvin, to attempt to force you into conforming to paradigms established by others."

"I found it," Melvin said, trying to look down his nose at Moira, "and I shall name it Fred if I choose to."

"Nosferatum Robustus," Moira said. "I like that! When we publish, that's gonna knock a lot of those old bastards on their collective ass."

"My intent exactly," Melvin said, "if we ever can publish. This is so huge, it may never be able to be made fully public. The antibody serum we give you, for instance. Can you imagine what the FDA would do with that? The big drug money would be flowing so freely, we could never keep control of it. Our work would be sold for exploitation to the highest bidder, or socked away in some governmental backwater so fast, our lives could even be in danger! The AMA would be scared to death of the economic repercussions in the greedy medical community, the drug manufacturers would have visions of ten-thousand percent profits, the Department of Defense would want to hide it, and the money involved would be almost as immense as the power that came with its control. How much do you think somebody like Bill Gates would pay to live an extra hundred years and never even have a cold? How much do you think one of these mid-eastern megalomaniacs would spend on a virus that killed as effectively as this one does? If what we're working with ever became common knowledge, the world would turn over! The possible scope of repercussions is horrific!"

"And all of this for one, very old, fourteen-year-old girl," Moira said.

"Speaking of that," Melvin said, pointing at the computer screen, "look at this!"

Three hours later, a disheveled Casey opened his door to their knock. "Melvin," he said, "I told you to have her home by eleven-thirty. You're grounded, young lady."

"Damn!" Moira said. "There goes the dirty weekend in Raytown. Make yourself useful, Casey. Fix food while we tell you what we know."

Casey kissed her and opened the fridge.

"Your daughter is beginning to suffer," Melvin said.

"Yeah, I know. I can feel it coming on in her."

"I took blood at fifteen minute intervals over two hours. Her adrenal function is erratic. That, of course, affects her kidneys. Her blood is losing some of its usually high level of acidity. She is flickering on the edges of a thyroid storm, blood sugar is all over the place, liver function is reduced, pituitary response is lagging, blood/oxygen level is depressed, white cell count is falling. All of these functions are, of course, still way above normal for a human being, but definitely not up to her usual standards. She has not fed in four or five days. Physically, that is putting a lot of pressure on her. I cannot guess what she must be going through emotionally."

"I can," Casey said, dropping a pat of butter into a warming skillet. "It's awful. Even when I did it, I knew I could leave. I was restrained in a manner befitting a human. They could not have kept me had I chosen to go. You can damn sure bet that Cat is completely aware of exactly how well she is secured. She's tried every square inch of her enclosure. She knows she can't get out."

"And that isn't all," Moira said. "Her pineal activity appears to be changing. It seems to be gaining a bit of organization."

"Like how?" Casey asked, removing a carton of eggs from the fridge.

"Suppose you have some water in one of those old fashioned wash tubs."

"Uh-huh."

"You start banging on the outside of the tub and the water becomes agitated, but in a random manner. Little waves and splashes pop up all over the surface. You use a fair amount of energy and you get considerable results, but the results are without discipline or continuity. Follow?"

"Sure," Casey said. He broke six eggs into the skillet and stirred them with a wooden spoon as Moira collected her thoughts.

"Now, instead of randomly beating on the side of the tub, put your hand in the water and, calling on the same energy that you used in all that pounding, sweep your hand through the water just once, from one side of the tub to the other. What happens?"

"One wave with much more power and water displacement."

"Exactly. Your pineal gland produces waves, Casey. And while you do not have the energy available that Cat seems to, yours does appear to be increasing slightly, possibly because of your ingestion of Michael's blood. Cat's pineal gland produces ripples and splashes, but she is pounding the hell out of the tub. It seems, as time goes on, that her energy transfer is becoming more efficient. Her ripples and splashes are increasingly regular and less fragmented."

Casey thought while he poured coffee for three and put bread in the toaster. "So my control is good and my energy is improving, while Cat's energy is good and her control is improving."

"Exactly," Melvin said. "And it all seems to be regulated by blood. Ingestion of Nosferati blood seems to raise the energy level, possibly permanently. We don't know when Cat ingested hers. Regular ingestion of significant amounts of human blood, however, seems to dilute the focus, or inhibit the ability to manage the pineal output, if you will. All just theory at this point, but that's how it looks."

"So Nosferati blood increases output and human blood decreases control."

"In a nutshell," Melvin said, "except that the twelve strands of DNA seem to increase pineal output well above humanly normal levels. Your pineal activity is way above mine, for instance. Cat's is four to five times yours."

Casey grinned. "How 'bout Moira's?"

Melvin's eyes twinkled. "Zilch," he said. "Nothing. Zero."

"I have other virtues," Moira replied, patting Casey on the butt as she moved behind him to the fridge for jelly.

"So, Moira and I have been discussing the magnitude of our discoveries," Melvin went on. "A great deal of the gross lab work has already been accomplished. Much of what is yet to come involves longer-term study. Truth be known, we already have what may be an acceptable widespread cure for infectious disease from just the work I did for Moira with your antibodies. Developing a way to mass-produce a synthesized serum will take time. Time is our enemy. The longer we work on this at someplace like Proteus or Provenance, the more likely it is that our security will be compromised. We need not only a more private facility, we need our own private facility."

"You don't think we're safe here?" Casey said.

"That would depend on what you mean by safe," Melvin replied. "I don't feel that we are in any personal danger or anything like that. As long as what we do here remains secret, we're fine. But secrecy in our situation is nearly impossible. We are not attempting to conceal only samples in a refrigeration unit someplace. We are attempting to conceal people, and their movements, and their relationships. That is much more difficult. You, Casey, are the subject of some speculation and rumor around the labs. You attract attention. The more attention we attract to ourselves, the more subject we are to discovery. The longer we remain here, the more subject we are to attention."

"So what do we do?"

"We leave. We take our research, our work, and leave."

"And set up somewhere else?"

"And set up somewhere else," Moira said.

"That can't be easy."

"It won't be when it comes to severing ties and relationships," Moira continued. "As long as we can obtain the equipment we need, the actual physical part of the relocation shouldn't be that difficult."

"I'm transient by nature," Casey said. "Are the two of you really prepared to turn your lives upside down?"

"And we haven't?" Melvin said. "I can't speak for Moira, of course, but as for me, my entire life has been within a very narrow scope. I view this as an opportunity. Anything I have to do to make the change is merely inconvenience."

"My priorities have changed," Moira said, patting Casey on the arm.

"Okay. What about money? Won't it be awfully expensive?" Casey asked, carrying plates with eggs and toast to the table.

"Considerably," Melvin said, "but we are not without resource. I have personal savings to fill my needs and much more. With my reputation, just the whisper of a possible break-through in the next few years should garner me significant funding from private sources greedy enough to cough up cash and stay out of my way."

"And I," Moira said, "should also be able to dig up some independent funding. Plus, I'm a long way from broke and, I have a place."

"A place?"

"Outside Glenwood Springs, Colorado. My great great-grandfather, a doctor, settled there in the late eighteen hundreds. He even worked for a time in the Tuberculosis Sanatorium where Doc Holiday died. He bought land cheap, Casey. Lots of it. Later my family leased portions for cattle and sheep ranching, but never sold any. I am the heir. There is a large house on that property that is big enough for us to have living quarters and a lab with room to spare."

"All of us?"

"Even Cat," she said. "When things are settled with her here, I suggest we move. We will be independent, we will be more secure, and we will be located in some of the loveliest country on the planet. In spite of its proximity to Vail and Aspen, it is not high enough to be overrun with snowfreaks and their ilk."

Casey grinned. "You'd leave Kansas City for security and scenery?"

"Just the kind of place where you'd like to watch your daughter grow up."

"I hope it comes to that," Casey said.

After breakfast, leaving Moira and Casey to their own devices, Melvin went to the sub-basement primate containment area. He found Cat sitting nude, with her back against a sidewall, and opened the speaker system.

"Hello," he said.

She turned her face to him and smiled.

"Hi," she said, with a small wave. "It's Melvin, isn't it?"

"That's correct," Melvin replied, keeping his eyes averted.

"Hi, Melvin. I'm afraid we never were introduced. I'm Catherine. I hope my appearance doesn't upset you. My clothes were so dirty, I just couldn't stand them. I washed up a bit with the drinking water. Is there any way I might be able to take a shower?"

"Sorry," said Melvin, not quite looking at her. "I will see to it that you receive clean clothing and more water before tomorrow morning, however."

"Well, after the way I've treated you, I don't suppose I've earned any trust," she said, turning her torso to face him. "That's fine. I appreciate anything you can do. Really. Could you tell me why I'm being held here?"

"Your father wants you to overcome your addiction."

"What addiction?"

"Your addiction to human blood."

Cat smiled. "I see. Well, I know he wants what he believes is best for me. I certainly can't fault him for being a dad, can I?" She chuckled and looked around the room. "I must say that his methods are a bit sterile though, don't you think?"

"He believes them to be necessary."

"Oh, I'm sure he does," Cat said. "Truth be known, I can live without room service, but it would be nice to have something to sleep on and perhaps a blanket. It's not very comfortable in here." She blushed and lowered her voice. "I mean, there's not even a toilet, Melvin. Can you imagine? Pretty primitive, wouldn't you say?"

"Would you mind if I asked you some questions?" Melvin said, changing the subject.

"Not at all," Cat replied, swiveling on her bottom to face him and moving into a cross-legged position. "Actually I'm glad for the company. My time is your time."

"On average," Melvin continued, looking past her, "how often would you say you fed in any given week?"

Cat chuckled. "Right to business, huh, Melvin?"

"I'm afraid so, yes."

"I guess at least every other day, to stay where I wanted to be physically. Sometimes more often, just for fun."

"Just for fun. You found it, ah, fun?"

"Sure. Girls just wanna have fun, Melvin. Or hadn't you heard that?"

"And when was it that you fed on another Nosferati?"

"My! You seem to be well acquainted with your subject! Anne Rice would be proud of you, so calmly discussing things with a genuine vampire." She laughed. "Tell me, does all this seem real to you, Melvin? Or is it just another laboratory study. I mean, am I under your microscope, or am I a person? No, wait. I'm sorry. I didn't answer your question, did I? I can't very well expect you to be candid with me, if I am not candid with you. Around 1805, Melvin. I don't remember the exact year, but it was about that time. Not long before the War of 1812."

"Did you know it was dangerous, that it could kill you?"

"Certainly."

"Then, why?"

"Girls just wanna have fun. No risk, no rush, no fun. Got something against fun, Melvin?"

"That would depend on the fun," he replied.

"Good answer. So, am I a person or a paramecium? Am I in the room or under a microscope?"

"I see you as a person," Melvin said quietly.

"That's very kind of you, Melvin," she replied, getting to her feet and walking toward the window. "Most people would think I'm a monster." She dropped her hands to her sides and looked at him. "Do I look like a monster to you, Melvin?"

Still looking past her, Melvin swallowed the excess saliva that had materialized in his mouth. "No," he said.

"Thank you," she dimpled, shyly lowering her eyes. "What do I look like to you, Melvin?" she whispered.

He didn't answer.

"I'm sorry. I'm embarrassing you. It must be difficult for you, me in here with no clothes on and all. Honestly, it really doesn't bother me very much. You can answer if you want. I won't be offended. What do I look like to you, Melvin?"

"A beautiful young girl," he said stiffly, still not quite looking directly at her.

Cat smiled and performed a small curtsy. "Thank you," she said. "That's sweet. Especially when you must have some idea of how old I really am. You're a very kind man, I think. Brave too. It took a lot of courage to jump on my back and stick me with that needle. Exciting, huh?"

She stooped to pick up a peach from the basket on the floor. "By the way," Cat continued, moving to within a foot of the large window and taking a bite from the fruit, "thanks for the food." Juice ran down her hand and chin, dripping onto her breast. "Oh," she said, wiping at her throat and taking another bite. "Now look at that. I'm going to be all sticky."

Cat finished half the peach, squeezing it so juice dripped down across her belly. "Are you afraid to look at me just because I'm naked, Melvin?" she asked, tracing patterns in the liquid between her breasts and licking the juice from her fingers. "You don't have to be shy. We're the only ones here. I don't mind if you look. Truth be told, I like it."

Past his control, Melvin's eyes found her. She smiled. "That's not so bad, is it?" Cat said, rocking back and forth on the balls of her feet. "It's just me, Melvin, with all this peach juice dripping everywhere." She traced a fingertip around a nipple. "If I could reach it, I'd lick it off, but I can't," she sighed. "Guess it's just going to have to stay where it is and get all sticky, since you won't let me take a shower. Now I'm gonna be all sweet and gooey, and it's your fault." Cat giggled. "Where's the love, Melvin? Where's the compassion?"

Melvin lurched to his feet and turned toward the door. "Aw," Cat complained, smearing the juice over her low belly and laughing. "Now I've driven you away. Or is it that you suddenly need a few minutes alone?"

Melvin turned back and looked into her eyes. "All this really isn't necessary," he said. "I find your courage amazing. I admire you. I would like to be your friend."

He shut off the lights and closed the door quietly behind him.

Cat sank to the floor and stared into the darkness, the remnants of the peach forgotten.

# TWENTY-FIVE

Breakdown

EVERY OTHER NIGHT Melvin and Moira tranquilized Cat in her sleep and continued their tests and samplings while Casey cleaned up the room, put out fresh food and water, and gave his daughter a sponge bath. Her condition deteriorated. By the end of thirteen days, she was eleven pounds lighter, losing some hair, and her skin had assumed a gray pallor. She ate almost nothing, drank little, and the doctor inside of Moira—despite Casey's assurances and Cat's superior body chemistry—was worried about the girl. On the morning of the fourteenth day, Moira and Melvin were in the lab.

"How often do you see her?" Moira asked.

"I drop by every day," Melvin replied. "She's come to expect it, I think. Even though she treats me horribly most of the time, I believe she appreciates our little visits. If nothing else, I would seem to be a diversion."

"She treats you horribly?"

"Oh, yes," Melvin replied, blushing slightly and clearing his throat. "She calls me various names typical of homosexual slang, exposes her genitals to me in the most lewd manners, and throws her own feces at me onto the glass. She tries very hard to make me angry or disgusted. It is, of course, just an attempt to gain some sort of control of her situation. If Casey and I are there together, she tries to pit us against each other. As time goes on, her attempts are becoming coarser. Her general condition seems to be allowing less subtlety. She's having more and more trouble controlling her rage and frustration. Quite sad, actually."

"Sad."

"Certainly."

Moira smiled. "Do the two of you talk?"

"Only a little. She occasionally rants at me and issues threats. Sometimes I spend an hour or more just sitting with her as she ignores me. I like to think that the contact, however remote, might bring her a measure of comfort. She is troubled and frightened."

"Can I come with you to see her this morning?"

"That might not be a wise idea. If she began to treat you badly, I would have to leave. I think very highly of you, Moira. I could not sit by and listen to her abuse you. Perhaps you should go this morning, and I will drop in later today. That, coupled with Casey's regular evening visits, would give her a rather full schedule. It might help take her mind off the pain for a while."

"The pain?"

"My latest data indicate that much of the neural tissue in her extremities is swelling a bit and constricting in the nerve sheaths. This is very similar to carpal tunnel syndrome, only spread through her arms, legs, neck, shoulders, hips, and such. It must be very painful. It will get worse."

"Jesus."

"She is attempting, however unwillingly, to defeat more than just one addiction. It has to be devastating. Plus she is suffering emotional instability in the extreme. Please try to keep all that in mind when you see her. She will, most probably, be less than pleasant."

"Perhaps I will be, too," Moira replied.

Gathering her courage and will, Moira entered the viewing room and turned on the lights. She had no idea what she was going to do or say, and attempted to put her trust in the moment. Cat, wearing a lab coat, was lying on the floor at the rear wall, facing away from the windows. Her legs looked very thin. She didn't move. She didn't speak. Moira took a chair and watched her through the slightly cloudy polymer. Cat made no acknowledgement that anyone else was around.

For nearly an hour, Moira studied the girl. She looked so small and frail, curled up on the cold floor at the rear of the room. A human in her condition would be unable even to walk. With a small sigh, Moira rose to go.

"Leaving so soon, Cow?" Cat asked, her voice thin through the speaker.

Startled, Moira swallowed before she answered. "You're awake."

"A trained scientific observer," Cat snorted, rolling over. The coat was unbuttoned and fell open. She stayed on her side and looked blankly at Moira. "I was wondering when you'd finally stop by. Don't get a lot of bovines in here," Cat said. "Moo."

Okay, if that's the way she wanted it. "I'd have been by earlier," Moira replied, putting as much disinterest in her tone as she could, "but I really don't give a shit. Been tough on you, huh? Not getting a good look at the competition."

"Competition?" Cat asked casually.

Moira grinned. "You know what I mean," she said. "Here's some news. There is no competition, Sweetpea. He's mine. You drove him away and now I won't let you have him back. Too bad, so sad, you've been had, and I'm glad. Little baby vamp can't play house with Daddy anymore."

"Fuck you!" Cat snarled.

"No," Moira said, laughing and leaning back in her chair, "fuck you. And you are fucked, Kid. You are so screwed, Sweetie. All those years of having it your way, and now it's over. Now you're in the box and the rest of us are free. And I put you there. Me! If it wasn't for me, you'd still be loose, you twisted little shit! I got your dad where I want him, and I got you where I want you. I have kicked your skinny little ass, you blood-sucking freak, and there isn't one damn thing you can do about it!"

In one bellowing bound from the back wall, Cat hit the glass with most of her body. Expecting the charge and steeled against flinching, Moira held her ground. "You seem to be showing some symptoms of frustration, you poor thing," she said. "I'm fucking your father, and now I've fucked you, too. Life do get tedious, don't it?"

"Bitch! Filthy, shit eating, bitch!" Cat raged, pacing back and forth. "If this fucking wall wasn't here!"

"But it is there," Moira sneered. "And poor little you is on the wrong side of it, right where I want you."

"You Goddamned cunt! You *Goddamned* cunt!" Cat screamed. "For almost four hundred years I've fed on sweet meat like you! For almost four hundred years, I've walked your streets and alleys, taking as many of you as I pleased! For almost four hundred years I've chewed and licked and drank your kind. You have no idea what I've done! You have no idea what I've been! *You have no idea what I am*! I've sucked the life out of thousands of you, you bitch! I've eaten your tongues while you thrashed and whined and cried and begged for mercy! I've slit your throats and bled you into my mouth, I've roasted your children while you watched, I've killed your fathers while they came, I've split hundreds better than you like roast pigs, you twisted fucking twat, and danced in their guts for fun!"

Moira yawned. "Yeah, yeah, yeah. Not any more, Sugar," she purred. "For almost four hundred years you've gotten by because of a genetic accident. For almost four hundred years you've gotten by because of a physical mistake. For almost four hundred years you've gotten by on adolescent tits and ass, you twisted fucking freak! You half-grown refugee from a carnival side show! You soulless, sickening, sad, little blood whore. I wouldn't waste pity on you if I had any."

"You're mine, Bitch," Cat spat, slamming a forearm into the glass. "When I get loose I'm coming for you. You're first, Cow. You're first! *You're first!*"

"Whatever, Girlfriend. Kiss my ass." Moira got to her feet and headed for the door. "By the way," she said. "You oughta eat more, Sweetie. You look like a corpse. Sorry to leave so soon, but the sight of you turns my stomach. Have a nice day."

Stepping into the hall, she gave a start. Casey was leaning against the wall, looking at her. "Think it'll work?" he asked.

"I don't know," Moira replied, tears collecting in her eyes. "I had to try something."

He held her while she cried.

After Moira collected herself, she and Casey met with Melvin in the lab. He was peering at the computer and muttering to himself.

"What's going on?" Moira asked.

"Her endocrine system is making wild swings. If she were human, she could not survive. It's been two weeks now and she hasn't taken in more than two or three thousand calories. Her water consumption is so low she should be dead of thirst. We've pumped enough tranquilizer through her to kill a small herd of elephants and still, she could crush Moira or me with her left hand. Amazing."

"Her judgment is beginning to fail, too," said Casey.

"How so?"

"Moira just spent some time bringing Cat into a rage and then lying to her. She didn't spot the lies."

"That's significant?"

"Oh, yeah. You can't lie to us, Melvin. We smell it."

"Yes, but those rooms are completely isolated from one another. She has her own independent air supply. Scent would not be a factor." He paused a moment, brow furrowed. "Unless, of course, our original assessment was more broadly correct than we assumed, and your body just interprets another more elevated sense as scent."

Casey looked at him and smiled.

"She's beginning to break down," Melvin said.

"She's beginning to break down," Casey agreed.

"And yet," Moira said, "her pineal activity is becoming more and more regular in pulse, and is losing none of its elevated productivity."

"Is that strange?" asked Casey.

"I would assume it is," Melvin replied, "even though I have nothing to compare it to."

"And," Moira continued, "if her blood pH continues to fall as it is now, in a week or two it will be within human parameters."

"Is that strange?" Casey asked.

"I have no idea," Moira said.

"I know one thing for sure," Casey went on. "She certainly doesn't like you."

"She has no reason to," Moira said.

By the beginning of the fourth week, Cat was feral. Half of her hair was gone, she paced constantly when not in her Nosferati period of sleep, she weighed only seventy-nine pounds, ate everything that was left in the cell, drank huge amounts of water, and still declined. Moira could not step into the observation room. Her appearance threw the girl into a blind rage and she would fling herself against the walls and windows with such force that she would break her own limbs. She still healed, but her body could ill afford the energy. On the evening of the twenty-third day, Casey sat, watching his daughter as she paced and talked to herself on the other side of the heavy polymer windows. She turned and looked at him from sunken, dark eyes. There were small droplets of blood around her lips where she constantly chewed and licked herself.

"You want me to beg, *Father?*"

Casey looked at the parody she had become and cursed himself for what he was doing to his child. "No," he said.

"You want me to whine for my freedom? To plead for my life?"

"No."

"Enjoying yourself, *Father*, watching me die?"

"You're not dying, Cat."

"She's doing this, that miserable, festering cunt! She's doing this! Must be some wild-assed pussy on that cow, for her to lead you around by the dick like this, *Father.*

She moo in your ear when she comes, *Father*? She twitch her tail when you shove it in, *Father*? She like pearl necklaces, or does she swallow, *Father*?"

"Cat, stop it!" Casey shouted, heartsick and angry.

She laughed at him. "You miserable, Holstein fucking, cuntsucker. I tell you this," she grinned. "Before this is over, I will have her, you limp-dick sonofabitch! I will fuck her and I will suck her and I will bleed her and I will drink her and I will spit her tongue at you, *Father*! And you, you weak-kneed pussy-whipped mother-fucker, will die washed in her blood and she will die washed in yours! You're no better than they are, you human-loving piece of shit, and you'll die squealing, just like they do!"

With great weariness, Casey rose to his feet. "I love you, Catherine," he said.

"Eat my shit!" Cat snarled, as he shut off the lights and left.

In the darkness, humming as she paced in tight circles, Cat methodically broke each finger on her left hand.

Twice.

During the following week, Cat lost the remainder of her hair and dropped to seventy-one pounds. Her color faded to a dull gray and she appeared to age into her sixties. Bathing her emaciated body, Casey could not hold back tears at the mere sight of what she had become. Melvin and Moira were able to maintain a certain level of clinical detachment from the daughter, but became very concerned about the father. They both did everything they could think of to offer support and strength, but Casey still withdrew, sitting for hours at a time, lost in memory and pain.

On the thirty-first day, Cat began to tear at her own flesh and lick the seeping blood. She was delirious and hallucinating freely, nearly blind and walking into walls. That night, as they tended to her, Casey spoke.

"Two more days," he said.

"What?" asked Moira.

"Two more days," he repeated. "If there is no change for the better in two more days, I'm going to put her out of my misery and her own."

"Oh, Casey," Moira replied, touching his arm.

He turned to her, his eyes and throat full. "This can't go on," he whispered. "This cannot go on. It's a living death for her, a screaming nightmare for me, and way above and beyond the call of duty for you and Melvin. She's even past going berserk when she sees any of us. She's a husk, Moira, a pathetic shrunken husk, and I can't stand it anymore. The only thing I can do is give her blood and that would just start the cycle all over again. I can't release her. If she survived, none of us would ever be safe. You and Melvin would be on borrowed time. God, I wish I'd never started this. I wish I'd just left it alone. I've made a terrible mistake that either you and Melvin or Cat has to suffer for. She'll pay the price, and I'll pay the piper for the rest of my life. Sweet Jesus."

The following night, Casey expressed a desire to be alone and Moira slept in her own room. It was not a night to treat Catherine, so Moira took a long shower and worked on her nails to keep occupied. A little after midnight she put down the

206

novel she was struggling through and turned off her small reading lamp. Moira tossed and turned for a while, then finally settled in. As sleep was about to claim her, she felt a shift in the timber of her room and a sour odor found her nostrils. Rousing, she turned on the reading lamp and peered into the gloom. Standing at the foot of her bed, eyes shining in the dim light, lips pulled back on her skull-like face in the parody of a grin, stood Cat.

"Hello, Cow," she rasped. "Surprised?"

Moira's heart thudded in her chest and blood roared in her ears. She choked back a scream and fought to contain her fear and shock.

"Hello, Catherine," she said to the skeletal figure.

"My, aren't we calm? Good control. You gotta be scared shitless. Go ahead and yell, human. *Father* won't hear you. He's in deep sleep. Melvin might, but that's okay. It'll just save me a trip to find him."

She grasped Moira's ankle through the covers and casually jerked her to the foot of the bed, Moira's legs dangling to the floor. Cat stepped between them and flung the blankets away.

"Let's just have a look at what Father likes so much, shall we?" she croaked, her laugh the grating cackle of a crone. Spreading Moira's legs apart and holding them there with amazing strength, Cat went on. "What a pretty little pussy, especially for a cow," she chuckled, roughly fondling Moira and forcing a knee between her legs. "And what udders!" she exclaimed, kneading Moira's breasts before lying full length upon her, their faces only inches apart.

Nearly mesmerized by her helplessness and the power that loomed over her, Moira turned her face away from Cat's rank breath. The blow to the side of her head was huge, stunning, and she blinked away tears as Cat pulled her face back and kissed her full and deeply on the mouth.

"Great tongue, Cow," she said. "I'll get to that later. I'm saving it for *Father*. First, it's time for a midnight snack. Just something to tide me over until I munch Melvin."

Cat, pulling Moira's head back by the hair, lightly traced a three-inch path down the side of her neck with a ragged fingernail. Blood welled to the surface.

Cat chuckled. "Ooh," she said, grinding her pelvis into Moira and clutching at a breast. "A little here, a little there, maybe a nip from a nipple, just to hear you squeal." She licked the ribbon of blood from Moira's neck and kissed her again. "Aw, don't cry," she teased. "We're just getting to know each other." She licked again as more blood filled the cut. "Ummm. I'm not usually partial to beef, but you taste good."

She sat up, straddling Moira's waist, and traced her finger through the blood, smearing a line of it down between Moira's breasts to her navel. Sliding down, she licked at the blood, working her way back to the neck wound. Moira began to struggle again and Cat cuffed her, laughing.

"The cow wants to fight? Careful, if you make noise, Melvin will come. And believe me, before I'm through, Melvin will come!" She giggled and licked Moira's neck again. "Maybe I'll bring you his cock, Sweetheart, so you can suck it before you …"

The girl sat bolt upright and sniffed, rubbing her throat. "What?" she said, appearing confused. Cat leaned forward and smelled Moira's neck, tentatively touching her tongue to the blood a few times. "No," she muttered, snorting, "it's not possible. No! It's not possible!"

She ripped Moira from the bed and held her upright by the throat.

"You bitch. *You filthy, evil bitch!*" she screamed, casting Moira back to the mattress with such force the woman blacked out.

When Moira returned to consciousness, she thought she'd had a nightmare. She lurched into the bathroom, saw her blood covered reflection, and screamed. Thirty seconds later she was still screaming, shaking Casey's limp form, trying to rouse him. Melvin staggered blearily into the room as Moira smeared her blood on Casey's face. Casey twitched, and opened his eyes.

"Wha?" he asked.

"*Cat's loose!*" Moira shouted. "She came to my room and was going to kill me! Then she started screaming that something was impossible and threw me away. When I woke up she wasn't there!"

Casey looked at her for a moment, then blurred and was gone.

Melvin peered at her and shifted his eyes quickly away.

"We need to tend to your neck," he said.

Only then did Moira realize she was nude.

Casey picked up Cat's scent in the hallway just outside Moira's room. He tracked her halfway around the quiet residence level to a maintenance closet and paused for a moment outside the closed door. This was it. He had to do what needed to be done. She was too wild, too far gone, too dangerous to be allowed to continue. Steeling himself for the task at hand and preparing to fend off an attack, he opened the door.

Cat crouched in the corner behind some mop buckets, holding her knees to her chest. She was shaking and appeared to be confused. Repeatedly licking her lips, she stared blankly at the wall. He dropped to one knee beside her. Slowly she turned to look at him and her eyes gained focus. She peered at him intently for a moment, then blinked rapidly a few times. Tears rolled down her sunken cheeks. Trembling, she tentatively extended a hand and gently touched his face.

"Daddy?" she whispered.

While they cried and then while she slept, Casey held his daughter in his arms.

## A  R o c k  a n d  a  H a r d  P l a c e

STANDING AROUND BOBBY LEE'S BODY, a frightened and elated Voorhees, knowing that he had far more resources at his disposal than did the foul-smelling pair before him, told Colin a very abridged version of whom he worked for and what he did. Trusting instincts honed over years of dealing with half-truths and hidden agendas, he did not lie. He merely didn't disclose everything. Voorhees knew he could not afford to alienate these people, for reasons of personal safety if nothing else, but there was something else. Whatever gave them their remarkable physical abilities was immensely marketable. And the first possible customer was that sterile slug living in his goddamned grade B castle. At Colin's request, Voorhees remained in the Jasper area waiting for Cat to return.

Roy and Lois Freeburton postponed their holiday until both their children were back in school, wanting to spend some time away from their combative daughter and whining son. After Lois' sister Allie consented to stay with the kids for two whole weeks, they gleefully loaded up their almost new Saturn and headed out on a child–free driving vacation to Branson, Missouri, the Mecca of the Ozarks. Looking at a map that described all the scenic wonders of the beautiful Ozark Mountains, they detoured south a ways to tour the magnificent Buffalo River Valley area.

Looking out her passenger window and fighting motion sickness as Roy snaked the Saturn through the twisty narrow roads, watching the shadow of the car skipping through the ditches in the late afternoon sun, Lois noticed the canvas roof-top luggage carrier seemed to be flapping. Irritated at another delay, Roy whipped the car into an overgrown side road and stopped, nearly rear-ending an old pickup truck parked in the way. He slammed the driver's door and stomped around to the passenger side to size up the problem, when he noticed a flash of color through the screen of saplings between him and a bend in the trail. Removing the tiny Personal Defense can of pepper spray from his left front pocket that he had faithfully carried throughout the entire drive, he walked around the thick undergrowth to investigate. Lois heard his strangled shout and the sound of her husband vomiting. The sight of Roy on his hands and knees in the shadow of a massive oak from which was suspended the bloated and headless body of Michael, would haunt her dreams for the rest of her life. When radio news of the Freeburton's grisly discovery became common knowledge, Colin showed up in Voorhees' motel room about an hour before dawn.

Colin stated that only one of his kind could have killed Michael. That left Cat as the obvious suspect, but it made no sense to believe Cat did the deed and then fled. Had she wanted to kill Michael, she could have easily done it a thousand times at home. Nobody would have cared. Michael was not a coveted or necessary member of the group. No. There was a rogue out there somewhere. Someone with whom Cat had allied herself, or who had done something to or with her.

That Melvin and Moira should be in the area when the incidents occurred was more than just happenstance, Voorhees was sure. But the killing of one of Colin's people was, according to Colin, well beyond their abilities. After what Voorhees had seen, he had no doubt such was the case. That left the probability a rogue was involved even more intact. Traveling in the company of Moira and Melvin was the unknown factor. The probable prison escapee who did not exist. In the back of his mind, Voorhees knew it all centered on that man. In the back of his mind, Voorhees knew he was into something very big. Visions of villas, fine wines, and disposable pretty boys flickered at the edge of his usually literal mind. He liked it. If he could keep his cards close to his vest and use the resources that both Colin and Unruh had to offer, his potential rewards were immense.

Voorhees was much too disgusted by Colin to have any loyalty to the man. He stank. He was filthy. He was probably illiterate. True, he had some amazing abilities, but they in no way made up for his liver colored lips, his pudgy body, or the fact that, beneath his t-shirt, the man had breasts. Voorhees knew his own limitations. With all his experience and training, with all his ruthlessness and lack of conscience, he could not stand against Colin physically for a moment. In truth, Voorhees felt very fortunate to have left that small farmhouse alive. Not that he was afraid. Voorhees' emotional make up was such that fear was nearly impossible for him. But, he was a realist. He knew he had two choices. Run, or continue to work for Unruh and kiss Colin's hermaphroditic ass. Always the profiteer, he chose to kiss.

He called Unruh and reported in, not mentioning his association with Colin, but hinting that the man accompanying Melvin and Moira might possess some truly unusual abilities. Unruh was intrigued and urged Voorhees to continue his investigations. By the time Voorhees got off the phone, Unruh was nearly panting with anticipation. Jesus! Voorhees was as repulsed by Unruh as he was by Colin. Disgusted by the power that surrounded him on both sides, power that certainly could punch his ticket, Voorhees balanced in the breeze. He'd been in tight spots before, and patience bolstered with ruthless response had always gotten him through. It was time for patience.

When he reached Kansas City, Voorhees drove downtown and registered under a fictitious name at the Marriott Hotel. Leaving his car parked in the basement garage, he wandered the underground walkway, finally emerging at the Holiday Inn, where he registered again under a false name, and called for a rental vehicle. He drove to the Kansas side, took a room under a third name at a La Quinta Inn, had dinner, and went to bed. The following morning he contacted Ted Plank of Provenance security. They met at The Machine Shed Restaurant for lunch.

"They came back around a week ago," Plank told him. "They've got something going on down on sublevel four. It's the old primate observation lab. Security is real tight. Even I can't get in there. The gate guard said that when they drove in there was something big and boxy under a tarp in the back of the van they were using. He had no idea what it was."

"Any way you can find out what they're doing?"

"Doubt it. Security is palm and retina ID at that level. I've seen all three of them a time or two in the cafeteria and halls, but that's all."

"What do you need?"

"Access to the security computer on a priority level. That requires a key to the containment area and a password."

"Alright," said Voorhees. He placed a plain brown envelope on the table between them, rose, and walked out.

Plank riffled through the crisp bills in the envelope and looked at his half-eaten sandwich. He had no appetite.

Nearly three weeks later, Ted Plank shut off the alarm clock and walked out into the living room of his apartment. He flipped on the TV to get an early morning weather report and yawned his way into the kitchen to make coffee. There, on top of the coffee maker, lay another plain brown envelope. Inside was a single key and a square of paper on which was written one word: Chrysalis. Blinking sleep from his eyes, he quickly checked his alarm system. Armed and functioning.

Ted Plank dropped into a kitchen chair and sat panting, sweat beading on his forehead.

# TWENTY-SIX

Catherine

CASEY CARRIED CAT DOWN to the observation area and sat holding her in the primate room. Melvin and Moira entered in a few moments and saw them through the glass. Moira spoke.

"Is she?"

"Sleeping," Casey said. "She's not quite unconscious. It's over."

Moira sank into a chair. "Thank God," she said.

Casey looked through the polymer at Moira's bandaged neck. "How 'bout you?" he said. "Your neck okay?"

"Melvin fixed me. Just a scratch."

"You were bleeding, and I just left you there. I'm sorry."

Moira shook her head. "You had no choice. Is it really over?"

"The worst of it, yeah," Casey said, weariness etching his face. "She called me Daddy. Jesus."

"Oh, Casey," Moira choked, tears leaping to her eyes.

"Yeah," Casey replied, shaking his head. "Just like that. After everything we've been through, just like that. Now we need to let her rest and give her some real nourishment. Is there a bed around here and someplace we can clean her up?"

Melvin brought in a narrow hospital bed and set it up as Casey held the girl over the drain and Moira soaped and rinsed her entire body. Thirty minutes later Cat was snoring softly on clean sheets and connected to a saline drip to which had been added twenty cc's of whole blood. Casey examined the door between the rooms and closed it.

"How the hell did she get out?" he said.

"Got me," Moira replied, adjusting a piece of tape on her throat. "Melvin and I looked it over before you and Cat came back. Couldn't find anything. It's like she never left."

"How badly are you hurt?" Casey asked, crossing to Moira and looking down at her.

"It's nothing."

Casey smelled the lie.

"Nine stitches," Melvin said. "Three inch tear within a half-inch of the common carotid."

"She was just playing," Moira said. "Oh, she was going to kill me, no doubt about that. She just wasn't going to kill me yet. Cat said she wanted a snack before she visited Melvin."

"Poor child," Melvin murmured.

"Poor Melvin," Casey replied, "if she hadn't run off. I'm really sorry you guys had to go through this." He thought a moment, then turned back to Moira. "What stopped her? I mean, abusing you would have been the most important thing on her mind. She would have toyed with you until you were crippled, done whatever she intended to do to Melvin before she killed him, then returned to finish her game with you. It was perfect. She couldn't miss. Yet, she didn't do it. That's unbelievable."

"All I remember was her shouting that something was impossible, and then she picked me up by the neck. When I woke up, she was gone."

The three of them looked through the glass at the small sleeping figure for a moment.

"So, do we lock her in again?" Melvin said.

"You lock *us* in," said Casey. "I'll stay with her in the chamber. I doubt that she'll be any threat, especially to me, but we'll play it as if she were, just in case. She'll probably sleep for a day or two. When she wakes up, she is going to be very hungry. I'm gonna need to move the small fridge in there. She'll require animal protein, bloody animal protein. Raw steaks would be good. I don't think she should get more than twenty cc's of human blood per day and not by mouth for three or four days. I'm pretty sure the cycle is broken, but there's no point in tempting fate. When she wakes up and I can speak with her, I'll know where her head is. If she says she won't hurt you and Moira, I'll know if she's telling the truth."

Cat slept for almost forty hours. Casey felt her body rhythms shift as she approached consciousness and looked down at his daughter. All of her wounds had healed, her color was nearly normal, and her hair had returned and was over a quarter of an inch long. Her eyes opened and, when the confusion cleared, crinkled at the corners.

"Good morrow, Pop. Long time no see."

"Hi, Sweetheart," Casey replied, stroking her forehead. "How doest thee fair?"

"Weak. Hungry. Confused." Pain shot through her eyes. "Oh, Daddy. I tried to kill you."

"Ancient history," he said.

"No, it isn't," she protested, tossing her head. "I tried to kill you! If that human, uh, Melvin, hadn't stopped me, I would have!"

"Possibly."

"And then *she* shot me."

"Moira."

"And then those same humans and you took care of me and ..." memory rushed over her, and Cat began to cry. She refused Casey's embrace and curled on her side in the fetal position, her thin body shaking with sobs.

Casey stroked her back for a time, easily feeling the vertebra in her spine, then removed two sixteen-ounce sirloins from the refrigerator. He put them on the top of the fridge to warm a bit and watched his daughter curled on the bed. His heart went out to her, but what she felt had to come out. It was only the tip of what she'd have to go through if she were to recover from her life. He'd done it. She could too. He'd help. So would Melvin and Moira.

He let her cry for over an hour, then cut the steaks in bite-sized pieces and carried them to her bedside. The smell of the meat forced its way through her tears and she turned to him, wiping her eyes with the palm of her hand.

"Enough crying for a while, Catherine. Eat," he said. "It'll help you get big and strong."

She began to wolf the beef as fast as she could, nearly snarling as the blood dripped off her chin.

"I know this isn't what you believe you need," Casey said, watching her snap at the beef. "No matter how it feels, your needs have changed. I'll help you get through it. So will Moira and Melvin. You have an opportunity to get control of your life in ways you aren't even aware of. I love you, Cat, but you must understand it can never again be the way it was. You're past all that now. So am I. You have a future that belongs to you. You are no longer a slave to the blood. Never again will you have to take an innocent human life."

Casey caressed his daughter's cheek.

"There is value in humans, Cat. They have honor. They care for one another, they love for the sheer joy of loving and give for the sheer pleasure of giving. Some of them are quite selfless, ready to lay their own lives on the line to help others. With all their frailties and faults, in spite of their weakness and fragility, they are often quite admirable. You were human once. You'll remember. Because of Melvin and Moira, I am happy. Happiness waits for you too, Sweetheart. You don't have to *take* it. You merely need to *accept* it."

She looked at him. "These humans, do they know what I am?"

"They know you are my daughter and that we are Nosferati."

"They know what I can do?"

"Yes. And the fact that you have killed thousands of their kind. They know the same about me."

"And still they came to get me. Why?"

"To help me and to help other humans."

"To wipe us out?"

"No—to possibly acquire information to help them overcome sickness and disease."

"Jesus," Cat muttered, shaking her head. "You actually trust these humans?"

"Absolutely."

"And they trust you?"

"Yes."

"God. This is so strange."

"Only compared to the way you have lived for so long," he went on, emotion clouding his voice. "Look at it. Was there ever a Nosferati you felt you could completely trust? Was there ever one who acted out of anything but self-interest? Was there ever one who actually cared if you were happy? Was there ever one that loved you?"

Tears filled her eyes. "Only you," Cat said.

"I was human for forty-two years, Catherine. Part of me still is. Part of you still is. That's what being a Nosferati represses, our humanness. It steals that from us, Cat. And no matter what the rewards are, no matter the nature of the benefits, it's not a fair trade. I hope you'll come to understand that, now that you're no longer a blood-slave. Then you can make your choice about how you want to live—with a clear mind, as I have."

Cat stared blankly at the ceiling for a moment before lifting her head to look at Casey. "Those humans took a terrible risk," she said.

"Melvin and Moira," Casey said. "They're people, Cat, just like you and I are people. And yes, they did."

"They're very brave."

"They were scared to death, but they were committed to a cause. Ever know a Nosferati who was committed to anything but blood?"

"No," she replied in a small voice, sinking back against the mattress.

"Rest," Casey said. "Sleep."

She took his hand. "Will you be here when I wake up?"

"Without a doubt."

"I love you, Daddy."

"It's been almost four hundred years since the last time I heard you say that," Casey whispered.

"I know." Cat smiled through fresh tears. "I remember."

"I fed her," Casey said, sitting across from Melvin and Moira in the cafeteria after they'd collected him from the lab. "She went straight back to sleep. No need to lock the door."

"How is she?" Moira asked

"Physically, much stronger. Her hair is growing back, her color is better. She'll eat massive amounts of protein and convert almost all of it to weight. Emotionally, she's pretty freaked at being helped by the livestock." He smiled. "She's having trouble dealing with humans being nice to her or friendly with me. Among our ex-circles, it simply isn't done, you know."

"When will she be up and around?"

"Tomorrow, I imagine. Things will progress pretty rapidly now." Casey paused, staring blankly at the tabletop. After a moment, he blinked, looked at Moira, and smiled.

"You okay?" she said.

"Yeah," he replied. "Just drifted for a minute. It was something Cat said. She, uh, she told me she loved me."

"Excellent!" Melvin said. "When can we see her?"

"A couple of days," Casey replied, unable to suppress a grin. "She'll gain back most of the weight by then and feel a little more confident. Being in the same room with the two of you will embarrass and confuse her. That's good. It'll give her more to think about. She needs her mind to go in as many different directions as possible right now, so she doesn't fixate on the blood. I've gotta get back down there and get more food ready for her. She'll wake up soon, eat three or four pounds of raw beef, and go to sleep again. You guys going to the lab?"

"I am," Melvin said. "I've got some cultures to go over."

"Me too," Moira replied. "I need to drop by my apartment for a few minutes, then I'll be with Melvin." She rose to leave, and Casey went with her to the elevator. When the door opened, Ted Plank stepped out.

Moira smiled. "Hi, Ted."

"Miss Flynn," he replied, returning her smile.

"What's new in the security business?" she asked.

"Just the same old boring stuff," he shrugged, nodding at Casey and stepping aside so they could enter the elevator. Casey frowned.

"Nothing exciting happening?" he inquired.

"Nope."

"No bad guys in the bushes, no undercover operations, no high level infiltrations, no clandestine meetings, no spies skulking in the stairwells?" Casey said. "Must get pretty tedious."

Ted laughed. "It does," he said. "Boring, too."

"Nice man," Moira said, after the elevator doors closed.

"Bullshit," Casey growled. "He's a liar."

"What?"

"He's a liar and he's frightened. There *are* bad guys in the bushes, there *have been* meetings, and there *is* some sort of operation in effect, and Mr. Plank is the spy. Judging by his reaction, that operation involves us."

"*What?*"

"We have evidently attracted some attention to ourselves. Somebody wants to know more about us, I suspect, and whoever that somebody is, they have some connection to Mr. Plank and probably Provenance."

"C'mon," Moira protested.

"I could smell it all over him," Casey went on. "The minute I brought it up, even in jest, his body temperature rose. That indicates increased heart rate and adrenalin output. No doubt about it. Good old Ted is hiding all sorts of stuff from us."

"Jesus," Moira muttered. "You're absolutely sure?"

"Absolutely. Who owns the company?"

"Provenance?"

"Yeah."

"The Proteus Trust."

"Who owns Proteus?"

"I have no idea."

"Can you find out?"

"Maybe. I'll call my pal, Marley. She might know people who can find out."

The elevator stopped on the residential level and Moira exited. Casey held the door open. "Check. Don't deal personally with anyone you haven't known for a long time," he said and let the door close.

When Cat woke up, Casey led her into the viewing area and let her use the restroom. He fed her nearly three pounds of raw beef and over a quart of fortified sports drink

216

and put her back to bed. She dropped off to sleep almost immediately. When he stepped out into the hall, he found Moira waiting for him. She was pale and trembling.

"What's wrong?"

"Marley's dead. Been dead for weeks."

"Aw, shit. I'm so sorry, Sweetheart. How'd she die?"

"Massive stroke," Moira replied, her face beginning to crumble. She wormed her way into his chest and began to cry quietly. "Two teen-age daughters. Her husband was killed in a light plane crash six or seven years ago. Now the girls have nobody."

"How old was she?"

"I don't know. Not forty yet. Great shape, ran four or five miles every day, watched her diet, used herbs and supplements. A stroke. A fucking stroke."

"Strange," Casey said.

"Christ. That's not all," Moira continued, pulling away and looking at him. "I checked with a contact over at NCIC to find out if anything unusual was going on down in Arkansas."

"Yeah."

"They found Michael's body."

"Uh-huh. You sure it was Michael?"

"Well, the head was missing. Nobody could find it."

"Coyotes."

"Sheriff Bobby Lee is dead, too."

"No kidding."

"Found his body out in the country at the place owned by Flavel and Aleen Potts."

"Oh?"

"Shot once in the back of the head. His gun was still in the holster. Nobody can seem to find any trace of the Potts couple."

"Hmm."

"Bobby Lee's feet were crushed."

"Oh, damn," Casey sighed.

"Whadaya mean, 'Oh, damn'?"

"That's a Nosferati thing," Casey explained. "If you wanna keep humans in one spot for an hour or two, you just break their feet. The physical trauma won't let them walk. The emotional trauma makes 'em think they're helpless. Very effective."

"Shit."

"And Bobby Lee being shot in the back of the head means there was another human there, too," Casey said.

"How do you know that?"

"A Nosferati wouldn't have used a gun to kill Bobby Lee. Too impersonal. No fun. Killing should be fun."

Moira shivered and looked at him. "So, you're saying that the Nosferati have another human working for them?"

"Looks like it. And one a damn sight better for their purposes than poor old Bobby Lee, or he'd still be alive."

"And now we have someone checking up on us?"

"And now we have someone checking up on us."

"Oh, hell," she said, squaring her shoulders. "This is starting to snowball. Damn." She shook her head. "I'm going to go call Marley's daughters and talk to them a few minutes," Moira went on. "Tell 'em how sorry I am about their mom."

"Rough, having a parent killed like that," said Casey.

"Killed? She died of a stroke."

Casey looked at her patiently.

"Oh, God!" Moira exclaimed, color draining from her face as recognition lit her eyes.

"You and Melvin mentioned that you wanted to relocate," Casey said quietly. "Soon would be good."

That evening as Cat slept, Casey and Moira apprised Melvin of the situation.

"But why would Ted Plank be interested in what we're doing?" he asked.

"He probably couldn't care less," Moira said. "Somebody pulling his strings is. And whoever is pulling *that* somebody's strings is most likely someplace in the upper levels of the Proteus Trust, or one of the companies that owns Proteus. I spent a little time on the internet this afternoon trying to get some idea of who actually controls Proteus, and therefore Provenance. Nothing. What a convoluted mess! Limited partnerships, corporations, holding companies, on and on."

"Since you can detect lies," Melvin continued, turning to Casey, "why don't you just talk with Ted. I'm sure you could get the truth out of him."

"I probably could, but he doesn't know enough of the truth to make exposing our own awareness of the situation worthwhile. I just hope he doesn't make some kind of move that I have to deal with. I don't want anyone to know that we're suspicious. Great Caesar, I hate this shit!"

"But maybe he could at least get you to the next level," Melvin protested.

Casey looked at him. "Melvin," he said, "if I question Ted Plank, I'll have to kill him to keep him quiet. I have no problem killing somebody who is moving against us, but I don't want to draw any more attention in our direction than it seems we already have. Virginia Marley is dead and she only talked to Moira on the phone. How much do you think your life would be worth once they got the information they needed from you?"

"Oh. I didn't understand."

"Neither does Plank. If he comes up with any serious stuff on us, his life isn't worth a nickel. Whoever is running him will kill his young ass to make sure he doesn't tell anyone else."

"We have to get to Colorado," Moira said.

"How many people know that you have property there?" Casey asked.

"Nobody around here. It's actually in my mother's sister's name. Aunt Louise is seventy-some years old and lives in Boston. An administrator handles the land for her, renting out pasture to pay for taxes and provide income. She hasn't been on the place in years. She's just holding it. When she dies it all goes to me."

"How much land is there?"

"Nearly four thousand acres. It's spread over an area north of Glenwood Springs. Still fairly secluded out that way. Access is limited. There aren't many roads in that neck of the woods."

"Could we hide?"

"Fairly well. We'll have to set up a lab, make some substantial purchases, and solicit funds, but we could do most of that through Denver or Boulder or someplace. We won't need an office or a public front. It'd be a bit of a hassle driving to Denver once or twice a week for a while, but it's not a deal breaker. A post office box in Denver, pre-paid cell phones, and we could be anywhere. We could just disappear."

Casey smiled. "That's what we need to do. You in, Melvin?"

"Of course. I began making copies of my work weeks ago. I've also designed a virus that will devour all of my computerized data in any of the system's computers. And I started liquidating my holdings in both Proteus and Provenance. I've done it relatively slowly so as not to attract attention. The amount will be considerable, I assure you."

Casey grinned. "You sly dog!"

"*Nosferatum Robustus* is the chance of a lifetime," Melvin continued. "I intend to keep working on it."

"Melvin!" Moira exclaimed, kissing him on the cheek. "You are a peach!"

"Ah, well," he colored. "I believe, that is to say, I thought it best to, uh, prepare for the possible, er, eventuality of our discovery, as it were."

"And so will I," Moira said. "I'll make a couple of calls tomorrow and get my end of things in motion."

"And we're off to Colorado," Melvin said.

"And Cat," Casey said.

"Certainly," Melvin went on, "and Catherine."

# TWENTY-SEVEN

### Occam's Razor

CAT SAT UP IN BED and pulled the sweatshirt down over her head. She swung her feet over the side and eased her legs into the sweatpants, sliding to put her bare feet on the floor. Standing, she shook herself to settle the clothes and ran the fingers of both hands through her curly hair, smiling shyly at her father.

"How ya doin'?" Casey asked, grinning at her.

"I'm scared," she replied, fidgeting a bit.

"You look great," Casey beamed, "except for ..."

"Except for what?" Cat asked, eyeing him suspiciously.

"Put on your shoes."

"I don't like shoes," she complained.

"Put 'em on anyway."

"Yes, Daddy Dear," she crooned, sticking her tongue out at him and pulling on a pair of Reeboks.

"Good. You look positively civilized."

"That's what I was going for," Cat replied, pushing the sweatshirt's sleeves up over her elbows.

"Nearly human," Casey teased.

"Oh, God," she shivered. "Is it time?"

"It's time. We'll go next door. There's a lounge that's much less sterile than here."

In the few days since her attack on Moira, Cat's weight had returned, her hair had grown back, color had blossomed in her cheeks, sparkle in her eyes, and she looked much as she had for many years. Some things were different, however. Her anger had abated. Her brittle edge had been blunted. As a Nosferati, Cat had always seemed to itch and was almost constantly touching herself. The light in her eyes came from need and want. She had projected a perpetual sexual energy, a heat that was never quiet, never still. All that was gone.

Not that Cat had regressed back to being Casey's fourteen-year-old daughter, although from time to time she played that role for amusement and to strengthen their bond. In some ways she was even younger and more naïve, more newly human. Coloring that was the experience of several lifetimes, ill spent to be sure, but with her nonetheless. She was a young woman who could remember the Revolu-

220

tionary War. A sensual female who had depended on her sexual allure for nearly four hundred years. A girl who had been human for only a decade and a half. A newly reborn stranger in a strange land.

And now, the cattle had caught her. And now, her prey of centuries had helped her. And now, those she had so ruthlessly used for her own purposes since the days of their great, great, great grandparents—those she would have so gladly and easily tortured and killed—were coming to meet her and offer her friendship.

"How can they stand to be near me, knowing what I am?" Cat asked.

"What you *were*," Casey corrected. "Humans have an amazing capacity for forgiveness. What you do is more important to them than what you've done. What you can be, in some ways, is more important than what you are. I came to Moira and Melvin as little more than a lab rat, and yet they have become my friends and more than just my friends. They are, in some respects, as much a part of my life as I am. I know that this is all very difficult for you, from several standpoints. Not the least of which is that it's hard for a wolf to be calm in the company of sheep."

Cat chuckled. "There's that."

"Of course there is," Casey said. "It's easier to deal with if you try to imagine how the sheep must feel. These people risked their lives to help you, Cat. They are risking their lives to help *us*. Compared to what they can lose, what they have to gain is less than nothing."

"Melvin and Moira?"

"Melvin and Moira."

"Okay, Pop," she said, putting her arm through his. "Let's get it over with."

The lounge was small and cozy, furnished with several padded Adirondack style chairs, some end tables, two empty vending machines, a cabinet containing a microwave oven, a coffee maker, and a few bottles of water. Casey and Cat walked in to find a nervous Moira and Melvin. The pair got to their feet.

"Cat," said Casey, "may I present Moira Marie Flynn and Melvin Foltz. Moira and Melvin, my daughter Catherine."

"It's nice to finally meet both of you," Cat said, not quite able to look either of them in the eye. "Dad has told me everything you've done for me, and a little of what I did to you. I'm just so sorry that I, that I, uh," She turned her face away, unable to continue, tears in her eyes.

Moira rose. "You are just lovely," she said, moving to stand in front of Cat. "You look wonderful! It's good to see you shine so."

She opened her arms and Cat slid between them, crying freely as the two women embraced.

"I'm so sorry," Cat choked. "I'm so sorry about the way I treated you."

"Hush," Moira replied, holding her and stroking the back of her head. "That wasn't you, Sweetheart. That was the Nosferati. There are no Nosferati in this room. Not one. Welcome back."

When Moira also began to cry, Casey and Melvin avoided each other's eyes and stood around swallowing and staring at the walls. At length, the crying reduced to sniffing and embarrassed laughter as Moira and Cat moved apart. The girl turned her attention to Melvin, who paled a bit and retreated half a step. Casey chuckled.

"And you, Melvin," Cat said, wiping her eyes, "who sat with me every day in spite of the way I abused you. You were so patient and kind. Please forgive me."

"Of course," Melvin said, clearing his throat and patting her gingerly on the arm. "I realize, certainly, the, uh, that is to say that, uh …"

"Melvin?" Cat said.

"Yes?"

"Hug me."

"Well, ah,"

"Open your arms."

"Yes, well," Melvin replied, doing as he was told.

They embraced for a moment, and when they separated, Melvin appeared to be quite moved.

"It would seem that I, too, am crying," he commented, wiping his eyes. "How unusual."

Cat reached out and thumbed a tear off his cheek. "Several weeks ago you said something to me that I am going to now say to you," she smiled. "Your courage is amazing. I admire you. I would like to be your friend."

"Uh," stammered Melvin. "It would, of course, be my honor to have you as a, surely, if that's what you'd, ah …"

Cat leaned forward and shyly kissed him on the cheek. "That's what I'd like, Melvin."

"Okay," he replied, only slightly lighter in color than a tomato.

Laughing, Casey slapped him gently on the back. "It's a bitch when they use your words against you like that, huh, Melvin?"

Melvin turned away from smiling at Cat and looked at Casey. "Oh, I don't know," he said. "I must admit that I found it quite pleasant, I suppose."

They talked for nearly two hours, telling Cat the entire story of how Casey came to be at Provenance, how they'd traced her, and the fact that they were probably being hunted. Cat confessed that Colin was the type of individual who would take her leaving personally and go to any lengths necessary to find and punish her.

"He won't let this lay. You can count on that," she said. "I'm not afraid for myself or Dad. Together, we can handle almost anything. But you and Melvin are not as equipped as we are. In taking care of us, you two are now in a position where we may need to take care of you." She smiled. "I think that's fair, don't you, Pop?"

"I think it's very fair," Casey said.

"So," Cat went on, "it looks like we're in this together. I hate to break up the visit, but I'm getting tired. I think I need to eat and then I need to sleep. Walk me home, Dad?"

"Every night, if you like."

"One more question, if I might?" said Moira.

"Sure."

"The night you came to my room to, ah …"

"To kill you," Cat said.

"To kill me. How did you get out of the containment area?"

Cat's brow furrowed. "I don't know," she said. "Now that you mention it, I don't know. I really don't. I guess I can't remember." She stood and Casey walked with her to the door.

"One more thing," Moira said as Cat and Casey stepped into the hall. "Why didn't you kill me?"

Cat looked at her. "The babies," she said.

"The babies?"

"Yes. The boy and the girl."

"The boy and the girl? What boy and girl?"

Cat beamed. "You don't know yet, do you?"

"Know what?" Moira nearly shouted.

"You're pregnant," Cat laughed. "You and Dad are going to have twins!"

She left Casey leaning against the wall and walked herself home.

An hour later in the lab, Melvin looked at Moira.

"You are," he said. "No doubt about it."

"Nosferati don't have babies. Nosferati don't father babies," Casey protested.

Moira patted his arm. "But you're not a Nosferati, Daddy."

"Just off the top of my head," Melvin said, "and this is only unsupported supposition, but I would suspect blood pH to be the determining factor."

Moira looked at him. "Ingestion of large amounts of blood?" she said.

"Raises it," Melvin countered.

"And reduced levels of consumption?"

"Allows it to return to more normal levels," Melvin said.

"That might also relate to the focus of pineal activity," Moira said.

"Why Casey's is higher than Cat's, and why Cat's is getting better."

"God. Could it be that simple?"

"Occam's Razor," Melvin said.

"Do you mean," Casey asked, "that the reason Nosferati don't have babies is because they drink too much blood?"

"Quite possibly."

"Jesus. That's the big bitch. For as long as I was among them, they always lamented the fact that no Nosferati ever had children, even if they consorted with humans. It just didn't work. There was always the fear that they would eventually die out because so few ever survive the infection. If you're right, all they have to do is lay off blood for a while, and they could have kids."

"That might be all," Melvin agreed. "Of course, we have no idea how long they would have to minimize consumption, or even if it would have to continue through the pregnancy."

"Ha!" Casey exclaimed, lightly punching the wall. "Talk about your Catch 22! All you have to do to have more Nosferati is to have less Nosferati."

"We're with child, Dear," said Moira, batting her eyes at Casey.

"Childs," he corrected, grinning at her.

"I think it's wonderful," Melvin beamed. "*Uncle* Melvin. Uncle *Melvin*. It has a nice ring to it."

"Yes, it does," said Moira, kissing him on the cheek. "We're going to need a nursery in the Glenwood Springs house. How did Cat know, I wonder?"

"Did she taste your blood?" Casey asked.

"Several times."

"That's it. And it stopped her from killing you. Our unborn children saved you from my daughter. Weird, huh?"

"Well, I certainly don't believe that we need to be concerned about Catherine at this point," mused Melvin.

"I don't think so either," Moira said. "You and Cat seemed to get along okay, huh, Melvin?"

"Well, yes," Melvin hesitated, swallowing and looking randomly about the room. " I, uh, I find her to be quite charming. She is ..."

"Really?" Moira said.

Casey sighed and shook his head.

## The Beat Goes On

IT WAS DARK, but they had no way to tell. It was quiet, but silence was all they knew. Tenuously tethered, they floated in their own private ocean, less than jellyfish in their Sargassian universe. They did not eat, they did not drink, they did not sleep, they did not wake, they did not contemplate. They did not realize. They merely waited, consciousness beyond them. They existed, but they did not know it.

It was the rhythm that made them real. They could not hear it, but it coursed through them in a pulse as ancient as life, as old as waves upon the shore. It called to them and, in their minute way, they responded with Lilliputian rhythms of their own, two tiny flutterings answering the massive one around them that was life. The tempo was different, but the pattern was the same. The beat of a billion years. A primordial cadence that wakened purpose. The beginning of two new brains became bombarded by the beating of two new hearts, mathematical certainty fell into place, entrainment melded the rhythms into life-sustaining compliance, and the vibration of millennia seeped through them. They knew they were.

From that instant they felt each other, were aware of each other in the rhythm flowing through the fluid in which they drifted. As the pulse of creation continued and they became more aware of the where of life, they knew more of the how of life and helped each other roam.

# TWENTY-EIGHT

MOIRA WAS GONE when Casey arose the next morning. A note on the counter said she'd be back by noon. He made coffee, dressed, drank his first cup, and was preparing to go visit Cat when Melvin knocked on the door.

"Good morning, Melvin. How's by you?"

"Uh, good morning. Have you seen Moira?"

"She'll be back around lunchtime."

"Oh, good. I need some blood."

"So do I," Casey said. "So does Cat. I think it's time to start her on a few cc's by mouth. She could use the energy, and I think she'll handle the real thing with no problem."

"I'll get what you need before I go out."

"You going out, too?"

"I must attend to the divestiture of additional stock, as well as some other financial matters before we relocate. After we leave here and take it on the lam, so to speak, I assume our location will be kept secret."

"If that's possible."

"So I must finish addressing the matter of our monetary needs. We will require a considerable amount of funds, I should think."

Casey smiled and shook his head. "Melvin, you are something else."

"How so?"

"Your generosity is amazing. You owe Cat and me absolutely nothing, and yet you're willing not only to move off into the wilds of Colorado somewhere and just leave your life behind, but also to foot the bill for the whole thing."

"Yes, well, Moira is not totally without resource, you know. She is also committed to this project. And, of course, to you."

"I know that you are an extraordinary person, Mr. Foltz," Casey replied, clasping Melvin lightly by the shoulder, "and that I am proud to call you my friend."

The small man looked up at Casey. "Ah, yes. There's, uh, always that, then, isn't there?" His eyes began to fill and he looked away. "We are friends, aren't we, Casey?"

"Only while I draw breath," Casey said, watching Melvin fidget and pace.

"I suppose you're my first real friend then," Melvin confessed. "I've always been something of a freak."

"Melvin, whatever else you are, you are not a freak. I've known plenty of freaks in my life. You do not qualify."

"Freakishness is relative, I suppose," Melvin commented, pouring himself a cup of Casey's coffee. His hands trembled slightly. "I'm very bright," he continued. "So were my parents. Very bright. I started school when I was three, did junior high level work by age six, began some college level courses by age ten, held the equivalent of two degrees by the time I was a teenager and acquired doctorate-level certification in microbiology and chemistry during my sixteenth year. By the time I was twenty-two, I had my medical degree, my PhD in immunology, and was the leading mind in the country in the areas of communicable disease. In the fifteen years since then, I have been nominated for the Nobel Prize, I have been published lavishly, I have acquired five patents, and my colleagues call me Doctor Blood. I have accomplished a great deal in my life, Casey. I have also been stuffed in school lockers, been pushed headfirst into toilets, and been repeatedly called faggot, geek, nerd, and the like, countless times. I have never been to a high school football game, never been to a dance or prom, never purchased a corsage, never driven a car over 75 miles an hour, and never been on a motorcycle."

Melvin looked around the room and rubbed his arms.

"I was regarded as a resource by the two cold academics who were my father and mother, and who, by the way, regarded themselves as resources also. I have never had a family, I live alone, I exist in laboratories and books, I've never owned a dog and, until I met you, had never been on an adventure. You not only saved my life, you have given me a life. I find it very gratifying that you consider me to be your friend. I am, you know."

Battling the lump in his throat, Casey smiled. "I know."

"And now I have this opportunity to not only continue my work, but to begin again in the association with some truly wonderful people who are becoming a family. If I can help with something as trivial as money, I would be a fool not to. I am not a fool."

"Melvin, you are not 'in association' with anything. You are part of it. A vital, necessary, appreciated part. My children are going to grow up in the company of their Uncle Melvin. I can think of no better influence for them than a man such as you. You are as much a part of this as anyone else."

Melvin, arms folded and staring at the floor, hesitated for a moment before speaking. "Yes, well," he said. "Ah, thank you. This is, ah, really wonderful, ah …"

"Blood, Melvin," Casey said. "I need some, so does Cat."

"Ah, yes. Blood. Well, perhaps I might, that is if you thought it prudent to do so, perhaps I might take Catherine's blood to her? Just ten cc's or so? Of course, it's absolutely your decision."

"I think that's fine. I'm sure she'll be glad to see you."

"Excellent! I'll be going then," Melvin replied, as he headed eagerly to the door. "I'll leave your blood out on the counter in the lab, Casey, and take Catherine's down to her straight away. She'll be awake and dressed, won't she? I don't want to intrude on her privacy."

"It'll be fine, Melvin."

"Good! I'm off then, I suppose," he replied, nearly skipping out of the room.

Casey chuckled and poured Melvin's untasted coffee down the sink.

A little after noon, Casey arrived at Cat's door with ham sandwiches and a container of German potato salad.

"You look great," he said, enjoying Cat's lopsided grin. She was sitting in one of the meeting room Adirondack chairs wearing sweat pants and a pink t-shirt. Her bare feet were propped up on the bed. He placed the tray on the mattress and gave her a hug.

"You brought food. You can stay," Cat said.

"Get some blood this morning?"

"Melvin brought me a little. Freaky how such a small amount can make a big difference in how I feel."

"When the addiction is gone, a little goes a long way. I take about twenty cc's a day. I believe he gave you ten. If things go okay, we'll raise your intake a little."

"He was so cute."

"What?"

"Melvin. He was so cute. He knocked on the outside door and yelled in to make sure I was decent. God! After everything he went through when I was coming down, and he treated me like I was a Sunday school teacher."

Casey laughed. "Melvin's a little unprepared," he said.

"A little? He could barely look at me. Couldn't get out a whole sentence without stammering. It was really sweet."

"He's a very sweet man," Casey agreed.

"He stayed for about a half an hour and tried to make small talk. What a struggle! He said something about us moving soon?"

"Yeah. Out to near some springs in Colorado. Glendale or Glenwood, something like that."

"Probably for the best. Gonna make a country girl outta me, Pop?"

"You could do worse."

"I have, for a long time. God, are we gonna be a family?"

"Moira's pregnant," he said.

"Yeah. What a rush, huh? Will they be Nosferati?"

"They'll be babies, Cat. Anything else, we'll deal with."

"My brother and sister. Wow. Babies! Felene wants kids so bad, and now I know she and Gunnar can have 'em. When all this settles down, maybe you and I should go tell them."

Smiling at the way she included him in her plans, Casey touched her cheek. "You could go alone, you know."

"I know. I'd just rather have you along."

"Insurance?"

"Maybe."

"Smart girl."

"Definitely."

"Eat," he said, standing. "I'm going to go bleed for Melvin. I'll drop by again later for a while. We'll get to stop all this sneaking around soon."

With a mouth full of sandwich, she stood and gave him a hug. "I love you, Dad."

Casey was still grinning when he got off the elevator. He walked to his room and stepped inside. Moira was hiding behind the door.

"Quiet," she hissed, her eyes raking the room. "Close the door. Make no sign that I'm here. Hide me."

"From what?"

"Whom."

"From whom?"

"From Melvin I-must-have-your-blood Foltz. He's stalking the halls like he's from Transyl-fucking-vania for chrissakes! Every time I pause for a minute, he's sticking a needle in my nearest appendage!"

"Ha! The price you pay for being with child, you shameless hussy!"

"The price I pay for consorting with the four hundred year old man! The least you could do is protect me. That should be the price you pay for open access to my feminine charms." She advanced on Casey and put her arms around his neck, leaning into him full length. "Whadaya say, Big Boy? Save me from Melvin and you could get lucky."

"I already got lucky."

"You could get luckier."

"Not possible," he said, putting his arms around her. "Nobody could be luckier than this."

"Aw. Silver-tongued devil."

"Who would know better than you?" Casey asked, kissing her on the tip of the nose. When the knock came they both flinched.

"Casey, are you in there?" Melvin's voice was muffled by the closed door.

"You open that door," Moira whispered, "and you will forevermore spill your seed on the dusty ground," she threatened.

"C'mon in, Melvin!" Casey shouted.

"Bastard!" Moira growled. Melvin's face lit up when he saw her.

"Moira," he beamed. "Just the lady I was looking for."

"You keep away from me," Moira threatened.

"Just twenty cc's," Melvin protested.

"Right. Then another twenty and another twenty," she accused, backing away from him. "Pretty soon I'll have nothing left."

"Now try to stay calm," Melvin said, advancing on her. "Just twenty, I promise."

She turned on Casey. "Are you gonna let this happen? Are you gonna allow the woman you profess to love to be set upon by this escapee from a Stephen King novel?"

"I have to. It's for the babies. Take her, Melvin. No fear. No mercy."

"For the babies," Moira sighed. "*For the babies*! Fatherhood speaks. All right, alright. I'll go peaceably," she said, hanging her head and shuffling toward the door. In the hall she turned again on Casey. "Here's the thing. Next time, *you* get pregnant, or the deal's off!" Moira gathered her dignity and strode off down the hall, Melvin trotting behind her.

That evening, Moira brought Cat dinner and the two women talked until nearly ten, Moira expounding on the beauties of Glenwood Springs, Colorado, and the preparations for going there. Cat listened raptly, but was overtaken by the need for sleep. She was in slumber within ten minutes after Moira left until, shortly after midnight, something woke her up.

Cat snapped into wakefulness and lay perfectly still, her acute hearing detecting the faint rasp of door hinges, far above the normal human frequency range. The door to the observation chamber opened slowly and the glare of a penlight swept the area. From behind nearly closed lids Cat observed the intruder. Wearing official looking slacks and a blazer, he moved cautiously through the observation room and through the open door between it and where Cat lay. Uncertain as to what to do and fearing discovery, Cat silenced her breathing. When the beam found her body on the bed, the intruder froze.

"You may as well turn on the light," Cat said, "before that little thing runs out of batteries and you get lost in the dark."

She felt him jump and immediately smelled fear. He cast the light around the room, but could locate no switches. Sighing, Cat sat up and swung her feet to the floor, wrapping a sheet around her nude body. She slipped off the bed and walked into the other room to turn on a lamp. He followed her with the penlight. As she passed through the massive connecting door, Cat slammed it behind her, leaving him trapped in the primate lab. She clicked on the overhead spotlights and the room exploded with brilliance. He stood, looking through the polymer, squinting in the glare. Cat opened the sound system.

"Gotcha," she said.

He ran to the door and uselessly tried it, then scanned the rest of the room for an exit. Finally he turned his attention to Cat.

"Let me out," he said.

Cat grinned at him. "Naw."

"C'mon. Let me out."

"You're fine right there."

"Unlock the door," Ted said, exasperation creeping into his voice. "I won't hurt you."

"That's for sure."

Plank looked at her for a moment and changed tactics.

"Who are you?" he asked.

"I'm not a burglar," Cat said. "Who are *you*?"

"My name is Plank. Ted Plank," he said. "I'm with security here at Provenance Center. Lemme out."

"That's okay. What brings you to my room?"

"Your room? This isn't your room. This building belongs to Provenance! What are you doing here?"

"I asked you first," Cat replied.

"It's part of my job! Just a routine sub-level security check."

Cat smelled the lie and her heart began to pound.

"I'm sorry I scared you," Plank went on. "I had no idea anybody was even down here."

A half-truth. Oh, Jesus. They'd been found!

"Who did you say you worked for?" Cat asked, keeping her voice calm.

"I work for the company that owns and operates this facility." Another half-truth. "Now open the goddamn door!"

"Who else?"

"Who else, what?"

"Who else do you work for?"

Plank hesitated for an instant before he replied. "Nobody," he said.

Blatant lie. In that split second, Cat saw the face of a man, sandy-haired and green-eyed. A thin face, not old, not young, but hard. A face with a scar across the chin. A face that contained no compassion or feeling. Fear slapped her like a wet towel, and in her mind she screamed: "*Daddy!*"

Plank couldn't believe what he saw. One moment the girl was wrapped in the sheet, talking to him through the window. In the next instant she was gone, so fast, so quickly, that the sheet actually held her shape for a moment before it slithered downward to the floor. Oh, shit! He sank to the edge of the bed and tried to stop the trembling in his hands. What the hell had he stumbled into?

Moira and Casey were in the middle of pillow talk in Moira's bedroom, when Cat flashed into substance beside the bed. Moira screamed. Casey lurched into a sitting position and stared at his nude daughter. She was near tears.

"Daddy! They found us! One of them came into my room! He's down there now. Hurry!"

In a rush, Casey hit the floor, grabbed his jeans, and was gone. Nearly as fast, Cat tore a sheet from the bed and followed. Moira sat panting for a moment. Then, muttering to herself, she put on a robe and headed for sub-level four.

Plank had been sitting on the bed for no more than thirty seconds when motion exploded behind the glass and the girl was back. With her was an older man wearing blue jeans and no shirt. Christ, it was Casey!

"Casey!" Plank yelled. "What the hell is going on? That little shit locked me in here. Open the door, willya?"

"Hey, Ted," Casey said, feeling considerable relief. "How ya doin'?" Casey's emotional shift communicated to Cat, and she settled down immediately.

"Not very damn well!" Plank spat. "Lemme out."

"That kinda depends on you, Ted," Casey said, sitting in a chair and leaning back.

"What? Goddammit! Open the goddam door!"

"You lied to me at the elevator, Ted. There is something new going on around here. There have been meetings, there are bad guys in the bushes, and you, my friend, are part of an operation. I suspect that you are working for someone who is interested in what Moira and Melvin are doing. Who ya working for, Ted?"

"I don't have to answer any of your questions!" Plank blustered, his voice cracking. "Open the fucking door!"

"Probably not. Somebody'll drop in here eventually and find your body. Later, Ted." He shut off the lights, took Cat by the arm, and headed for the door.

"What the fuck! You can't just leave me here!"

Silhouetted in the doorway, Casey laughed. "I can't? Why, sure I can, Ted. This whole area is totally soundproof and designed to hold gorillas. I just shut the door and walk away. You cease to exist. You know how often anybody comes down here. Enjoy the next three or four days."

"Wait! Wait a minute!" Ted protested, his voice shaking. "Okay! Let's talk. Turn the light back on."

"Who ya working for, Ted?" Casey asked, leaving the frightened man standing in the dark.

"A guy that's connected with the company that owns Provenance. I've never seen him. I just get my instructions over the phone."

Cat stepped up beside Casey in the doorframe. "You're lying," she said. "Light brown hair, green eyes, scar on his chin. What's his name?"

"Who the fuck *are* you?" Ted snarled.

Cat heard the name in her head and grinned. "Voorhees is gonna be pretty pissed at the way you blew this whole operation, Asshole. I'd hate to get on his bad side. Boy, is your shit weak. You better think up a real good story. Oh, sorry. Forget the story. You'll be dead of thirst in a few days."

"I don't need a fucking story. I'm security! I have the right to check up on anything that goes on in this building!"

"Not so," said Moira, moving into the patch of light from where she'd been standing in the hall. "You have no clearance for this level and no right to be here. That indicates you run errands for some pretty powerful people."

"Powerful people," Casey continued, "who will dust your ass the minute they believe you are no longer useful or know too much. You know too much, Plank. If you tell them all you know, you're dead. You will simply disappear."

"Alright," Plank agreed, the scent of his fear permeating the lab. "How 'bout I tell *you* all I know?"

"You don't know enough to interest me, Teddy," Casey said, "and you know too much for them to let you live. I'll give you some time to work on your story. Somebody'll let you outta there in four or five days. Have fun."

Plank's scream of protest was clipped off by the closing of the door.

# TWENTY-NINE

## Goodnight Trail

THE THREE OF THEM STOOD IN THE HALLWAY looking at each other. Moira spoke first.

"He'll die in there in the dark."

"Naw," grinned Cat. "He'll think he's going to, but he'll stumble around with his little flashlight and find the water. There's fruit and stuff in a basket, too. He'll be fine for a few days."

"One of us can make an anonymous call and get him out," Casey said. "If he opens his mouth, he's a dead man anyway. It's up to him."

"And you," said Moira, turning to Cat. "How did you do that?"

"Do what?"

"Show up in my room out of nowhere. You scared the shit outta me!"

"I don't know. I really needed Dad, and then I was just there."

"We can worry about it later," Casey said. "Right now, Cat and I both have to have our beauty sleep. She can bunk in my room. Then we gotta hustle. We need to be out of here in no more than three days."

"You guys go on," Moira said. "I couldn't sleep if my life depended on it. I'm gonna wake Melvin up and get things started."

"Do whatever you need to," Casey said, "but make no phone calls from this building or from your cell phone. Go someplace else and use a public telephone, a different one for each call. Whatever money you're going to get, make it cash. Your credit cards are now useless. Very soon, we will be hunted. Don't leave a trail."

"You know," Moira said, "I used to have a normal life."

"Pretty boring, huh?" Casey replied.

"Now I'm pregnant, on the run with two ex-vampires and Doctor Blood, and can't even use my Visa card."

"What fun!"

"Ha!" She kissed Cat on the cheek, Casey on the mouth, and headed for the elevator. "See ya at breakfast. Make it good."

Breakfast was good. Cheese and red pepper omelets, corned beef hash, and Johnny Cakes with blackberry jam. Conversation was at a minimum during the meal as everyone watched Moira eat everything in sight. When she finally finished, Melvin sipped at his coffee and leaned back.

"Today," he said, "I am going to make sure I have all I need on personal hard storage, then I am going to remove anything on the company computer system installed since a week before Casey arrived. I will also delete his identification from the security unit. It shall be as if he has never been."

"Will it be safe for me to use the ID that you had made for me?" Casey asked.

"Probably," Moira said. "Your appearance is changed, but not too much. You can always pop the contacts back in if necessary. The paperwork is all valid, if fictitious."

"Good. I'm the only one of the three of us who may still be unknown."

"Last night I created false identification for both Moira and myself, driver's licenses, social security cards and such," Melvin went on. "No credit cards or anything like that, but enough to withstand casual inspection from traffic police and the like."

"How 'bout me?" Cat asked. "Do I get a driver's license?"

"Can you make yourself look older?" Melvin asked.

"Than what?" came the reply. There was a split second of silence, then Moira began to chuckle.

"The Statue of Liberty?" she asked. Infectious laughter took them, and they found release in it, voiding themselves of pent up emotion and fear, laughing for no other reason than because they could. When things settled down, Cat looked at Melvin and smiled.

"Yes," she said, "I can make myself look older if Moira has some make-up I can borrow."

"Of course."

"Splendid," said Melvin, rising to his feet. "Find me sometime this afternoon and I will take your photo. Right now, I must be off. I have much to do if we are going to depart the day after tomorrow."

After Melvin left, Cat wandered off and Moira finished her coffee. "I have to call and have the house opened up," she said.

"Got a neighbor that takes care of it?" Casey asked.

"That part of the country is riddled with vacation homes and part-time residences," Moira replied, beginning to pace. "There are several companies that take care of such places. It's been over ten years since anybody has lived in the house. Twice a year it's cleaned and set up for the season. If I hurry and call today, it'll be aired out and freshened, put in working order, and stocked with food by the time we get there. I assume we'll be taking very little with us."

"Cat and I have nothing," Casey said.

"Most of my stuff is in Chicago anyway," Moira continued, biting her lip. "I'll just buy what I need when we get there. The house is completely furnished. Everything Melvin has is on disc. We'll travel light. It'll be good to travel light. We'll attract less attention to ourselves that way."

Casey looked at her, concern on his face. "Sweetheart, what's wrong?"

"Wrong? Nothing's wrong," she replied. "There's just so much to do. We've got to keep a low profile, we've got to get out of Provenance without being seen, we've gotta get clear out to Glenwood Springs. Could you ask Cat to, no, never mind. I'll ask her myself. I hope Melvin got all his …"

"Hey," Casey interrupted, grasping Moira gently by the shoulders.

"What?" she replied, her train of thought derailed by his action.

"Settle down a little bit. You're prattling. You never prattle."

"I don't think you understand how much …"

"I understand more than you believe I do. Take it easy. Everybody's got their shit together. All you have to take care of is you."

"But somebody has to be responsible for all …"

"What's going on here?" Casey asked. "You got some kinda Mother complex or something? You can't take care of everything and everybody, and you don't need to! Relax a little bit."

Moira flared and stared at him. Casey held her gaze and smiled. Tears filled her eyes.

"Sorry," Moira said, slumping against him.

"Hormone storm?"

"Yeah," she replied. "Let's blame it on that."

The next thirty-six hours were a flurry of activity for Moira and Melvin as they pared down their belongings to the absolute minimum, packing only what was necessary for the relocation, and attended to the balance of their respective financial situations. Cat and Casey helped when they could, stayed out of the way when they couldn't, and offered as much moral support as possible. They all reunited for a late dinner, the mood nearly festive because of the impending departure.

"Melvin and I agree," Moira said. "We leave tonight."

"I thought we were going tomorrow," Casey said.

"Have you ever driven from Kaycee to Denver?" asked Moira.

"No."

"We leave tonight. The only thing more boring than driving across Kansas at night is driving across it in the daytime. Darkness is more entertaining than Kansas. A sore tooth is more entertaining than Kansas. Melvin says he has secured a vehicle. We will meet him at midnight in the Home Depot parking lot. The three of us will take a company vehicle to our rendezvous and abandon it there. We will then just disappear." She looked at Casey and Cat. "Now would be a good time for you two to gather up anything you'd like to take along. A change of clothes, toiletries, blood. You know, the essentials. We'll stop on the way and get you coats. It will be cold where we're going."

Cat grinned at Casey. "What kind of coat ya want, Pop? Don't wantcha to take a chill," she said. Casey laughed.

"What's so funny," asked Moira.

"We don't really wear coats," Casey said. "I guess we'll have to if we want to keep up appearances."

"You don't get cold?"

"No. Cold doesn't make much difference to us. Neither does heat."

"I should have known," Moira snorted. "Alright. We leave in three hours. You all set, Melvin?"

"Yes. I'm packed and loaded. All that remains is for you to deliver me and my bags to the dealership so I can get my new car."

"Fine. Let's do that now. You can lay on the floor in the back seat until we're clear of the lot. The guard will see me leave alone and return alone. Later, when Casey and Cat go out with me, I'll put them in the trunk."

Casey looked at his daughter. "She's afraid to be seen with us," he muttered. "Oh, sure, we're okay when nobody else is around, but the minute she goes out in public, we're not good enough for her."

"Bitch," Cat smiled.

"I'm sorry you had to see the truth about her so soon. God knows I tried to spare you."

"You two can work on the rest of your comedy routine while I'm gone," Moira said. "Actually, now might be a good time for you to sleep if possible. That way you can entertain us all the way across Kansas. C'mon, Melvin."

"She's even afraid to be seen with me," Melvin said, heading for the door.

At 11:41 p.m. Moira drove the company Impala out of the Provenance lot, casually waving at the guard. Two blocks down the street she made a right turn and stopped in front of a body shop. She popped the trunk release and Casey and Cat climbed into the car. Nine minutes later, they parked at the south end of the Home Depot parking lot, midway between two overhead lights, shielded from the street by several newly landscaped evergreens. The rest of the lot was empty, save for vehicles driven by the night stocking crew that were parked at the other end of the seven acre expanse. Light rain began to fall. Moira fidgeted.

"Melvin should be here," she yawned, peering through the droplets on the windshield.

"We're early," Casey said.

"Melvin should be here," Moira repeated.

"We're early," Casey said again. "Take it easy. Nobody knows we've run off. Nobody's sneaking up behind us."

"Yet."

"Yet."

At two minutes after midnight, a dull green Humvee pulled into the lot and turned in a ninety-degree arc, raking the area with its headlamps on bright. When they crossed the Impala, the sweep stopped and steadied on the car. From eighty yards, the Humvee crouched on its immense suspension and peered at them, primeval and threatening. Dull light reflected from the massive grill guard, glistening in the soft rain.

"Oh, shit," said Moira, and Casey felt her tense.

"Relax," he said. "Probably private security or something like that."

Slowly, the Humvee began to roll toward them, a lumbering behemoth on heavy cleated tires, the interior black and impenetrable. At thirty yards it stopped again, hunkered on the dark wet asphalt, watching, waiting. Four off-road lights on the overhead rack clicked on. The Impala shivered in the rain-augmented glare.

Moira reached for the ignition. "No," Casey said. He could feel Cat shift her position slightly.

"I'll take the left side," she murmured.

"Goddammit Casey!" Moira growled, groping around on the floorboard between her feet.

"Leave your gun where it is, please," Casey said.

"I don't fucking like this! Do something!"

"Cat and I will handle it. Stay still."

Again, the Humvee rolled ponderously forward, a steel triceratops glistening with drizzle. It moved to within twenty feet, then turned sideways to the Chevy. Slowly, the driver's door opened, and Melvin, wearing Levi's, a red and white flannel shirt, hiking boots, and a smile, stepped out of the cab.

"Goddamn you, Foltz!" shouted Moira, rolling down her window.

"How do you like my new car?" beamed Melvin.

"Car? *Car*! That's a fucking dinosaur, you repressed juvenile! God, help! Boys and their toys."

"It's beautiful, Melvin," laughed Casey, climbing out of the Impala. "Roomy, tough, built to do a job. Wonderful!"

"What are you wearing?" Moira squawked. "Melvin, we're not going to Alaska!"

"New car, new clothes, new life," Melvin said. "I even have a compass and a pocket knife!

"A compass?" Moira said.

"Sure. I could have gotten one of those GPS systems in the truck, but I didn't think that would be a good idea since we want to keep our location secret. You guys ready to go?"

"You bet we are," Casey said, grabbing his duffel from the back seat.

Melvin looked at the Impala. "What about the car?" he asked.

"Leave it," Casey said. "It'll add to the mystery." He grinned at Moira. "Coming, Pookie?"

Casey and Moira, bickering at each other, climbed into the Humvee's front and rear seats on the passenger side as Cat walked to the driver's side rear door. Melvin opened it for her.

"Your truck is cute, Melvin," she said. "So are you."

"Yes. Well, ah,"

Even before they were halfway to Lawrence, Kansas, Moira was snoring in the back seat.

"She okay?" Casey asked.

"Fine," Melvin replied, the dash lights reflecting off his smile. "She's nearly exhausted, but that's to be expected as hectic as the last couple of days have been for her. She needs rest and food. She eating for three, you know."

"Or four, or five," Casey chuckled.

"It's the way it is," Melvin went on. "Hormones kicking up, eating twice as much as she used to, wearing herself out, the emotional conflict of leaving her life. At least she doesn't have morning sickness."

"You're right," Casey shrugged.

"She'll probably kick into some sort of mothering mode before long."

"Already has," Casey said.

"Well," Melvin went on, "the plain truth is, there's very little she can do about it."

"Melvin," Casey sighed, "there's very little we can do about it either."

Dawn showed them the distant Rocky Mountains. As they approached Denver around ten a.m. Moira awakened.

"Food," she gurgled, rubbing her eyes. "Restroom."

They stopped at a 7-11 for gas and sandwiches. As Moira—chewing on a Snickers bar and carrying a large bag of munchies—walked back toward the Humvee, Melvin looked at the dirty sky.

"Where's all the clean air?" he asked.

"Chamber of Commerce propaganda," scowled Moira, stretching her back and opening a box of donuts. "Denver's a dump. Too much traffic, too much pollution, too many people, and it's all in a basin. Unless the wind is right, it just lays here."

"Not what I was anticipating," Melvin complained.

"You'll get your mountain air, Melvin," Moira said. "Another three or four hours and you'll be surrounded by it. We're going into some tall country on one of the prettiest drives in the world. Ike's road is gorgeous."

"Ike's road?"

"Eisenhower Expressway. We'll get over twice as high as we are here when we get to Vail, then down into the Glenwood Springs valley. You'll love it."

Cat sauntered up to Moira, carrying a cell phone. "What's the main number at Provenance?" she asked.

"Where'd you get the cell phone?" Moira replied around a mouthful of donut, powered sugar smearing her chin and the front of her blouse.

"From that car over there. California plates. Let 'em trace the call if they can."

Moira laughed and gave her the number, shaking her head as Cat called.

"Hello? Is this Provenance Center? My name is Mary Ellen Davis. I was in Kansas City visiting my cousin? And she fixed me up on a blind date with a guy named Ted Plank that works there, okay? Well, we went out a couple of nights ago and Ted got me kinda drunk and, like, took me over to where he works there at you guys' place, and drug me way deep into the basement six or seven stories down to this, like, secret lab, y'know, and tried to get my clothes off and, like, get me onto this hospital bed thing? I ran and slammed this big old door and locked him in this room. Then I, like, wandered around and finally got out of the place and took a cab back to my cousin's house over in Merriam. I just wanted to let all of you know that he was, like, locked up down there cause I don't want the rat bastard to die, I want the fucker around when I sue *his* ass, and *your* ass, and *everybody's* ass that is even connected with your company! I've already contacted the Enquirer and done an interview about my brush with rape and death in your secret laboratory. My lawyer'll be in touch. Oh, and when you see Ted, tell him my dick is bigger'n his, and I'm a fucking girl!"

"Jesus, Cat," Moira said. "That was beautiful."

"Just wanted to give Ted something to remember me by."

Melvin loved the mountains, including their passage through the Eisenhower tunnel, a segment of the drive that even had Casey squirming a bit. The long descent into Glenwood Springs allowed both Moira and Melvin the luxury of comfortable breathing, and made a relaxing end to the drive. As they left I-70, Melvin began to pull into a grocery parking lot, but Moira urged him onward.

"There'll be plenty of food at the house. Do we have gas?"

"Over half a tank."

"Then keep going. I need to avoid Glenwood Springs as much as possible. I haven't been here in years, but I still don't want to take a chance on being recognized."

They picked up 325 on the northwest side of town and drove north across the Garfield County line on 17 almost halfway to Buford, climbed east on a one lane road called Goodnight Trail, forded a shallow stream called Kingstone Creek, turned south on what was little more than an abandoned logging road, bounced through another shallow stream that had no name, followed the twisting trail another mile or two through a section of what Moira said was the White River National Forest, and came out on a shallow hillside about two hundred feet below a hodgepodge of a house, flanked by a couple of rickety loafing sheds and one small barn. The house was part stone, part log, part frame, and all big.

"Home, sweet home," Moira said, looking up the gentle hill toward the house. The sadness in her voice was colored with hope. Casey put his hand on her shoulder and she shrugged into his palm, enjoying the feel of his touch.

Melvin turned left, and the Humvee began its easy climb up the slope.

The center section of the house was fieldstone on the ground floor, cement chinked log on the top story and a half. The front door was surrounded by an immense porch that faced almost due south. Inside was an entry room with a living room behind it and a kitchen behind that. To the left, a large parlor sat off the entry and a library next to the living room. To the right, a study and behind it a large dining room. The second floor contained three bedrooms and one bath, the top half-story consisted of storage and a smaller, fourth bedroom. Off the rear of the house, behind the kitchen, had been added a large framed mudroom containing a second bath, and a combined pantry and canning kitchen. To the west side a glass enclosed sun porch had been connected to the original structure. To the east, a fieldstone patio stretched almost thirty feet out into the yard.

Moira led the tour as her companions gaped and gawked.

"This place has got to be nearly six thousand square feet," Casey said.

"A little over seven, if you count the cellar," Moira replied.

"The cellar?"

"The dry sink in the kitchen slides to the side and under it is a trap door. Under the trap door is the cellar. It's pretty well shot. I suppose it held up fairly well for the first hundred years or so, but it's useless now."

"Guess you know how that feels, huh, Pop?" Cat said.

"If I get curious I can just ask you, Brat, uh, Cat," Casey countered.

Moira and Casey took the master bedroom, Melvin took the one farthest from it, and Cat claimed the half-story bedroom at the top of the second flight of stairs, stating that teenagers needed their privacy.

The place was clean and freshly dusted, the cabinets and two freezers loaded with necessities, the electricity on, the propane tank topped off, the pilot lights burning in the stove and furnace, the well-house had been serviced, and the pressure system turned on. While Casey carried their bags and Melvin's computer cases into the house, it began to snow. Moira put milk on to simmer for hot chocolate and went onto the sun porch to build a small fire in a round clay fireplace tucked into a corner of the room. They sat in padded wicker chairs, sipping the sweet brew, and watched the day fade away behind the mountains.

"This is wonderful," Casey said, sinking lower into his chair. "Beautiful country."

"Kit Carson supposedly spent some time in this area," Moira ventured, looking at Casey from the corner of her eye.

"Yeah," Casey replied, taking a swallow of his chocolate. "That's what he claimed. Never did care much for ol' Kit. Bragged a lot. Lotsa room here, huh Melvin?"

"All the space I need," Melvin agreed, as Moira stared blankly out the window. "Of course we have no place to dry anyone out, but that is probably a moot point."

"Out below the west loafing shed," Moira said, "is a bomb shelter. My grandfather built it in the early sixties. Reinforced concrete over lead-lined steel. If we need a place it could probably be made to work."

"The space I need and a detention facility, too," grinned Melvin. "All I lack now is a gas chromatograph, a couple of autoclaves, a sequencer, a spectrum analyzer, a centrifuge, a couple of hundred terabytes of computer space, bunch of odds and ends, and a truckload of other things I have taken totally for granted."

"Not to mention blood," said Casey.

"Ah, yes. Blood."

"No sweat. There have got to be several hospitals not excessively far from here. For the rest of the stuff, Cat and I just have to visit midnight laboratory supply."

"Midnight laboratory supply?"

"A little homework and two or three forays to Denver and Boulder, and we should be able to get everything you need. If not, we can actually order and pay for the stuff. I'm not above honesty if it suits our purpose."

"You have a larcenous heart, Casey," Moira grinned.

They sat quietly for a time, watching the large snowflakes drifting downward past the windows. An elk walked out of the tree line a quarter mile down the slope, then disappeared in the snow-induced distant blur.

"Lonesome up here," Melvin ventured to the silent room. "If someone came after us, nobody would hear us if we yelled for help."

Cat stretched and cracked her knuckles. "That's okay," she said. "Nobody'd hear them either."

"My little girl," Casey said.

# THIRTY

Love in Bloom

DURING THE NEXT TWO WEEKS, Cat and Casey made a total of five trips to both Denver and Colorado Springs, securing equipment for Melvin's research. Police and newspersons alike were baffled at the string of burglaries and at the impudence of the burglars. No matter how rapid the response time, no matter how many officers dispatched, never was any perpetrator found at the scene. This gang—and because of their efficiency it was assumed it was a gang—was *fast*.

Items that had to be ordered were handled through an independent postal service in Denver and picked up there after delivery. Midway through the third week, Melvin conducted a sonogram on Moira. He peered at the screen.

"How pregnant can you possibly be?" he asked.

"You're either pregnant or you're not, Melvin."

"That's true, but speaking in weeks ..."

"Five or six, I suppose."

"Hmmmm."

"Whadaya mean, 'Hmmmm?'" Moira asked.

"This is very unusual," Melvin replied, furrowing his brow. "That is to say, I've never even heard of anything like this. Quite remarkable, actually."

Moira craned her neck to see the screen. "What?"

"Your babies, and they appear to be quite well, are, uh, too large, it would seem."

"Too large?"

"That's an oversimplification, actually. They appear to be too developed for their age. It's not just their size, although that was the first thing I noticed. If I knew nothing of the history of this pregnancy or of the participants in its, ah, consummation, as it were, I would assume you to be nearing the end of your first trimester."

"*What?*"

"Indeed. You appear to be twelve or thirteen weeks along. At the present rate of growth and development, should it continue on its current course, I would assume a full-term pregnancy at four and a half to five months' gestation. Very strange."

Casey came walking in. "What's strange?" he asked.

"Moira is three months pregnant," Melvin replied, wiping the jelly off her tummy with a fistful of paper towels.

"Three months?"

240

"For all intents and purposes," Melvin replied.

"Uh-*huh*," Casey muttered, raising an eyebrow at Moira. "Well. I guess that pretty much tells the tale. I want a divorce."

"Bite me," Moira grinned.

"Okay, but then can I have a divorce?"

"We're not married."

"Moira, will you marry me?"

"No."

"How the hell can you be three months pregnant?"

"I'm not. I'm five or six weeks pregnant."

"In that case, I rescind my request."

"It seems that our babies are growing and maturing at roughly twice the normal rate."

Casey grinned and stuck out his chest. "Ugh," he grunted. "Me man."

Moira sat up and pulled down her t-shirt. "Neanderthal applies," she muttered.

"Moira should come to term around the middle of March," said Melvin.

"That's comforting," Casey said. "I've certainly never come to terms with her."

"I don't think you understand," Melvin said, exasperation creeping into his voice.

"I understand that the woman that I love is pregnant with two of our babies and that these babies are doing well and will be born. She will have them when she has them. When things are right between these babies and their mother, they will come into this world. Nine months, five months, two weeks … it makes no difference to me, Melvin. As long as their mother is fine and the babies are healthy, I don't give a damn about anything else."

"We have to make arrangements," Melvin blurted. "We have to find a facility. None of this can be left to chance, Casey! These children are too important!"

Casey shook his head. "I delivered Catherine from her mother on a dusty corn shuck mattress after two days of labor," he said. "I tied the cord with twine spun from raw wool and buried the placenta behind my forge. There was no medicine, no painkillers, no oxygen, no coach, no epidural, no disinfectant, no doctor, no nurse, no clean sheets, and certainly no Melvin. This time I have you, we have this facility, and we have two family members that are healers such as the world has not seen since the days of the ancients. Do you think Cat and I are going to allow anything to happen to Moira or those babies?"

"Well, uh, no. Of course not."

"There ya go. Relax."

Moira put her arm across Melvin's back and kissed him on the cheek. "Melvin, you have no idea how much your concern means to me. Thank you."

"Yes, well," he flushed, "I'm very gratified that you, that is to say, I've got to, ah," he retreated from the room and wandered off.

Casey looked at Moira. "So, how ya doin'?"

"Scared to death."

"Me too. Great, huh?"

"Yeah, Dad. It really is."

By the first of the year, the household had settled into a comfortable routine. Casey did the necessary traveling for supplies and to their mail service in Denver. Moira mothered everybody, including the unborn twins, and assisted Melvin. Melvin peered at his computers, drew blood from everyone, clucked over Moira, and walked around looking perplexed. Cat roamed the mountains, sometimes staying gone for two or three days at a time.

Casey was sitting in the kitchen one morning, enjoying an after breakfast cup of coffee and watching a blizzard raging in its second day through a frosty window, when Moira came in and kissed the back of his neck. She was wearing two layers of sweat clothes, a robe, and fuzzy house slippers about the size of snowshoes.

"Cold," she said. "The furnace has been running constantly since lunch yesterday. When this snow stops, we'll hit twenty-five or thirty below."

Casey smiled at her. "I'll go split a rick of wood or so in a little while and start a fire. We can sit on the couch, and you can tell me how wonderful I am."

"That won't take long. Seen Cat?"

"Not since yesterday morning. Probably went for another hike."

"I was born and raised here, and she knows these mountains and passes ten times better than I ever did."

"Cat's a natural warrior," Casey said, pride in his voice. "The better she knows the terrain, the better she'll be able to defend us if we're found."

"Will they find us?"

"I don't know. A lot of it depends on who 'they' is. I'm not very concerned about being located by humans. Nosferati could be a real problem, though. This apparent alliance between humans and Nosferati that started in Arkansas might be the worst of both worlds. It could easily be a situation where the whole is much greater than the sum of its parts. Truthfully, the longer we're here, or in any one spot for that matter, the greater the chance we'll be found, but also the more secure we become."

"Does all this worry you?"

"'Tiz but a trifle. I'm always concerned about discovery, but that's my natural condition. If I worry about anything, I worry about becoming complacent. But, complacent I'm not. We don't have enough manpower to make complacency much of a problem."

"So we need more manpower."

"Vamp power actually," Casey nodded. "Maybe Melvin can figure a way to clone Cat and me."

"Cat would be okay," Moira snorted.

"Actually, Cat and I have discussed contacting Gunnar and Felene in Chicago and offering them the opportunity of having a child. Cat thinks they might go for drying out if it meant they could have a baby. We've talked about going up there after the twins are born."

"Gunnar and Felene are Nosferati?"

"Yep."

"Wow. Two twelve-stranders making a baby. That could be interesting."

"Would that make twenty-four strands of DNA in the child?"

"Maybe. Maybe one hundred forty-four strands. Maybe something in between. Who knows? There's no precedent."

"What about our babies? Twelve strands like me?"

"Possibly. Maybe six strands, maybe twenty-four. Maybe latent strands. God knows. Of course, none of what we're talking about takes the pineal factor into account either. Melvin's been theorizing on that a bit."

"Oh yeah?"

"He thinks that's how Cat managed to show up in my room both those times. She was able to slip dimension, or astrally project, or escape time and distance, or something."

"Slip dimension?"

"Melvin likes to play with the String Theory."

"The what?"

"The String Theory. Multi dimensional concepts. Particles that transmit forces and particles that make up matter. You know, gravitons as opposed to electrons, photons as opposed to muons. Supersymmetry."

Casey allowed his eyes to glaze over. "Sure," he said. "Gotcha."

Moira smiled. "Whether we have ten dimensions or eleven. The nature of reality and existence."

"Beam me up?"

"For want of a better description. He thinks you might be able to do it too, when your pineal output reaches a high enough level."

"And mine is climbing?"

"Yes, but very slowly. It could take a long time for it to get strong enough. Cat ingested Nosferati Blood around two hundred years ago."

Casey thought for a moment. "But, Cat can't control it," he said.

"No. It seems to be spontaneous when a certain level of desire or stress is reached."

"What about the babies?"

"I have them in advanced pineal training right now," Moira said.

"Is that right?"

"Yep. We're gonna bypass that entire birth canal thing and go straight for the old immaculate delivery. They'll just appear in swaddling clothes, lying in a manger."

"Ha! I think you're confused. That was the immaculate conception."

"No. I liked the conception part," Moira said, leaning into Casey and putting her hand on his thigh. "It's the delivery I want to be immaculate."

"You enjoyed conception?" he asked.

"Sure. Wanna go concept right now?"

"Too late. You're already concepted."

"We could pretend I'm not," she replied, bumping her eyebrows. "Do you realize that underneath all these layers, I'm naked?"

"Coulda fooled me," he said, eyeballing her sweats and robe.

"It's true. Wanna see?"

"Always and forever."

"Great," she replied, lifting herself from the couch.

The mudroom door slammed open and Cat stepped into the kitchen. She was carrying eight frozen trout strung on a willow branch.

"Lunch," she beamed, and closed the door. "Fish is very good for expectant mommies." She clunked the catch into the sink and kissed Moira on the cheek. "Gotta take good care of you and the little guys," she continued, putting her hands on Moira's belly through the robe. "I can feel them, you know."

Melvin wandered in and looked in the sink.

"Fish?" he asked.

"Not just fish, Melvin," Cat answered. "Trout. Flash frozen and very fresh. Good for Moira."

"Where did you get them?"

"Southeast of here is Ute Creek. If you follow it about five or six miles, it forks. A mile or so farther on the east fork, it runs into a little lake. That little lake is alive with trout."

"You went fishing?"

"Sorta."

Melvin raised an eyebrow. "But isn't the lake frozen?"

"Sure. You just punch a hole in the ice, dive in, and chase 'em around until you grab a few. It's fun!"

"But you get all wet!"

"That's okay. I take off my clothes first."

"You take off your, uh …" Melvin colored.

"Sure. Don't want my jeans and t-shirt to freeze and shrink."

"It's below zero!"

"Aw," Cat smiled, advancing on Melvin. "You're worried about me. That's so sweet."

"Yes, uh," Melvin stammered, holding his ground as Cat placed a wrist on each of his shoulders.

"Thank you, Melvin," she said, leaning in and kissing him gently on the mouth. Instantly Melvin turned pale purple.

"We were just on the way upstairs," Moira grinned, tugging on Casey's sleeve and heading for the stairway.

"You go ahead," Cat said. "Melvin and I will clean the fish and he can help me fix lunch. We'll eat around one."

"Whenever, Sweetie, take your time." Moira replied, pushing Casey up the stairs.

After Moira nearly stuffed him through the bedroom door, Casey turned and looked at her.

"What's with the bum's rush?"

"We needed to vacate the area," Moira replied. "Give Melvin and Cat a little space."

"Space?"

"Yeah," Moira replied, raising an eyebrow.

"What in the hell is going on?"

"Nothing yet," Moira replied, "but soon I expect. We're about to find out if you have any papa paranoia."

"What?"

Moira smiled. "Relax, Dad. It shouldn't take Cat long. Melvin doesn't stand much of a chance."

"Huh?"

She patted him on the arm and smiled indulgently. "Everything's fine, Sweetie," she cooed. "Don't you worry your pretty little head about it."

Lunch was excellent. Pan-fried trout, American fries, steamed carrots, and baked apples for desert. All through the meal, Melvin stole shy glances at Cat, who was unusually bubbly. After lunch, Casey spent a leisurely hour splitting wood and filling the huge two-cord bin. When he returned to the house, he found Moira arguing with Melvin in front of a computer, but could not locate Cat. Feeling her nearby, he walked back outside and down to the small barn. Inside, he encountered her working on the hanging carcass of an elk.

"Jesus," he said.

She grinned. "I took her about a week ago," Cat said. "What a rush! Been saving it as a surprise. Elk stew tonight, and tomorrow, and the next day, if I make enough. I'm gonna strip some out for jerky, grind some up for sausage and, if I can find some wild serviceberries this spring, I'll make pemmican."

Casey felt his eyes fill. "I'm proud of you, Cat," he said.

"Just your basic domestic kitten, Pop."

Casey smiled. "Can I help with the stew?"

"You can dice the potatoes," she replied, slipping her free arm around his waist and snuggling against his chest. "I'm happy, Daddy," she murmured. "I'm so glad you found me."

The next morning, it was Casey's turn to fix breakfast. When the flapjacks and bacon were ready, he walked into the living room to find Moira sitting on the couch, as Cat lay with her ear pressed against Moira's stomach.

"Soup's on," he said.

"They respond to your voice," Cat said, getting up. "I can feel them react to it," she continued, helping Moira to her feet. "It's really wonderful."

Melvin met them at the table and seated himself next to Cat as Casey served from the kitchen. They both ate in a hurry, it seemed to Casey, exchanging furtive looks and sitting much closer together than he'd ever noticed before. Almost before they had started to eat, they were done. Melvin excused himself, went upstairs, and not to the computer bank in the study. As usual, Cat simply disappeared.

Moira gave the meal her undivided attention, consuming even more than usual, smiling as she ate. Casey carried dishes into the kitchen while she finished. She picked up her plate and followed him to the sink.

"Where's Melvin?" he asked.

"Upstairs, I think."

"Not feeling well?"

"No," Moira said. "I expect ol' Melvin feels pretty fine about now."

"Seen Cat?"

"Not for a while."

"Wonder where she went?"

"She's upstairs too, I think."

"What's the big fascination with upstairs," Casey muttered, mostly to himself.

Moira grinned at him and bumped her eyebrows.

He stared at her for a moment, then dropped a dish in the sink.

"No!" he exclaimed.

"Yeah," she giggled.

"Cat and, uh, Melvin?"

"Sure. She's been working on him for weeks."

"No."

"Yes."

"No!"

"*Yes!*"

"But, he's ... Melvin!"

"Yes, he is," Moira laughed.

"My God!"

"Don't you approve?" Moira asked.

"Well, I, uh, sure, I ... *approve*. It's just that ... *Melvin?*"

"I think it's terrific," Moira beamed.

"Jesus! Melvin. Melvin! Ha! Oh, shit! What about the virus?"

"Melvin started his shots a week or two after I did. He handles too much of your blood not to take precautions. Everything's fine."

"Yeah," Casey laughed, "I guess it is. Melvin. Damn!"

"Stranger things have happened," Moira said. "Look at me, you escaped convict, you."

# THIRTY-ONE

Puddie Power

"IT'S GETTING A LITTLE CROWDED IN THERE," Melvin mused, peering at the computer screen.

Moira lay on her back, her stomach towering over her, and snorted. "Ya think?"

Melvin moved the sending unit through the jelly on her tummy. "Unusual," he muttered.

"Unusual?"

"They turn toward the wand."

"They what?"

"The babies. They appear to turn toward the wand as I move it from place to place. It's almost as if they can hear or feel the ultrasonic waves."

"Why couldn't they?" Cat asked from her position at the end of the table.

"It's beyond the range of human audio reception," explained Melvin. "Oh! You can hear the ultrasound?"

"Sure," Cat replied. "You can't?"

"No."

"Moira, can you?"

"Nope."

"Wow. I didn't know that. I thought everybody heard it."

"No. Probably just you and your dad."

"And now the kids," Cat said. "Cleo and Leo."

She put a hand on Moira's belly and the distorted figures on the screen moved.

"Cleo and Leo, my ass," Moira grinned.

"Look at them move when I touch you," Cat said.

"Unusual," Melvin commented.

"Not for Cat," Moira replied. "They've noticed her since the end of my second month. She and the babies have a connection, in most ways as strong as their father's, in many ways stronger than mine."

Cat pulled back her hand. "Does that upset you?" she asked.

Moira smiled. "Not in the least, Sweetie. I think it's wonderful that they respond so positively to their Aunt Catherine."

"Ah!" exclaimed Casey, walking into the room. "Baby pictures. How's everybody?"

247

"Everybody is just fine," Moira said.

"Monique and Unique doing okay?" he asked.

"Who?" Moira growled.

"Kanga and Roo?"

"*Who?*" Moira growled again.

"And our little mommy?" Casey continued, patting her cheek, "is she doing well today?"

"Better than you will be if Melvin ever lets me up."

Casey smiled at her. "How 'bout Elizabeth Anne and Sean Robert?"

Moira looked at him for a moment before she spoke. "Cat's mother and my brother."

"Yeah," Casey replied. "Whatcha think?"

"You are a marvelous man," she whispered, tears collecting in her eyes.

"I'm gonna let that one go," he said, smiling down into her shining face. "Too easy."

That evening the four of them sat in front of the fireplace, staring into the flames. Casey roused himself and looked at Melvin.

"So, will they need blood?" he asked.

"Hmmm?" Melvin replied, rising out of his fire-watching stupor.

"The babies. Will they need blood?"

"Oh. Uh, I don't really know. If there is a thriving problem, we can always feed them a small amount and see what happens, I suppose. A lot will depend on their digestive systems. Human babies' digestive capabilities and dietary requirements change rather rapidly as they grow. That may be the case with these children."

"But they have the virus?"

"Oh, yes. I'm certain they do. It could be that Moira's breast-feeding will totally sustain them, at least for a while. There is so much that I just don't know."

"What about the DNA?" Casey went on. "How many strands?"

"Again, I don't know. I could easily draw a small amount of blood from each of them and determine the answer, but I am reluctant to do so. We don't know their strength. To alarm them, or to cause them pain might, depending on their reaction, be dangerous for Moira. If they have even a fraction of your physical abilities and were to thrash around, well."

"We'll know soon enough," Cat said. "They're fine. They know where they are, they know all of us, they're comfortable with each other."

"How can you be sure?" Melvin asked.

"I communicate with them," she said. "Not with words or anything like that. I feel them. When I press my head on Moira's stomach, I can almost hear them. They're very much alike, but different, too. She is more precocious, he more contemplative. She is more impatient, he more introspective. They balance each other. The connection between them is very strong. They're good together."

"How long 'til the delivery?" Casey asked.

"Two or three weeks, I should think," Melvin said. "Not long."

"Will they continue their accelerated growth after they're born?"

"I wouldn't be surprised. I don't expect them to be giants or anything that mundane, but I believe we can anticipate a certain level of advanced maturity and such. Again, it's hard to make any predictions. Whatever unusual abilities they may have could change again when they approach puberty. In their case that could be as early as ages six or seven."

"Six or seven?" Casey asked.

"Possibly. Carrying that possibility a bit farther would indicate that they would, at that age, appear to be in their early teens. I would imagine emotional maturity to be even greater, but again, this is the rankest speculation. Time will tell."

Time began its tale a little less than three weeks later, on March thirteenth.

Moira's water broke as she sat at the breakfast table. By noon, her contractions were at four minutes, and she was on a bed in the lab, Melvin fluttering about like a wounded pigeon. The first child, the girl, was born a little after 6:45 p.m. as Cat attended to Moira's emotional and Casey to her physical needs. The boy, slightly larger than the little girl at five pounds four ounces, arrived at 7:14 p.m. There was minimal bleeding or tearing, considerable name-calling, extensive perspiration, two broken nails, significant emotionality, and no complications. By 9:00 p.m. Moira and the babies had been cleaned up for the second time; she was holding Sean and Casey held Beth. Both babies were sleeping.

Moira smiled. "I hope you realize that you are not all of those horrible things I accused you of earlier in the evening," she said.

Casey looked down into her pale and happy face. "Not all of them, huh?"

"No. Not all. 'Blood-sucking emotional dwarf,' for instance. I have never considered you to be a dwarf, Daddy."

"Thank you."

"You're welcome. Gonna lay hands on me, so I can get out of this bed tomorrow and go back to work in the fields?"

"I don't think so. Melvin and I discussed it. He believes your recovery should come at its own pace unless you get in some kind of trouble. Since you're breastfeeding, he wants as little outside interference in your body's natural state as possible, at least for the first few days. I'm inclined to agree with him. Sorry."

"So, you gonna sleep on the couch for a while?"

"What?"

"No healing, no touching. Right?"

"Oh, no," Casey said. "You don't get off that easy. We can cuddle and touch all we want to. I just won't do any healing stuff."

"Oh," Moira replied, raising her eyebrows. "You can control it then?"

"Sure. I though you knew that."

"No. That's very interesting. So your healing involves will."

"I guess so," Casey replied. "I never really thought about it that way, but yeah. When I want it to, it works. If not, nothing happens."

"Hmmm," Moira pondered. "Floating brain and conscious brain connection. Melvin needs to know about this." The baby squirmed against her shoulder. "Just not right this minute," she smiled, stroking the back of the child's head.

"You have other things to think about," Casey said.

"And you are gonna make me suffer through this like a woman."

"Yep. No miracles for you, Mom."

"You are *so* wrong, Casey."

"I am?"

"There already are miracles. The biggest one is holding Beth and sitting on the edge of my bed. You are my miracle, Casey. And you have presented me with many more."

"I'll bet you say that to all the fathers of your little miracles."

The little miracles did very well. They were in highchairs by three months, had their first teeth by four, and multi-word vocabularies as they tottered around the house by six. Other than their accelerated growth and development, they seemed quite normal. Beth most often took the lead, Sean being the more deliberate and thoughtful of the two. They did not appear to require any raw blood and suffered no illness whatsoever, not even normal childhood complaints. They were doted on by the adults, accepted it as their due, and were most drawn to Aunt Cat who spent much of her time with the children. While they exhibited better muscular control and a higher level of coordination than children two to three times their age, they showed none of their father's exceptional physical abilities. During spring and summer, the six occupants of the house became a true family. There was no indication that they were being watched. Melvin sent brief letters of inquiry to some possible sources of research money through their postal drop in Denver, and life went on. The research progressed, the family settled in, and autumn came to the mountains.

One morning in late October, Melvin drew blood from each of the twins and disappeared into the lab. Early that afternoon, while Moira prepared lunch, Casey sat at the table, watching Cat as she attempted to feed the kids in their highchairs. They were engaged in a dietary discussion.

"Puddie," Beth said.

"Eat your carrots and meat, and you can have pudding for dessert."

"Puddie," Beth repeated, pointing to the refrigerator.

"Not yet. Eat your carrots and meat."

"Puddie," Sean chimed in, grinning at Cat.

"I'm gonna lock you two up and never give you pudding ever again!" Cat teased. "Eat!"

"Puddie now," giggled Beth, bouncing in her chair and reaching for the fridge.

"Puddie now," echoed Sean.

"No," Cat said.

"Yes," insisted Beth.

"Not pudding now. Meat and carrots now."

"Puddie now," Sean repeated, looking at the refrigerator.

"Now," Beth said, following his gaze.

Everybody in the room watched as the refrigerator door swung open and a container of chocolate pudding slid across a shelf and fell to the floor.

"Puddie!" Beth crowed, clapping her tiny hands. Sean grinned and pointed at the fallen container.

"Jesus Christ," Casey murmured.

Except for a wide-eyed glance at her father, Cat kept her cool. She picked up the container and put it back in the fridge. Moira removed her hand from over her mouth.

"All right, you two," she said. "Eat your lunch and you can each have a cookie. Please don't get in the fridge again without permission. If you want something, ask for it, okay?"

Sean immediately began to eat his carrots. Beth looked at her mother for a moment and thought it over. "Okay," she said.

Moira smiled. "I love you," she said. "Did you know that?"

Beth returned her smile and began to eat, the pudding incident forgotten.

"Telekinesis?" Melvin asked, his eyebrows rising.

It was mid-afternoon and the kids were down for their nap. The adults were gathered in the living room.

"That's what it appeared to be," Moira said. "Opened the door to the fridge and slid that pudding right out onto the floor."

"Any idea which one of them did it?"

"Both of them," Cat said. "It was a joint effort. I could feel it."

"Can you or your father do such a thing?"

"I can't. Dad?"

"Never have."

"Maybe it takes two," Melvin mused. "That vase on the mantle, try to move it together."

"Pick something else," Moira said. "That vase belonged to my grandmother. There's a pencil on the table. See if you can make it roll or something."

Cat and Casey concentrated on the pencil until Cat started laughing. The pencil didn't budge.

"Couple of no talent bums, Pop," she said.

"Maybe we should try pudding," Casey added.

"Interesting," Melvin said. "They show none of the speed or strength that each of you possess, yet they seem to be able to do things with their minds that you two cannot do. Puberty should be enlightening."

"Why puberty?" Moira asked.

"Casey, have you ever known a Nosferati that was young?" Melvin said.

"Ah ... no. I think Cat is the youngest."

"And you've never known one who was very old either, I believe you said once."

"That's true. Most of them are physically in their late teens and twenties."

"Catherine, would you agree with that?"

"Sure. I've never met one as young as I am, and never one even close to Dad's age. Thirty is about the top end I guess."

"Puberty is probably the determining factor on the low end," Melvin said. "The children both have six strands of DNA. I have sequenced both of them and can find no difference in their makeup whatsoever. There, of course, has to be a difference. They are not of the same sex, but it does not appear in my examination."

"How is that possible?" Moira asked.

"It isn't. And yet we have the proof that it has occurred napping upstairs. The computerized electron scan shows something unusual, however. Their respective helixes seem to have shadows."

"Shadows?"

"That's the best way I can think of to describe it. They're ghosts, other unformed, foggy strands entwined within or around the existing ones. I've never seen anything like it."

"Computer malfunction?"

"Possibly. But if it is, it's the same malfunction on two separate sequences. I'll run it again tomorrow from scratch, but I suspect the results will be the same."

Moira looked at him. "And you think?"

"And I think that the additional strands are dependent on puberty."

"That with puberty they'll manifest?"

"And?" Melvin encouraged.

"And that their physical attributes will come with that manifestation."

"And?"

"And that they will then need blood like Cat and Casey do!"

"Exactly!" Melvin said. "But now?"

"But now," Moira muttered. "But now, *but now* … because the strands that are in evidence seem to be identical, they can combine their mental abilities together and create a phenomenon like what we saw today!"

"Yes!" Melvin pounced. "Twins have always been known to have unusual abilities and connections with each other. Even two-strand twins can do things nobody can explain. But these children are not just two-strand twins."

"They're six-strand twins!"

"And, I suspect that their combination is not mere addition."

"It's multiplication?" Moira blurted.

"Precisely!" Melvin shouted.

"Oh, my God!" Moira exclaimed, looking at Cat and Casey with big eyes. "Oh, my God," she repeated in a whisper.

"What?" Cat asked. "*What?*"

"What we saw today was the manifestation of what can happen with tiny, untrained minds when they can, even unconsciously, draw on thirty-six strands of DNA."

Casey looked at her for a moment as it sunk in what Moira said.

"And they haven't even reached puberty yet," he said. "Think of that."

The group was silent for a moment until Cat spoke up.

"Felene wants a child," she said, "and she and Gunnar are both twelve-stranders. Think of that."

# THIRTY-TWO

## Norse-Indian

CASEY DUSTED SNOW FROM HIS CLOTHES and entered the kitchen from the mud-room. Cat and Moira sat around the kitchen table drinking tea.

"Where's Melvin?" he asked.

"Melvin is muttering in the lab," Cat said. "He heard back from his friend at Fischer Laboratories in your last mail run. The guy's excited about the little bit that Melvin told him and is going to the company bigwigs to check into funding. We won't see Melvin for a day or two. You know how he is. Kids are upstairs. How goes the dungeon?"

"Great. I'll have it ready before long. That diesel generator is perfect, and plain old Halon fire extinguishers will do fine for the gas. It's a far cry from the primate lab at Provenance, but between the blast area, living area, and the airlock, we've got what we need."

"I'm just glad my grandfather was paranoid," Moira said. "He built that thing clear back in the 60's during some sort of nuclear threat."

"Probably because of the Cuban missile crisis," Cat said. "Everybody was scared to death back then."

"He did a hell of a job," Casey said. "The thing is like a bank vault. Most of the stuff that has gone bad I won't have to replace. We won't need the water purification processor or the air and particulate filters. We don't have to keep things out."

"Just keep things in," Cat said.

"You really think Gunnar and Felene will go for it?" Casey asked.

"I think Felene will, and if she does, so will Gunnar. They're actually married, you know."

"Really?"

"Yep. Tied the knot around the time Custer got his at Little Big Horn. I stood up for her. Last ceremony that preacher ever performed," she said, shaking her head.

"Hey," Casey said, lifting her face by the chin and looking into his daughter's eyes. "Days past, times past. You can't change it. That's who you were, not who you are."

"Then," Moira said, "we stand a good chance of having more Nosferati."

"Lucky for us," Cat replied. "We could use Felene. She can fight."

"Fight?"

Cat looked at Casey. He nodded. "Yeah," Cat went on. "If Colin shows up, we're gonna need more troops."

"Colin will come here?"

"It's possible," Cat replied. "Hell, it's probable. You gotta understand that Colin, even for a Nosferati, is not normal. His, uh, penis is deformed."

"What?"

"Yeah. It's small and the hole isn't at the end. It's about in the middle on the bottom. He has to sit down to pee. When he gets hard, which is not very often, his penis curves downward."

Moira thought for a moment. "Hypospadias," she said.

"Hypo who?"

"Hypospadias," Moira went on. "It's a birth defect. Not uncommon. The meatus, the opening through which the urine passes, is located on the underside of the penis anywhere from near the tip to all the way back to the scrotum. A condition called Chordee, a downward curve of the member, especially when erect, is common with the condition. In the extreme, it makes intercourse impossible. But it's easily correctable by surgery, usually at an early age. That's a disgrace! Where were his parents?"

"Colin is nearly three-hundred-years old," Cat said. "Not a lot of corrective surgery in those days."

"He could have it done now, though."

"Nosferati don't go to doctors," Casey said.

"Besides," Cat went on, "that's not all. He's also a morphadite, or hermaphrodite, or whatever."

"Describe him," Moira said. "His build, I mean."

"Three or four inches taller that Dad, kinda pear-shaped, a little flabby, soft. No muscle definition."

"It he weak?"

"He's Nosferati. Weak is not a factor. Also, he's got breasts. His tits are about half as big as mine."

"Uh-huh. How about body hair?"

"Head and eyebrows. No beard to speak of. No pit hair, very little pubic hair."

"Does he have testicles?"

"Sort of, but they're small and kinda up inside him. It sorta like he's got a shallow vagina where they should be, and they're inside it a little." Cat flushed. "It's hard to describe. Hammond called 'em 'pussy peas' once, and had to leave for a while so Colin wouldn't kill him. He's real sensitive about the whole thing. And yet, he flaunts it, just waiting for somebody to say something."

"Horrible," Moira said. "It's probably either Androgen Insensitivity Syndrome or Kleinfelter Syndrome, depending on whether he has one or two X chromosomes. Breasts, deformed penis, no obvious testicular formation, sparse body hair, tall, overweight. Does he have difficulty putting his thoughts into words?"

"No, but he doesn't read or write."

"That's understandable. Considering when he was born, he would not have received any of the help he needed to develop normally. Poor man."

254

"Poor man, my ass!" Cat flared. "Colin is the nastiest bastard I have ever known! He will not take it well that I left. Most Nosferati come and go as they please. They don't form real attachments. Not so with Colin where I'm concerned. He'll consider it betrayal. Chances are pretty good he'll never find me, but he'll look. And if he does manage to locate me, he'll show up. Count on it. That's why it'll be good to have Felene around."

"So," Moira said, "if Felene goes for it, so will Gunnar?"

"Without a doubt," Cat replied, shaking herself. "Gunnar is as much like her child as he is her mate. She infected him."

"What?"

"Yep. In Boston, before the Revolutionary War. Found him wandering around a couple of weeks after she fed on him."

"Jesus!" blurted Casey. "I didn't know that."

"Yeah. Scary, huh? Said she just about freaked out. When she got over the shock and figured out he didn't intend to hurt her, she felt responsible for him and tucked him under her wing. They've been together ever since."

"That was nice of her," Moira said.

Casey and Cat looked at each other and began to laugh.

"Guess maybe *nice* wasn't the right word?" Moira said.

"Nice is the perfect word," Casey said. "It's just not one often applied to Nosferati."

"You've gotta understand about Felene," Cat said. "She is *old*. Really old. At least a thousand years. Maybe more. Probably a lot more. She doesn't know."

"Jesus!" Moira said.

"She was taken into slavery on a Norse raid into the Misty Isles."

Moira looked at her. "What?"

"The Vikings captured her and some others from a village in Wales when she was a child. She was traded a few times as she got older and wound up with the Phoenicians. While she was aboard ship, they stopped at several ports in North Africa and she escaped. She hung around the area for a couple of years, doing whatever she had to do to survive. It was there that she came in contact with the virus. As time went on, she made her way back to Finland or wherever and traveled with the Norsemen as a warrior. She went to Iceland and Greenland and finally to North America, long before Columbus. When the North American settlement went bust, she stayed. Eventually European civilization came to her."

"My, Lord," said Moira. "All those years alone."

Cat smiled. "You're thinking like a human," she said. "Perspective on years changes when you have a relatively limitless lifetime. She was far from alone. This hemisphere had thriving civilizations. Imagine what effect a white woman with nearly supernatural powers would have on the native cultures of the time. Felene roamed from the woodland Indians of the northeast, south to the Mayans and the Incas. She went west long before the plains civilizations had horses! Cultural anthropology relates tale after tale of mythical beings in Native American culture. Some of those wild stories may have been true, Moira. Some of them were Felene."

"That's so hard to believe. A thousand years old!"

"Maybe a lot more than that. Felene doesn't really have any idea how old she is."

"And she's coming here."

"She is if she wants a child badly enough," Casey said.

"God. What do you say to somebody like that? Someone who's seen what she has, and done what she has, and been around as long as she has? How do you treat someone like that?"

Cat grinned. "No sweat," she said. "Felene's pretty laid back."

Moira smiled. "It'll be good to have her, especially with Colin out there. What's his special attraction to you, anyway?"

Cat looked away for a moment, then resettled her eyes on Moira.

"I could make him come," she said.

About a week after the twins' first birthday—an occasion celebrated with copious amounts of pudding—Casey, Melvin, and Cat loaded up in the Humvee and headed east. In Denver, Melvin dropped them off at the airport and Casey rented a Lincoln Towne Car from Avis. They said goodbye to Melvin, took I-76 to I-80 at the Nebraska state line, and got through Ogallala to North Platte by dinnertime. They stopped at a Steak n' Shake, found a Days Inn, got adjoining rooms, and Casey called home. Moira answered.

"Do you realize I miss you?"

"Already?" He could hear the smile in her voice.

"Don't let it go to your head," he chided. "Kids okay?"

"They keep asking for you and Aunt Cat. Of course, they like you better than I do."

"Smart kids."

"Where are you?"

"Deep in the heart of Nebraska."

"How can you tell?"

"There's nothing here. We'll be in Chicago by late afternoon tomorrow. Probably look for Felene and Gunnar the day after, then head home. Melvin get back alright?"

"Record time. I think he was afraid of leaving me alone too long. He's putting the kids to bed. Last I heard, they were winning."

"All's well, hug the twins, give Melvin a thank you. I love you, Pookie."

"Ah. Sleep well, asshole of my dreams. I love you, too. Lemme talk to Cat."

Casey walked through the open connecting door, handed Cat the phone and went in to take a shower. When he got out of his bathroom, Cat, wearing an oversized man's dress shirt strolled in toweling her short hair dry. She was grinning.

"What?" Casey asked.

"Among other things, Moira told me to listen to you, you'd been clean and sober longer than I have. She also made me promise to take care of you, out among all them there evil Nosferati."

Casey smiled sadly. "Part of her is afraid that we won't come back."

"Yep."

"That you and I will be together in the old home town and just keep going. The lure of the blood and memories of our life together will be too strong."

"It gets pretty strong," Cat admitted.

"Yeah, it does."

Cat smiled. "But not that strong," she said.

"She's also concerned that we might stumble into more than we can handle."

"Felene and Gunnar? Please."

"We all have our fears. I'm worried about leaving Moira and the babies out there by themselves."

"You mean with just Melvin."

"Yeah. No offense."

"None taken," Cat said. "He'd die to protect them, but he's only human. That's probably what I like best about him," she murmured thoughtfully. "He's only human."

"Melvin is a good man."

"Yes, he is. He'll be a good father, too."

Casey looked at her. "You're not …"

"No, *Daddy*, I'm not pregnant. Someday, Melvin says. After my homogoblins and hermanglecrits align with Jupiter and Mars, or some such crap. Half the time I don't know what he's talking about, but it cracks me up to listen. Hell, his socks hardly ever match, and the other day he was walking around with his glasses on his forehead while he looked for his glasses. As far as kids go, we've got plenty of time. It makes sense to see what happens with the twins first. He's scared to death for us to go off like this, too. Told me to be careful not to get into more trouble than we could handle."

"That, Daughter," Casey said, "would be a shitload of trouble."

They giggled their way through a re-run of Frank Langella's *Dracula* on the badly tuned motel TV and fell asleep, hugging each other on top of Casey's bed.

The following morning, as Casey re-iced the cooler, Cat brought the car around in a dismal drizzle. The light rain stayed with them all the way to Omaha. They ate a fast-food lunch in the car. As they crossed into Iowa, it began to rain in earnest. The hiss of the tires, the repetition of the wipers, and the rhythm of the rain cocooned the car closely around them and created an aura of intimacy. Cat wrapped herself in it like a blanket, sliding down in the passenger seat and leaning on the center console, her left hand lightly on the outside of Casey's thigh, craving contact with her father.

"How ya doin', Pop?"

"Fine, Sweetheart."

"Us against them again, huh?"

Casey smiled. "Yep. Whoever them is. Are?"

"Never in my wildest dreams would I have imagined the two of us on the way to offer Gunnar and Felene a chance to straighten out and have a family."

"Us against them."

"Or imagined us living in the freaking mountains, you a daddy again with a human, and me. Me! Jesus. I'm sharing my life and my bed with Melvin! Dad, they don't come any more human than Melvin." She laughed. "A couple of years ago I would have had Melvin shredded for lunch! Now I ask that wonderful little geek what he wants for breakfast, and then, and then *I go fix it*! God, help. Us against them, and they are winning."

"How could we have come to this?" Casey said.

"I don't know. I do know that I love it. I love you and Moira and the twins and Melvin and my life. I really do love my life." Cat smiled, her mouth quivering with emotion. "Dad, you know how I was. Christ, you know how we were. What we did, how we lived. If is wasn't for you, if you hadn't ganged up with Moira and Melvin and found me, I'd still be that way. You gave me life, and now you've given me back my life."

"As much as it's been us against them, Cat, it's been us against ourselves," Casey said. "And we're the ones who are winning. Just don't let the past pollute the victory, Hon. Don't allow what we were to diminish what we are, or what we may yet come to be. I didn't give you anything but a chance. You did the work. You did the suffering."

"And now I can offer Gunnar and Felene the same chance, if they'll take it."

Casey grinned. "How absolutely noble and selfless of you," he said.

"Bullshit!" Cat laughed, "and you know it. It'll be a trade-off. They want a family and we need troops."

"Troops would be good," Casey said. "I think you're right about that bunch you ran with and the people Moira and Melvin worked for probably haven't just given up."

"They'll find us, won't they?"

"Eventually."

"And they'll come."

"Eventually."

She sat up and looked at him. He saw the old flash of joy in her eyes and felt a crackle of psychic energy pulse through her.

"You knock 'em down, Pop," Cat said, "and I'll stomp on 'em."

Casey grinned. "Together again," he said.

"So, about Gunnar and Felene." Cat said. They were in a Comfort Inn suite on the outskirts of Davenport, their progress slowed by the rain that had been with them all day.

"What about 'em?" Casey asked.

"We can't dry both of them out at once, can we?"

"No. They'd be too much of a danger to each other, to say nothing of us."

"That's what I thought. And we can't have a Nosferati running around loose out at the place while his partner dries out. Too much potential for disaster with Moira, Melvin, and the kids right there."

"I agree."

"Why not take Felene back with us and leave Gunnar behind until she's okay, then go back and get him?"

"You know them better than I do. If you think so."

"Gunnar is very dependent on Felene. He could handle a month without her a lot better if he were left in familiar surroundings. That way, she'd be straight and ready to help him through the whole detox thing. She's much stronger than he is. We should do her first."

"Suits me."

"And you should call the mother of your children," Cat continued, handing him the phone.

Moira answered on the second ring. He could hear tension in her first word.

"Casey?"

"Hi, Babe. How ya doin'?"

"Oh, I'm fine. Where are you?"

"In Iowa at the Illinois state line. We've had terrible weather. It slowed us down quite a bit. What's wrong?"

"Probably nothing. The twins don't seem to feel quite up to par."

"What's going on?"

"They miss you and Cat terribly. They keep asking for you. And, they're a little listless. They act sorta like they have colds. They're not running temperatures or anything like that, they just seem tired and a little cranky. They don't want to play and raise their usual brand of hell."

"Moira, our kids don't get colds or anything. They can't."

"I know. Melvin's been over them with a fine-tooth comb. He says that if they're not doing better tomorrow, he's gonna draw some blood. Now, don't get all shook up. It's not that they're sick, it's just that they're not exactly well. I don't know how else to describe it."

"Alright. We'll go on into Chicago tonight and hurry every chance we can. Tell Beth and Sean we love them and we'll be home soon."

"Okay, Sweetheart. Hug Cat for me. I love you."

Cat and Casey were back on the road in ten minutes.

Casey and Cat were on Lakeshore Drive before dawn. They stopped at Columbia Michael Reese Hospital to snatch some blood and left the car in the Shedd Aquarium visitor's lot just as the sun was coming up. On foot, Cat led Casey across the lawn and parking areas toward the Field Museum of Natural History. Approaching a small copse of pine trees, she detoured into their midst. There, surrounded by weeds, was a vertical concrete culvert covered by a rusting iron grate.

"This is it," she said, lifting the barred cover. It rose noiselessly on well-oiled hinges.

"This is what?" Casey asked, looking down into a dark shaft with iron rungs bolted into one side.

"This is the front door to Felene and Gunnar's house. It used to be a steam tunnel. Now it's just an old abandoned cement pipe that dumps out in the second sub-basement of the museum. Gunnar helped build the place. He and Felene have lived there for years and years. Felene loves it. A lot of the anthropological exhibits are of places and times she's lived through. It's like her life on display. There have been rumors for over a hundred years of a ghost that haunts the museum. Felene."

Casey grinned. "A real live ghost."

"Yeah. Hoot, huh?"

"What's our reception going to be like?"

"Fine, I think. Gunnar may get squirrelly, but he'll defer to Felene. If he's fed recently he might be a little hard to handle."

"He'll also be faster and stronger than either one of us. That worries me a bit."

"Scared?" Cat teased.

"Yeah, to be honest, I am. Nosferati scare the shit out of me. I know how crazy I used to be. I'm gonna charge up. You can join me if you like."

She thought for a moment. "No, I'll pass. One of us is enough. I'll take a swallow or two, it's real dark down there, but you've been dry a lot longer than I have. I don't wanna push my luck."

He took two bags of blood from his jacket pockets and consumed the first one. He drank half the second and handed it to Cat. She took two swallows and passed it back just as the rush hit him. Casey dropped the bag and fell to one knee, trembling with the surge of power and awareness that flooded through him. His cells sparked and fired, his synapses rattled and shook, and he stifled the howl that ripped upward from his diaphragm, bolting to his feet and trembling, his face overloaded with gleeful eyes and bloody teeth. He turned away toward a tree and emptied his bladder, then shook himself like a dog. When he turned back, Cat was grinning at him.

"Man!" she said. "Just two swallows hit me like a ton of bricks. What'd you do, a pint and a half?"

"Almost," he growled.

"Shit! You've gotta be sailing! You with me?"

"Oh, yeah," Casey replied, inhaling deeply through his nose.

"Ready to go?"

"Uh-huh," he snorted.

"Then pick up your trash and dispose of it properly in that barrel over there. We don't want the litter police on our ass," she said.

Casey could feel his anger flash at being told what to do and repressed the snarl that leapt to his lips. Instead, he looked at his daughter and smiled. Something inside him shifted, and he was fine. Still high, still more than ready, but not brittle or edgy. Nosferati in his ability, human in his judgment, he did as she asked.

When he returned, he found Cat standing on the raised edge of the shaft.

"Watch out for the rats," she said, "and follow me."

Ignoring the iron rungs on the side of the shaft, Cat stepped off the cement and disappeared straight down into the darkness. Casey gave her a moment to land and move out of the way and followed in the same manner, the shaft's walls flying upward around him as he grinned with joy at his empty-handed leap into the void.

# THIRTY-THREE

## Death Under Glass

THE SHAFT WENT STRAIGHT DOWN for about forty feet. Casey landed lightly in two inches of water and mud. In the half-light he could see Cat crouching slightly in the five-foot connecting tunnel.

"We've got a couple of hundred yards 'til we reach the museum. Be glad you didn't wear your good suit." She grinned, then turned on her heel, and began trotting away.

They were in total darkness after the first sixty feet. Shuffling along in a crouch, Casey relied on his proximity sense to keep him in the center of the narrow passageway. He saw Cat as a faint glow in front of him. The tunnel smelled of mildew and rats, rot and decay. The old cement seeped ground water and dripped constantly, exuding a layer of slime that covered the walls and made footing treacherous. They easily covered the two hundred yards in less than twenty seconds, but for Casey that was twenty seconds too long. At length, Cat stopped beneath an ascending shaft. The tunnel continued on.

"Up here," she said, "about twenty feet. I'll go first and open the manhole."

She disappeared upward, and in a few seconds, Casey heard metal scrape on metal. Above him, the darkness became less dense. He climbed the rusting rungs on the side of the shaft and entered a large columned room through the floor. There was enough light filtering through grates overhead for his vision to return. What he saw made him stop and gape.

"Something, huh?" Cat said. "Storage for all things dead."

That's exactly what it was. The room was large, possibly half an acre, and it was randomly full of glass cases containing everything from aardvarks to zebras. Grime clung to the exposed surfaces, clouding the contents. Glassy eyes peered through the murky gloom, and yellow teeth gleamed in the partial light. Monkeys and apes, lions and leopards, warthogs and lemurs, bears and buffalo, and abominations in large jars of formaldehyde watched their tentative progress, dust rising from the floor with their passage, drifting behind them in the swirl of their wake.

"*Jesus*!" whispered Casey. "We're surrounded by corpses. This place gives me the creeps!"

"Me, too," breathed Cat, leading the way. "I've been through here a hundred times, and I still get a little freaked. I guess this is where they put the stuff that gets too old for display."

"From what I've glimpsed in some of these jars," Casey muttered, "a lot of it is too gross for display. Christ! I wonder if anybody from the museum ever visits this hell?"

"Not for a long time, Herriott," said a soft and feminine voice off to his left. "How have you been for the last century and a half?"

In spite of himself, Casey flinched, then chuckled, and turned to the speaker as she came out from between two camels and a family of chimpanzees.

"Fair morrow to thee, Good Gentle," he said. "No Alzheimer's yet, Felene. How 'bout you? You don't look a day over eight hundred."

"You always were gallant," she replied, slowly stepping up in front of him and carefully offering her hand.

Casey took it and held it briefly. She returned his smile, then backed a respectful distance away and turned to Cat.

"Hey, Girl. If I knew you were coming, I would have baked a tourist."

"That's okay," Cat replied, exchanging an embrace. "I'm kinda on a restricted diet these days."

"Well, c'mon to the place anyway, and we'll chew the fat, so to speak. Never thought I'd see you and Herriott together again. The change in your scents have anything to do with that?" She finger combed her long chestnut hair and rocked side to side, her peasant skirt swinging around her ankles.

"A little," Casey said, "and please call me Casey. That's the name I've been using for some time."

"Sure. I'll call you whatever you like. I figure that the two of you being back together again, and here, means life as I know it is probably due for a big shake-up. You two didn't get religion or something, did you?" She smiled, moving a large glass display of ratty butterflies aside to open a heavy oak door set flush into the wall. The hinges groaned and echoed through the brittle space.

"Not exactly," Cat said. "We just came by to ask you a question."

Felene stopped in the doorway and turned to face them.

"Like what?"

"Like, how would you like to make a baby?" Casey asked.

"Out of what?" Felene replied.

Casey smiled and tried again. "How would you like to make a baby?"

Felene looked at him for a moment. "This is so sudden," she said, straightening up and adjusting her blouse. "You trying to sweep me off my pretty feet?"

"Not that the prospect isn't appealing," Casey said, as he smiled into her Nordic blue eyes, "but that's not exactly what I had in mind."

"Perhaps not," she teased, "at least not this time. Ah, but I do have my memories."

"And I have mine," Casey countered.

"The nice thing about memories," Felene went on, "is that fresh ones are waiting just around the corner. Wanna go for a walk in the park, you brown-eyed devil?"

"What would you say," Casey said, "if I told you that motherhood could possibly be in your future?"

"I'd say that you're nuts and that you should have some wine and tell me more," Felene replied, leading them through the door.

The room had originally been a storage area for boiler parts, and it was exceptionally neat and clean for a Nosferati lair. About twice as big as the average motel room and with a ten foot ceiling, it contained a rumpled bed, two old armchairs, a hanging rack for clothes, a couple of small tables, and an ancient buffet. Felene lit a candle, opened the lower cabinet, and removed a dusty bottle of Burgundy. Using her little finger, she pushed the cork down into the wine and took a sip, then passed the bottle to Cat. Cat also drank a little and handed it to Casey who followed suit, sweeping debris off a chair and sitting down. He was struck by the near absence of foreign odor. Usually Nosferati lived in filth and decay. This place, while very dirty by human standards, was nearly pristine compared to most Nosferati digs.

"Comfortable," he observed.

"Bathroom and such one flight up," Felene said, pointing to the ceiling. "Cat knows the way if you need to avail yourself. Excuse me while I slip out of something less comfortable." She removed her Birkenstocks, blouse and skirt, and sat nude on the end of the bed facing Casey.

"I had to go out for breakfast early this morning," she smiled, arching her low back and stretching. "Didn't want to alarm the natives. What brings the two of you to Chicago?"

"You do," said Cat.

"I'm flattered," Felene grinned, shifting to a cross-legged position. "Is it my feminine charms, my womanly wiles, or are you after my family fortune?"

Cat looked at her with serious eyes. "Felene, would you like to have a baby?"

"Whose?"

"Yours."

"Not possible."

"Yes, it is. I'm an aunt. Dad has twins a little over a year old."

"No kidding?"

"No kidding."

"Is the mother alive?"

"And kicking."

"Who is she?"

"A human."

"*What?*"

"Yep."

"A *human?*"

"A human."

"Oh, please!"

"It's true," Cat said.

Felene looked at Casey. He grinned at her. "Let me get this straight," she said. "You have actually fathered babies?"

"Exactly."

"Human babies."

"Well," he hesitated, "they're more than human. They may be more than we are, Felene. Time will tell."

"Is he serious?" Felene asked, turning to Cat and rising to her feet.

"Very," Cat replied. "I fully expect to get pregnant in the near future myself. There really seems no reason I can't."

"Picked out the father?"

"Yeah. He's human, too."

"Bullshit!" Felene flared. "Humans don't survive us! We fuck 'em 'til they die and move on. I know! And so do both of you!"

"We have a way around that, Felene," Casey said. "We have a vaccine that overcomes the fatality problem. It also seems to make humans as disease resistant as we are. I can expect, barring accident, for the mother of my children to live a century and a half. Possibly more."

"That's not very long."

"It's a damn sight longer than without it!"

"You're serious about this? You're not, excuse the expression, pulling my shapely leg?"

"Very serious," Cat said.

"I could have a baby?"

"Possibly."

"With a human."

"Yes, or with Gunnar, probably," Cat replied, "if that's what you'd like."

Felene sat heavily on the bed and stared at the floor for a moment. When she finally raised her face, tears in her eyes.

"Really?" she whispered. "This isn't some kind of obscene joke?"

"No guarantees," Cat said. "But you'd be as likely to get pregnant as any human would."

Felene dropped to her knees in front of Casey. "This is true. This is really true."

Smiling, he stroked her hair then cupped her chin in his hand and looked deeply into her eyes. "Yes, it is, Sweetheart," Casey whispered. "It's really, really true."

"God," she said, sinking back on her heels and taking his hand. "I have lived for so long. I have watched dozens of generations pass before my eyes, countless mothers and children. I am old. Three, maybe four times older than either of you. Life has long since lost most of its meaning for me. For over a thousand years I've wanted to have a baby. The fate that granted me all the power that we have, has denied me the one thing I want more than anything else. Just to feel that heartbeat inside me. To *create* life for a change. And now the two of you show up out of nowhere and say that it's possible. I just can't believe it."

"Believe it," Cat said.

Felene shook her head in wonder. "But Nosferati can't have children."

"That's true," Cat replied.

Felene looked at Cat. "You guys tell me I can get pregnant, and then you tell me that I can't. What's the catch?"

"To get pregnant, you can't be Nosferati."

"But I am."

"But you don't have to be. You can stop."

"After all these years?"

"Yep."

"And live?"

"And live."

"C'mon."

"You won't be weak. You'll still retain most of your abilities. You just won't be able to continue to live the way you have. Your life will have to change radically."

Felene looked back and forth between the two of them. "You're telling the truth, huh?"

"Yep," Cat said.

Felene smiled. "Where do I sign?" she said.

"So it'll take about a month to dry me out?" Felene asked. The three of them had been talking for well over two hours.

"That's roughly how long it took for Cat and for me," Casey said. "It will not be easy. You'll suffer a lot, I'm afraid."

"But in thirty days or so it will be over. Small price to pay to get pregnant."

"What about Gunnar?" Cat asked. "Will he agree to this?"

"Gunnar will do whatever I decide to do. He's a sweet boy. Sometimes I feel as if I already have a child. I've got some regrets with Gunnar. I don't know. Perhaps I should have let him go his own way instead of looking out for him. He might be stronger for it."

"We can't take you both at the same time," Casey said. "It would be too dangerous for you to be in withdrawal together, and I can't allow a Nosferati around my children or the humans who live with us."

"Of course not," Felene agreed. "I understand completely."

"Cat and I have discussed it, and we believe the most practical arrangement would be for you to come back with us now. When you've dried out, we'll return for Gunnar and put him through the process. Of course, we'll provide you both with a place to live and such for as long as you care to stay. In return we expect the normal contributions to the maintenance of the household and assistance with any of the possible trouble that may come our way."

"The group from Arkansas and your lady's ex-employer."

"That's correct."

"Sounds like fun," Felene said. "A commune of ex-vamps. You got me, guys."

"What about Gunnar?

"Gunnar's wandering around someplace. Every so often, he takes off for a day or two. He left last night."

"Felene," Cat said, "we can't wait on him. We have to get home as soon as possible."

"I'll leave him a note, to hang around until I get back. I'm not going to tell him what's going on. I'll do that when we come back for him. He'll handle it a lot better if I've already gone through it. As soon as I get dressed and throw some clothes in a garbage bag, I'm ready to go. I fed early this morning, so I'm good for two or three days. There's certainly nothing to keep me here."

"Great!" Casey said. "Back through the tunnel."

"Oh no," Felene smiled. "The museum opens in a few minutes. By the time I collect my stuff and write the note, we'll just go upstairs and walk out the door like we own the joint."

As they passed the magnificent African elephants in the museum rotunda, Casey pulled out his cell phone and called home. Melvin answered.

"Ah, Casey. Good of you to call. Moira is upstairs with the twins. Shall I summon her?"

"How are the kids, Melvin?"

"Well, it's quite unusual. I ran blood tests on both of them early this morning. They seem to be anemic."

"Anemic?"

"Yes. Considerably reduced red cell count. I can find no reason for it. Moira and I decided to give each of them a bit of whole blood in their breakfast juice bottles, but they rejected it. Threw up all over their highchairs. They're quite listless, and the only thing we can get them to eat is pudding. They continually ask for you and Cat. Beth even went so far as to say something like 'Aunt Cat make me better.' Very perplexing."

"Are they in danger, Melvin?"

"No, not yet. If necessary, I can transfuse both of them here. Obviously, we cannot take them to a hospital. I don't understand this failure to thrive. I'm continuing tests, Casey. I'll do everything I can."

"I have not the slightest doubt of that, Melvin. We're on the way home. We'll drive in shifts and come straight through. Tell Moira I called. I'll phone again in a few hours."

"Very well. Give my love to Catherine and drive carefully."

"Make sure the shelter is unlocked. We have a new resident coming with us. I'll call when we get close to home. I don't want to attempt to get this rental boat all the way to the house. You can meet us in Glenwood Springs. We'll return the car to Denver after we deal with the children."

"Fine. We'll speak later then. I'll tell Moira."

"Thanks, Melvin."

When they crossed the Illinois line, Casey called home again. Moira answered, and the tension in her voice was palpable.

"How ya holdin' up, Sweetie?"

"Oh, Casey. Beth and Sean aren't well at all. I just picked Sean up and I had to support his head. They're both getting weaker. They won't eat, their red cell count is still dropping. Where are you?"

"We just crossed into Iowa, and we're not stopping for anything but gas. We should be there by noon tomorrow at the very latest. Felene is with us. I need you or Melvin to put out some bottled water and fresh fruit in the shelter before we arrive. She will go directly there and begin drying out. She will not come to the house until she has recovered."

"Alright. Please hurry, Casey. I'm so frightened. Melvin is going to start the kids on IV-feeding in a few moments and begin transfusing them in a couple of hours. I feel like we're losing our babies!"

They crossed Iowa and Nebraska in excess of a hundred miles an hour. No highway patrolmen pursued them, no massive traffic tie-ups slowed them down. The miles flew by. An hour outside of Denver, with Casey at the wheel rocketing through the night, Cat simply disappeared. On the passenger seat were her clothes, on the passenger floorboard were her shoes. Cat was gone.

"*Jesus!*" sputtered Felene. "*What* the hell is going on? Where's Cat?"

"Take it easy," Casey soothed. "I think she went on ahead."

"Went on ahead? Whadaya mean she *went on ahead* for crissakes?"

In spite of himself and the situation, Casey laughed. "Don't blow a gasket, Felene. I think Cat went home to help with the twins. It's not the first time something like this has happened. Crawl on up here in the front seat, and I'll tell you a story."

Looking somewhat less than gruntled, Felene clambered over the seat back, moved Cat's clothes and shoes, and settled in, staring at Casey.

"Okay," she said. "What the hell just happened?"

Casey smiled. "What do you know about the pineal gland?" he said.

On the outskirts of Denver, Casey's phone rang.

"Yeah?"

"The kids are better," said Moira, sounding nasal and stopped up.

"Guess Cat made it, huh?"

"Popped up right in the lab. Melvin almost fell down. He's still not over it."

"Beth and Sean better?"

"Much. It seems they really did need you and Cat. Melvin thinks, because they can't digest blood yet, they need the physical support that comes from twelve-stranders like you and Cat. You two hold them and love on them so much, we never even considered that your support was anything more than psychological. Evidently it is. The minute Cat got her hands on them, they both started to perk up. Melvin has both of them off IV's and they're recovering nicely. I'm gonna dump Cat and them in our bed for the night. He thinks they'll be fine by morning."

"So it's part of the healing thing."

"More than just healing. It's an actual process, or lack of one, in their bodies that makes contact with you or Cat necessary. When Felene and Gunnar get straight, we might find that it works with them, too. No way to tell right now."

"And how are you?"

"I'm a wreck. A very happy, very relieved wreck. Every so often, I just cry for a while."

"Well, Wreck, we're about four hours out. I'll call when we need somebody to come pick us up in the Humvee. Rest."

"Okay. See you soon. I love you."

Casey didn't call for a ride. He and Felene left the car in a grocery store parking lot and went cross-country to the house, covering eleven miles in around thirty minutes, enjoying the morning air. Felene went directly to the shelter, seemingly eager to start the process. After securing Felene, Casey walked to the house, went in through the mudroom, and sat in the kitchen smiling out the window. Hearing the pitter-patter of tiny feet, he looked up to see Sean coming down the stairs backwards. When the boy saw Casey, he ran to him and grabbed his leg. Casey picked him up and kissed him until he squirmed, then put him down. Sean scampered to the fridge and began to pat the door, smiling over his shoulder at his daddy.

"Puddie," he said.

Pursuit

A WHITE-GLOVED HAND PUSHED A SWITCH beside a blinking blue light, and a pale tongue licked nearly bloodless lips. The thin voice rasped. "Yes, Voorhees?"

"Good evening, Mr. Unruh." Voorhees' voice was metallic through the speaker-phone.

"Is it really? I wonder."

"I regret that it has been so long since we last spoke, Sir. Until now I have had very little to report."

"You have something now, I assume?"

"Yessir. Several things."

"How comforting. Please."

"I finally located my asset from the security department of Provenance. I found him working as a security consultant for a small firm in Seattle."

"Did Mr. Plank offer you any enlightening information?"

"It would seem that Mr. Foltz and Ms. Flynn were keeping some unusual company at that facility, Sir. Not only their male companion—who we may safely assume is the escaped prisoner from near Indianapolis known as Casey—but also the young woman described to me by the unfortunate sheriff from Jasper, Arkansas, now deceased. The assets I managed to develop from the Arkansas area have also been searching for the girl. We may assume she remains with Foltz and Flynn. I am not sure what her connection to your ex-employees is, but that is being investigated at this time. As we speak, I have agents on the way to Chicago, attempting to unearth that very information."

"What do we know about this young woman?"

"The only name we have for her is Cat, Sir."

"Cat?"

"Yessir, as in Feline. According to Mr. Plank, she does seem to possess unusual abilities."

"Example, please."

"Plank swore he saw her disappear, Sir."

"Disappear?"

"Yessir. It seems that he encountered the young woman in the unused great ape facility at Provenance. When he attempted to question her, he claimed she vanished before his eyes."

"Indeed?"

"And returned to the lab only a few seconds later in the company of Mr. Casey. This is unusual in the fact that Mr. Casey was a good five minute walk from Plank's location, and yet he and Cat arrived in a tiny fraction of that time, much faster that what would be considered possible."

"Could Plank account for that?"

"He could not, Sir. He also stated that they both seemed to have prior knowledge of our investigation. He could not account for that either, except to say he believed that Cat could read his mind."

"Really?"

"She spoke my name, Sir."

"Could she have known your name, Voorhees?"

"Nossir. She could not."

"Hmmm."

"Casey and Cat frightened Mr. Plank very badly, Sir. They, and his fear of me, are the reasons he left the area and hid himself away in the Pacific Northwest."

"Was he able to tell you anything else of consequence?"

"Nossir, he was not."

"And where is Mr. Plank now?"

"I believe the expression is 'He sleeps with the fishes,' Sir."

"Ah. The eloquence of Puzo," Unruh chuckled dryly.

"And we have another lead. It seems that Melvin Foltz has contacted Fischer Laboratories in search of funding for continued research."

"What exactly is our connection with Fischer Laboratories?"

"You own it, Sir."

"Ah."

"His letter claims that he may be on the trail of a cure, not only for Ebola, but also AIDS, and possibly every currently infectious disease known to exist."

"All disease?"

"Yessir. That is what Mr. Foltz claimed."

"He is the leader in his field," Unruh said, gasping a bit with excitement. "How many dollars did he request?"

"Some four millions, Sir."

"See to it that he gets one million as soon as possible, with an additional million to follow every six months until the full investment is reached. Where is he?"

"We don't actually know. The letter requesting funding came from Denver, Colorado. I checked the address. It is a postal service that offers mail drops and a re-mailing facility. I'll have Fischer reply and follow the mail trail. I would think, unless things are being re-mailed to him, that he, and therefore Ms. Flynn and company, are someplace in the Denver area."

"I want him, Voorhees."

"Yessir.

"I want him. He could be worth billions. Bring him to me."

"Yessir."

"And this … Cat. I want her, too. She could be an interesting diversion. Fetch her also."

If she is what Colin claims she is, Voorhees thought, she'll tear your head off and shit down your neck, you fucking freak.

"Yessir," Voorhees said, swallowing his smile. "It will take time, but I'll find them."

"I'm certain of it. Time, while valuable, is not of the essence. Mr. Foltz continues his work. You have never failed me. Know that you shall have any and every resource that you need to affect my will. We have devastated entire countries in the past, Voorhees," Unruh continued, the faintest trace of humor in his voice. "I am certain that we shall prevail. Use whatever means and methods you choose to accomplish that end. You are under no restrictions."

"Thank you, Sir. I won't fail."

"Of course you won't, Voorhees. Of course you won't."

# THIRTY-FOUR

Vlad Dracul

COLIN DIDN'T USE THE STEAM TUNNEL, he didn't know it existed. The only reason he knew about the Field Museum was because he'd heard Cat speak of Gunnar and Felene and the fact that they lived in the bowels of the building. Colin was not a frequenter of museums because, as with most Nosferati, culture of almost any kind was not part of his life. In the months since her disappearance, he and Hammond had traveled to every place he could remember Cat mentioning. The Field Museum was the last.

They bought tickets at the entrance, just like everybody else, and spent several hours walking around, gaping at the exhibits with the other tourists, and attempting to meld with the crowds in spite of the scents and presence of so many humans. Both of them had fed the evening before, taking a jogger off of Lakeshore Drive; they could easily afford to wile away some time. The stress, however, kept them both on edge. Late afternoon, they began investigating doors marked 'Employees Only' and finally found their way into the first sub-basement of the building just before closing. They settled in behind some large packing crates until the employees left. Then they began to look around. Security patrols were confined to the offices and public floors. They roamed undisturbed.

"Smell that?" Colin asked as they moved past the taxidermy repair area.

"I smell all kinds of things in here I've never smelt before," Hammond replied, rubbing his chin, "and a lot of things I have."

"No, you numb-nosed git!" Colin said. "Open up your nostrils, Love. There's a nest around here. A male and a female. I think it's below us."

A ten-minute search revealed a door near a staff locker room that opened onto an unlighted flight of stairs leading downward. The odors of formaldehyde, dust, decay, and other things drifted up the gloomy passage.

"Knees up, Mother Brown," breathed Colin, taking the first downward step. "This would be it, then. Like a little mouse, Bucko," he cautioned. "Just like a tiny little mouse."

At the bottom of the stairs was another door. Colin eased it open slowly, and the two of them stepped into the second sub-basement.

"Jesus," whispered Hammond, scanning the immense room in the dim light.

"Look at all this," Colin replied. "Cor, this must be the edge of hell. I'll bet Judas hisself is in here somewhere."

They moved slowly through the collection of grimy, glass enclosed cases and grubby taxidermy, stirring up dust as they went.

Hammond shuddered. "I don't much like this," he murmured. "I feel like I'm bein' watched. Too many eyes."

"We probably are, Dearie," Colin answered, scanning the floor. "Lookit them tracks in the dirt."

"Whole place makes me itch."

"*God's holy trousers*!" whispered Colin, peering into a smudged, ten-gallon, glass jar containing a small, deformed human figure. "It's me Uncle Bill! I'd know him anywhere," he grinned. "Mum always said he'd end up dead *of* the bottle, but I didn't think he'd end up dead *in* one!"

A flicker of movement glimmered at the far end of the room, and Colin was off, flashing down a long aisle, Hammond on his heels. "The game's afoot, Love!" he rasped. "Go left!"

They split up, each heading for opposite corners of the space, and a dark figure shot between them. Hammond slipped on the grimy floor and slowed, dodging a zebra thrown in his direction. Colin closed on their prey and brought the runner down, pinning him until Hammond could lend his bulk and strength to the capture.

It was a young man, thin and pale, wearing only ratty Levi shorts. His brown hair was long and tangled, and a sparse beard sprouted from his face. They flipped him over on his back and Hammond held him.

"Now then," said Colin, grinning down at the youth, "stop thrashin' about. Nobody wants to hurt you, Mate. I expect your name would be Gunnar, right?"

The young man settled and looked up at him. "Yes," he said, his voice breaking a bit. "Who are you?"

"Ah. Now that's a proper question, that is. Well, I guess you could call me a friend of a friend. I'm Colin and this fine specimen what's pinnin' you like a butterfly is Hammond. We're partners with someone of your acquaintance, I believe. A lovely blond child by the name of Cat. Have you seen her lately?"

"Lemme up!"

"That's a distinct possibility," Colin said, patting the lad gently on the side of his face, "as soon as I'm sure you won't go tearin' off and make us catch you again. Answer me question. Have you seen Cat lately?"

"*Lemme up*!" Gunner yelled and began to struggle.

Colin nodded at Hammond, who backhanded Gunnar with such force that the young man's jaw shattered and his head struck the floor with a sickening crack. Gunnar lost consciousness for a moment. When he opened his eyes, he saw Colin grinning down at him.

"Right," said Colin. "That is the only lesson you get, Love. Stop muckin' about! Lay still for a minute while your jaw heals. When you can speak, you'll give me some answers, and we can be friends. It's nice to be me friend. I kill me enemies. There's a good cobber. Felene around?"

Slowly the boy shook his head.

"See? That wasn't so hard, and it didn't hurt a bit. I'm startin' to feel friendly toward you already, Bucko. Now for the big question again. Seen Cat lately?"

"No," Gunnar replied through clenched teeth.

"Fair dinkum. I love open communication. Let him up, Hammond, so we can visit. If he runs again, tear off his ears."

Hammond chuckled and released Gunnar, who eased himself into a sitting position and rubbed his jaw.

"So," Colin continued, "Cat hasn't been here."

"I didn't say that," Gunnar muttered. "I just said I hadn't seen her. She *was* here." Gunnar glared at the two men.

"When?"

"Two or three weeks ago. I was gone. When I came back, I found a note from Felene. She took off with Cat for a while."

"For how long?"

"I don't know. The note said she'd be back in a month or so."

"Cat comin' back with her?"

"I don't know."

"Where'd they get off to?"

"I don't know."

"Who's buried in Grant's tomb?"

"I don't ... what?"

Colin nodded to Hammond, who casually reached out and broke Gunnar's thumb. As the lad clutched his hand and fell back onto the floor, Hammond quickly got to his feet and stamped on both the boy's knees. The kneecaps came apart with audible cracks. Gunnar shrieked as his body went into spasm, then he curled on his side and began to cry.

"There, there," cooed Colin, leaning over Gunnar and stroking his hair. "Hurts, doesn't it, Love? There's a bushel more where that came from. You'll be right as rain in a few minutes, or Hammond'll keep goin' at you 'til some of the damage is permanent. Big strong bloke like him could cripple a soft young thing like you for life. It's entirely up to you. Now, if you can stop blubberin' long enough to say somethin' to me except 'I don't know,' we can get on with our friendship. Ignorance ain't bliss, Bucko. I'm getting' bloody tired of you not knowin' anything."

Tears in his eyes, Gunnar raised up on one elbow and looked at Colin.

"Cat's father was with her," he said.

"Father! Whatdaya mean, her Father? Her dear old dad?"

"I mean her father," Gunnar grimaced. "Her male parent!"

"Right! Her dad. Now stop and think. How could that be? We outlive our mums and dads. Cat's older than me, you lyin' little shit!" Colin nodded to Hammond who reached for the boy.

"He's one of us!" Gunnar squeaked, showering spittle over his two tormentors and throwing up his hands. "Her father's Nosferati! He and Cat were taken at the same time and both of them came back. *Both of them!*"

"Blackbeard's balls! I never heard of such a thing!"

"Well, it's true. I've known Cat for over two hundred years. She and her dad used to live near here before he went away."

"Bloody Hell! That's one for the books, that is. What's his name, then?"

"Herriott," Gunnar replied, flexing his legs. "Can I get up?"

"Up you go," Colin replied, assisting the lad to his feet and brushing some of the grime from his body. "Herriott, you say?"

"Yes."

"Ever heard him called Casey?"

"No. Just Herriott."

"Describe him."

"Five-ten or so, dark hair, dark complexion. Old for one of us. Over forty when he was taken."

"Over forty?"

"Yes."

"That's him," Colin grinned at Hammond. "That's him. That shit-filled little twat ran off with her dear old dad! Ha! Pints to persimmons, I bet she's with her father right now, bouncin' on his lovely knee after she's fetched him his pipe and slippers." He turned back to Gunnar. "You don't know where they are or when they'll return, or if Cat is even coming back, is that right?"

"Yes," said Gunnar, taking a step backward.

Colin smiled. "Now, don't be afraid, Laddie-buck. You've been very helpful for someone who doesn't know anything. Hammond and me will leave you to your knittin'. You've nothing to fear from us. We're friends. Of course, as friends, we expect you to keep your mouth shut about our little visit, right?" He put his arm lightly across Gunnar's shoulders and leaned in, his lips almost touching the young man's ear. "Now, not a word to anyone, Love. Not the tiniest itsy-bitsy word. Right? This is our little secret."

"Sure. Not a word."

"There's a good lad," Colin continued, grasping the back of Gunnar's neck. "See, if we find out you've flapped your gums, what you got today will be a walk in the bleedin' park. And whatever we do to you, we'll do twice to your lady friend. Got me?"

"Yes," Gunnar said, licking his lips and shuddering, visions of permanent mutilations dancing in his head. "I won't say anything to anyone. I promise."

"Right," Colin said, releasing the youth's neck and kissing him on the cheek. "There's a good lad. Now how do we get out of this place without alertin' any members of the constabulary?"

Gunnar led them to the manhole and opened it. Colin and Hammond peered downward into the darkness.

"At the bottom of this shaft is a tunnel," Gunnar said, pointing down into the hole. "It runs out under the side lawn six or seven hundred feet to another shaft that comes up in a small grove of trees into a culvert that's covered by a grate. All you have to do is lift the grate and climb out."

"How do ya keep bums and the homeless from comin' in?"

"The grate weighs five or six hundred pounds. What human is gonna lift it?"

"What human indeed?" Colin said. "Well, that's it, then. Not a word, Love."

"Not a word," Gunnar agreed, nodding his head.

"Behave yourself, and when we get done with Cat, maybe I'll bring you a piece as a souvenir. Something you can put in one of those bloody jars."

Colin lowered himself into the shaft and Hammond followed. Gunnar replaced the cover, sat back on his heels, and fought to keep from shaking.

Casey watched his daughter walk into the kitchen from the mud room, the early morning sun streaming through the window giving her skin a golden glow. She looked at him, sitting at the table.

"What are you smiling about?" she asked.

"It's just such a treat to see you clean and shining and happy. I love you, Kiddo."

"I love you too, Pop," she smiled, picking up an apple off the counter and crossing to him. She kissed him on the back of his neck and folded into a chair, arm akimbo on a bent knee.

"Been down to see Felene?" Casey asked.

"Yup. She's still sleeping. About twenty hours now. It may be over."

Felene had had an easier time of it than Cat. She was not as angry, less driven by need for the attack and kill. Even during her worst moments, the knowledge she had entered withdrawal by choice seemed to stay with her, softening the experience. She did not mutilate herself or offer seething threats against her captors. Felene's suffering was more internal. She also lost a great deal of weight through both malnutrition and dehydration and was very weak. When she had fallen into a deep sleep the afternoon before, relief among the other members of the group had been palpable. The crisis point had been reached in only a little over three weeks; rehabilitation of another Nosferati had begun.

Three days after Felene's crisis and collapse, she had recovered so well that Cat brought her to the house for breakfast. Moira met them at the kitchen door.

"Welcome, Felene," she smiled. "It is good to have you here and see you well."

Felene flushed a bit and took her offered hand. "May I compliment you on your graciousness and selflessness," Felene replied, her voice shaking. "To be invited into your home is very humbling for me. There has been little kindness in my life for a long time. I have not received or offered compassion for many years."

"Better late than never," piped Casey, striding through the door.

"And you," Felene smiled, advancing on Casey and capturing his neck in her arms, "to see you now and know you now ..." She began to cry and buried her face in his shoulder.

Casey patted her back and kissed the top of her head. "You'll be purging for a while, Sweetheart," he said. "Just let it happen. You're also going to need a lot of calories. C'mon, let's eat."

"So you're going tomorrow?" Casey asked as he cleared the breakfast dishes away.

"Yes," Felene replied, lowering her cup to the table. "Cat and I both believe it would be the best. Gunnar doesn't do well without me, and I've been gone for nearly four weeks. It's best if I get back there as soon as possible. You're not coming with us?"

"No. Cat's the logical choice. Gunnar knows her a lot better than he does me, and one of us has to stay with the kids. Besides, it'll give the two of you some time together. Cat can fill you in on exactly what we're doing here and the possibilities for the future. I'll drive you to Denver and rent a car for the trip. I have to go to the city anyway. It's my bi-weekly mail run, and I need to pick up some blood."

"Blood?" Felene asked.

"Yes," Melvin replied, carrying a jug of milk to the fridge. "Beginning tomorrow morning, we'll start you on ten to fifteen cc's of blood orally per day. It should give you more energy and strength. Of course, your old level of ability will not be present unless you actually feed, but we'll be able to keep you at sixty to seventy percent and still allow your pH to achieve a status where you will viably ovulate."

"I'll feel good and be able to get pregnant."

Melvin smiled. "Exactly," he said.

"Great."

"Plus, I'll need to draw blood from you on a regular basis, to monitor your progress, conduct my research, and make sure we have no surprises."

"Where do you get the blood that I'll drink?"

"I steal it," Casey said.

"What?"

"Yeah. Hospitals, clinics, blood banks." He raised an eyebrow and peered at her. "*Vereffer dere iss blut, I lurk in de night.*"

Felene laughed. "Those acting lessons were a waste of money. You *steal* blood?"

"Yep."

"That's certainly the lesser of two evils."

That evening, Moira knocked on the door to the third bedroom. Felene opened it and motioned her inside.

"Come in, please."

"I don't want to bother you," Moira said. "I just thought I'd check and see if you needed anything."

"Bother me? How could you, who has taken me into her home and family, possibly be any kind of bother? Sit. Kick back. Tell me about yourself."

The women chatted for a while, and Moira explained how she and Casey had come to be together.

"So you didn't reform Herriott, uh, Casey," Felene said.

"No," Moira replied. "He did that himself."

"But you civilized him."

"As much as can be expected."

"Ha! That's a hell of an undertaking!" Felene laughed. "He's a piece of work, that man. I can't believe what you people have accomplished for yourselves, or for me either. It's wonderful. I don't know how to thank you, and I certainly have no idea how I can ever repay you."

"Don't concern yourself with that," Moira replied. "You'll be part of our support system."

"Ah. A less than bloodthirsty commune. That's a change of pace."

They sat in silence for a moment before Moira spoke.

"May I ask you a personal question?"

"Certainly."

"How old are you?"

"You know, I'm not really sure. Twelve or thirteen hundred years probably. Certainly well over a thousand."

"Cat said you came to North America with the Vikings?"

Felene nodded. "With the Norsemen. 'Viking' is actually a verb. *Viking* was something the Norsemen did, not who they were."

"And you stayed in the new world all those years?" Moira asked, watching Felene stifle a yawn.

"A lot of the time. I went back and forth to Europe on several occasions."

"Amazing, Moira said. "Well, you're tired and need some rest," she went on, rising to her feet and walking to the door. "One more question and I'll get out of your way."

"Anything."

"Casey claims he knew Kit Carson. Didn't you ever know any famous people?" Moira blushed. "Please excuse my curiosity. I feel sorta like a history groupie."

"Let's see," Felene said. "I knew one famous person, but he was really more of a notorious asshole."

"Really? Who?"

"Vlad Tempes."

"Who?"

Felene smiled. "It was in the last half of the fourteen hundreds," she went on, "in Romania. You might know him better as Vlad Dracul. Vlad the Impaler?"

"Vlad the Impaler!" Moira exclaimed. "Him?"

"Yeah. Real sweetheart. Killed more people than Cecil B. DeMille. Had a castle in the Carpathians. Used to line the sides of the road with pikes and ram captive Turks down on top of 'em. Miles of impaled dead and dying. Quite an attraction."

"Attraction?" Moira asked, repressing a shudder.

"Sure," Felene said. "That's why we hung around."

"We?"

"Me and three or four other Nosferati. We were in that area for a hundred years or so, freaking the locals out."

"And the atrocities drew you to Vlad?"

"All those dying Turks. Free lunch," Felene said.

"I see," Moira said, carefully controlled.

"He knew we were there," Felene went on, her eyes looking far away. "Christ, he knew what we were! He loved it! Hell, he's the one who is credited with starting the vampire legend in the first place. Some people believe Vlad actually *was* Count Dracula!"

"And he wasn't?" Moira ventured, fascinated by the tale.

"Lord, no!" said Felene, laughing at the memory. "He wanted to be. He'd make sure to impale the ones near his hangout slowly. That way, he could enjoy their screams and suffering, and maybe get a peek at us when we showed up. He even got so bold that, now and then, he'd eat a late meal outside at twilight underneath the hanging bodies, hoping to get a closer look at us. Fucker was weird! He'd even call to us, inviting us to his table. I never went, but a guy named Rimsky actually sat with Vlad occasionally, just for kicks. Said old Vlad nearly worshipped us. He told me that one night the bug-eyed little freak even tried blood himself. Had one of his lackeys collect some in a goblet. Made the nasty little bastard sick. Threw up all over the place. Nosferatu, my ass! Vlad the Impaler was nothing more than a mass murderer and a Nosferati wannabee. History says he was assassinated. That much is true, but not by humans. We ate him. Twisted fucker."

"Ah," Moira replied. It was the only thing she could think of to say.

"They claim," Felene continued, "that he's buried near the altar in this old Romanian church, or that his skeleton is in one of several other places, including a museum in Hollywood, for crissakes! Bullshit. We scattered his bones for the wolves, creepy little shit!"

Felene paused briefly and seemed to return to current reality. "Well," she said, gathering herself and standing. "Thanks for dropping by, and thank you again for all you've done for me," she continued, moving to Moira's side and kissing her on the cheek. "Pleasant dreams, Sweetie."

A little numb, Moira stepped into the hall and closed the door.

Cat spent most of the time during the drive to Chicago dealing with Felene's deep feelings of sorrow and regret for the life she had led, but it was uplifting nonetheless. Watching Felene's understanding of her situation grow and blossom, and associating with a perspective fed by the woman's immense lifetime, was also a purge for Cat. At a motel in Omaha, Felene declined the opportunity to go out for a drink, shy among so many humans. Cat left long enough to bring back both Chinese food and pizza, and they talked and laughed until deep sleep claimed them. The following morning they lazed around, went out for brunch, and didn't get on the road until nearly noon. Ten p.m. found them on Lakeshore Drive in Chicago. By ten-thirty they stood beside the entrance to the steam tunnel. Cat grabbed the grate to lift it, and paused.

"Something's not right," she said, shaking her head and sniffing.

"What?"

"Something's not right. Oh, hell. I need to get my shit together. God. I've come so far. I hate to do this, but I gotta have some blood. I'll be right back."

She walked to the car, opened the trunk, and lifted out the cooler. Both frightened and curious, she removed the top from a half-pint container and drank.

Jesus! The half-pint hit her like a quart did in the past. The stars quadrupled in brightness, the traffic thundered vibrations through the earth, the scent of the city ripped through her nostrils. She leaned on the rear of the car and trembled, then almost urinated in her jeans. Panting, she collected herself, peed in the grass, replaced the cooler, and returned to Felene.

"You okay?" Felene asked.

"Oh, yeah," Cat grinned, rubbing her arms. "God, what a rush. Emergency use only," she laughed, then stepped up to the shaft and lifted the grate. "*Shit!*"

"What?"

"*Oh, shit!* Shit. Shit. *Shit!*"

"What *shit?*"

"Colin's been here. Hammond, too. In the tunnel!"

"The Nosferati from Arkansas?"

"The Nosferati from Arkansas. Dammit! I could probably handle Colin, I might even be able to handle Hammond if I got real lucky, but not both of them."

"I'm here."

"Aw, Sweetie, you wouldn't stand a ghost of a chance against either one of them. You've just dried out. You haven't fed in over a month!"

"So, I'll just drink some blood."

"No, you won't! You drink right now, and you are back where you started! Colin's scent isn't that strong. He's probably not down there right now."

"What about Gunnar?"

"We have to hurry, but we can't just break into the museum. We'll have cops all over the place. And I don't want to risk running into Colin and Hammond in case they show up in the tunnel. Is there another way in?"

"Sort of."

"Sort of?"

"Yeah. We take a sump shaft over by the Shedd Aquarium to a drainage duct that used to dump into the lake. It's awful."

"How awful?"

"The runoff culverts have been sealed from the lake side. The water that's trapped in there seeps in from sewers and the ground water table. It's really nasty. The tunnel connects to the level below ours at the opposite end of the museum."

"There's a level below yours?"

"Yeah. It's about half filled with slime and god knows what, but it's a way in."

"And a way out. One that Colin doesn't know about."

"Okay," said Felene, walking toward the aquarium. "It's also totally dark. No ambient light at all. We'll be blind."

Cat shrugged.

The women walked for nearly a half-mile through an eight-foot tunnel, stepping in muck on things that moved and things that didn't, in water that was thicker than blood. The air was viscous with odors of putrefying garbage and flesh. Chin deep, sometimes swimming through liquid decomposition, surrounded by moldering walls that dripped gelatinous residue, they kept on, breathing through their mouths, both on the ragged edge of control. After an eternity that lasted only a few minutes, they encountered a four-foot feeder drain that sloped upward to their right and pulled themselves from the mire.

"Jesus," said Cat, trying to scrape slime from her jeans. Something flopped onto the crumbling cement beside her and wiggled away into the dark. "That was awful."

Felene was trembling. "The worst is over," she said. "We can clean up at my place. On the way back, we'll bring extra clothes in a plastic bag for the return trip."

"Fuck that!" Cat exclaimed. "We'll leave by a window or something. I am not going back through that mess. We can break out a lot easier that we could have broken in. Now what?"

"No more water. Just lots of mud and slime."

"Let's do it."

Gunnar was not in evidence when Cat and Felene finally arrived. They went upstairs to clean up. Cat took a shower with her clothes on and another with her clothes off, then put her wet togs over an air vent to dry. Back downstairs, Felene provided Cat with a caftan. She'd just slipped it over her head when Gunnar walked in. He gave a start and flushed.

"Cat, hi."

"Hello, Gunnar," Cat replied, scenting confusion and fear.

He crossed to Felene and hugged her, then stepped back. "Welcome home," he said, then looked at her with a puzzled expression on his face. "What's going on? You're different."

"We'll talk about it later, Sweetie," Felene said. "Gather up some clothes and things, and all the money you have. We're leaving."

"Leaving? Why?"

"Later, Gunnar. Just trust me. We have to hurry."

"I just got here!"

"So did we, and now we're leaving."

"I don't wanna leave. I live here! What's the matter with you, Felene? You were fine 'til you left with her, and now, all of a sudden, you want to go someplace else? This is bullshit."

"C'mon, Gunnar," Cat said. "Shake a leg."

"And you," he protested, "you're not the same either. You smell different! What's going on?"

Cat leveled her gaze on the young man. "Gunnar, we have to get out of here. We're in danger."

"I'm not in danger," he snapped. "You may be, but I'm not!"

Cat smiled. "You think Colin won't kill you?"

Gunnar flushed. "Wh-who?"

"Who? *Who?* Your feet fit a limb, Asshole?"

"I don't know what you're talking about!"

"His scent is in the tunnel and all over this level of the building. He and his dumbass sidekick, Hammond. You can't lie to me! You can't lie to Felene either! How long ago was he here?"

Gunnar flopped into a chair and took his head in his hands. "He hurt me."

"How long ago was he here?"

"He hurt me and made me promise," Gunnar complained.

Felene looked at Cat and gave her a quick nod. "I'm going for a walk," she said, opening the door. "I'll be back in about ten minutes."

Gunnar flinched when the door slammed and kept his eyes on the floor.

Cat smiled and sat on the edge of the bed. "Tell me," she said.

"I can't."

"Tell me."

"I can't! He'll come back and hurt me and Felene!"

"If he finds Felene, he will kill her no matter what you do or don't do. Then he'll kill you. He'll try to kill me, too. Tell me."

"I can't!"

280

"You have one chance to get out of this, Gunnar. One chance. *Me.* You get your shit together, tell me when he was here and what happened, and I'll take you with us when we leave. Make no mistake. Felene and I are leaving. You wanna stay here all by yourself? You wanna be here when Colin and Hammond come back? You wanna face them alone?"

Gunner looked at her, his eyes rimmed with tears. "No," he said.

"Tell me."

He did.

Thirty minutes later, the three of them had worked their way to the third floor storage area, past roaming guards and alarmed doors, and opened an unsecured window. The heavy stone walls provided excellent footing, and in a matter of moments they had descended low enough that Felene could safely make the thirty foot drop to the side lawn of the Field Museum of Natural History.

Hammond lifted the grate on the entrance shaft, and Colin stepped forward to the edge. He paused and wrinkled his nose.

"Cat!" he hissed, looking at Hammond. "She's been here! Bloody hell! Her scent has changed a bit, but it's her. Right, Bucko. Let's go."

Colin jumped down the shaft and hit the tunnel running, Hammond on his heels. He was almost all the way to the museum before he realized that Cat had not passed that way. He slid to a stop and Hammond collided with him, both of them crashing to the floor. Before Hammond could protest, Colin was up and gone, back toward the entrance at best speed. He fairly flew up the shaft, his nostrils working like a hound's, and set off, sniffing his way across the lawn toward the Shedd Aquarium. The headlights of a car leaving the parking lot about fifty feet away raked over the two of them, but the Nosferati paid no attention. Inside the car, Cat laughed.

"Have fun in the drainage tunnel, Boys," she said. "You'll love it."

# THIRTY-FIVE

Gunnar

ON THE DRIVE BACK FROM CHICAGO, Felene explained to Gunnar what she had been through in the converted bomb shelter, and why she had done it.

"We can have a baby?" he asked.

"Melvin tells me it's as possible for us as it is for humans."

"But, look," Gunnar protested, "if we don't feed, we'll be weak. I don't want to be weak."

"No," Felene said patiently, "we won't be weak. We just won't be as strong as we are after we feed. Once the addiction is broken, just a couple of swallows a day is all you'll need to remain way above human levels. Feeding, unless it is some sort of life threatening emergency, is out. No more kills, Gunnar. The Nosferati life is over for me. Once you dry out, it will be over for you, too."

"But everything will be so different!"

"Yes, it will. You have no idea how different. You will think differently, act differently, see the world differently, but let me tell you the single biggest difference between humans and Nosferati. It's not the blood, it's not the strength or the speed or the power or the life span. It's much more simple and much more complicated than that."

"Well, what is it?" Gunnar asked, rolling his eyes.

Felene smiled at him tolerantly. "Love," she said.

"Love?" Gunnar complained. "I know about love. I love you."

Felene stroked his arm. "No, you don't. You're dependent on me. You're lost without me. That's not love. That's fear. Fear is the opposite of love. It masquerades as anger, hate, need, and a thousand other things, but it's just fear, and it is what the Nosferati base their entire existence upon.

"Nosferati are the most fearsome predators on the planet, and the most dishonest. They not only kill to sustain themselves, they kill to promote themselves, to reassure themselves that they can! To reinforce the knowledge that they have the power, the ability, the will to do whatever they want with all these puny little humans. When a lioness makes a kill, she's going to the grocery. When a Nosferati makes a kill, he's celebrating his superiority! He craves it! Gunnar, the only reason anybody ever needs to feel superior is the fear of being inferior. And they're right, Sweetheart. Those poor, wretched bastards are so inferior that God won't even allow them to procreate. Through some fluke, a few survive and perpetuate a virus that should have killed itself off thousands of years ago. It shouldn't still be alive! It's an aberration."

Felene looked deeply into his eyes, willing him to understand. "And now," she said, "because of Moira and Casey, because of Melvin and the twins, because of Cat, we have the opportunity to do something right with this whole mess: to change that aberration into our salvation, to create a better reality for all of us, to relieve disease, to elevate the consciousness, to raise the level of human awareness and understanding and ability. This could be the beginning of events that can literally change the world. If you want to change your surroundings, you must first change yourself. Do you understand?"

"I like things the way they are," Gunnar muttered, picking at a wrinkle in his jeans.

"Part of that's my fault," Felene said. "In my effort to protect you, I sheltered you too much. Plus, you don't have much life experience. You can't begin to have my perspective on the world. You haven't lived long enough."

"I've lived over three times longer than a fucking human does!"

Felene smiled patiently at him. "And I was three times your age when Columbus came to the new world. I sailed with the Phoenicians, Gunnar! I'd been living among *Los Indios* for over fifty years when Ponce de Leon came ashore. I have seen more war and famine and progress and failure than you can imagine. I've watched nations grow and prosper and whole civilizations decline and decay. I have roamed this planet from one end to the other, living lifetimes among people that you have never heard of, seeing things you cannot imagine. I was with Leif Erickson on his first voyage to North America. I was old when Longshanks went after the Scots! I was ancient during the Inquisition! Do you understand? Does any of this make sense to you? Do you have any appreciation for my perspective?"

"I just don't wanna be weak," Gunnar muttered, staring out the window.

They found Gunnar in a deep coma on the eleventh morning of his treatment. He had opened the veins in his wrists and drank his own blood until he lost consciousness. Even Casey couldn't bring him back.

# THIRTY-SIX

## American Dream

THEY BURIED GUNNAR in a small clearing about half a mile from the house, the grave marked only with one large stone and surrounded by aspens. Felene stayed by the spot for three days and nights. On the fourth morning, she ambled into the kitchen, said hello to everyone, kissed the twins, and went upstairs. An hour later, freshly showered and changed, she stopped by the lab, drank about twenty cc's of blood, and announced she was going to town.

"Need a ride?" asked Casey. "I'm heading for Denver today. Be glad to drop you off on the way."

"No, thanks. I think I'll go on foot. I could use the walk."

Moira slipped an arm around Felene's waist. "Are you okay, Dear?"

"Almost. Gunnar was too weak for this life. His understanding of power was misguided. Even if he had survived breaking the addiction, he wasn't strong enough or secure enough to have stayed clean. We grieve most when we lose a future. Gunnar and I had no future; we never did. He leaned too heavily on me, and I allowed it, thinking I had to atone for something."

Moira hugged her. "You seem to be doing very well," she said.

"Christ, Moira, I predate Marco Polo! When you're that old, you have a tendency to roll with the punches. Need anything from town? I'm clean there. Nobody knows me. I fit right in with the artists and potters. The natives think I'm a tourist, the tourists think I'm a native. I can infiltrate. Got a grocery list or something?"

"I'll make a short one," Moira said. "Just take a minute."

It was almost dark by the time Casey returned from Denver. Cat helped him unload the Hummer and they walked into the kitchen together. Melvin and Moira were at the table feeding the kids.

"Where's Felene?" Casey asked, handing Melvin a letter.

"She hasn't come back from town yet," Moira replied, wiping a wet glob of cheese off her shoulder and kissing him on the chin.

"Is that good?"

"I don't know if it is or not. Felene's actions can't be judged by my standards. She has a much different view of the world than I do."

"I got it," Melvin interrupted, waving his letter. "I got the money for the facility! I'll have the first million in around thirty days."

"Great!" Cat beamed, hugging him. "Now you can take me away from all this. Paris? Monaco? Cleveland? You decide."

"Cleveland, I should think," Melvin said.

Moira laughed. "That's wonderful, Melvin. Fischer Labs?"

"Yes."

"How are they going to pay you?"

"Well, they didn't say. An open account from their bank, I suppose, or a, oh!"

"Uh-huh," Casey said. "Tomorrow we go for a drive, Melvin. We'll go to Colorado Springs or somewhere, set up a second mail drop, and have the mail service in Denver forward all the stuff to it. You can call the money people on the phone from there and set up payment. I'd suggest a cashier's check. Fischer will send it to Denver, Denver sends it to Colorado Springs, we cash it someplace like Fort Collins, and open a business account for you in Boulder or Pueblo. Lotsa blind alleys and no connection to Glenwood Springs at all. Okay?"

"Well, that's probably ..."

"Quiet!" hissed Cat, cocking her head. "Dad?"

Casey froze for a moment, staring sightlessly at the floor. "Crossing the creek," he murmured.

Cat looked at Moira. "Strange truck coming," she said. "Get the kids upstairs, stay inside." She and Casey left the house so fast the air pressure fluctuated, causing the twins to cry.

Less than ten minutes later, they returned in the company of a smiling Felene. Moira and Melvin heard them and came downstairs.

"Sorry to cause any hassle," Felene apologized, watching Moira put her .45 back on top of the dining room china cabinet. "I guess I should have called ahead or something. I bought a truck."

"A truck?"

"Yep. A '99 Chevy. It's got less than a hundred thousand miles on it, new brakes and tires, and a rebuilt motor."

"Good for you," Moira said. "I had no idea you even wanted a vehicle."

"It's my first one," Felene said. "The American dream. Get a job and get a car, or a truck in my case."

Moira's eyebrows rose. "A job?"

"Yep. A place called The Troll and the Sandrider. It's a pottery shop. The gal that owns it is too busy throwing clay to wait on all the customers. We chatted, I told her about some glazing techniques, and she offered me a gig on the spot. I am gainfully employed. Or I will be as of next Monday."

"You know about pottery?"

"I know about glazing. I spent some time in Japan a while back. Some of those guys could glaze a running cat."

"How long ago is 'a while back?'" Moira asked.

"I don't know," Felene said, "two or three hundred years before Vlad. So, now I have a truck and a job. I'll wait on customers when we have some, and sit on the stoop and play guitar when we don't. Cool, huh?"

"Very cool," Moira said. "Very, very cool."

During the next few weeks the twins, looking and acting very much like four-year-olds, celebrated their second birthday. Melvin received his first payment, he and Casey began construction on the research facility, and everyone enjoyed watching Felene blossom. She worked at the pottery shop Wednesday through Sunday, brought home a bag or two of groceries a couple of times a week, bought a used Martin guitar, Birkenstocks, baggy blouses, peasant's skirts, smiled a lot, and seemed to be very happy with her new life.

"She's a hippie," Casey observed at the dinner table one evening.

"That's it," Cat said. "She even said 'far out' the other day."

"Neither of you are old enough to remember real Hippies," Casey said to Moira and Melvin, "but Felene qualifies. She is living history from the 1960's. A flower child, for God's sake. Groovy."

"Make love, not war," chuckled Cat.

"Speaking of that," Moira said, "the chances of us getting a child from two twelve-stranders went out the window with Gunnar's death."

"Yeah," Cat agreed, "but she could still have a baby, couldn't she Melvin?"

"Her system is running perfectly, her blood pH is within acceptable limits, she's ovulating." He shrugged. "No reason she couldn't get pregnant."

"Would that be safe?" Moira asked. "What about the chance of infection? I mean, if she were intimate with a human, couldn't he get the virus?"

"Possible," Melvin said. "But not probable. There has to be blood involved, his blood. It would be much more likely for a male Nosferati to infect a female human than vice versa. Very low risk, as long as she didn't, uh, that is to say, get out of hand, so to speak."

"She's a very gentle person," Cat said, raising her voice. "Considerate, too. As we speak, she's trying to sneak through the mudroom so we won't know she heard us talking about her. Whatcha think, Felene? You gonna drag some unsuspecting young swain into the giggle grass and get outta hand?"

Felene walked in from the kitchen, trying to look offended. "Catherine," she said, raising an eyebrow, "how could you, of all people, think such a thing of me?"

"I've known you too long to think anything else," Cat laughed, "and I am excessively familiar with your appetites." She turned to Moira and bumped her eyebrows. "I could tell you stories that would curl your hair."

"Or your toes," chimed Casey.

"Oh, goody!" Moira said. "Give."

"I don't think a discussion of past transgressions is appropriate conversation, all things considered," Felene snorted, taking the high road.

"What things considered?" asked Cat.

"I'm pregnant."

"What?"

"At least I think so. I'm ten days late."

Questions came from every direction. Felene held up a hand and the melee quieted. "No, I won't be bringing anyone home to meet the family. Yes, he's human, very human. No, he doesn't know about the child. Yes, he's not a native. His name is Gerald, he's a theatre arts professor at Bard College. He came to Glenwood Springs for the waters and he doesn't even know my real name. He's very smart, he's very pretty, and he's very gone. The last thing I want is a relationship. The first thing I want is a baby. At your convenience, Melvin, we will confirm what I already know. I am now going upstairs to change and allow the four of you some time to gossip behind my back. And yes, Cat, he was a tremendous piece of ass, for a human. The other two weren't bad either, but I'm pretty sure Gerald is the father." She bestowed a saintly smile on the four stunned faces, turned on her heel, and left the room.

Cat broke the silence. "Ha!" she said. "Too good! Felene always did know how to pick 'em." She grinned at Casey. "Didn't she, Father?"

When Casey didn't answer, Moira spoke up. "Hmmm. Is there something here I should know?"

"Curl your hair," Cat replied.

"Toes," said Casey, then he, too, left the room.

The pregnancy was confirmed. Felene glowed. The twins were fascinated by her growing stomach, often positioning themselves on either side of her as she sat on the couch, pressing their ears and cheeks against her tolerant belly. One evening in late June, they were so engaged they both broke into laughter. From across the room, Moira smiled at them. "What's so funny?" she asked.

"The baby," Beth said. "The baby wiggles."

Sean raised up and patted Felene's stomach. "She likes it when we laugh," he said.

"She?" asked Felene.

"Uh-huh," said Beth. "She."

Felene looked at the child. "It's a girl, Lizzy?"

"A girl," Beth replied.

"How do you know?"

"Just is," Beth shrugged, then clambered off the couch and went into the kitchen in search of pudding. Sean hung around for a moment, patting Felene's tummy, before leaving to join his sister.

The next day, Melvin's ultrasound confirmed that the baby was female.


Found


THE HEAVILY GLOVED HAND PUSHED THE SEND BUTTON, and the sound of digital tones echoed through the white room. There was a click.

"Voorhees here."

"Ah, dear boy, are you well?"

"Mr. Unruh. I was going to phone you tomorrow, Sir."

"Where are you?"

"Denver, Sir."

"You have news, Voorhees?"

"Some, Sir. After the debacle in Chicago, my agents have nowhere else to look. We have established that the young woman called Cat and the subject known as Casey are, most probably, father and daughter. It would also seem likely that they have added two others to their number, a male called Gunnar and a female named Felene. They are now six."

"Felene. Lovely name."

"Yessir. Melvin Foltz went for the funding deal with Fischer Labs and accepted the first installment. It was sent to him at an address in Denver that turns out to be a mail drop and re-mailing service. It was sent from there to an unknown destination. I'll be going into the building this evening, Sir, to attempt to find out where the payment was posted."

"Not necessary, Voorhees."

"Sir?"

"Not necessary. It is possible that we know where Ms. Flynn and company are hiding."

"Good news, Sir."

"Most probably. An operative I control, who labors in the human resources office of The Proteus Trust, received an interesting phone call from the legal firm of Dobbs, Wainwright, Felding and Dobbs of Boston only yesterday. It was an inquiry seeking after Ms. Flynn. My operative was able to learn that these lawyers are responsible for the estate of one Louise Agatha Durbin, the aunt and last living relative of Ms. Flynn. It would seem that Ms. Durbin, now deceased, was holding a considerable piece of land and a home in trust for Ms. Flynn. Through other sources, I have been able to determine that this acreage lies not overly far from your present location, Voorhees, north-northwest of Glenwood Springs, Colorado. Are you familiar with that area?"

"Mildly, Sir. You could pass through Glenwood Springs were you to drive from Vail to Aspen."

"Quite. I have been in touch with certain operatives at a company in Urbana, Illinois known as HAL Devices. They are in contact with, among other technology, an observation satellite known as Pegasus III. Pegasus' tasked orbital path takes it over the Glenwood Springs area several times a day. The good people at HAL Devices will start providing me with digital scans of the area within the hour. We should be able to determine not only if anyone is living on Ms. Flynn's property, but also who he or she is. I will, of course, relay this information to you with utmost dispatch. If Mr. Foltz is there, Voorhees, I desire his company. You shall acquire him for me, and anyone else that could be of interest to us."

"Indeed, Sir."

"The area is quite remote with limited avenues of conventional approach. Begin your plans. Anything you need is approved."

"Thank you, Sir."

"Indeed. Don't fail me, Voorhees. It's not allowed."

"Yessir."

Voorhees turned on his computer, awaiting transmission from Unruh, and made a phone call. The voice that answered was quiet to the point of being nearly a whisper.

"Yeah?"

"Hello. Do you know who this is?"

"Yeah. Whatcha need?"

"Helicopter."

"How big?"

"Eight to ten passenger capability. Military function."

"Gotta a re-built Huey coming in about a month. Too late?"

"No."

"What else?"

"Pilot and three or four weekend warriors. Expendable. Cannon fodder only."

"Ha. Commin' out my ears. Everybody wants to be a hero. What else?"

"Gun. Shoulder weapon. Big. Long range. Knock down an elephant."

"Got it. Some secret shit from our friends at the Browning Company. Sixty caliber, auto loader, five round mag, shells copper-jacketed with lead dust in Teflon backed by a core of depleted uranium. When the round hits, it explodes and the uranium pushes the explosion through the target. Around four thousand fps. Ten power scope with a laser sight and distance compensation. Point and shoot to fifteen hundred yards."

"How much?"

"Lots. How soon?"

"At least a month."

"Foreign or domestic?"

"Domestic."

"How long?"

"Thirty minutes or less on site."

"A helo, warm bodies, big gun. Anything else?"

"As of now, no."

"Keep in touch, Mr. V."

"Count on it."

Voorhees looked at a series of six photographs that scrolled out of his printer. Jesus! The technology was amazing. He put his computer and the photos in a case, grabbed a bag, and headed for the car. He needed help, and it was always prudent to fight fire with fire. It was time for a trip to Jasper.

# THIRTY-SEVEN

## Death and Birth

FELENE'S PREGNANCY followed the same rapid growth pattern Moira's had, and by mid July she was huge. The twins followed her around like puppies, Moira and Cat doted on her, Melvin and Casey worried about her, and high summer in the mountains was a glorious time. With the lab nearly completed in the barn loft, most of the equipment was removed from the house to provide more ground floor space and a nursery. The expectant mother left her job in anticipation of an early August delivery and lumbered around the house, smiling. Because Felene no longer spent her days in Glenwood Springs, she wasn't in a position to notice the new faces drifting in and out of town. The odd, black-haired young man with the strange accent, feral eyes, and cruel mouth did not catch her attention, nor did she see his oversized lumbering companion. The quiet older gentleman with sandy hair, green eyes, and a scar on his chin also escaped her notice.

He saw her many times in high resolution courtesy of HAL Devices and their connection with Pegasus, just as he saw everyone else in Casey's extended family. All through June, he watched them. All through July he plotted their habits, observed vehicles, noted their comings and goings. He peered at them every day, planning his course of action, assembling his tools, preparing his people, making periodic calls to the keep in Austria to advise his master of the proceedings. Voorhees watched and Voorhees waited, maintaining his thin hold on Colin through promise and greed. It was difficult work, but he was good at it.

At the house, all was well. Moira had never been located by the law firm of Dobbs, Wainwright, Felding and Dobbs on the matter of Louise Agatha Durbin's death. The lawyers continued to send monthly payments from the estate to the property management company in Boulder that handled the account, their bureaucratic myopia never noticing the increase in expenses over the past two years. In their insular little Colorado world, Moira, Casey, Cat, and Melvin went about their business as if their lives were normal. They were not. They never could be.

The two, Cat and Casey, who should have known better, didn't. Family life had claimed them. Apparent security had seduced them. In displacing their need to be predators, they had also released the mindset of prey. They succumbed to the one thing that could not be overcome by their frightening speed, their awesome strength, or their amazing abilities. They became complacent. That complacency, and his association with the Nosferati from Arkansas, gave Voorhees the edge he needed.

Casey heard the distant whump of helicopter rotors as he came downstairs for breakfast, but gave the sound only passing notice. Helicopters were common all year round, coming and going from both Vail and Aspen. It was a beautiful morning, already nearly sixty degrees. He kissed Moira, hugged the twins, rubbed Cat's neck, smiled at Melvin, said hello to Felene, and sat. He felt nothing of portent, no impending sense of tragedy, no harbinger of grim events. It was breakfast time, and he was content.

After the meal, Moira took Sean upstairs to remove a splinter from the web of his thumb. Casey carried the dirty dishes to the sink and spent a moment looking out the back window, watching Cat push Beth on the tire swing, as Melvin stopped to join them on his way to the lab. Smiling, Casey lit a cigarette and wandered out onto the deeply shadowed front porch. The meadow stretched away nearly two hundred yards down the gentle hill, sunlight coloring the trees on the west side, already bright on the rise another two hundred yards distant. Felene stood barefoot in the grass sixty feet down the slope, facing away from the house, slowly bending her swollen body from side to side, her ankle length skirt swaying gently with the motion, hanging well away from her feet because of the size of her belly. She was due any day.

"Now, touch your toes," Casey said.

She turned sideways and grinned at him. Just as she raised her hand to deliver an obscene gesture, the bullet arrived.

Beginning its journey from a little over a half mile away, the sixty caliber round entered Felene's leg from the outside of her upper right thigh at slightly over thirty-four hundred feet per second. Within the first inch of penetration, the thin copper jacket peeled away releasing the Teflon core with its cargo of lead dust. Her thighbone sheared off just below the hip, expanding the mass even more, so that when the diabolical projectile exited the inside of the thigh, it destroyed all the soft tissue on that side of her leg. The damage was hideous, Felene's right leg remaining attached only by skin around the entry site. The thin wafer of depleted uranium propelled the rapidly disintegrating mass of Teflon and lead through her left thigh from the inside outward, severing that appendage completely, tearing her skirt away to land ten feet distant wrapped around the left leg. In a tiny fraction of a second, Felene was ruined. With a quiet thud, her legless torso dropped to the earth, and she toppled silently to her back.

Casey was moving even before the sound of the shot reached his ears, zigzagging his way across the meadow toward the trees, his last visual image of Felene destroyed burning his retinas. Small arms fire broke out from three locations in front of him, one round even nicking his elbow, and he made for them, knowing that what had happened to Felene had not come from any of those weapons, realizing that they were a diversion to allow the sniper to escape, but unable to ignore them for fear of what might occur should the men behind those weapons gain the house. It took him less than two minutes to find and deal with the three shooters, in spite of their M-16's and camouflage clothing, regardless of their superior number and training, heedless of the sound of the helicopter so close to the house. He left them ripped and dead in the trees and streaked back to the yard.

Cat was pushing Beth in the tire swing when she heard the heavy report of the sniper's weapon. Leaving Melvin with the child, she was halfway around the house when Hammond appeared from behind the barn to her right. Without breaking stride, she swerved and tore straight into him. Hammond swatted her away like a child.

"Long time, no see, Cat," he said, circling her as she rose to her feet. "You're slow. Miss breakfast?"

"Where's your master, Dog Boy?" Cat snorted, popping a dislocated elbow back in place. "You don't go anywhere without your tongue up Colin's butt."

"He's around someplace. You'll see him later."

"God, you smell bad!" Cat replied. "You ever take a bath?"

Hammond sneered. "There was times you didn't mind."

"Another life, Asshole. This is now. Leave while you can."

"I'm gonna leave, all right, but you're comin' with me."

"Fat chance."

"Got some people wanna meet you, Cat."

"Not today, Hammond. Get outta here and take your stink with you."

"You're gonna have my smell all over you before I'm through, little girl," he laughed. "I'm gonna wear you out!"

It was an exercise in futility. Five times Cat closed with him. Five times he hurled her away, ever more broken, ever more bleeding. She stood before him, panting and clutching a shattered and slashed arm, swaying to keep her feet as he advanced, pressing his advantage before her wounds could heal. Just as he got within range, the sun crested the top of the trees behind the house, its glare striking Hammond full in the eyes. When he blinked and turned his head away, Cat, marshaling all that was left of her will and power, struck.

Ducking under his outstretched reach, she leapt to his back, anchored herself with her legs and good arm, she sank her teeth into the nape of his neck, and began to chew. Hammond shrieked and reeled, flinging himself backwards time and again into the stone side of the house, flailing and writhing to rid himself of the snorting banshee gnawing her way into his neck. Cat heard her bones pop and snap, felt the blood running from her nose and bubbling out of her side where ribs came through the skin, and still she hung on, riding the storm in grim determination.

Dropping to the ground, Hammond rolled across the earth in desperation to be rid of her. She clung to him, her clothing shredding from her crimson stained body, a leopard on a buffalo, gnashing ever deeper into the back of his muscular neck, knowing this could easily be her last battle, realizing death was licking at her, committed to the depth of her reptile brain to do it, or die. She did it. As Hammond lurched back to his feet, Cat felt his vertebrae crunch between her teeth, followed by the warm gush of spinal fluid. The cord severed and Hammond stiffened, and he fell onto his face. She bounced from atop his body and rolled to her back, her nose, jaw, and cheek fractured, her arm mangled, blood bubbling from around exposed ribs protruding from her lacerated side. Her heart had lost its rhythm, fluttering like a bird in her breast, when Moira appeared above her. Cat felt herself being pulled along the ground, then rolled onto her side. The bloody back of Hammond's neck came into her narrowing field of vision, and her face was pushed into the gore. From a million miles away she heard Moira's command.

"*Drink!* Goddamn it, Cat, I love you and I need you. Drink! Don't you die on me, you selfish little shit. Don't you let go! *Drink! Drink!!*"

Cat opened her mouth and began to suck.

Casey returned to Felene and found her lying on her back looking at the sky.

"I never realized it was so blue," she said.

"Hang on, Sweetheart," Casey whispered, his thoughts on Moira, but unable to leave the stricken woman's side. "Give me some time and I can probably get you through this okay."

"What about the baby?"

"I don't know. You've lost a lot of blood."

"And both legs," Felene said.

"And both legs," Casey admitted.

"Get the baby out, Casey."

"What?"

"Take the baby. Save her life."

"Felene, if I remove the baby in your condition, you'll die."

"Gee. And I'm so young. Save the baby. Please. All these years finally mean something. It's a fitting end. Let me go, Casey. It's the perfect time."

"If that's what you want, Sweetheart," Casey replied.

"It's what I want." Felene smiled. "I love you all. Thanks for helping me be human." She blinked back tears. "It's wonderful," she whispered. "First you save the mother. Now you save the child."

And there, kneeling beside the broken body of a woman who had lived for over a thousand years, using his thumbnail as a scalpel for a Cesarean section, Casey delivered a squalling six-pound eleven-ounce human being into the world. Holding the baby girl as he removed a shoelace to tie the cord, he looked at her mother's lovely face. Even in death, Felene smiled.

Casey was cleaning the baby with his shirt when Cat walked out from around the back of the house. Nude and dripping with well water, she smiled at him.

"Whatcha got there, *Father*?" Cat said, pulling wet hair back from her face.

Instantly, Casey was on guard. "Felene's baby," he replied. "Felene didn't make it, I'm afraid."

"Bummer," Cat pouted. "She was a great piece of ass."

"How are you, Cat?" Casey asked.

"Me? I haven't been this good in years." She laughed. "Hammond damn near did me, *Father*. I drank him. Wow."

"Uh-huh," Casey replied, wiping the baby's chest and neck and rising slowly to his feet. "Melvin okay?"

"Melvin's gone. Beth, too. I guess Colin got 'em. I was a little busy at the time."

"Melvin and Beth are gone?"

"Yeah. Zip. The old family took a hell of a hit today, huh, Pop? Bet you feel pretty inadequate, doncha? Big bad alpha male got a limp dick, Daddy?"

Casey struggled with his composure, then felt tremendous relief as he saw Moira step out onto the porch with Sean. She remained silent and watched from a distance.

"And you drank Hammond."

"No shit. I am so cranked right now! You wouldn't believe it. I absolutely guarantee that I am the baddest sonofabitch in the whole fucking valley! Think I'll go to town for a snack or ten."

"No."

"No? *No?* Who the hell do you think you are?" Cat snarled. "You disgusting piece of shit! You're no better than a human! How the fuck you gonna stop me? I can kick your tired old ass and not break a sweat, *Father.*"

"I know you can, Cat," Casey replied, forcing calm into his voice. "You can kill all of us and go do what you please. I don't deny that. But you won't."

"I won't?" She grinned, stepping to within five feet and taunting him.

"No."

"And why won't I, *Father?*"

"Because you're human."

"Ha! Doesn't mean a fucking thing."

"Sure it does. It means love and understanding and compassion and empathy."

"Bullshit."

"All qualities that you have in abundance, Daughter."

"*Bullshit.*"

"Alright," Casey sighed. "If being human is meaningless and blood is all that matters, then why not start with her." Gently, he tossed the baby at Cat's chest.

Out of reflex, Cat caught the child and held her. "Cheap shot, Pop."

The baby, also out of reflex, did what babies do. She began to nuzzle between Cat's breasts. Cat looked stunned.

"Finish cleaning her up," Casey said, laying his shirt over Cat's shoulder and gently touching her cheek. "I'm going to talk to Moira." He began to walk to the house.

Cat looked down at the baby, then her eyes traveled to Felene's broken corpse.

"Aw, Jesus," she whispered, and sank to a sitting position on the earth. She wrapped the baby tenderly in Casey's shirt and held her carefully, feeling the tiny warm body moving against her chest. "Aw, Jesus," she whispered again, and began to cry.

"I can't find Melvin or Beth," Moira blurted, throwing herself into Casey's arms as he climbed the steps up to the porch.

"Cat thinks Colin took them," he replied, rubbing her back.

"That Nosferatl! He has my baby?"

"And Melvin."

"And Melvin. God, Casey, what are we going to do? *What are we going to do?*"

He pushed her back a bit and looked into her eyes. "We are going to do what we have to do. Is Hammond's body around here?"

"Behind the house," Moira replied with a faint wave over her shoulder.

"Get a kit and collect at least a pint of his blood and refrigerate it. We may need it later. I'm going back out to the tree line and bury three bodies. I'll be back in a few minutes. By then Cat will have settled down, we can get rid of Hammond and I'll put Felene up by Gunnar. When all that's done, we'll talk about all this. Okay?"

"They took Beth, Casey," Moira said, stepping in front of him.

"Yes, they did," Casey answered, taking her by the shoulders. "They also took Melvin. If Colin masterminded the attack, Melvin wouldn't have been a factor. Whoever is behind all this wants more than just Melvin and Beth. They'll be in touch. This is a long way from over." He kissed her gently on the cheek and loped off down the slope.

Twenty minutes later, Casey returned from his burial detail and carried Felene's body to the house. Cat was sitting on the porch holding the baby, now wrapped in a light cotton blanket. She smiled at him.

"You okay, Pop?"

"Marginally. How 'bout you?"

"Getting there. Sorry."

"S'alright, Cat. Musta been something you drank."

"Musta been," she said.

Casey wrapped Felene in a clean white sheet and went inside to wash up. He looked out the kitchen window in time to see Moira rise from beside Hammond's body with a bag of blood in her left hand. As she stood, she pulled her .45 from the waistband of her shorts and fired seven rounds into the back of Hammond's head. Walking into the kitchen, she laid the gun on the counter and opened the refrigerator to place the blood inside. Looking over the door, she noticed Casey.

"Just wanted to make sure," she said, her voice flat and emotionless.

"Good idea," Casey replied as she closed the fridge.

She moved into his arms, the side of her face against his chest.

"I'd kill 'em all if I could, Casey. Every one of those fucking bastards."

He held her through anger and tears. When Moira finally settled down, the two of them joined Cat on the porch.

"This isn't finished," Cat said, when they walked outside. "Through Hammond I got a good picture of our old friend Voorhees. He's masterminding all of this for somebody else. Colin is working for him. This is a lot bigger than just a couple of Nosferati."

"That's what your father thinks, too," Moira said. "He believes they'll be in touch with us." She glanced down at the fluffy bundle against Cat's chest. "How's the baby?"

"Nursing," Cat said.

"What?"

"Yep," she replied, shifting the blanket so Moira and Casey could see the child at her breast. "Right after Dad handed her to me, everything swelled up and I began lactating."

"That quickly?" Moira asked, her eyebrows rising.

"Weird, huh?" Cat said. "What the hell," she grinned, rubbing the baby's back as it nursed. "I always did want bigger boobs."

# THIRTY-EIGHT

Sorrow and Hope

THE BUMBLEBEE SETTLED ON MOIRA'S ARM, and she shooed it away, afraid for the baby she held against her breast. The anger that had sustained her had leaked away. Fear for babies seemed to be the biggest thing in her life, consuming her world, filling her from emotional horizon to emotional horizon. Looking down in the valley, she could see the afternoon sun splashing against Glenwood Springs, but it brought her no comfort. Beth was gone, taken by a vampire. Of their own accord, her feet had carried her among the aspens to the spot she had last visited the day after Bobby's death so many years before. She stood there, nearly numb, holding Felene's child, a less than one day old Nosferati-human crossbred ripped from the womb of her dying mother only hours before. As Felene lay legless and bleeding on the ground, Moira's child had been stolen. And Casey, poor Casey, who fought to save the family and could do nothing to stop the theft, who was equally despondent over the events of the day, had done his best to comfort her. Controlling his anger and outrage, he'd offered her all the love he had, and it wasn't enough. Nothing was.

Even Cat, who had almost died in the attack and then nearly been lost to the blood, tried to comfort her. Cat, whose lover and friend, dear Melvin, had also been taken, pushed back her grief and rage and tried to help. A few drops of water cannot prevail against a forest fire. Rice paper cannot stand against a hurricane. Father and daughter tried. Father and daughter failed.

The emotional vacuum of Bobby's death, still so near after all the years, washed over her and Moira became empty. Standing on that hillside among the aspens, everything she had, everything she was, just leaked away. She saw the prison where she met Casey as if through a haze. The events in Indianapolis, the search for Cat and her resurrection, the birth of the twins, the events that had made the last few years the most rewarding and gratifying of her life, swirled about her in an emotional fog, then wisped away on a despondent breeze. Vacant, she stood holding the newborn for immeasurable time. Hollow, she huddled on the hill.

Eventually the child stirred and fussed, pulling Moira partway back. She shifted the infant in her arms, dropping her right hand to her side. Feeling a warm clasp enfold her fingers, she glanced down. Her *son*, Sean, stood beside her, looking across the valley.

"Felene is worried, Mom," he said.

Jolted by the words, Moira kneeled to see his face. "Felene is not here any more, Sean," she replied, her eyes searching his features as he stared, unseeing, out over the valley.

"Yes, she is, Mom. She's here. In the baby."

"How do you know?"

"When I put my head in the baby, I can feel her," he replied, his unfocused gaze never shifting. "She's worried."

Gooseflesh rose on the back of Moira's arms. She looked into Sean's eyes, but he seemed not to see her. "Is your head in the baby now?"

"Yep."

"Do you know what Felene is worried about?"

The baby writhed, then settled. "Uh-huh," Sean said.

Moira swallowed. "What?"

"She's worried you'll be too sad to be brave. Dad and Aunt Cat need you to be brave, Mom. So do Beth and Uncle Melvin."

A tiny smile teased her lips. "You think so, huh?"

Sean shrugged. "Felene thinks so," he replied.

A brief dizziness surged through Moira, and she shook her head to clear her vision. "Felene thinks so."

"Yep," Sean answered, turning to look at her with blank eyes. Again the baby squirmed and quivered, then relaxed.

"It's time to go back to the house, back to the family, and back to the world," the boy said. "For everyone's sake, you have to be strong. You have to have hope, Moira. The strength of the human is what binds all this together. Your humanity binds all of us. You, above all others, have to have hope."

Rocked to her core, Moira braced herself to keep from sprawling on the ground. Panting, she looked at her son as he shivered for a moment. Focus returned to his eyes. He blinked rapidly a few times, and smiled at her.

"Mommy," he asked, "can we go back to the house now?"

"Sure," Moira replied, weaving to her feet. "It's time we did."

Moira and Sean were holding hands when they entered the kitchen. Moira looked at Cat and Casey sitting across from each other in the living room.

"If you two will tend to the baby, I'll fix us some dinner," she said.

Cat smiled. "How are you?" she asked, walking over to take the child.

"Better," Moira replied, returning her smile. "How 'bout cheeseburgers, fries, and pudding for desert?"

"Sounds perfect," Casey said, rising to embrace her. "Just perfect."

Tears leapt from Moira's eyes as she looked up at him. "We'll get through this," she whispered. "We'll get through this."

"C'mon, Kid," said Cat, carrying the baby to the couch. "Need a snack?"

"You can call the baby by her name, you know," Moira said.

"And what would that be?"

"Hope," Sean said, skipping off down the hall.

Early the next morning, after a long night of little sleep and less rest, Casey's phone rang as they sat down to coffee.

"Yes."

"Casey, it's Melvin."

"Thank God. Are you alright?"

"I'm fine. So is Beth."

"Beth and Melvin are alright," Casey said to the room, then clicked on the speaker. "Where are you?"

"Ah, Austria, I think." Melvin's voice echoed through the kitchen.

"Austria?"

"So it would seem. Everyone, save a strange young man called Colin, has been quite hospitable. I am tasked to assure you that we have been well treated and put you in the, ah, correct frame of mind, as it were, to speak with a representative of the individual who is responsible for these events."

"Okay."

"Yes. Well, I'll give him the floor, then."

There was the sound of a phone changing hands, and a dry controlled voice came on the line.

"Mr. Casey?"

"That's correct."

"Mr. Casey, my name is Voorhees ..."

"Got your will made out, Voorhees?" Casey interrupted.

"Please let me assure you," Voorhees went on, ignoring Casey's question, "that, in spite of the unpleasantness of yesterday, my employer intends no harm toward you or any member of your group."

"Cheap talk from a kidnapper and murderer."

"I fully understand your attitude."

"You don't know shit about my attitude, Motherfucker."

"Mr. Casey, this type of behavior on your part is counterproductive to the resolution of our current situation."

"Is it?"

"You know it is, Mr. Casey."

"I assume that you have at least some understanding of my capabilities?"

"I do."

"Then let me say this. Whatever you think you understand is just the tip of the iceberg, *Mister* Voorhees. Now, if that doesn't frighten you, ask that miserable piece of shit, Colin, about what my daughter is capable of. Once you come to grasp that, you'll appreciate what I am about to say. Your life is in my hands, Voorhees. *My hands!* You do anything to harm my child or my friend, and there is no power on this planet that will keep you from dying very slowly. Understand?"

"Are you attempting to intimidate me, Mr. Casey?"

"I already intimidate you, Asshole. I'm trying to save your life."

"I see."

"You better hope to God you do, you worthless fuck."

"If we may dispense with the theatrics, Mr. Casey, let me explain what is required of you to ease your current difficulties. I understand from Mr. Foltz that it is necessary for the health of your child that she come in contact with you or your daughter on a regular basis."

"That's correct."

"Allow me to invite your daughter to drop by for a visit so we may insure the health of the child."

"No."

"I beg your pardon?"

"No."

"May I suggest that you are in no position to bargain, Mr. Casey?"

"Listen, asshole. I am in every position to bargain. You take all of us, when you expect us, when you're ready for us, or we'll come late some night on our own terms. I hang up, and in twenty minutes, I'll know exactly where you are. You've got a choice to make, Voorhees. You can cooperate and live through this, or you can attempt to bargain with the life of my friend and my child, and you will shit your pants while I watch you die. What'll it be?"

"Very well, Mr. Casey. Transport for your party is on the way to the Denver Airport as we speak and should arrive about noon, your time. We will fly you from there to New York, and from New York to Innsbruck. Passports are not necessary. At Innsbruck you will be taken by helicopter the few kilometers to this location and ..."

"No."

"Now what?"

"At Innsbruck we will require a hotel and a car. We have a new baby to worry about. Moira will remain at the hotel with the child, Cat and I will drive to your location. Leave directions with the vehicle that you'll provide for us. We will come and go on our own terms."

"Very well."

"Say again, Voorhees?"

"Very well. Your conditions are acceptable."

"We will leave for Denver within an hour."

"Very good, Mr. Casey. How many in your party?"

"Three adults, one child, one infant."

"It shall be done."

"Oh. And Voorhees?"

"Yes?"

"If this goes to hell, you'll be the first one to fall."

Casey disconnected.

"Way to go, Pop!" blurted Cat.

"Not too strong?" Casey said.

"Ooh, my big ol' tough daddy!"

"Is he telling the truth?" asked Moira.

"So far. We won't leave you in the hotel of his choice, though. We'll move you and Hope to a location of our choosing."

"God, Casey," Moira continued, a little pale, "you abused that man."

"I want him to goddam well know that he is an underling, and I don't deal well with underlings. I also want him to be frightened of both me and Cat. He'll be more

299

likely to give us access to the head guy. Good old winning through intimidation. We'll get Melvin and Beth back, Sweetheart. Whatever it takes, they'll come home with us."

Cat looked at him, a thoughtful expression on her face. "Question," she said.

"Sure."

"You can't smell him. How do you know he's telling the truth?"

"Can't tell you," Casey said.

"Can't tell me?"

"Nope."

"Why not?"

Casey smiled. "Pineal envy," he said.

Immediately after Casey disconnected, the overhead speaker in the conference room crackled to life.

"Voorhees?"

"Yes, Mr. Unruh."

"Voorhees, it would seem that our Mr. Casey is a man of fortitude and purpose."

"It would seem so, Sir."

"I will see him upon his arrival. After he and I visit, you and he may work out the details of our arrangement."

"Yessir."

"Is Mr. Foltz available?"

"I'm here," Melvin said.

"Ah. Very good, Mr. Foltz. I wonder if you would do me the honor of chatting with me for a while? You and I have much to offer one another. I would be pleased if we could meet face to face and begin an amicable relationship."

"Since I probably have no choice, I would find that agreeable, I'm ah, certain, Sir, but I must be allowed to bring my niece. She is frightened and feels some security in being with me."

"Quite understandable. Shall we say in thirty minutes?"

"That will be fine."

"Voorhees?"

"Yessir?"

"See to it."

"If you think it wise, Sir."

"Conversation with an intelligent man? Very wise. Unusual too, Voorhees. That's all."

# THIRTY-NINE

## The Touch of a Child

MELVIN SETTLED INTO THE GREEN CHAIR and took Beth on his lap. She seemed quite calm and not at all frightened by the fact they were enclosed in a clear cubicle protruding into Unruh's white plastic sanctuary. Unruh slowly rose from behind his desk and shuffled tenuously to a seat ten feet on the other side of the Lucite wall. His bulky white suit, gloves, and slippers made him appear physically large. His thin neck and drawn face told the truth. Carefully, he eased himself into a chair, regarded them through level eyes, and spoke.

"Mr. Foltz. Kind of you to come."

"Your invitation was irresistible."

Unruh's smile was nearly invisible. "I have followed your career with high interest for several years," he said. "And, to a lesser extent, that of Ms. Flynn. Up until the two of you moved to Colorado, you both worked for me."

"Really?"

"Among other things, I own the Proteus Trust and, therefore, Provenance. When you and she acquired Mr. Casey, I felt you might be onto something. When all of you fled to Glenwood Springs, I became very curious. When you entered into your relationship with Fischer Laboratories, another of my holdings, I became convinced the notable Doctor Blood was making heavy progress. Are you, Mr. Foltz? Has there been a break-through? Have you constructed a Magic Bullet, Mr. Foltz?"

Melvin looked through the glass at the pathetic figure before him, feeling Unruh's withered power, his need, his immense will. "There is, ah, significant reason to believe that infectious disease may be reduced to the level of annoyance instead of catastrophe in the next few years, and that conditions such as you appear to be suffering from, hemophilia and reduced immune efficiency, can be easily managed with very comfortable protocols."

Unruh stared at him for a moment. "You're serious."

"Oh, yes."

"Encapsulate it for me, if you would, Sir. Tell me how you got from where you were to where you are, but please, with brevity. We do not want the child to become restive or uncomfortable and, therefore, an annoyance. Continue, Mr. Foltz."

"Why should I?" Melvin asked.

"I beg your pardon?"

"Why should I?" Melvin repeated.

The briefest of smiles flickered across Unruh's face. "Because I wish it, Sir," he replied.

"Just as you wished to attack our location at Glenwood Springs?"

"It was not my wish to attack your home," Unruh replied. "It was my wish that you be brought to me. I have no interest in the methodology that secures my will. I concern myself with outcomes. You are here, are you not, Mr. Foltz?"

Melvin looked at the withered figure on the other side of the transparent barrier. "And you are prepared to do whatever is necessary to secure from me the information that you require?"

"Oh, no," Unruh protested. "All I am prepared to do is summon Mr. Voorhees. It is he that will do whatever is necessary to obtain the information."

"That would entail using drugs or inflicting some sort of pain upon me, I assume," Melvin replied, trying to appear calm in spite of his increasing heart rate.

"Whatever," Unruh shrugged. "I suppose that, while that scenario is possible, Voorhees would most probably direct his attention toward the young woman on your lap. As I understand it, a screaming child offers many people extreme motivation."

"My God," Melvin gasped around the lump that had materialized in his throat.

"You see, Mr. Foltz, it really is up to you. We can have a comfortable conversation. An exchange between two civilized, learned men, as it were. It is possible that you and I might even find some common ground between us."

"I doubt it," Melvin muttered, holding Beth close to his chest.

"Or," Unruh went on, ignoring the comment, "you may attempt to resist my wishes. Either way, I assure you, I shall obtain what I want. The choice is yours, Mr. Foltz."

"Call me Melvin," Melvin whispered.

Over the next thirty minutes, Melvin related a great deal of what they had been up to. Their discoveries, their conclusions, their assumptions were laid out in a precise and orderly manner. He told Unruh almost everything.

"And these Nosferati you speak of, one of whom would be that distasteful young man called Colin, cannot have children?"

"That is the paradox," Melvin replied. "As long as they are actively feeding, they cannot. For the Nosferati to produce more Nosferati, they must stop being Nosferati."

"And the only other way is through the rare survivor of the infection."

"Very rare."

"Vampires," Unruh mused.

"The origin of the myth, I would assume," Melvin replied.

"Fantastic. And Mr. Casey, his daughter, and this other woman, Felene, are all ex-Nosferati."

"I would call them non-active Nosferati," Melvin said. "It is always with them. While they must ingest a small amount of blood on a regular basis, large amounts have a very profound effect on them. The monster still lurks within, as it were. I suspect that only a small percentage of the Nosferati could even survive the drying-out process. Another subject, a young man called Gunnar, did not."

"No?"

"No. Halfway into the treatment, he drank his own blood until he died from it."

"Had he been totally restrained, would he have survived?"

"I think not."

"Why?"

"Ah. I have given that very question considerable thought. My conclusions are somewhat less than scientific, I'm afraid," Melvin said.

"Please continue," Unruh encouraged. "I have confidence in your mind."

"To overcome the addiction, the subject must be, uh, humanized, as it were. That is to say, he must possess some vestige of human value and content to survive the ordeal. Chief among these requirements, I believe, is love."

"Love?"

"Indeed. Casey, for instance. Casey had the advantage of being human for forty-two years before he was infected. He is, by far, the oldest survivor of the infection of whom we are aware. That humanity, those years of being human, weighed heavily on his ability to survive the drying out process. Besides, his daughter was still around. He loved her. It was his need to find and possibly rehabilitate her that caused him to cast his lot with Moira."

"And his daughter?"

"She was young when taken, just fourteen. Much more typical. However, she and her father are the only two known blood relatives to ever become Nosferati. This indicates a very strong physical and emotional connection between the two of them. The love she had for her father, and he for her, allowed her to reform."

"And what about the other woman?"

"Felene?"

"Yes."

"Felene is very old. Even she does not know how many years she has lived, but certainly well over a thousand. During that time, she developed a certain under-standing of the human condition. She, above all else in her extraordinary life, wanted a child. When Casey and Catherine offered her the opportunity to have one, she jumped at the chance, willingly entering treatment. The love she possessed for her not only unborn, but also unconceived baby provided the strength to do what had to be done. She is due any day."

Unruh stared at the floor for a moment, then raised his gaze to Melvin. "Mr. Foltz," he said. "Information indicates that Mr. Casey, Ms. Flynn and Casey's daughter will join us soon, as you know, in the company of one child and one in-fant. We may assume that the infant is the newborn child of Ms. Felene. She, how-ever, did not survive the events in Colorado."

"You killed her?"

"She was killed."

"Oh, no. No," Melvin replied, tears leaping to his eyes. Unruh shrugged.

"Obviously, you feel a certain sense of loss," he commented dryly.

"A certain sense of loss?" Melvin blurted, shifting in the chair and moving Beth on his lap. "That's how you'd categorize it? A certain sense of loss! My God, man, this is tragic! Not only was Felene probably the oldest living sentient creature to have ever drawn breath, a woman who resided on this continent hundreds of years before Columbus, a human being that covered a sweep of history in her lifetime that you or I cannot begin to imagine, she was the kindest, most gentle soul I have ever encountered." Melvin shook his head and wrapped an arm tightly around Beth.

"A certain sense of loss," he muttered. "You poor, cold, fool. I loved her. We all loved her. Humanity is reduced by her passing, as I am. As *you* are, Mr. Unruh, you *civilized* freak. I do not expect your myopic conception of the world to do more than even slightly acknowledge her life or death, but I assure you, the loss of that shining woman is a blow to us all."

Beth patted his hand. "It's alright, Uncle Melvin," she whispered. "She's in the baby. She's still here. I know."

Melvin looked at the child's solemn face. "How do you know, Sweetie?" he asked.

"Sean told me."

"Sean told you?"

"Uh-huh."

"How?"

"Just did," she smiled, and returned her attention to Unruh, who had not been privy to the exchange.

"I know I must appear callous and unfeeling to you, Melvin," said Unruh, "and, in truth, I probably am. All my life I have been a prisoner of my blood. All my life I have been shut away from contact with other people. I am the original boy in the plastic bubble. My entire existence has been a struggle against death from small things. A simple cut, a common cold. I understand greed, jealously, envy, fear, and the like, but I have little appreciation for love. I suppose some would consider that my largest failing. I, on the other hand, am relatively neutral on the subject. It is difficult to miss something that one has never had, and of which one can only barely conceive. Do you understand?"

Melvin stared at him for a moment. "Sadly, yes," he replied.

"Then understand this," Unruh continued. "It is not my desire to bring pain or suffering to you or any of your fellows. That was not my purpose for bringing you here."

"What was?"

"To reach an agreement of mutual benefit. You mentioned that the reformed Nosferati have an uncanny ability to heal others?"

"Yes, they do."

"Me, for instance?"

"Possibly, but I doubt it. You are not suffering from a disease, Mr. Unruh. You are suffering from a condition of incompleteness, as it were, that I assume has been present since your birth."

"You and Ms. Flynn are immunized against the virus, I believe you said."

"That's correct. We both take monthly boosters to insure it."

"And both of you are immune to disease."

"So far," Melvin admitted. "Even colds and flu."

"Remarkable. Would this immunization work for me?"

"I don't know. I am not familiar with your blood."

"How about the healing process from a non-active Nosferati?"

"Again, I don't know. I would be more inclined to try the healing, as it is non-invasive. There would be a much smaller personal risk for you. The benefits, should there be any, would be temporary only, I believe. Symptomatic relief, as it were."

"This child, Beth. She's what, about four or five years old?"

"Two, actually."

"Two?"

"Two."

"Remarkable. Accelerated growth due to her altered DNA, I suppose."

"So it would seem."

"Could she effect a healing on my person?"

"Possibly."

"How?"

"I'm not at all sure of the mechanics of it," Melvin confessed. "Perhaps it's a direct exchange of DNA information that influences the floating brain, perhaps it's communication on some level with the immune system, who knows? I'm just scratching the surface at this time."

"No," Unruh responded. "What I am asking is, how might the healing be done. What must the healer do and what must the subject do?"

"Oh, … touch."

"Ah. Would she touch me?"

"That's up to her," Melvin replied, feeling Beth stiffen a bit.

"Child," Unruh said, peering at the Beth through the clear barrier that separated them, his rasping voice echoing through the overhead speaker, "would you touch my hand?"

"You don't have to," Melvin said.

Beth sat very still for a moment, then smiled. "It's okay," she said. "Aunt Felene would."

"Yes, she would," Melvin replied, tears in his eyes again.

"Then so will I," Beth stated.

Unruh adjusted his seat to a position in front of a pass-through on the sidewall of the cubicle, and Melvin moved his chair near the same apparatus.

"There will be a slight influx of air on your side when the portal is opened," Unruh said rather nervously. "We maintain positive air pressure in my chamber."

He carefully removed the glove from his right hand. "This is different for me," Unruh went on. "It has been over sixty years since bare skin has contacted my own. I have never felt the touch of a child."

With his gloved hand, he released the latch on the pass-through and allowed the small door to fall away. Swallowing nervously, he extended his bare hand through the opening. His nails were overlong and ragged, the skin pale, punctuated by blue-green veins pulsating just beneath the surface. He held his hand flat and rigid, unable to control the tremors that vibrated through it. Without hesitation, Beth took his hand in her own.

"Think of your mommy and daddy," Melvin murmured, "and of everybody who loves you, and everyone you love."

Beth did.

If Unruh had not been seated, he would have fallen. A roaring filled his ears, the sound of a distant waterfall. Colors splashed on his closed eyelids in counterpoint, and he felt his head loll to one side and his body slump in the chair. Alarm was quashed by curiosity and sensation, and he gave himself over to the touch of the child, the quiet assurance of her two tiny hands.

After a time, the colors coalesced into vision. He saw and knew Casey, Cat, Moira, Melvin, Sean, and Felene. He viewed them from a child's perspective. He was rolled on the floor, tickled on the bed, held at arm's length, tossed in the air, kissed, hugged, rumpled and pummeled. He walked around the house holding Moira's hand. He felt Casey's whiskers against his cheek. He giggled as Cat pushed him in the tire swing and ate pudding while Felene played guitar and sang to him on the porch. He wrestled with Sean, had his diaper changed, and ate Cheerios from his high-chair tray while giants rumbled at the kitchen table. He rolled in new grass, smelled with the clear nose of a child, sneaked up on Uncle Melvin, spoke to his brother without words, heard the baby in Felene's womb, and felt love from every single person he knew. It washed over him, it ripped through him. It gave him peace and refused him rest, slapping against what he was as a tsunami onto an unsuspecting atoll; it overwhelmed his futile resistance, leaving change foaming in its wake. When Beth released his hand he felt such a momentary loss, he was almost afraid to open his eyes.

At length, Unruh blinked a few times then looked at Melvin and the child sleeping curled up on his lap. "Oh, my," he said.

Melvin smiled.

"How long did that take?" Unruh continued.

"Less than thirty seconds. Beth let go of your hand when she fell asleep."

"I see," Unruh responded, clearing his throat and adjusting his posture as he flexed his bare hand. "Perhaps you should put her to bed and get some rest yourself, Mr. Foltz. You also must be fatigued. Someone will be waiting for you in the hall."

Melvin lifted the child as he rose. "Are you alright?" he asked.

"I suspect," Unruh replied with a hint of a smile, "that in many ways, I have never felt better. Goodnight, Sir, and thank you."

"Goodnight, Mr. Unruh," Melvin said and opened the door into the waiting hall.

Unruh sat very still for some time, his mind awash in memory and sensation, then leaned over in his chair and shook his head. "I am sorry, Ms. Felene," he murmured, and wiped a tear onto the palm of his strangely gloveless right hand.

# FORTY

Tiny Tim

VOORHEES WALKED DOWN THE HALLWAY past the room where Melvin and the child were installed and paused to check the door. Locked. Good. He would soon have to order breakfast for them and check in with Unruh about the coming events. Their visitors should arrive shortly. Things needed to be put in place. As he rounded the corner heading for the kitchen, he came face to face with Colin.

"Good mornin', Love," Colin said. "Have a pleasant night?"

"Fine. You?"

"I went for a nice long walk. Met some lovely tourists. Had a wonderful time."

"Oh, good," Voorhees sighed.

"Now, don't be that way. I cleaned up my mess. Left not a trace, Bucko. Cat and company arrive today, right?"

"In a couple of hours."

"Looking forward to that. Haven't seen her in a while. Can't wait to meet her dear old dad."

"Yeah," Voorhees responded, disgusted by Colin as usual. "Well, you just keep your shit together, Goddammit! There's a lot riding on this for all of us."

Colin smiled a slow smile. "Was that a threat, Love?" he purred. "Did you just threaten me?"

"Oh, Christ. I'm trying to get you to understand that there is a lot more in the works here than some petty emotional vendetta. I don't give a fuck what you do on your own time and on your own turf, but this is here and now! It's a lot bigger than your delicate feelings or some little blood-sucking blonde bitch! You get stupid and you'll screw this up for everybody. You stay cool and you win big time. Plus, you can go ahead and do whatever you want down the road a ways. This is the chance of a lifetime. Any lifetime. Just keep control of yourself, and don't fucking blow it!"

"Cat's mine," Colin hissed. "Just remember that. She's mine."

"Fine! She's yours. Terrific. Take her! I couldn't care less. Just not yet, Colin. Not yet! This whole thing is worth literally billions of dollars. Billions! A little patience and you can spend the next thousand years in ways even Caligula couldn't imagine! You can bathe in blood while nuns suck your dick, for chrissakes! You can make a dozen kills a day if you like. That kind of money can bring you more power than you can possibly imagine. Just be patient and control yourself!"

Colin studied him thoughtfully for a moment. "Well," he said, "I just suppose I'll have to get a grip then, won't I? Take it easy, Voorhees. Don't get your knickers in a twist."

Voorhees' belt pager began to vibrate. "Christ," he snapped, shutting it off. "The freak wants me."

When Voorhees entered the cubicle, he was stunned to see Unruh on his feet, swinging his arms and pacing about the room.

"Good morning, Sir. Is everything alright?"

"Ah, Voorhees!" Unruh beamed. "Everything is fine. Are we prepared to receive our guests?"

"Yessir. As we planned, the child and Melvin will be in my and Colin's company to forestall rash action on the part of Casey or his daughter. Shouldn't you be sitting down, Sir?"

"I have too much energy to sit right now. I've been pacing for the last two hours."

Voorhees couldn't believe what he was hearing. "Perhaps you should rest a bit, Sir."

"I slept for seven consecutive hours last night, Voorhees. Seven! Amazing, don't you think?"

"Uh, yessir. How are you feeling, Sir?"

"Never better. Literally, never better. About our visitors. None of them are to be harmed in any way, not Beth or Melvin, not Mr. Casey or his daughter. Am I clear?"

"Certainly, Sir, but that leaves us in a rather awkward position. We have no power over any of them if they cannot be put in harm's way."

"We won't need it, Voorhees. Send Mr. Casey and company directly to me when he arrives. I will speak with him and his daughter, then direct them to you in the conference room when we are through. There they may be joined by Melvin and that amazing little girl."

"I'm confused, Sir."

"Of course you are. Things have changed since last we spoke. I can't go into it right now, I have a technician on the way to draw blood and bring me some clothing."

"Clothing, Sir?"

"Yes, Voorhees," Unruh nearly chuckled, "clothing. You know, slacks, shoes, shirt, jacket, clothing, Dear Boy, clothing!"

"Isn't that taking a big chance, Mr. Unruh?"

"I feel like it, Voorhees. I feel like a lot of things. Just remember, no one is to get hurt. We'll use the threat toward Melvin and Beth long enough to gain time for me to speak with Casey, but it is only a threat. Is that clear?"

"Nossir, but it is your order."

"Very good. When all this is done, I'll explain. That's all."

"Thank you, Sir," Voorhees muttered and left the chamber.

After the Lear landed in Innsbruck, a limo picked up Casey, Moira, Cat, Sean, and Hope, and delivered them to their hotel. Rooms were reserved, and a car was waiting. They stood in the lobby and Casey found an assistant manager who spoke English.

"Do you accept American Express?"

"Of course."

"Then I would like to make two purchases."

"Your rooms are already paid for, Sir."

"It's not the rooms that concern me," Casey said. "I need to buy cooperation and discretion. Please keep the money for the rooms and charge them again on my companion's card. Then make sure she is moved to another hotel of your choice where she will be as comfortable as she would have been here. You may distribute the additional monies to your staff or whatever you see fit. When I return from my business and find her safe and sound, I will stop by your hotel and rent the same rooms again for another ten days, then leave immediately without asking for a refund."

The manager stepped close to Casey and dropped his voice to a whisper. "This is highly irregular, Sir."

"And highly profitable," Casey said. "The offer will be withdrawn in two minutes. I suggest you make a call. I'll want to know where she'll be staying before I leave, and I must leave momentarily."

"If you will ask gnädige Frau to join me at the desk, I will attend to this matter in the utmost haste."

"Thank you."

"Thank you, Sir. Everything will be exactly as you requested."

Moira returned from the front desk and took Hope from Cat. "A hotel car will be here in a few minutes to move me," she said, handing Casey a memo containing the address and room number.

"Good," he said. "Stay in the room. As soon as we're through, we'll see you there. All of us." He bent to the cooler and slipped a half-pint bag of blood into each jacket pocket. "We've got to go, Sweetie. The less time they have to prepare for us, the better our chances are."

"You be careful, Casey," Moira whispered. "You too, Cat. We're counting on you."

"I'm going, too," piped Sean. Casey looked down at him.

"Sorry, Slugger. You have to stay with Mom."

"No," the boy replied. "I'm coming with you."

"Sorry."

"Yes!"

"Sean, *no*."

"I *have* to! Beth is there. Beth needs me!"

Casey squatted down in front of his son. "Sean, where we are going there are some bad men. You can't come with us."

Sean looked at Cat. "Tell him I'm not stupid," he said. "I'm just little."

Cat grinned. "He's not stupid. He's just little."

"Sean," Casey smiled, "I know you want to go, but …"

"Dad," Sean pleaded, "I *have* to go. I have to be there, I *have* to!"

Feeling the intensity of the child, Casey looked at Moira. She shrugged. "Okay," he said. "Just stay with me, right with me, all the time. Clear?"

"Yessir."

The hotel van pulled up in front of the lobby and Moira and the baby got on board. "You come back to me, all of you," she said, tears in her eyes.

Casey kissed her. "Never a doubt," he said, and closed the sliding door.

Their Mercedes was waiting at the curb, directions taped to the steering wheel.

Motoring through the Tirolean Alps, Casey drove northeast through Schwaz and Wörgl, then east to the hamlet of Kitzbühel. If he'd had less on his mind, he would have enjoyed the Disneyesque scenery, the neat little towns, the immaculate homes and gardens, but it was lost on both him and Cat. They drove southward through Mitters and into the Hohe Tauern National Park. Passing a sign advising them they were eight kilometers from Lienz, they began to look for a small side road to the west, as described in the directions. It was surprisingly easy to find. With less than two kilometers to go, Casey stopped the car. He and Cat got out. Sean, as asked, stayed in the vehicle. Leading Cat to the rear of the Mercedes, Casey handed her a pouch of Hammond's blood.

"Pick me up?" he asked.

"Considering where we're going, you bet," she replied.

When the Nosferati euphoria wore off, Cat turned to her father.

"This could get rough, Dad. Just remember that Colin is the slimiest sonofabitch on the planet. Better than anyone, I know. I suspect there are no other Nosferati on hand. If there were, he'd have used them when they attacked the house. You're faster and stronger than I am. If the feces hit the fan, you protect Sean and try for Melvin and Beth. I'll take care of Colin. I know how he operates."

"Suits me, Champ," Casey said. "Kinda like old times, huh?"

"You tip 'em over, Pop. I'll rub dirt in their hair."

The last two kilometers were excessively tall. The Mercedes complained a bit, its engine laboring in low gear to maintain movement up the grade. After slow progress on switchbacks and rutted turns, they pulled into a stone courtyard in front of what could best be described as an undersized castle. There was no thick wooden door or bannered parapets, but it towered over the landscape, thrusting out of the living rock. The mountain fell almost vertically downward from two sides, the keep clinging to the stone, a manmade icon of determination and will. In spite of a sunny sky and warm breezes, the heavy image it created brought forth visions of chain mail, sounding trumpets, long sieges, and cold steel. Bleak, barren, and ancient, its walls towered eighty feet above their heads, dwarfed by the unyielding mountain rising above it.

"Jesus," shivered Cat, "talk about vampire country."

They were met by a white-coated houseman before they reached the doorway and led through renovated halls to an elevator. Smiling, he went inside with them, and they rose three stories. When the door opened again, they were facing a carpeted hall that could have been plucked from any quality hotel on the planet. The houseman led them around a corner and to another door. He motioned them to enter, turned, and went back the way they had come. Casey looked at Cat, took Sean's hand, and opened the door. They stepped into Unruh's Lucite cubicle.

A bit overwhelmed by Unruh's coldly hygienic nest, they stared for a moment, taking in the surreal technology that glistened before them. After giving them a moment to adjust, Unruh stepped out from behind a bed screen and walked to within ten feet of the glass. He smiled.

"Mr. Casey, Miss Catherine, Master Sean," he said. "Good of you to come. My name is Unruh. Accept my apologies for remaining behind my sterile barrier. While my condition has greatly improved over the past few hours, until I receive the results of recent tests, it is prudent that I remain sequestered."

"Melvin and Beth," Casey growled, "where are they?"

"Be at ease, Mr. Casey. They are safe and you will join in their company before long. I know you have the ability to discern if I am telling the truth. I tell you now that they are well and comfortable. Do you believe me?"

Casey looked at the pale thin man before him. "Yes," he replied.

"Good. Please take a seat," Unruh continued, gesturing to the gray loveseat that had replaced the green armchair and moving to a stool in front of them. "I wish to speak with you for a time and tell you a story. I shall not lie to you for two reasons. First of all, you could easily detect a lie, but more importantly, it is my desire to be honest. I have lived in deceit for many years, good people, and I find it suddenly distasteful. Your marvelous child, Elizabeth, has freed me from myself. May I explain?"

Casey looked at him—Unruh's white suit several sizes too big, his skeletal frame angling against the linen as sticks in a sack—and took pity. Cat's hand found his shoulder and they both sat, Sean leaning against Casey's knees. "Alright," he said. "Tell us a story."

"Thank you," Unruh replied. "Are you familiar with a Dickens character called Ebenezer Scrooge?"

Casey was puzzled. "Uh, yes. A Christmas Carol."

"Exactly!" pounced Unruh. "I spent last night with my ghosts and I sit before you a changed man. I have my Tiny Tim, Mr. Casey. Her name is Elizabeth."

For the next hour, Unruh talked. He confessed his life to Cat and Casey, what he had done to amass his fortune, acts he'd ordered to increase his power. He laid it all out before them. They listened in silence.

"So," said Unruh, "there you have it. I ask for no pardon, I seek no sympathy, I require no empathy. I have been as inhuman as a human can be, I suppose, and I cannot atone. I cannot heal the wounds I have caused. I cannot resurrect, I cannot restore. What I did, I did from greed, from avarice, from fear, and from ignorance. As is often said, ignorance is no excuse. Most recently, I authored the attack on your home in Colorado that resulted in the kidnapping of Melvin and Elizabeth and the death of Ms. Felene. I engineered that tragedy for one reason. Personal gain. I thought to coerce your group into cooperation so that I might expand my tentacles, strengthen my grasp, and ameliorate my personal illness. These were my motivations. And then something marvelous happened. A small child held my hand and thought of love."

Unruh paused to wipe his eyes on a tissue. "Mr. Casey, Miss Catherine, my life is yours if you require it. I will give it without struggle and without condition. I, who have caused so much pain to so many souls, will reunite you with Melvin and Elizabeth and gladly accept any penance you require." He smiled. "Should that be my death, I expect, in many ways, it shall be relief."

Cat squeezed Casey's hand, and he looked at her, seeing the light shining in her eyes. Unruh waited quietly.

"Well," Casey said, "as I see it, one of the first things we have to do is to get you healthy."

"I beg your pardon?"

Cat leaned forward, her eyes glistening with tears. "You'll never find two people who understand how you feel better than we do," she said. "And you're right. There is nothing you can do to fix what you've done. We committed our sins too, and we can't fix them either."

"You have offered your life to us, Mr. Unruh," Casey said. "We'll take it. We have good use for it. Melvin thinks the eradication of infectious disease is possible if enough resources can be found. He and Moira are also excited about some unusual developments in human DNA. That research will require heavy funding. You have the money and assets he needs. It would be a shame if you were not around to see the work bear fruit. You were correct when you said you could not atone, but you can achieve. We have plenty of room near Glenwood Springs for a research facility. Doctor Melvin Foltz and Doctor Moira Flynn are already on staff. We'd like you to join us. What do you say?"

Unruh got to his feet. "Felene Laboratories is what I say, Mr. Casey. Oh, my. This is truly wonderful. Now, perhaps you'd like to see Melvin and Elizabeth." He turned toward his desk. "Allow me to summon someone to deliver you to the conference room so that you may be reunited with your family."

# FORTY-ONE

Pudding

"*FUCK!*" SPAT VOORHEES, snapping off the intercom connection to Unruh's suite and whirling to glare at Colin. The Nosferati eased away from the conference room wall and raised an eyebrow.

"What's the matter, Love?"

"*What's the matter?*" Voorhees bellowed, flinging a plastic chair across the room, nearly hitting Melvin and Beth where they sat near open French doors that led outside to a stone balcony. "I'll tell you what's the matter," he hissed. "The freak just sold the whole fucking thing right down the river! He just screwed us, you goddamn dim bulb! That's what's *the fucking matter!*"

Colin smiled his cold smile. "Really?"

"You think you're invincible? You think you can't be had? Jesus Christ. Over two years of work, billions of dollars in potential profits. Gone. *Gone!*" Voorhees paced to the French doors and stood in the sunlight for a moment, seething. "And now, Casey and his fucking daughter are on their way to get these two back!" He waved an arm toward Melvin and Beth. "Shit! I gotta get outta here!"

He bolted for the door only to find Colin standing in front of it. "What's the hurry, Cobber?"

"Get out of the way," Voorhees snarled.

"No, no, no, Love. You don't tell me what to do."

"*Holy shit!*" shouted Voorhees, his frustration from months of dealing with Colin roaring to the surface. "I don't believe you, I really don't. Look, you mental midget, it is over! Do you understand *over?* Do you grasp *over?* Do you have the slightest ability to comprehend *over?*"

"Be nice, Bucko. Don't call me names," Colin whispered. His left hand lazily connected with Voorhees chest, sending the man sliding across the room scattering chairs like tenpins.

Gasping, Voorhees rolled to one knee. "Try and get this in your brain," he wheezed, struggling to catch his breath. "This isn't about you, you egomaniacal dumbass! Unruh has dumped the deal. Cat and Casey are on the way to this room right now! We have no edge, we have no leverage! The best thing we can do is get the fuck out of here while we still can. Jesus Christ! Don't be stupid! Put your God-dammed ego away, and let's go!"

313

Smiling, Colin crossed to him and lifted Voorhees to eye level by one arm. "Stupid?" he said. "Call me stupid? I don't like that, Bucko!" He casually tossed Voorhees toward the far wall. The stricken man tumbled across the floor and struck the baseboard feet first. Everyone in the room heard his ankle break.

Spittle running from his panting mouth, Voorhees again raised himself to a knee, his body quivering with stress. "*You idiot!*" he seethed. "You just crippled the only ally you have left! For two fucking years I have played up to your vanity, pandered to your twisted personality, put up with your stupidity! For two fucking years I have done everything I could to keep you from fucking this whole thing up, and now this. *And now this!*" Gasping with pain, he grabbed a chair and clawed his way to his feet.

"You somnambulistic, pea-brained, mindless, petulant shithead!" he rasped. "Even now, you have no idea the trouble you're in! Even now, the only thing you grasp is that I called you stupid! Well, you are! You are so Goddammed stupid that you've killed us both! Cat and Casey are coming, you double-breasted Dumbo! All this time, you've been crying about Cat. *Wanting* to find Cat. *Needing* to see Cat. You're about to, you fucking retarded Hermaphrodite, and I hope she tears your heart out! You're too fucking stupid to live!" Exhausted, Voorhees lost his grip on the chair and collapsed to the floor.

As Melvin recoiled in horror, turning Beth's face away and covering her eyes with his hand, Colin crossed to Voorhees' limp form and lifted the wounded man to a standing position.

"Well, Love," Colin said. "If I'm in so much trouble, perhaps a bit of a snack would be called for."

He twisted Voorhees' head to one side and buried his face in the exposed neck. For nearly a full minute he stood thus, easily overcoming Voorhees' weakening struggles. When he finished, Colin flung the body away from him. It struck the wall headfirst with a sickening crunch and thudded to the floor. He turned toward Melvin and the child and grinned through blood-covered teeth. Urine soaked his pants and dripped on the floor.

"Now then, Missy," he hissed, his body trembling with pleasure as he extended a quivering hand. "Come to Uncle Colin. There's a good girl."

When Cat and Casey arrived at the room, they were both fully aware mayhem had occurred inside. Casey stopped the houseman from opening the door, flinging it wide himself, and Cat entered the room at best speed with he and Sean close behind. Melvin lay in a corner clutching a dislocated shoulder. Across the room, Voorhees' body sprawled, slowing oozing blood onto the tile. Colin stood with his back to the open balcony outside the French doors—Beth in front of him—his right hand lazily around her throat. He was grinning.

"You must be dear old dad," he said.

"Don't," said Casey, his gaze flicking from Elizabeth and fixing on Colin's face. "Don't you dare." Sean and Beth locked eyes. Neither child spoke.

"And Cat," Colin continued. "It's good to see you again, Love. I thought I'd lost you."

"You never had me, Asshole," she growled. "Let Beth go."

"That would depend on you, then, wouldn't it?" Colin smirked.

"Me?" Cat replied, glancing at Beth. The girl's eyes were still locked on her brother.

"Aye," Colin answered, tightening his grip on the child's throat a little. Beth and Sean continued to stare at each other. "How 'bout a trade?" Colin continued.

"A trade?"

"A fair one, too. You for the girl. You come with me, she stays. She's free to return to the bosom of her lovin' family, you and I leave together."

"What makes you think I wouldn't kill you as soon as we were alone?" Cat asked, smelling Colin's lies and malevolence.

"Only your word, me Darlin'. Only your word. You and me, Cat. Just like old times. You need me. You know you do."

"Jesus," sneered Cat. "You're sicker than I thought. I don't need you. I never needed you." She flicked her eyes to Melvin who picked up the cue.

"She needs a real man," he said, trying to divert Colin's attention. "A real man. Not some half-witted, impotent, blood-sucking cheap imitation that has to sit down to pee!"

"You're with him?" Colin blurted. "You're with this pathetic little human?"

"I love him, Colin. I can't even work up pity for you."

"No! Nooo!" Colin shouted, lifting Beth off the floor and retreating toward the French doors. "You're mine, say it! *Say it!* Say it, or this little fucking git goes over the side!" He backed out onto the balcony.

"No," growled Casey, leaving Sean and advancing slowly on Colin's position. The two children continued to stare at each other.

"Put her down, Colin, and you walk out of here as free as a bird," Cat said. "No harm, no foul."

"You come with me, Cat," Colin snarled, "or I'll throw this little bitch over the edge."

Casey and Cat both started to crouch.

"Ah, ah, ah, ah," Colin cautioned. "I'm just as fast as either of you. Back on your heels, ladies and gents, or over she …" A puzzled expression washed over his face and his hand began to loosen from around Beth's neck. He struggled against the opening of his grip as if grappling with an unseen enemy, but to no avail. Shocked and panting, Colin watched his fingers spread against his will, as Beth slipped from his grasp and slid to the balcony floor. Silently she turned to look at him.

Slowly, Colin's feet left the stone beneath them and he began to elevate. Gasping for breath, he strived to speak but could not. His eyes started from their sockets in terror as his body lifted clear of the balcony and swung out over the abyss. There he hung, motionless in the air, poised over the rocks far below.

"Jesus," whispered Cat, looking at the children.

Casey followed her gaze and saw Sean and Beth both staring at Colin as if in trance. Grasping the situation, a tiny smile flickered across his face.

"Hey, kids," he said. "Want some pudding?"

The fall was almost two thousand feet. Colin screamed for the first three hundred.

# EPILOGUE

CAT, CASEY, MELVIN, AND THE CHILDREN visited with Unruh for an hour or so after they fixed Melvin's shoulder and Casey called Moira to assure her everything was all right. According to the blood tests, Unruh's immune system was soaring to new heights and his blood was coagulating with record efficiency. He met the group in a common room, sitting in direct proximity with other people for the first time since early childhood. When they parted company, he joyfully shook hands with everyone, including several times with Beth and Sean.

Melvin and Cat promised to return in a few weeks with serum, lists, needs, and wants. Unruh provided a driver to return them to Innsbruck, put a plane at their disposal for the trip home, and even promised to install an airstrip on the Glenwood Springs property, should such a thing be feasible.

He felt an immense sense of loss when his guests departed, and a surprising amount of hope for the future as he mused over the events of the day. Staff was put to work cleaning up after the happenings in the conference room and Unruh was startled when he received word that Voorhees was not dead.

"What?" he asked.

"Nossir," answered his chief medical officer. "He's lost over half the blood in his body, has a badly lacerated neck, a dislocated knee, three broken ribs, a fractured sternum, a broken ankle, and the rear left quadrant of his skull is crushed to the point of brain exposure through the cranium. He will never recover from coma, Sir. He is, in common parlance, a vegetable, and will remain so, but he is alive."

"Do whatever is necessary to maintain him for as long as he lives," Unruh answered. "The man served me for years. Do not prolong his life with artificial respiration or circulation, but do nothing that will, in any way, hasten his demise. Is that clear?"

"Yessir. Quite clear."

"Thank you," Unruh replied. "I appreciate your efforts and concern."

The man looked at him as if he'd seen a ghost. Unruh was amused. "And tell the staff that all of you receive a fifty percent raise, effective immediately."

"Uh, yessir! Thank you, Sir."

"It's nothing," Unruh replied, a smile lighting his face. "I only wish I had a fat Christmas goose for you." He waved the confused man away as he chuckled to himself.

Voorhees lasted a little less than two weeks, finally succumbing to a widespread infection. When Unruh received the news, he ordered the body placed in the walk-in cooler until funeral arrangements could be made in Wolfsberg, a suitable distance from the keep.

Four days later, wrapped in plastic and lying on the cooler floor, Voorhees opened his eyes and smiled.

He was hungry.